BRUCE CHATWIN

... s born in Sheffield in 1940. After attending Marlborough School he began work as a porter at Sotheby's. Eight years later, having become one of Sotheby's youngest directors, he abandoned his job to pursue his passion for world travel. Between 1972 and 1975 he worked for the *Sunday Times*, before announcing his next departure in a telegram: 'Gone to Patagonia for six months.' This trip inspired the first of Chatwin's books, *In Patagonia*, which won the Hawthornden Prize and the E.M. Forster award and launched his writing career. Two of his books have been made into feature films: *The Viceroy of Ouidah* (retitled *Cobra Verde*), directed by Werner Herzog, and Andrew Grieve's *On the Black Hill*. On publication *The Songlines* went straight to No. 1 in the *Sunday Times* bestseller list and stayed in the top ten for nine months. His novel, *Utz*, was shortlisted for the 1988 Booker Prize. He died in January 1989.

BRUCE CHATWIN

The Novels

WITH AN INTRODUCTION BY
Hanya Yanagihara

VINTAGE

1 3 5 7 9 10 8 6 4 2

Vintage
20 Vauxhall Bridge Road,
London SW1V 2SA

Vintage is part of the Penguin Random House group of companies
whose addresses can be found at global.penguinrandomhouse.com

Penguin
Random House
UK

On the Black Hill
First published in Great Britain by Jonathan Cape in 1982
Copyright © Bruce Chatwin 1982

The author and publisher are grateful to Faber & Faber for permission
to print lines from Ezra Pound's version of 'Exile's Letter', from
Selected Poems 1908–1969, 1975

Utz
First published in Great Britain by Jonathan Cape in 1988
Copyright © Bruce Chatwin 1988

The Viceroy of Ouidah
First published in Great Britain by Jonathan Cape in 1980
Copyright © Bruce Chatwin 1980

Introduction copyright © Hanya Yanagihara 2017

This omnibus edition first published in Vintage in 2017

Bruce Chatwin has asserted his right to be identified as the author of this
Work in accordance with the Copyright, Designs and Patents Act 1988

penguin.co.uk/vintage

A CIP catalogue record for this book is available from the British Library

ISBN 9781784705831

Typeset in 10.75/15 pt Quadraat by Jouve (UK), Milton Keynes
Printed and bound by Clays Ltd, St Ives plc

Introduction

In 1972, Bruce Chatwin left England and began to travel. This was not so long ago, and yet the world back then was still so unmapped: a traveller could, and did, wander through it as Pausanias, as Ibn Battuta, as the explorers who wrote the first drafts of the romance of movement, of the twinned danger and delight of finding yourself in a place where you were at the mercy of unfriendly but intriguing strangers. A traveller, back then, was far less likely to find traces of the familiar in the foreign. Depending on where he ventured, he had significantly fewer guarantees of safety and, equally thrillingly, only limited ways of communicating with those he knew and had left behind. And it wasn't only that you could (and, indeed, would) travel as Ibn Battuta had, but, crucially, you could travel *where* he had, as well: Sana'a and Baghdad and Damascus, all of which are now treacherous or off-limits, cities in countries forced, by war or disaster or bad governance, to deny their cultures' extravagant senses of hospitality.

Chatwin was thirty-two when he began this, the latest of his reinventions – from an Englishman of England, to an Englishman of elsewhere – and for the rest of his life he would remain (more or less) in that elsewhere. Great travellers are recessive personalities; the best are unmemorable. This ability to shape-shift, to adapt oneself to one's context instead of imposing oneself upon it, is a necessary skill – the gift of self-erasure ensures one will see and hear things one ought not. One's goal as a traveller is to be forgettable, to leave no footsteps in the sand.

Though Chatwin may not have been forgettable, he *was* adaptable. Before embarking on his new life, he had been a student in archeology at the University of Edinburgh, and, before that, an expert in antiquities and Impressionist art at Sotheby's in London. He was not forgettable in appearance, either, in his particularly English brand of soft blond beauty, the kind destined to spoil quickly in equatorial sun, the kind in which one could see the remnants of a too-pretty boy wearing short pants and round-toed black shoes that gleamed like beetles. (Part of the enjoyment of inhabiting *The Songlines* and *In Patagonia*, Chatwin's inimitably vivid travelogues, is imagining their author moving through those baked and lonely landscapes, a slim white flame licking his way across such scarily empty territory.)

Chatwin also possessed another quality that all great travellers have: the ability to remain completely who he was, even as he proved himself ceaselessly malleable. Writers who deliberately seek out the company of those foreign to them need to be armed with an unshakable sense of self-possession and a certain sense of arrogance; you need to be able to walk into a place (be it a city or a souk or a tundra) without wondering whether who you are is actually where you're from, because you already know that where you're from doesn't matter. This kind of writer is certain that his identity has resulted not from where he was raised, but in spite of it. We think of travellers as people who have no attachment to things, but true travellers are people who really have no attachment to place. Home is not a beloved memory or something to yearn for and fetishise, but merely a matter of circumstance: a piece of land (sometimes large, but usually small) on which one eats and sleeps, sometimes for a lifetime, and sometimes for a day. Home, therefore, is anywhere, and yet nowhere as well. Chatwin was powerfully attracted to nomadism, and you might view his collective writing as a struggle to discard this idea of home as a kind of heaven, and to replace it with the radical notion that the person who found himself adrift, in perpetual motion, might already be at home – that *movement* itself might be the ideal human state.

This sense of certainty, the feeling the reader has that a place is being used as a mirror to reflect the author's own image, is also what made Chatwin's travelogues so controversial. His critics called them self-absorbed confabulations, fiction presented as fact. This isn't untrue, but it is also incidental to the works' resonance and beauty. Writings about place are almost *always* about the writer: the most rigorous are a series of self-exposures, revelations of their chronicler's prejudices and ignorances. The genius of *The Songlines* is not its veracity, but its artificiality, of plot, character and storytelling: it is a book that feels like what it is, a performative diary, a person trying to prove to himself a thesis about the human condition. Chatwin doesn't claim to be an expert on Australia, or nomadism, or Aboriginal culture – he doesn't even claim to be an expert on himself.

But the reader allows herself to be guided by him anyway, because what is being revealed is not a physical terrain so much as the twisty, dead-endy pathways of the author's own subconscious, and it is a glorious maze to be in, sparky and colourful and punctuated with unexpected roundabouts.

That is Chatwin's so-called non-fiction. But in fiction, he finally cedes the stage. His three novels are remarkable for the distinctiveness of their styles – *The Viceroy of Ouidah* (1980) is a humid, grotesque fable of African colonialism that reads like a third-hand rumour; *Utz* (1988) is a linked chain of dispatches that evokes the absurdist, bleak humour of the Eastern European Soviet age; and *On the Black Hill* (1982), the most traditional and conventionally beautiful of the trio, is a perfectly calibrated history of two brothers, as well as of England in the twentieth century – but also for their especial uncanniness, their relentless omniscience. The reader senses a dedication to honesty in these works, as if within them are the most astonishing, the most haunting of the anecdotes Chatwin had heard on his travels and, thinking them too improbable for non-fiction, he saved them for a realm in which they might be taken more seriously, or might be allowed to chime most loudly. *The Viceroy of Ouidah*, which concerns the brief rise and ignominious decline of a Brazilian slave-baron in the short-lived and brutal Dahomey kingdom, is in particular replete with these curious and exposing details, the kind of fabulist and dangerously intimate family secrets one would confess only to a stranger one was certain never to encounter again: the jilted ancestor gone mad with waiting for her beloved; the treasured daughters who were sent back to Brazil as wards of a trusted friend, who instead made them into whores; the blood pacts and curses and long-ago vengeances. With this book, the reader also imagines Chatwin, but this time she sees him near a fire, or in someone's home, aware that when he was listening to these stories, he was on the knife-edge of peril, and that in those moments only his attentiveness, his ability to sit still and say nothing, spared him his life.

The novels are a reminder, too, that fiction provides a kind of safety; it allows the writer to create outlandish stories and characters without fear (not reasonable fear, anyway) that they might be taken as representative of an entire culture or ethnicity or race – indeed, in these books Chatwin says more about colonialism, and tin-can monarchies, and failed systems of government, than you find in either The Songlines or In Patagonia. They are also more relaxed, more revealing of obsessions from Chatwin's own life, than his non-fiction: behind the scrim of fiction, the writer is able to stop performing as an author and devote his energies to being a storyteller instead. Chatwin had a keen appreciation for objects, and all three novels are decorated with lovingly, precisely described material goods, evidence of his ability to conjure an entire history by noting the stuff of people's lives. Utz, for example, is a sad, sweetly funny elegy for Mitteleuropa, told through the story of a maniacally single-minded collector of Meissen porcelain, a collection that imprisons him in both Prague and, by extension, socialism itself. In Ouidah, the titular viceroy's daughter hoards some of her father's possessions, a catalogue – '. . . his silver-mounted cigar case; his pink opaline chamber pot; his ivory-handled slave-brand with the initials F.S.; his rosary of carnauba nuts; some scraps of paper covered with his handwriting; a lithograph of the Emperor Dom Pedro II; a picture of a Brazilian house, and a particularly bloodthirsty canvas of Judith hacking off the head of Holophernes' – that forms its own miniature portrait, a biography of a man found not in the people he sired or the land he conquered, but in the things he cherished.

But of all his books, it is perhaps *On the Black Hill* that displays Chatwin at his finest and most surprising: certainly it is the most disciplined of his novels, the least dazzling in setting or circumstance, but told with an economy and elegance of language and, most strikingly, a deep tenderness. Here, the location is not some impossible land, but a farm in rural Wales. Here, the people are not eccentric collectors or sadistic potentates, but twin brothers, farmers and sons of a farmer, who, through first the Great War and then the next, never leave home for any significant period of time. The world moves into modernity, but Lewis and Benjamin largely remain behind, sometimes scrabbling forward to catch it, but mostly just clinging to its tail, being dragged reluctantly forward. Though they, too, are Chatwinesque oddities, their lives are not sources of irony, but instead of wonder.

The book is also a reminder of how lovely Chatwin's language could be, how years of seeing had given him the power to describe in terms both startling and true: a 'pewter sun' hangs low over the cold Black Hill, the rooks' 'wingtips glinting like flakes of ice'; an Afro-Brazilian boy in *Ouidah* is notable for his 'wad of blonde hair'; and in *The Songlines* a prized possession of childhood, a conch shell from the West Indies that Chatwin named Mona, is rendered as a 'sheeny pink vulva' in which he first heard the sea's shushing slush. Such instances are testament to how Chatwin could isolate the most revealing detail from the people and places and situations he observed: he may have been writing about himself, but that didn't mean he wasn't watching everything around him. A writer, like a traveller, is a thief. He waits and waits, and at the moment of divulgence – as there inevitably is, should he be able to wait long enough – he seizes the secret or confession that he came for, magpie-like, and flits away, a glossy black shadow. Someone else's story becomes his own, and his to tell and share. And when there were no appropriate words for a tale, when English provided no exact match? Well, then, Chatwin simply invented (or resurrected) the language he needed, sometimes so evocatively, with such charm and precision – such as the flies on a hot day in June 'zooming and zizzing' around the twins' barn – that one forgets one is encountering them for the first time here, that they are Chatwin's own creations. (Resourcefulness: another of the traveller's necessary qualities. When something doesn't exist, be it shelter or friends or words, one learns to make them with whatever's available.)

It is never quite a satisfying exercise – and at any rate, a rather insulting one – to try to excavate from a work of fiction evidence of the author's regrets and misgivings about his own life. But On the Black Hill makes it near-impossible not to indulge. By the time the novel was published, Chatwin had been a professional peripatetic for a decade; seven years later, at the age of forty-eight, he would be dead of an AIDS-related illness. One cannot help but wonder if, in Lewis, an armchair traveller and geography lover who is never quite able to venture far from home, Chatwin was writing himself an alternative narrative. For this is a book about the difficult work of standing still; it is a book that suggests that although (maybe?) the ideal human state may in fact be movement, the more challenging one is remaining exactly where you were born, that accepting that the earth may not be yours to occupy is its own kind of nobility. 'The planet was now full of bickering little countries with unpronounceable names,' Lewis comforts himself. 'The real journeys only existed in the imagination.' But for Chatwin, the journeys were both real and imaginary: fact became fiction, and fiction fact, and the terra incognita he travelled between them was where the true adventure lay.

Hanya Yanagihara
May 2017

On the Black Hill

For Francis Wyndham and for Diana Melly

Since we stay not here, being people but of a dayes
abode, and our age is like that of a flie, and
contemporary with a gourd, we must look some
where else for an abiding city, a place in another
countrey to fix our house in . . .

Jeremy Taylor

One

For forty-two years, Lewis and Benjamin Jones slept side by side, in their parents' bed, at their farm which was known as 'The Vision'.

The bedstead, an oak four-poster, came from their mother's home at Bryn-Draenog when she married in 1899. Its faded cretonne hangings, printed with a design of larkspur and roses, shut out the mosquitoes of summer, and the draughts in winter. Calloused heels had worn holes in the linen sheets, and parts of the patchwork quilt had frayed. Under the goose-feather mattress, there was a second mattress, of horsehair, and this had sunk into two troughs, leaving a ridge between the sleepers.

The room was always dark and smelled of lavender and mothballs.

The smell of mothballs came from a pyramid of hatboxes piled up beside the washstand. On the bed-table lay a pin-cushion still stuck with Mrs Jones's hatpins; and on the end wall hung an engraving of Holman Hunt's 'Light of the World', enclosed in an ebonized frame.

One of the windows looked out over the green fields of England: the other looked back into Wales, past a dump of larches, at the Black Hill.

Both the brothers' hair was even whiter than the pillow-cases.

Every morning their alarm went off at six. They listened to the farmers' broadcast as they shaved and dressed. Downstairs, they tapped the barometer, lit the fire and boiled a kettle for tea. Then they did the milking and foddering before coming back for breakfast.

The house had roughcast walls and a roof of mossy stone tiles and stood at the far end of the farmyard in the shade of an old Scots pine. Below the cowshed there was an orchard of wind-stunted apple-trees, and then the fields slanted down to the dingle, and there were birches and alders along the stream.

Long ago, the place had been called Ty-Cradoc – and Caractacus is still a name in these parts – but in 1737 an ailing girl called Alice Morgan saw the Virgin hovering over a patch of rhubarb, and ran back to the kitchen, cured. To celebrate the miracle, her father renamed his farm 'The Vision' and carved the initials A.M. with the date and a cross on the lintel above the porch. The border of Radnor and Hereford was said to run right through the middle of the staircase.

The brothers were identical twins.

As boys, only their mother could tell them apart: now age and accidents had weathered them in different ways.

Lewis was tall and stringy, with shoulders set square and a steady long-limbed stride. Even at eighty he could walk over the hills all day, or wield an axe all day, and not get tired.

He gave off a strong smell. His eyes – grey, dreamy and astygmatic – were set well back into the skull, and capped with thick round lenses in white metal frames. He bore the scar of a cycling accident on his nose and, ever since, its tip had curved downwards and turned purple in cold weather.

His head would wobble as he spoke: unless he was fumbling with his watch-chain, he had no idea what to do with his hands. In company he always wore a puzzled look; and if anyone made a statement of fact, he'd say, 'Thank you!' or 'Very kind of you!' Everyone agreed he had a wonderful way with sheepdogs.

Benjamin was shorter, pinker, neater and sharper-tongued. His chin fell into his neck, but he still possessed the full stretch of his nose, which he would use in conversation as a weapon. He had less hair.

He did all the cooking, the darning and the ironing; and he kept the accounts. No one could be fiercer in a haggle over stock-prices and he would go on, arguing for hours, until the dealer threw up his hands and said, 'Come off, you old skinflint!' and he'd smile and say, 'What can you mean by that?'

For miles around the twins had the reputation of being incredibly stingy – but this was not always so.

They refused, for example, to make a penny out of hay. Hay, they said, was God's gift to the farmer; and providing The Vision had hay to spare, their poorer neighbours were welcome to what they needed. Even in the foul days of January, old Miss Fifield the Tump had only to send a message with the postman, and Lewis would drive the tractor over with a load of bales.

Benjamin's favourite occupation was delivering lambs. All the long winter, he waited for the end of March, when the curlews started calling and the lambing began. It was he, not Lewis, who stayed awake to watch the ewes. It was he who would pull a lamb at a difficult birth. Sometimes, he had to thrust his forearm into the womb to disentangle a pair of twins; and afterwards, he would sit by the fireside, unwashed and contented, and let the cat lick the afterbirth off his hands.

In winter and summer, the brothers went to work in striped flannel shirts with copper studs to fasten them at the neck. Their jackets and waistcoats were made of brown whipcord, and their trousers were of darker corduroy. They wore their moleskin hats with the brims turned down; but since Lewis had the habit of lifting his to every stranger, his fingers had rubbed the nap off the peak.

From time to time, with a show of mock solemnity, they consulted their silver watches – not to tell the hour but to see whose watch was beating faster. On Saturday nights they took turns to have a hip-bath in front of the fire; and they lived for the memory of their mother.

Because they knew each other's thoughts, they even quarrelled without speaking. And sometimes – perhaps after one of these silent quarrels, when they needed their mother to unite them – they would stand over her patchwork quilt and peer at the black velvet stars and the hexagons of printed calico that had once been her dresses. And without saying a word they could see her again – in pink, walking through the oatfield with a jug of draught cider for the reapers. Or in green, at a sheep-shearers' lunch. Or in a blue-striped apron bending over the fire. But the black stars brought back a memory of their father's coffin, laid out on the kitchen table, and the chalk-faced women, crying.

Nothing in the kitchen had changed since the day of his funeral. The wallpaper, with its pattern of Iceland poppies and russet fern, had darkened over with smoke-resin; and though the brass knobs shone as brightly as ever, the brown paint had chipped from the doors and skirting.

The twins never thought of renewing these threadbare decorations for fear of cancelling out the memory of that bright spring morning, over seventy years before, when they had helped their mother stir a bucket of flour-and-water paste, and watched the whitewash caking on her scarf.

Benjamin kept her flagstones scrubbed, the iron grate gleaming with black lead polish, and a copper kettle always hissing on the hob.

Friday was his baking day – as it had once been hers – and on Friday afternoons he would roll up his sleeves to make Welsh cakes or cottage loaves, pummelling the dough so vigorously that the cornflowers on the oilcloth cover had almost worn away.

On the mantelpiece stood a pair of Staffordshire spaniels, five brass candlesticks, a ship-in-a-bottle and a tea-caddy painted with a Chinese lady. A glass-fronted cabinet – one pane repaired with Scotch tape – contained china ornaments, silver-plated teapots, and mugs from every Coronation and Jubilee. A flitch of bacon was rammed into a rack in the rafters. The Georgian pianoforte was proof of idler days and past accomplishments.

Lewis kept a twelve-bore shotgun propped up beside the grandfather clock: both the brothers were terrified of thieves and antique-dealers.

Their father's only hobby – in fact, his only interest apart from farming and the Bible – had been to carve wooden frames for the pictures and family photographs that covered every spare stretch of wall. To Mrs Jones it had been a miracle that a man of her husband's temper and clumsy hands should have had the patience for such intricate work. Yet, from the moment he took up his chisels, from the moment the tiny white shavings flew, all the meanness went out of him.

He had carved a 'gothic' frame for the religious colour

print 'The Broad and Narrow Path'. He had invented some 'biblical' motifs for the watercolour of the Pool of Bethesda; and when his brother sent an oleograph from Canada, he smeared the surface with linseed oil to make it look like an Old Master, and spent a whole winter working up a surround of maple leaves.

And it was this picture, with its Red Indian, its birchbark, its pines and a crimson sky – to say nothing of its association with the legendary Uncle Eddie – that first awoke in Lewis a yearning for far-off places.

Apart from a holiday at the seaside in 1910, neither of the twins had ever strayed further than Hereford. Yet these restricted horizons merely inflamed Lewis's passion for geography. He would pester visitors for their opinions on 'them savages in Africky'; for news of Siberia, Salonika or Sri Lanka; and when someone spoke of President Carter's failure to rescue the Teheran hostages, he folded his arms and said, decisively, 'Him should'a gone to get 'em through Odessa.'

His image of the outside world derived from a Bartholomew's atlas of 1925 when the two great colonial empires were coloured pink and mauve, and the Soviet Union was a dull sage green. And it offended his sense of order to find that the planet was now full of bickering little countries with unpronounceable names. So, as if to suggest that real journeys only existed in the imagination – and perhaps to show off – he would close his eyes and chant the lines his mother taught him:

> *Westward, westward, Hiawatha*
> *Sailed into the fiery sunset*
> *Sailed into the purple vapours*
> *Sailed into the dusk of evening.*

Too often the twins had fretted at the thought of dying childless – yet they had only to glance at their wall of photographs to get rid of the gloomiest thoughts. They knew the names of all the sitters and never tired of finding likenesses between people born a hundred years apart.

Hanging to the left of their parents' wedding group was a picture of themselves at the age of six, gaping like baby barn-owls and dressed in identical page-boy collars for the fête in Lurkenhope Park. But the one that gave them most pleasure was a colour snapshot of their great-nephew Kevin, also aged six, and got up in a wash-towel turban, as Joseph in a nativity play.

Since then, fourteen years had passed and Kevin had grown into a tall, black-haired young man with bushy eyebrows that met in the middle, and slaty grey-blue eyes. In a few months the farm would be his.

So now, when they looked at that faded wedding picture; when they saw their father's face framed in fiery red sideburns (even in a sepia photo you could tell he had bright red hair); when they saw the leg-o'-mutton sleeves of their mother's dress, the roses in her hat, and the ox-eye daisies in her bouquet; and when they compared her sweet smile with Kevin's, they knew that their lives had not been wasted and that time, in its healing circle, had wiped away the pain and the anger, the shame and the sterility, and had broken into the future with the promise of new things.

Two

Of all the people who posed outside the Red Dragon at Rhulen, that sweltering afternoon in August 1899, none had better reason for looking pleased with himself than Amos Jones, the bridegroom. In one week, he had achieved two of his three ambitions: he had married a beautiful wife, and had signed the lease of a farm.

His father, a garrulous old cider-drinker, known round the pubs of Radnorshire as Sam the Waggon, had started life as a drover; had failed to make a living as a carter; and now lived, cooped up with his wife, in a tiny cottage on Rhulen Hill.

Hannah Jones was not an agreeable woman. As a young bride, she had loved her husband to distraction; had put up with his absences and infidelities, and, thanks to a monumental meanness, had always managed to thwart the bailiffs.

Then came the catastrophes that hardened her into a mould of unrelieved bitterness and left her mouth as sharp and twisted as a leaf of holly.

Of her five children, a daughter had died of consumption; another married a Catholic; the eldest son was killed in a Rhondda coalpit; her favourite, Eddie, stole her savings and skipped to Canada – and that left only Amos to support her old age.

Because he was her final fledgling, she coddled him more carefully than the others, and sent him to Sunday School to learn letters and fear of the Lord. He was not a stupid boy, but, by the age of fifteen, he had disappointed her hopes for his education; and she booted him from the house and sent him to earn his own keep.

Twice a year, in May and November, he hung round the Rhulen Fair, waiting for a farmer to hire him, with a wisp of sheep's wool in his cap and a clean Sunday smock folded over his arm.

He found work on several farms in Radnorshire and Montgomery, where he learned to handle a plough; to sow, reap and shear; to butcher hogs and dig the sheep out of snowdrifts. When his boots fell apart, he had to bind his feet with strips of felt. He would come back in the evenings, aching at every joint, to a supper of bacon broth and potatoes, and a few stale crusts. The owners were far too mean to provide a cup of tea.

He slept on bales of hay, in the granary or stable-loft, and would lie awake on winter nights, shivering under a damp blanket: there was no fire to dry his clothes. One Monday morning, his employer horsewhipped him for stealing some slices of cold mutton while the family was out at Chapel – a crime of which the cat, not he, was guilty.

He ran away three times and three times forfeited his wages. And yet he walked with a swagger, wore his cap at a rakish angle, and, hoping to attract a pretty farmer's daughter, spent his spare pennies on brightly coloured handkerchiefs.

His first attempt at seduction failed.

To wake the girl he threw a twig against her bedroom window, and she slipped him the key. Then, tiptoeing through the kitchen, his shin caught on a stool, and he tripped. A copper pot crashed to the floor; the dog barked, and a man's deep voice called out: her father was on the staircase as he bolted from the house.

At twenty-eight, he spoke of emigrating to Argentina where there were rumours of land and horses – at which his mother panicked and found him a bride.

She was a plain, dull-witted woman, ten years older than he, who sat all day staring at her hands and was already a burden on her family.

Hannah haggled for three days until the bride's father agreed that Amos should take her, as well as thirty breeding ewes, the lease of a smallholding called Cwmcoynant, and grazing rights on Rhulen Hill.

But the land was sour. It lay on a sunless slope and, at the snowmelt, streams of icy water came pouring through the cottage. Yet by renting a patch of ground here, another patch there; by buying stock in shares with other farmers, Amos managed to make a living and hope for better times.

There were no joys in that marriage.

Rachel Jones obeyed her husband with the passive movements of an automaton. She mucked out the pigsties in a torn tweed coat tied up with a bit of twine. She never smiled. She never cried when he hit her. She replied to his questions with grunts or monosyllables; and even in the agony of childbirth, she clenched her mouth so tightly that she uttered not a sound.

The baby was a boy. Having no milk, she sent him away to nurse, and he died. In November 1898, she stopped eating and set her face against the living world. There were snowdrops in the graveyard when they buried her.

From that day Amos Jones was a regular churchgoer.

Three

One Sunday matins, not a month after the funeral, the vicar of Rhulen announced that he had to attend a service in Llandaff Cathedral and that, next Sunday, the rector of Bryn-Draenog would preach the sermon.

This was the Reverend Latimer, an Old Testament scholar, who had retired from mission work in India and settled in this remote hill parish to be alone with his daughter and his books.

From time to time, Amos Jones had seen him on the mountain – a hollow-chested figure with white hair blowing about like cotton-grass, striding over the heather and shouting to himself so loudly that he frightened off the sheep. He had not seen the daughter, who was said to be sad and beautiful. He took his seat at the end of the pew.

On the way, the Latimers had to shelter from a cloudburst and, by the time their dog-cart drew up outside the church, they were twenty minutes late. While the rector changed in the vestry, Miss Latimer walked towards the choir-stalls, lowering her eyes to the strip of wine-red carpet, and avoiding the stares of the congregation. She brushed against Amos Jones's shoulder, and she stopped. She took half a step forwards, another step sideways, and then sat down, one pew in front of him, but across the aisle.

Drops of water sparkled on her black beaver hat, and her chignon of chestnut hair. Her grey serge coat was also streaked with rain.

On one of the stained-glass windows was a figure of the Prophet Elijah and his raven. Outside, on the sill, a pair of pigeons were billing and cooing and pecking at the pane.

The first hymn was 'Guide Me, O Thou Great Jehovah' and as the voices swelled in chorus, Amos caught her clear, quavering soprano while she felt his baritone murmuring like a bumblebee round the nape of her neck. All through the Lord's Prayer he stared at her long, white, tapering fingers. After the Second Lesson she risked a sidelong glance and saw his red hands on the red buckram binding of his prayerbook.

She blushed in confusion and slipped on her gloves.

Then her father was in the pulpit, twisting his mouth:

' "Though your sins be as scarlet, they shall be as white as snow; though they be red like crimson, they shall be as wool. If ye be willing and obedient . . ." '

She gazed at her hassock and felt her heart was breaking. After the service Amos passed her in the lych-gate, but she flashed her eyes and turned her back and peered into the boughs of a yew.

He forgot her – he tried to forget her – until one Thursday in April, he went to Rhulen market to sell some hoggets and exchange the news.

Along the length of Broad Street the farmers who had driven in from the country were tethering their ponies, and chatting in groups. Carts stood empty with their shafts in the air. From the bakery came the smell of freshly baked bread.

In front of the Town Hall there were booths with red-striped awnings, and black hats bobbing round them. In Castle Street the crowds were even thicker as people jostled forward to inspect the lots of Welsh and Hereford cattle. The sheep and pigs were penned behind hurdles. There was a nip in the air, and clouds of steam rose up off the animals' flanks.

Outside the Red Dragon two greybeards were drinking cider and moaning about 'them bloomin' rogues in Parliament'. A nasal voice called out the price of wicker chairs, and a purple-faced stock-dealer pumped the hand of a thin man in a brown derby.

'And 'ow's you?'

'Middling.'

'And the wife?'

'Poor.'

Two blue farm waggons, strewn with straw and piled with dressed poultry, were parked beside the municipal clock; and their owners, a pair of women in plaid shawls, were gossiping away, trying hard to feign indifference to the Birmingham buyer, who circled around them, twirling his malacca cane.

As Amos passed, he heard one of them say: 'And the poor thing! To think she's alone in the world!'

On the Saturday, a shepherd riding on the hill had found the Reverend Latimer's body, face downward in a pool. He had slipped in the peat bog and drowned. They had buried him at Bryn-Draenog on the Tuesday.

Amos sold his hoggets for what they would fetch and, as he put the coins into his waistcoat pocket, he saw that his hand was shaking.

Next morning, after foddering, he took a stick and walked the nine miles to Bryn-Draenog Hill. On reaching the line of rocks that crown the summit, he sat down out of the wind and retied a bootlace. Overhead, puffy clouds were streaming out of Wales, their shadows plunging down the slopes of gorse and heather, slowing up as they moved across the fields of winter wheat.

He felt light-headed, almost happy, as if his life, too, would begin afresh.

To the east was the River Wye, a silver ribbon snaking through water-meadows, and the whole countryside dotted with white or red-brick farmhouses. A thatched roof made a little patch of yellow in a foam of apple-blossom, and there were gloomy stands of conifers that shrouded the homes of the gentry.

A few hundred yards below, the sun caught the slates of Bryn-Draenog rectory and reflected back to the hill-top a parallelogram of open sky. Two buzzards were wheeling and falling in the blue air, and there were lambs and crows in a bright green field.

In the graveyard, a woman in black was moving in and out among the headstones. Then she passed through the wicket gate and walked up the overgrown garden. She was halfway across the lawn when a little dog came bounding out to greet her, yapping and pawing at her skirt. She threw a stick into the shrubbery and the dog raced off and came back, without the stick, and pawed again at her skirt. Something seemed to stop her from entering the house.

He raced downhill, his heel-irons clattering over the loose stones. Then he leaned over the garden fence, panting to catch his breath, and she was still standing, motionless among the laurels, with the dog lying quietly at her feet.

'Oh! It's you!' she said as she turned to face him.

'Your father,' he stammered. 'I'm sorry, Miss——'

'I know,' she stopped him. 'Do please come inside.'

He made an excuse for the mud on his boots.

'Mud!' she laughed. 'Mud can't dirty this house. And besides, I have to leave it.'

She showed him into her father's study. The room was dusty and lined with books. Outside the window, the bracts of a monkey-puzzle blocked out the sunlight. Tufts of horsehair spilled from the sofa on to a worn Turkey carpet. The desk was littered with yellowing papers and, on a revolving stand, there were Bibles and Commentaries on the Bible. On the black marble mantelpiece lay a few flint axeheads, and some bits of Roman pottery.

She went up to the piano, snatched the contents of a vase, and threw them in the grate.

'What horrible things they are!' she said. 'How I hate everlasting flowers!'

She eyed him as he looked at a watercolour – of white arches, a date palm, and women with pitchers.

'It's the Pool of Bethesda,' she said. 'We went there. We went all over the Holy Land on our way back from India. We saw Nazareth and Bethlehem and the Sea of Galilee. We saw Jerusalem. It was my father's dream.'

'I'd like some water,' he said.

She led the way down a passage to the kitchen. The table was scrubbed and bare; and there was not a sign of food.

She said, 'To think I can't even offer you a cup of tea!'

Outside again in the sunlight, he saw that her hair was streaked with grey, and there were crow's-feet spreading to her cheekbones. But he liked her smile, and the brown eyes shining between long black lashes. Around her waist there curled a tight black patent leather belt. His breeder's eye meandered from her shoulders to her hips.

'And I don't even know your name,' she said, and stretched out her hand.

'But Amos Jones is a wonderful name,' she continued, strolling beside him to the garden gate. Then she waved and ran back to the house. The last he saw of her, she was standing in the study. The black tentacles of the monkey-puzzle, reflected in the window, seemed to hold her white face prisoner as she pressed it to the pane.

He climbed the hill, then bounded from one grassy hummock to the next, shouting at the top of his voice: 'Mary Latimer! Mary Jones! Mary Latimer! Mary Jones!, Mary! . . . Mary! . . . Mary . . . !

Two days later he was back at the rectory with the present of a chicken he had plucked and drawn himself.

She was waiting on the porch, in a long blue wool dress, a Kashmiri shawl round her shoulders and a cameo, of Minerva, on a brown velvet ribbon round her neck.

'I missed to come yesterday,' he said.

'But I knew you'd come today.'

She threw back her head and laughed, and the dog caught a whiff of the chicken and jumped up and down, and scratched its paws on Amos's trousers. He pulled the chicken from his knapsack. She saw the cold pimply flesh. The smile fell from her face, and she stood rooted to the doorstep, shuddering.

They tried to talk in the hall, but she wrung her hands and stared at the red-tiled floor, while he shifted from foot to foot and felt himself colouring from his neck to his ears.

Both were bursting with things to say to each other. Both felt, at that moment, there was nothing more to say; that nothing would come of their meeting; that their two accents would never make one whole voice; and that they would both creep back to their shells – as if the flash of recognition in church were a trick of fate, or a temptation of the Devil to ruin them. They stammered on, and gradually their words spaced themselves into silence: their eyes did not meet as he edged out backwards and ran for the hill.

She was hungry. That evening, she roasted the chicken and tried to force herself to eat it. After the first mouthful, she dropped her knife and fork, set the dish down for the dog and rushed upstairs to her room.

She lay, face down on the narrow bed, sobbing into the pillow with the blue dress spread round her and the wind howling through the chimney-pots.

Towards midnight, she thought she heard the crunch of footsteps on gravel. 'He's come back,' she cried out loud, gasping with happiness, only to realize it was a rambler rose, scratching its barbs against the window. She tried counting sheep over a fence but instead of sending her to sleep the silly animals awoke another memory – of her other love, in a dusty town in India.

He was a Eurasian – a streak of a man with syrupy eyes and a mouth full of apologies. She saw him first in the telegraph office where he worked as a clerk. Then, when the cholera took her mother and his young wife, they exchanged condolences at the Anglican Cemetery. After that, they used to meet in the evenings and take a stroll beside the sluggish river. He took her to his house and gave her tea with buffalo milk and too much sugar. He recited speeches from

21

Shakespeare. He spoke, hopefully, of Platonic love. His little girl wore golden earrings, and her nostrils were bunged up with mucus.

'Strumpet!' her father had bellowed when the postmaster warned him of his daughter's 'indiscretion'. For three weeks he shut her in a stifling room, till she repented, on a diet of bread and water.

Around two in the morning, the wind changed direction and whined in a different key. She heard a branch breaking – *cra-ack!* – and at the sound of splitting wood, she sat up, suddenly:

'Oh my God! He's choked on a chicken bone!'

She groped her way downstairs. A draught blew out the candle as she opened the kitchen door. She stood shivering in the darkness. Above the screaming wind she could hear the little dog snoring steadily in his basket.

At dawn, she looked beyond the bedrail and brooded on the Holman Hunt engraving. 'Knock, and it shall be opened unto you,' He had said. And had she not knocked and waved her lantern outside the cottage door? Yet, at the moment when sleep did, finally, come, the tunnel down which she had wandered seemed longer and darker than ever.

Four

Amos hid his anger. All that summer, he lost himself in work, as if to wipe away the memory of the contemptuous woman who had raised his hopes and ruined them. Often, at the thought of her grey kid gloves, he banged his fist on the lonely table.

In the hay-making season, he went to help a farmer on the Black Hill, and met a girl called Liza Bevan.

They would meet in the dingle, and lie under the alders. She plastered his forehead with kisses and ran her stubby fingers through his hair. But nothing he could do – or she could do – could rub away the image of Mary Latimer, puckering her eyebrows in a pained reproach. At nights – awake, alone – how he longed for her smooth white body between himself and the wall!

One day, at the summer pony fair in Rhulen, he struck up a conversation with the shepherd who had found the rector's body.

'And the daughter?' he asked, making a show of shrugging his shoulders.

'Be leaving,' the man said. 'Packing up the house and all.'

It began to rain next morning as Amos reached

Bryn-Draenog. The rain washed down his cheeks and pattered on the leaves of the laurels. In the beeches round the rectory young rooks were learning to flex their wings, and their parents were flying round and round, cawing calls of encouragement. On the carriage-drive stood a tilbury. The groom waved his curry-comb at the red-headed stranger who strode into the house.

She was in the study with a ravaged, scant-haired gentleman in pince-nez, who was leafing through a leather-bound book.

'Professor Gethyn-Jones,' she introduced him without a flicker of surprise. 'And this is plain Mr Jones who has come to take me for a walk. Do please excuse us! Do go on with your reading!'

The professor slurred some words through his teeth. His handshake was dry and leathery. Grey veins ran round his knuckles like roots over rocks, and his breath was foul.

She went out and came back, her cheeks flushed, in wellington boots and an oiled drabbet cape.

'A friend of Father's,' she whispered once they were out of earshot. 'Now you see what I've suffered. And he wants me to give him the books – for nothing!'

'Sell them,' Amos said.

They walked up a sheeptrack, in the rain. The hill was in cloud and tassels of white water came streaming out of the cloud-bank. He walked ahead, brushing aside the gorse and the bracken, and she planted her footsteps in his.

They rested by the rocks, and then followed the old drove-road, arm in arm, talking with the ease of childhood friends. Sometimes, she strained to catch a word of his Radnor dialect. Sometimes, he asked her to repeat a phrase. But both knew, now, that the barrier between them was down.

He spoke of his ambitions and she spoke about her fears. He wanted a wife and a farm, and sons to inherit the farm. She dreaded being dependent on her relatives, or having to go into service. She had been happy in India before her mother died. She told him about the Mission, and of the terrible days before the monsoon broke:

'The heat! How we nearly died of heat!'

'And I,' he said, 'I'd not a fire all winter but the fire in the pub where they hired me.'

'Perhaps I should go back to India?' she said, but in a tone of such uncertainty that he knew that was not what she wanted.

The clouds broke and columns of brassy light slanted downward on to the peat bog.

'Look!' he called, pointing to a skylark above their heads, spiralling higher and higher, as if to greet the sun. 'Lark'll have a nest hereabouts.'

She heard a soft crack and saw a yellow smear on the toe of her boot.

'Oh no!' she cried. 'Now look what I've done!'

Her foot had crushed the nestful of eggs. She sat down on a tuft of grass. The tears stained her cheeks and she only stopped crying when he folded his arm around her shoulders.

At the Mawn Pool they played ducks-and-drakes on the dark water. Black-headed gulls flew up from the reed-beds, filling the air with mournful cries. When he lifted her across a patch of bog, she felt as light and insubstantial as the drifting mist.

Back at the rectory – as though to quieten her father's shade – they addressed one another in cold, terse phrases. They did not disturb the professor, who was buried in the books.

'Sell them!' said Amos, as he left her on the porch.

She nodded. She did not wave. She knew now when, and for what, he would be coming.

He came on the Saturday afternoon, on a Welsh bay cob. At the end of a lead-rein he held a piebald gelding with a side-saddle. She called from the bedroom the second she heard the sound of hoofs. He shouted, 'Hurry now! There's a farm for rent on the Black Hill.'

'I am hurrying,' she called back, and flew down the banisters in a riding habit of dove-grey Indian cotton. Her straw hat was crowned with roses, and a pink satin ribbon tied under her chin.

He had dipped into his savings to buy a new pair of boots, and she said, 'My! What boots!'

The scents of summer had clotted in the lanes. In the hedgerows, the honeysuckle had tangled with the dog-rose; and there were cloud-blue crane's-bills and purple foxgloves. In the farmyards, ducks waddled out of their way; sheepdogs barked, and ganders hissed and craned their necks. He broke off a branch of elder to whisk away the horseflies.

They passed a cottage with hollyhocks round the porch and a border ablaze with nasturtiums. An old woman in a goffered cap looked up from her knitting and croaked a few words to the travellers.

'Old Mary Prosser,' he whispered, and, when they were out of earshot, 'them do say as she's a witch.'

They crossed the Hereford road at Fiddler's Elbow; crossed the railway line, and then climbed the quarrymen's track that zigzags up the scarp of Cefn Hill.

At the edge of the pine plantation, they paused to rest the horses and looked back down over the town of Rhulen – at the jumble of slate roofs, the broken walls of the castle, the spire of the Bickerton Memorial, and the church weathercock glinting in a watery sun. A bonfire was burning in the vicarage garden, and a scarf of grey woodsmoke floated over the chimneys and streamed away along the river valley.

It was cold and dark among the pines. The horses scuffed the dead pine-needles. Midges whined, and there were frills of yellow fungus on the fallen branches. She shuddered as she looked along the long aisles of pine-trunks and said, 'It's dead in here.'

They rode to the edge of the wood and they rode on in the sunlight, out onto an open slope and, when the horses felt the grass underfoot, they broke into a canter and kicked up crescents of turf that flew out behind them, like swallows.

They cantered over the hill and trotted down into a valley of scattered farms, down through lines of late-flowering hawthorns, to the Lurkenhope lane. Each time they passed a gate, Amos made some comment on the owner: 'Morgan the Bailey. Very tidy person.' 'Williams the Vron, as married his cousin.' Or 'Griffiths Cwm Cringlyn what the father died of drink.'

In one field, boys were gathering hay into cocks and, by the roadside, a red-faced man was whetting his scythe, his shirt-front open to the navel.

'Nice mate o' yours!' he winked at Amos as they went by. They watered the horses in the brook; and then they stood on the bridge and watched the waterweeds wavering in the current, and the brown trout darting upstream. Half a mile further, Amos opened a mossy gate. Beyond it, a cart-track wound uphill to a house in a clump of larches.

'Them do call it "The Vision",' he said. 'And there be a hundred and twenty acre, and half gone to fern.'

Five

The Vision was an outlying farm on the Lurkenhope Estate, whose owners, the Bickertons, were an old Catholic family made rich by the West India trade.

The tenant had died in 1896, leaving an old unmarried sister who had carried on alone until they fetched her to a madhouse. In the yard, a young ash-tree reared its trunk through the boards of a hay-waggon. The roofs of the buildings were yellow with stonecrop; and the dungheap was overgrown with grass. At the end of the garden stood a brick-built privy. Amos slashed down the nettles to clear a path to the porch.

A broken hinge prevented the door from opening properly and, as he lifted it, a gust of fetid air flew in their faces.

They went into the kitchen and saw a bundle of the old woman's possessions, rotting away in a corner. The plaster was flaking and the flagstones had grown a film of slime. Twigs from a jackdaw's nest up the chimney were choking the grate. The table was still laid, with two places, for tea; but the cups were covered with spiders' webs, and the cloth was in shreds.

Amos took a napkin and flicked away the mouse-droppings.

'And rats!' said Mary cheerfully, as they heard the scuttle of feet in the rafters. 'But I'm used to rats. In India you have to get used to rats.'

In one of the bedrooms she found an old rag doll and handed it to him, laughing. He made a move to chuck it from the window; but she stayed his hand and said, 'No, I shall keep it.'

They went outside to inspect the buildings and the orchard. There'd be a good crop of damsons, he said, but the apple-trees would have to be replanted. Peering through the brambles, she saw a row of mouldering beehives.

'And I', she said, 'shall learn the secrets of the bee.'

He helped her over a stile and they walked uphill across two fields overgrown with gorse and blackthorn. The sun had dropped behind the escarpment, and swirls of coppery cloud were trailing over the rim. The thorns bit her ankles and tiny beads of blood burst through the white of her stockings. She said, 'I can manage,' when he offered to carry her.

The moon was up by the time they came back to the horses. The moonlight caught the curve of her neck, and a nightingale flung liquid notes into the darkness. He slipped an arm around her waist and said, 'Could you live in this?'

'I could,' she said, turning to face him, as he knotted his hands in the small of her back.

Next morning, she called on the vicar of Rhulen and asked him to publish the banns: on her finger she wore a ring of plaited grass stems.

The clergyman, who was having breakfast, spilled egg down his cassock and stuttered, 'It would not have been your father's wish.' He advised her to wait six months before deciding – at which she pursed her lips and answered, 'Winter is coming. We have no time to lose.'

Later in the day, a group of townswomen watched Amos helping her into his trap. The draper's wife squinted angrily, as if eyeing the eye of a needle, and pronounced her 'four months gone'. Another woman said, 'For shame!' – and all of them wondered what Amos Jones could see in 'that hussy'.

At dawn on the Monday, long before anyone was about, Mary stood outside the Lurkenhope Estate Office, waiting for the Bickertons' land-agent to discuss the terms of the lease. She was alone. Amos had little control of his manners when confronted with the presence of the gentry.

The agent was a jowly, wine-faced man, a distant cousin of the family, who had been cashiered from the Indian Army, and had lost his pension. They paid him a wretched salary; but since he had a head for figures and a method for dealing with 'uppity' tenants, they allowed him to shoot their pheasants and drink their port.

He prided himself on his humour and, when Mary explained her visit, he rammed his thumbs into his waistcoat and roared with laughter:

'So you're thinking of joining the peasants? Ha! I wouldn't!'

She blushed. High on the wall, there was a moth-eaten fox's mask, snarling. He drummed his fingers on the leather top of his desk.

'The Vision!' he said abruptly. 'Can't say I've ever been to The Vision. Can't even think where The Vision is! Let's look it up on the map!'

He heaved himself to his feet and led her by the hand to the estate map that covered one end of the room. His fingernails were stained with nicotine.

He stood beside her, breathing hoarsely: 'Rather cold up there on the mountain, what?'

'Safer than on the plain,' she said, disentangling her fingers from his.

He sat down again. He did not motion her to a chair. He muttered of 'other applicants on the list' and told her to wait four months for Colonel Bickerton's reply.

'Too late, I'm afraid,' she smiled, and slipped away.

She walked back to the North Lodge and asked the keeper's wife for a sheet of paper. She penned a note to Mrs Bickerton, whom she had met once with her father. The agent was furious to learn that a manservant had driven down from the castle inviting Mary to tea that same afternoon.

Mrs Bickerton was a frail, fair-skinned woman in her late thirties. As a girl, she had devoted herself to painting, and had lived in Florence. Then, when her talent seemed to desert her, she married a handsome but brainless cavalry officer, possibly for his collection of Old Masters, possibly to annoy her artist friends.

The Colonel had recently resigned his commission without ever having fired at an enemy. They had a son called Reggie, and two daughters – Nancy and Isobel. The butler showed Mary through the rose-garden gate.

Mrs Bickerton was sheltering from the hot sun, beside a bamboo tea-table, in the shade of a cedar of Lebanon. Pink rambler roses tumbled over the south front, but holland-blinds were drawn in all the windows, and the castle looked uninhabited. It was a 'fake' castle, built in the 1820s. From another lawn came the knock of croquet balls and the noise of young, moneyed laughter.

'China or Indian?' Mrs Bickerton had to repeat the

question. Three ropes of pearls fell into the ruffles of her grey chiffon blouse.

'India,' her guest replied vaguely; and as the older woman poured from the silver teapot, Mary heard her say, 'Are you sure it's the right thing?'

'I am sure,' she said, and bit her lip.

'I like the Welsh,' Mrs Bickerton went on. 'But they do seem to get so angry, later. It must be to do with the climate.'

'No,' repeated Mary. 'I am sure.'

Mrs Bickerton's face was sad and drawn, and her hand was trembling. She tried to offer Mary the post of governess to her children: it was useless to argue.

'I shall speak to my husband,' she said. 'You can count on the farm.'

As the gate swung open, Mary wondered if the same pink roses would flower so freely, high up on her side of the mountain. Before the month was out, she and Amos had made plans to last the rest of their lives.

Her father's library contained a number of rare volumes; and these, sold to an antiquarian bookseller from Oxford, paid for two years' rent, a pair of draught horses, four milch cows, twenty fattening cattle, a plough and a second-hand chaff-cutter. The lease was signed. The house was scrubbed and whitewashed, and the front door painted brown. Amos hung up a branch of rowan to 'keep off the bad eyes' and bought a flock of white pigeons for the dovecote.

One day, he and his father carted the piano and four-poster from Bryn-Draenog. They had the 'Devil's job' getting the bed upstairs; and, afterwards in the pub, Old Sam bragged to his cronies that The Vision was 'God's own little love-nest'.

The bride had one anxiety: that her sister might come from Cheltenham and ruin the wedding. She sighed with relief to read the letter of refusal and, when she came to the words 'beneath you', burst into a fit of uncontrollable laughter and tossed it in the fire with the last of her father's papers.

By the time of the first frosts, the new Mrs Jones was pregnant.

Six

She spent the first months of her marriage making improvements to the house.

The winter was hard. From January to April the snow never melted off the hill and the frozen leaves of foxgloves drooped like dead donkeys' ears. Every morning she peered from the bedroom window to see if the larches were black or crisped with rime. The animals were silent in the deep cold, and the chatter of her sewing machine could be heard as far as the lambing paddock.

She made cretonne curtains for the four-poster and green plush curtains for the parlour. She cut up an old red flannel petticoat and made a rag rug, of roses, to go in the kitchen hearth. After supper, she would sit on the upright settle, her knees covered in crochet-work, while he gazed in adoration at his clever little spider.

He worked in all weathers – ploughing, fencing, ditching, laying drainage pipes, or building a drystone wall. At six in the evening, dog-tired and dirty, he came back to a mug of hot tea and a pair of warmed carpet slippers. Sometimes, he came back soaked to the skin and clouds of steam would billow upwards to the rafters.

She never knew how tough he really was.

'Do take off those clothes,' she'd scold him. 'You'll catch your death of pneumonia.'

'I expect,' he'd smile, and puff rings of tobacco smoke in her face.

He treated her as a fragile object that had come by chance into his possession and might easily break in his hands. He was terrified of hurting her, or of letting his hot blood carry him away. The sight of her whalebone corset was enough to unman him completely.

Before his marriage, he had doused himself once a week in the wash-house. Now, for fear of upsetting her sensibilities, he insisted on having hot water in the bedroom.

A Minton jug and basin, stencilled with a trellis of ivy leaves, stood on the wash-stand under the Holman Hunt engraving. And before putting on his nightshirt, he would strip to the waist and lather his chest and armpits. A candle stood beside the soap-dish; and Mary would lie back on the pillow watching the candlelight as it flickered red through his sideburns, threw a golden rim around his shoulders, and cast a big, dark shadow on the ceiling.

Yet he felt so awkward when washing, that if ever he sensed her eyeing him through the bed-curtains, he would wring out the sponge and snuff the candle, and bring to bed both the smell of animals and the scent of lavender soap.

On Sunday mornings, they drove down to Lurkenhope to take Holy Communion in the parish church. Reverently, she let the wafer moisten on her tongue: 'The Body of Our Lord Jesus Christ which is given for you . . .' Reverently, she raised the chalice to her lips: 'The Blood of Our Lord Jesus Christ which is shed for you . . .' Then, lifting her gaze to the brass cross on the altar, she tried to concentrate on the Passion, but her thoughts would wander to the hard, breathing body beside her.

As for their neighbours, most of them were Chapel-folk whose mistrust of the English went back, centuries before Non-conformism, to the days of the Border Barons. The women especially were suspicious of Mary; but she soon won them over.

Her housekeeping was the envy of the valley; and at teatime on Sundays, providing the lanes were clear of ice, four or five pony traps would drive up to The Vision yard. The Reuben Joneses were regulars, as were Ruth and Dai Morgan the Bailey; young Haines of Red Daren, and Watkins the Coffin, a despairing pox-pitted fellow, who despite his club-foot would hobble over the mountain from Craig-y-Fedw.

The guests came in with solemn faces and Bibles under their arms: their piety soon vanished as they tucked into Mary's fruitcake, or the fingers of cinnamon toast, or the scones with thick fresh cream and strawberry jam.

Presiding over these tea-parties, Mary felt that she had been a farmer's wife for years, and that her daily activities – of churning milk, drenching calves, or feeding poultry – were not things she had learned but had come as second nature. Gaily, she would chatter away about scab, or colic, or laminitis. 'Really,' she'd say, 'I can't think why the mangolds are so small this year.' Or 'There's so little hay, I don't know how we'll last the winter through.'

Up at the end of the table, Amos would be terribly embarrassed. He hated to hear his clever wife making a fool of herself. And if she saw him bridling with annoyance, she would change the subject and amuse her guests with the watercolours in her Indian sketchbook.

She showed them the Taj Mahal, the Burning Ghats and the naked yogis who sat on beds of nails.

'And 'ow big's them elephants?' asked Watkins the Coffin.

'About three times the size of a carthorse,' she said, and the cripple creased with laughter at the absurdity of the idea.

India was too far, too big and too confused to appeal to the Welshmen's imagination. Yet – as Amos never tired of reminding them – her feet had trodden in the steps of His Feet; she, too, had seen the real Rose of Sharon; and for her, Carmel, Tabor, Hebron and Galilee were as real as, say, Rhulen, or Glascwm, or Llanfihangel-nant-Melan.

Most Radnorshire farmers knew chapter and verse of the Bible, preferring the Old Testament to the New, because in the Old Testament there were many more stories about sheep-farming. And Mary had such a talent for describing the Holy Land that all their favourite characters seemed to float before their eyes: Ruth in the cornfield; Jacob and Esau; Joseph in his patchwork coat; or Hagar, the Rejected One, gasping for water in the shade of a thornbush.

Not everyone, of course, believed her – least of all her mother-in-law, Hannah Jones.

She and Sam had the habit of turning up uninvited; and she would brood over the table, wrapped in a fringed black shawl, gobbling up the sandwiches and making everyone feel uncomfortable.

One Sunday, she interrupted Mary to ask whether 'by any chance' she'd been to Babylon.

'No, Mother. Babylon is not in the Holy Land.'

'No,' echoed Haines of Red Daren. 'It be not in the Holy Land.'

*

No matter how hard Mary tried to be pleasant, the old woman had hated her son's new wife on sight. She ruined the wedding-breakfast by calling her 'Your Ladyship!' to her face. The first family lunch ended in tears when she crooked her finger and sneered, 'Past the age of childbearing, I would have said.'

She never set foot in The Vision without finding something to scorn: the napkins folded like waterlilies, the marmalade pot, or the caper sauce for mutton. And when she ridiculed the silver toast-rack, Amos warned his wife to put it away 'or you'll have us the laughing-stock'.

He dreaded his mother's visits. Once, she jabbed Mary's terrier with the ferrule of her umbrella and, from that day, the little dog would bare its teeth, and try to scuttle under her skirt and nip her ankle.

The final break came when she snatched some butter from her daughter-in-law's hand and screamed, 'You don't waste good butter on pastry!' – and Mary, whose nerves were on edge, screamed back, 'Well, what do you waste it on? You, I suppose?'

Though he loved his wife, though he knew she was in the right, Amos flew to his mother's defence. 'Mother means well,' he'd say. Or 'She's had a hard life.' And when Hannah took him aside to complain of Mary's extravagance and 'stuck-up' ways, he let her finish her diatribe and – in spite of himself – agreed with it.

The truth was that Mary's 'improvements' made him more, not less, uncomfortable. Her spotless flagstones were a barrier to be crossed. Her damask table-cloths were a reproach to his table-manners. He was bored by the novels she read aloud after supper – and her food was, frankly, uneatable.

As a wedding present, Mrs Bickerton had sent a copy of *Mrs Beeton's Book of Household Management* – and though its recipes were quite unsuited to a farmhouse kitchen, Mary read it from cover to cover, and took to planning menus in advance.

So, instead of the predictable round of boiled bacon, dumplings and potatoes, she served up dishes he'd never even heard of – a fricassee of chicken or a jugged hare, or mutton with rowanberry sauce. When he complained of constipation, she said, 'That means we must grow green vegetables,' and made out a list of seeds to order for the garden. But when she suggested planting an asparagus bed, he flew into a towering rage. Who did she think she was? Did she think she'd married into the gentry?

The crisis came when she experimented with a mild Indian curry. He took one mouthful and spat it out. 'I want none of your filthy Indian food,' he snarled, and smashed the serving dish on the floor.

She did not pick up the bits. She ran upstairs and buried her face in the pillow. He did not join her. He did not, in the morning, make amends. He took to sleeping rough and went for long walks at night with a bottle in his pocket. One wet night, he came home drunk and sat staring savagely at the table-cloth, clenching and unclenching his fists. Then he got to his feet and lurched towards her.

She cringed and raised her elbow.

'Don't hit me,' she cried.

'I won't hit you,' he roared, and rushed out into the dark.

At the end of April there were pink buds in the orchard, and a vizor of cloud above the mountain.

Mary shivered by the grate and listened to the tireless lapping of the rain. The house absorbed the damp like a sponge. Mouldy rings disfigured the whitewash, and the wallpaper bulged.

There were days when it occurred to her that she had sat for years in the same damp, dark room, in the same trap, living with the same bad-tempered man. She looked at her chapped and blistered hands, and felt she would grow old and coarse and ugly before her time. She even lost the memory of having a father and mother. The colours of India had faded; and she began to identify herself with the one, wind-battered thorn-bush that she could see from her window, silhouetted on the lip of the escarpment.

Seven

Then came the fine weather.

On the 18th of May – even though it was not a Sunday – they heard the peal of church bells on the far side of the hill. Amos harnessed the pony and they drove down to Rhulen, where Union Jacks were fluttering from every window to celebrate the Relief of Mafeking. A brass band was playing and a parade of schoolchildren passed down Broad Street with pictures of the Queen and Baden-Powell. Even the dogs wore patriotic ribbons tied to their collars.

As the procession passed, she nudged him in the ribs, and he smiled.

'Be the winter as makes me mad.' He appeared to be pleading with her. 'Some winters seem as they'll never end.'

'Well, next winter', she said, 'we shall have someone else to think about.'

He planted a kiss on her forehead, and she threw her arms around his neck.

When she woke next morning, a breeze was ruffling the net curtains; a thrush sang in the pear-tree; pigeons were burbling on the roof, and patches of white light wandered over the bed-cover. Amos was asleep in his calico nightshirt. The buttons had come undone, and his chest was bare. Squinting sideways, she glanced at the heaving ribcage, the red hairs round his nipples, the pink dimple left by his shirtstud, and the line where the sunburned neck met the milky thorax.

She cupped her hand over his biceps muscle, and withdrew it.

'To think I might have left him' – she held the words within her teeth and, blushing, turned her face to the wall.

As for Amos, he now thought of nothing but his baby boy – and, in his imagination, pictured a brawny little fellow who would muck out the cowshed.

Mary also hoped for a boy, and already had plans for his career. Somehow, she would send him to boarding-school. He'd win scholarships. He'd grow up to be a statesman or a lawyer or a surgeon who would save people's lives.

Walking down the lane one day, she absent-mindedly tugged at the branch of an ash-tree; and as she looked at the tiny transparent leaves breaking from the smoky black buds, she was reminded that he, too, was reaching for the sunlight.

Her one close friend was Ruth Morgan the Bailey, a small homely woman with a face of great simplicity and flaxen hair tied up in a coif. She was the best midwife in the valley, and she assisted Mary to prepare the layette.

On sunny days, they sat on wicker chairs in the front garden, sewing flannels and binders; trimming vests, petticoats and bonnets; or knitting blue wool bootees that tied with satin ribbon.

Sometimes, to exercise her stiff hands, Mary played Chopin waltzes on the piano that badly needed tuning. Her fingers ran up and down the keyboard, and a flight of jangling chords flew out of the window, and up among the pigeons. Ruth Morgan heaved with emotion and said it was the loveliest music in the world.

Only when the layette was finished did they spread it out for Amos to admire:

'But them's not for a boy,' he said, indignantly.

'Oh yes!' they cried in unison. 'For a boy!'

Two weeks later, Sam the Waggon came to lend a hand with the shearing and, rather than go back home, stayed on to help in the kitchen-garden. He sowed and hoed. He pricked out lettuce seedlings, and cut pea-sticks and bean-poles. One day, he and Mary dressed up a scarecrow in one of the missionary's tropical suits.

Sam had the face of a sad old clown.

Fifty years of fisticuffs had flattened his nose. A lonely incisor lingered in his lower jaw. Nets of red string covered his eyeballs and his eyelids seemed to rustle as he blinked. The presence of an attractive woman drove him to acts of reckless flirtation.

Mary liked his gallantries and laughed at his yarns – for he, too, had 'run about the world'. Every morning he picked her a bouquet from her own front flower-bed; and every night, as Amos passed him on the way upstairs, he'd rub his hands and cackle, 'Lucky dog! Ooh! If I were a younger man . . . !'

He still owned an ancient fiddle – a relic of his droving days – and when he took it from its case, he would caress the gleaming wood as if it were a woman's body. He knew how to knit his eyebrows like a concert violinist and to make the instrument quaver and sob – though when he hit the high notes, Mary's terrier would raise its snout and howl.

Occasionally, if Amos was away, they practised

duets – 'Lord Thomas and Fair Eleanor' or 'The Unquiet Grave'; and once he caught them polka-ing on the flagstones.

'Stop that!' he shouted. 'Will ye hurt the baby?'

Sam's behaviour made Hannah so angry that she fell ill.

Before Mary's appearance, she had only to call out, 'Sam!' for her husband to hang his head, mutter 'Aye, m'dear!' and shuffle off on some trivial errand. Now, the people of Rhulen saw her storming down to the Red Dragon, filling the street with deep-throated cries, 'Saa-am! . . . Saa-am!' – but Sam would be out on the hillside gathering mushrooms for his daughter-in-law.

One muggy evening – it was the first week in July – a clatter of wheel rims sounded in the lane, and Hughes the Carter drove up with Hannah and a pair of bundles. Amos was screwing a new hinge to the stable-door. He dropped the screwdriver and asked why she had come.

She answered gloomily, 'I belong by the bedside.'

A day or two later, Mary woke with an attack of nausea and throbbing pains that raced up and down her spine. As Amos left the bedroom, she clung to his arm and pleaded, 'Please ask her to go. I'd feel better if she'd go. I beg you. Or I'll ——'

'No,' he said, lifting the latch. 'Mother belongs here. She must stay.'

All that month there was a heatwave. The wind blew from the east and the sky was a hard and cloudless blue. The pump ran dry. The mud cracked. Swarms of horseflies buzzed about the nettles, and the pains in Mary's spine grew worse. Night after night, she dreamed the same dream – of blood and nasturtiums.

She felt that her strength was draining away. She felt that something had snapped inside; that the baby would be born deformed, or born dead, or that she herself would die. She wished she had died in India, for the poor. Propped up on pillows, she prayed to the Redeemer to take her life but – Lord! Lord! – to let him live.

Old Hannah spent the heat of the day in the kitchen, shivering under a black shawl, knitting – knitting very slowly – a pair of long white woollen socks. When Amos beat to death an adder that had been sunning itself by the porch, she curled her lip and said, 'That means a death in the family!'

The 15th of July was Mary's birthday; and because she was feeling a little better, she came downstairs and tried to make conversation with her mother-in-law. Hannah hooded her eyes and said, 'Read to me!'

'What shall I read, Mother?'

'The floral tributes.'

So Mary turned to the funeral columns of the *Hereford Times* and began:

' "The funeral of Miss Violet Gooch who died tragically last Thursday at the age of seventeen was held at St Asaph's Church——" '

'I said the floral tributes.'

'Yes, Mother,' she corrected herself, and began again:

' "Wreath of arum lilies from Auntie Vi and Uncle Arthur. 'Nevermore!' . . . Wreath of yellow roses. 'With ever loving memory from Poppet, Winnie and Stanley . . .' Artificial wreath in glass case. 'With kind remembrance from the Hooson Emporium . . .' Bouquet of Gloire de Dijon roses. 'Sleep softly, my dearest. From Auntie Mavis, Mostyn Hotel, Llandrindod . . .' Bouquet of wild flowers. 'Only good-night, Belovèd, not farewell! Your loving sister, Cissie . . .'

'Well, go on!' Hannah had opened an eyelid. 'What's the matter with you? Go on! Finish it!'

'Yes, Mother . . . "The coffin, of beautifully polished oak with brass fittings, was made by Messrs Lloyd and Lloyd of Presteigne with the following inscription on the lid: 'A harp! A magnificent harp! With a broken string!'"'

'Ah!' the old woman said.

The preparations for Mary's confinement made Sam so jittery anyone would have thought that he, not his son, were the father. He was always thinking of ways to please her: indeed, his was the one face that made her smile. He spent the last of his savings commissioning a rocking cradle from Watkins the Coffin. It was painted red, with blue and white stripes, and had four carved finials in the form of songbirds.

'Father, you shouldn't have . . .' Mary clapped her hands, as he tried it out on the kitchen flags.

'And it's a coffin, not a cradle, she'll be needing,' Hannah mumbled, and went on with her knitting.

For over fifty years she had kept, from her bridal trousseau, a single unlaundered white cotton nightdress to wear with the white socks when they laid her out as a corpse. On August 1st, she turned the heel of the second sock and, from then on, knitted slower and slower, sighing between the stitches and croaking, 'Not long now!'

Her skin, papery at the best of times, appeared to be transparent. Her breath came in cracked bursts, and she had difficulty moving her tongue. It was obvious to everyone but Amos that she had come to The Vision to die.

On the 8th of August the weather broke. Stacks of smoky, silver-lidded clouds piled up behind the hill. At six in the evening, Amos and Dai Morgan were scything the last of the oats. All the birds were silent in the stillness that precedes a storm. Thistledown floated upwards, and a shriek tore out across the valley.

The labour pains had begun. Upstairs in the bedroom, Mary lay writhing, moaning, kicking off the sheets and biting the pillow. Ruth Morgan tried to calm her. Sam was in the kitchen, boiling water. Hannah sat on the settle, and counted her stitches.

Amos saddled the cob and cantered over the hill, helter-skelter down the quarrymen's track to Rhulen.

'Courage, man!' said Dr Bulmer, as he divided his forceps and slid each half down one of his riding-boots. Then, shoving a flask of ergot into one pocket, a bottle of chloroform into the other, he buttoned the collar of his mackintosh cape, and both men set their faces to the storm.

The rainwater hissed on the rooftiles as they tethered their horses to the garden fence.

Amos attempted to follow upstairs. The doctor pushed him back, and he dropped on to the rocking-chair as if he'd been hit on the chest.

'Please God it be a boy,' he moaned. 'An' I'll never touch her again.' He grabbed at Ruth Morgan's apron as she went by with a water-jug. 'Be she all right?' he pleaded, but she shook him off and told him not to be silly.

Twenty minutes later, the bedroom door opened and a voice boomed out:

'Any more newspaper? An oilskin? Anything'll do!'

'Be it a boy?'

'Two of them.'

That night, Hannah rounded off the toe of her second sock and, three days later, died.

Eight

The twins' first memory – a shared memory which both remembered equally well – was of the day they were stung by the wasp.

They were perched on high-chairs at the tea-table. It must have been teatime because the sun was streaming in from the west, bouncing off the table-cloth and making them blink. It must have been late in the year, perhaps as late as October, when wasps are drowsy. Outside the window, a magpie hung from the sky, and bunches of red rowanberries thrashed in the gale. Inside, the slabs of bread-and-butter glistened the colour of primroses. Mary was spooning egg-yolk into Lewis's mouth and Benjamin, in a fit of jealousy, was waving his hands to attract attention when his left hand hit the wasp, and was stung.

Mary rummaged in the medicine cupboard for cotton-wool and ammonia, dabbed the hand and, as it swelled and turned scarlet, said soothingly, 'Be brave, little man! Be brave!'

But Benjamin did not cry. He simply pursed his mouth and turned his sad grey eyes on his brother. For it was Lewis, not he, who was whimpering with pain, and stroking his own left hand as if it were a wounded bird. He went on snivelling till bedtime. Only when they were locked in each other's arms did the twins doze off – and from then on, they associated eggs with wasps and mistrusted anything yellow.

This was the first time Lewis demonstrated his power to draw the pain from his brother, and take it on himself.

He was the stronger twin, and the firstborn.

To show he was the firstborn, Dr Bulmer nicked a cross on his wrist; and even in the cradle he was the stronger. He was unafraid of the dark and of strangers. He loved to rough-and-tumble with the sheepdogs. One day, when nobody was about, he squeezed through the door of the beast-house, where Mary found him, several hours later, gabbling away to the bull.

By contrast, Benjamin was a terrible coward who sucked his thumb, screamed if separated from his brother, and was always having nightmares – of getting caught in a chaff-cutter, or trampled by carthorses. Yet whenever he really did get hurt – if he fell in the nettles or walloped his shin – it was Lewis who cried instead.

They slept in a truckle bed, in a low-beamed room along the landing, where, in another early memory, they woke one morning to find that the ceiling was an unusual shade of grey. Peering out, they saw the snow on the larches, and the snowflakes spiralling down.

When Mary came in to dress them, they were curled, head to toe, in a heap at the bottom of the bed.

'Don't be silly,' she said. 'It's only snow.'

'No, Mama,' came two muffled voices from under the blankets. 'God's spitting.'

*

Apart from Sunday drives to Lurkenhope, their first excursion into the outside world was a visit to the Flower Show of 1903 when the pony shied at a dead hedgehog in the lane, and their mother won First Prize for runner beans.

They had never seen such a crowd and were bewildered by the shouts, the laughter, the flapping canvas and jingling harness, and the strangers who gave them pickaback rides round the exhibits.

They were wearing sailor-suits; and with their grave grey eyes and black hair cut in a fringe, they soon attracted a circle of admirers. Even Colonel Bickerton came up:

'Ho! Ho! My Jolly Jack Tars!' he said, and chucked them under the chin.

Later, he took them for a spin in his phaeton; and when he asked their names, Lewis answered Benjamin and Benjamin answered Lewis.

Then they got lost.

At four o'clock, Amos went off to pull for Rhulen in the tug-of-war; and since Mary had entered for the Ladies' Egg-and-Spoon Race, she left the twins in charge of Mrs Griffiths Cwm Cringlyn.

Mrs Griffiths was a big, bossy, shiny-faced woman, who had twin nieces of her own and prided herself as an expert. Lining the boys up side by side, she scrutinized them all over until she found a tiny mole behind Benjamin's right ear.

'There now!' she called out loud. 'I found a difference!' – whereupon Benjamin shot a despairing glance at his brother, who grabbed his hand, and they both dived through the spectators' legs and hid in the marquee.

They hid under a cloth-covered trestle, under the prize-winning vegetable marrows, and so much enjoyed the view of ladies' and gentlemen's feet that they went on hiding until they heard their mother's voice calling and calling in a voice more cracked and anxious than a bleating ewe.

On the way home, huddled in the back of the dog-cart, they discussed their adventure in their own secret language. And when Amos bawled out, 'Stop that nonsense, will ye?' Lewis piped up, 'It's not nonsense, Papa. It's the language of the angels. We were born with it.'

Mary tried to drill into their heads the difference between 'yours' and 'mine'. She bought them Sunday suits – a grey tweed for Lewis and blue serge for Benjamin. They wore them for half an hour, then sneaked off and came back wearing each other's jackets. They persisted in sharing everything. They even split their sandwiches in two, and swapped the halves.

One Christmas, their presents were a fluffy teddy-bear and a felt Humpty-Dumpty, but on the afternoon of Boxing Day, they decided to sacrifice the teddy on a bonfire, and concentrate their love on 'The Dump'.

The Dump slept on their pillow, and they took him for walks. In March, however – on a grey blustery day with catkins on the branches and slush in the lane – they decided that he, too, had come between them. So the moment Mary's back was turned, they sat him on the bridge, and tipped him in the brook.

'Look, Mama!' they cried, two stony faces peeping over the parapet at the black thing bobbing downstream.

Mary saw The Dump get caught in an eddy and stick on a branch.

'Stay there!' she called and rushed to the rescue, only to miss her footing and almost fall into the scummy brown flood-water. Pale and dishevelled, she ran to the twins and hugged them.

'Never mind, Mama,' they said. 'We never liked The Dump.'

Nor, in the following autumn, did they like their new baby sister, Rebecca.

They had pestered their mother to give them a baby sister; and when, at last, she arrived, they climbed up to the bedroom, each carrying a coppery chrysanthemum in an egg-cup full of water. They saw an angry pink creature biting Mary's breast. They dropped their offerings on the floor, and dashed downstairs.

'Send her away,' they sobbed. For a whole month, they lapsed into their private language and it took them a year to tolerate her presence. One day, when Mrs Griffiths Cwm Cringlyn came to call, she found them writhing convulsively on the kitchen floor.

'What's up with the twins?' she asked in alarm.

'Take absolutely no notice,' said Mary. 'They're playing at having babies.'

By the age of five, they were helping with the housework, to knead the bread dough, shape the butter-pats, and spread the sugar icing on a sponge cake. Before bedtime, Mary would reward them with a story from the Brothers Grimm or Hans Christian Andersen: their favourite was the story of the mermaid who went to live in the Mer-King's palace at the bottom of the sea.

By six, they were reading on their own.

Amos Jones mistrusted book-learning and would growl at Mary not to 'mollycoddle the kids'.

He gave them bird-scarers and left them alone in the oatfield to shoo away the woodpigeons. He made them mix the chicken-mash, and pluck and dress the birds for market. Fine weather or foul, he would sit them on his pony, one in front and one behind, and ride around the hill-flock. In autumn, they watched the ewes being tupped: five months later, they witnessed the birth of the lambs.

They had always recognized their affinity with twin lambs. Like lambs, too, they played the 'I'm the King of the Castle' game; and one breezy morning, as Mary was pegging up her laundry, they slipped under her apron, butted their heads against her thighs, and made noises as if suckling an udder.

'None of that, you two,' she laughed, and pushed them away. 'Go and find your grandfather!'

Nine

Old Sam had come to live at The Vision, and slipped into second childhood.

He wore a moleskin waistcoat, a floppy black cap, and went around everywhere with a buckthorn stick. He slept in a cobwebby attic no bigger than a cupboard, surrounded by the few possessions he had bothered to keep: the fiddle, a pipe, a tobacco-box and a porcelain statuette picked up somewhere on his travels – of a portly gentleman with a portmanteau and an inscription round the base reading, 'I shall start on a long journey.'

His principal occupation was to look after Amos's pigs. Pigs, he said, 'was more intelligent than persons'; and certainly all his six sows adored him, snorted when he rattled their swill-pail and answered, each one, to their names.

His favourite was a Large Black called Hannah; and while Hannah rootled for grubs under the apple-trees, he would scratch behind her ears and recall the more agreeable moments of his marriage.

Hannah, however, was hopeless as a mother. She crushed her first litter to death. The second time, having swelled to a colossal size, she produced a solitary male piglet, whom the twins called Hoggage and adopted as their own.

One day, when Hoggage was three months old, they decided it was time to baptize him.

'I'll be vicar,' said Lewis.

'I bags be vicar,' said Benjamin.

'All right! Be the vicar, then!'

It was a boiling hot day in June. The dogs lay panting in the shade of the barn. Flies were zooming and zizzing. Black cows were grazing below the farmhouse. The hawthorns were in flower. The whole field was black and white and green.

The twins stole out of the kitchen with an apron to wear as a surplice and a stripy towel for the christening robe. After a mad chase round the orchard, they cornered Hoggage by the hen-house and carried him squealing to the dingle. Lewis held him, while Benjamin wetted his finger and planted a cross above his snout.

But though they dosed Hoggage with worm-powders, though they stuffed him with stolen cake, and though Hoggage made up for his smallness with an amenable personality – to the extent of letting the twins take rides on his back – Hoggage remained a runt; and Amos had no use for runts. One morning in November, Sam went to the meal-shed for barley and found his son sharpening the blade of a meat-cleaver. He tried to protest, but Amos scowled and ground his whetstone even harder.

'No sense to keep a runt,' he said.

'But not Hoggage?' Sam stammered.

'I said, no sense to keep a runt.'

To get them out of earshot, the old man took his grandsons mushrooming on the hill. When they came home at dusk,

Benjamin saw the pool of blood beside the meal-shed door and, through a chink, saw Hoggage's carcass hanging from a hook.

Both boys held back their tears until bedtime; and then they soaked their pillow through.

Later, Mary came to believe they never forgave their father for the murder. They acted dumb if he taught them some job on the farm. They cringed when he tried to pet them; and when he petted their sister Rebecca, they hated him even more. They planned to run away. They spoke in low, conspiratorial whispers behind his back. Finally, even Mary lost patience and pleaded, 'Please be nice to Papa.' But their eyes spat venom and they said, 'He killed our Hoggage.'

Ten

The twins loved to go on walks with their grandfather, and had two particular favourites – a 'Welsh walk' up the mountain, and an 'English walk' to Lurkenhope Park.

The 'Welsh walk' was only practical in fine weather. Often, they would set out in sunshine, only to come home soaked to the skin. And equally often, when walking down to Lurkenhope, they would look back at the veil of grey rain to the west while, overhead, the clouds broke into blue and butterflies fluttered over the sunlit cow-parsley.

Half a mile before the village, they passed the mill of Maesyfelin and the Congregational Chapel beside it. Then came two ranks of estate workers' cottages, with leggy red-brick chimneys and gardens full of cabbages and lupins. Across the village green a second, Baptist Chapel squinted at the church, the vicarage and the Bannut Tree Inn. There was a screen of ancient yews around the Anglican graveyard: the half-timbering of the belfry was said to represent the Three Crosses of Golgotha.

Sam always stopped at the pub for a pint of cider and a game of skittles with Mr Godber the publican. And sometimes, if the game dragged on, old Mrs Godber would come out with mugs of lemonade for the twins. She made them bawl into her ear-trumpet and, if she liked what they said, she'd give them each a threepenny bit and tell them not to spend it on sweeties – whereupon they would race to the Post Office, and race back again, their chins smudged over with chocolate.

Another five minutes' walk brought them to the West Lodge of the park. From there, a carriage-drive looped downhill through stands of oaks and chestnuts. Fallow deer browsed under the branches, flicking their tails at the flies, their bellies shining silvery in the deep pools of shade. The sound of human voices scared them, and their white scuts bobbed away through the bracken.

The twins had a friend in Mr Earnshaw, the head-gardener, a short, sinewy man with china-blue eyes, who was a frequent guest at Mary's tea-parties. They usually found him in the potting-shed, in a leather apron, with crescents of black loam under his fingernails.

They loved to inhale the balmy tropical air of the hothouse; to stroke the bloom on white peaches, or peer at orchids with faces like monkeys in picture books. They never came away without a present – a cineraria or a waxy red begonia – and even seventy years later, Benjamin could point to a pink geranium and say, 'That's from a cutting we had off of Earnshaw.'

The lawns of the castle fell away in terraces towards the lake. On the shore stood a boathouse built of pine-logs and, one day, hiding in the rhododendrons, the twins saw the boat!

Its varnished hull came whispering towards them through the waterlilies. Combs of water fell from the oars. The oarsman was a boy in a red-striped blazer; and in the stern, half-hidden under a white parasol, sat a girl in a lilac dress. Her fair hair hung in thick tresses, and she trailed her fingers through the lapping green wavelets.

Back at The Vision, the twins rushed up to Mary:

'We've seen Miss Bickerton,' they clamoured in unison. As she kissed them goodnight, Lewis whispered, 'Mama, when I grow up I'm going to marry Miss Bickerton,' and Benjamin burst into tears.

To go on the 'Welsh walk' they used to tramp over the fields to Cock-a-loftie, a shepherd's cottage left derelict since the land-enclosures. Then they crossed a stone stile on to the moor, and followed a pony-trail northwards, with the screes of the mountain rising steeply on the left. Beyond a spinney of birches, they came to a barn and longhouse, standing amid heaps of broken wall. A jet of smoke streamed sideways from the chimney. There were a few contorted ash-trees, a few pussy-willows, and the rim of the muddy pond was covered with bits of goose fluff.

This was the homestead of the Watkins family, Craig-y-Fedw, 'The Rock of the Birches' – better known locally as 'The Rock'.

On the twins' first visit, sheepdogs barked and yanked at their chains; a scrawny red-haired boy ran for the house; and Aggie Watkins came out, blocking the doorway in a long black skirt and an apron made of gunny-sack.

She blinked into the sun but on recognizing the walkers she smiled.

'Oh! It's thee, Sam,' she said. 'An' you'll stay and have a cup of tea.'

She was a thin, stooped woman with wens on her face, a bluish complexion and strands of loose, lichenous hair that blew about in the breeze.

Outside the door were the stacks of planks that Tom Watkins used for making his coffins.

'An' it's a pity you missed Old Tom,' she went on. 'Him and the mule be gone with a coffin for poor Mrs Williams Cringoed as died of her lungs.'

Tom Watkins made the cheapest coffins in the county, and sold them to people who were too mean or too poor to pay for a proper funeral.

'And them be the twins!' she said, folding her arms. 'Church-folk, same as Amos and Mary?'

'Church,' said Sam.

'And the Lord have mercy! Bring 'em in!'

The kitchen wall had been freshly whitewashed, but the rafters were black with soot and the dirt floor was scabbed with dried fowl-droppings. Ash-grey bantams strutted in and out, pecking up the scraps that had fallen from the table. In the room beyond, a box-bed was piled with blankets and overcoats; and above it hung a framed text: 'The Voice of One Crying in the Wilderness. Prepare Ye the Way of the Lord, make His Paths straight . . .'

In another room – in what had once been the parlour – two heifers were munching hay; and an acrid smell oozed round the kitchen door and mingled with the smell of peat and curds. Aggie Watkins wiped her hands on her apron before putting a pinch of tea in the pot:

'An' the weather,' she said. 'Bloomin' freezing for June!'

'Freezing!' said Sam.

Lewis and Benjamin sat on the edge of a chair, while the

red-haired boy crouched over a kettle and fanned the flames with a goose's wing.

The boy's name was Jim. He stuck out his tongue and spat. 'Aagh! The devil!' Aggie Watkins raised her fist and sent him scampering for the door. 'Take ye no notice,' she said, unfolding a clean linen table-cloth; for, no matter how hard the times, she always spread a clean white linen cloth for tea.

She was a good woman who hoped the world was not as bad as everyone said. She had a bad heart brought on by poverty and overwork. Sometimes, she took her spinning-wheel up the mountain and spun the wisps of sheep's wool that had caught in the gorse and heather.

She never forgot an insult and she never forgot a kindness. Once, when she was laid up, Mary sent Sam over with some oranges and a packet of Smyrna figs. Aggie had never tasted figs before and, to her, they were like manna from Heaven.

From that day, she never let Sam go back without a present in return. 'Take her a pot of blackberry jam,' she'd say. Or 'What about some Welsh cakes? I know she likes Welsh cakes.' Or 'Would she have some duck eggs this time?' And when her one scraggy lilac was in bloom, she heaped him with branches as if hers were the only lilac in creation.

The Watkinses were Chapel-folk and they were childless.

Perhaps it was because they were childless that they were always looking for souls to save. After the Great War, Aggie managed to 'save' several children; and if anyone said, 'He was raised at The Rock,' or 'She was reared at The Rock,' you knew for sure the child was illegitimate or loony. But in those days the Watkinses had only 'saved' the boy Jim and a girl called Ethel – a big girl of ten or so, who would spread her thighs and stare at the twins with glum fascination, covering one eye, then the other, as if she were seeing double.

From The Rock a drovers' trail wound up the north shoulder of the Black Hill, in places so sharply that the old man had to pause and catch his breath.

Lewis and Benjamin gambolled ahead, put up grouse, played finger-football with rabbit-droppings, peered over the precipice onto the backs of kestrels and ravens and, every now and then, crept off into the bracken, and hid.

They liked to pretend they were lost in a forest, like the Twins in Grimms' fairy-tale, and that each stalk of bracken was the trunk of a forest tree. Everything was calm and damp and cool in the green shade. Toadstools reared their caps through the dross of last year's growth; and the wind whistled far above their heads.

They lay on their backs and gazed at the clouds that crossed the fretted patches of sky; at the zig-zagging dots which were flies; and, way above, the other black dots which were the swallows wheeling.

Or they would dribble their saliva onto a gob of cuckoo-spit; and when their mouths ran dry, they would press their foreheads together, each twin losing himself in the other's grey eye, until their grandfather roused them from their reverie. Then they bounded out along the path and pretended to have been there all the time.

On fine summer evenings, Sam walked them as far as the Eagle Stone – a menhir of grey granite, splotched with orange lichen, which, in the raking light, resembled a perching eagle.

Sam said there was an 'Old 'Un' buried there. Or else it was a horses' grave, or a place where the 'Pharisees' danced. His father had once seen the fairies – 'Them as 'ad wings like dragonflies' – but he could never remember where.

Lifting the boys onto the stone, Sam would point out farms and chapels and Father Ambrosius's monastery nestling in the valley below. Some evenings, the valley was shrouded in mist; but beyond rose the Radnor Hills, their humped outlines receding grey on grey towards the end of the world.

Sam knew all their names: the Whimble, the Bach and the Black Mixen – 'and that be the Smatcher nearby where I was born'. He told them stories of Prince Llewellyn and his dog, or more shadowy figures like Arthur or Merlin or the Black Vaughan; by some stretch of the imagination, he had got William the Conqueror mixed up with Napoleon Bonaparte.

The twins looked on the path to the Eagle Stone as their own private property. 'It's Our Path!' they'd shout, if they happened to meet a party of hikers. The sight of a bootprint in the mud was enough to put them in a towering rage, and they'd try to rub it out with a stick.

One sunset, as they came over the crest of the hill, instead of the familiar silhouette, they saw a pair of boaters. Two young ladies, arms akimbo, sat perched on top of the stone; a few paces off, a young man in grey flannels was bending behind a camera tripod.

'Keep still,' he called out from under the flapping black cloth. 'Smile when I say so! One . . . Two . . . Three . . . Smile!'

Suddenly, before Sam could stop him, Lewis had grabbed his stick and walloped the photographer behind the knees.

The tripod lurched, the camera fell, and the girls, convulsed with giggles, almost fell off the stone.

Reggie Bickerton, however – it was he who was the cameraman – turned crimson in the face and chased Lewis through the heather, shouting, 'I'll skin the blighter!' And though his sisters called out, 'No, Reggie! No! No! Don't hurt him!' he bent the little boy over his knee and spanked him.

On the way home, Sam taught his grandsons the Welsh for 'dirty Saxon', but Mary was crestfallen at the news.

She felt crushed and ashamed – ashamed of her boys and ashamed of being ashamed of them. She tried to write a note of apology to Mrs Bickerton but the nib scratched and the words would not come.

Eleven

That autumn, already wearied by the weight of the oncoming winter, Mary went on frequent visits to the vicar. The Reverend Thomas Tuke was a classical scholar of private means, who had chosen the living of Lurkenhope because the squire was a Catholic, and because the vicarage garden lay on greensand – a soil that was perfect for growing rare Himalayan shrubs.

A tall, bony man with a mass of snowy curls, he had the habit of fixing his parishioners with an amber stare before offering them the glory of his profile.

His rooms bore witness to a well-ordered mind and, since his housekeeper was stone-deaf, he was under no obligation to speak to her. The shelves of his library were lined with sets of the classics. He knew the whole of Homer by heart: each morning, between a cold bath and breakfast, he would compose a few hexameters of his own. On the wall of the staircase was a fan-shaped arrangement of oars – he had been a Cambridge rowing blue – and in the front hall, ranked like a colony of penguins, were several pairs of riding boots, for he was also Joint Master of the Rhulen Vale Hunt.

To the villagers their vicar was a mystery. Most of the

women were in love with him – or transported by the timbre of his voice. But he was far too busy to attend to their spiritual needs, and his actions often outraged them.

One Sunday, before Holy Communion, some women in flowery hats were approaching the church door, their features reverently composed to receive the Sacrament. Suddenly, a window of the vicarage banged open; the vicar's voice bawled out, 'Mind your heads!' and he fired off a couple of barrels at the wood-pigeons crooning in the elms.

The shot fell pattering among the tombstones. 'Bloody heathen!' muttered Amos; and Mary hardly held back her giggles.

She liked the vicar's sense of the ridiculous, and his sharp turn of phrase. To him – and him alone – she confessed that farm life depressed her; that she was starved of conversation and ideas.

'You're not the only one,' he said, squeezing her hand. 'So we'd better make the best of it.'

He lent her books. Shakespeare or Euripides, the Upanishads or Zola – her mind ranged freely over the length and breadth of literature. Never, he said, had he met a more intelligent woman, as if this in itself were a contradiction in terms.

He spoke with regret of his youthful decision to take Holy Orders. He even regretted the Bible – to the extent of distributing translations of the *Odyssey* round the village:

'And who, after all, were the Israelites? Sheep-thieves, my dear! A tribe of wandering sheep-thieves!'

His hobby was bee-keeping; and in a corner of his garden he had planted a border of pollen-bearing flowers.

'There you are!' he'd exclaim as he opened a hive. 'The Athens of the Insect World!' Then, gesturing to the architecture of honey-cells, he would hold forth on the essential nature of civilization, its rulers and ruled, its wars and conquests, its cities and suburbs, and the relays of workers, on which the cities lived.

'And the drones,' he'd say. 'How well we know the drones!'

'Yes,' said Mary. 'I have known drones.'

He encouraged her to replace her own hives. Halfway through the first season, one of them was attacked by wax-moth, and the bees swarmed.

Amos ambled into the kitchen and, with an amused grin, said, 'Your bees is all knit up on the damsons.'

His offer of help was worse than useless. Mary posted the boys to keep watch in case the swarm flew off, and hurried to Lurkenhope to fetch the vicar: Benjamin would never forget the sight of the old man descending the ladder, his arms, his chest and neck enveloped in a buzzing brown mass of bees.

'Aren't you afraid?' he asked, as the vicar scooped them up in handfuls and put them in a sack.

'Certainly not! Bees only sting cowards!'

In another corner of his garden, the vicar had made a rockery for the flowering bulbs he had collected on his travels in Greece. In March there were crocuses and scillas; in April, cyclamen, tulips and dog's-tooth violets; and there was a huge dark purple arum that stank of old meat.

Mary loved to picture these flowers growing wild, in sheets of colour, on the mountains; and she pitied them, exiled on the rockery.

One blustery afternoon, as the boys were booting a

football round the lawn, the vicar took her to see a fritillary from the slopes of Mount Ida in Crete.

'Very rare in cultivation,' he said. 'Had to send half my bulbs to Kew!'

Suddenly, Lewis lobbed the ball in the air; a gust carried it sideways, and it landed on the rockery where it smashed the fragile bell-flower.

Mary dropped to her knees and tried to straighten the stem, stifling a sob, not so much for the flower as for the future of her sons.

'Yokels!' she said, bitterly. 'That's what they'll grow up to be! That's if their father has his way!'

'Not if I have my way,' said the vicar, and lifted her to her feet.

After Matins that Sunday, he stood by the south porch shaking hands with his parishioners and, when Amos's turn came, said: 'Wait for me a minute, would you, Jones? I only want a word or two.'

'Yes, sir!' said Amos, and paced around the font, shooting nervous glances up at the bell-ropes.

The vicar beckoned him into the vestry. 'It's about your boys,' he said, pulling the surplice over his head. 'Bright boys, both of them! High time they were in school!'

'Yes, sir!' Amos stammered. He had not meant to say 'Yes!' or 'Sir!' The vicar's tone had caught him off his guard.

'There's a good man! So that settles it! Term begins on Monday.'

'Yes, sir!' he had said it again, this time in irony, or as a reflection of his rage. He rammed on his hat and strode out among the sunwashed tombstones.

Jackdaws were wheeling round the belfry, and the elm-trees were creaking in the wind. Mary and the children had already mounted the trap. Amos cracked his whip over the pony's back, and they lurched up the street, swerving and scattering some Baptists.

Little Rebecca yelled with fright.

'Why must you drive so fast?' Mary tugged at his sleeve.

'Because you make me mad!'

After a silent lunch, he went out walking on the hill. He would have liked to work, but it was the Sabbath. So he walked alone, over and round the Black Hill. It was dark when he came home and he was still cursing Mary and the vicar.

Twelve

All the same, the twins went off to school.

At seven in the morning, they set off in black Norfolk jackets and knickerbockers, and starched Eton collars that chafed their necks and were tied with grosgrain bows. On the damp days Mary dosed them with cod-liver oil and made them wrap up in scarves. She packed their sandwiches in greaseproof paper, and slipped them in their satchels, along with their books.

They sat in a draughty classroom where a black clock hammered out the hours and Mr Birds taught geography, history and English; and Miss Clifton taught mathematics, science and scripture.

They did not like Mr Birds.

His purple face, the veins on his temples, his bad breath and his habit of spitting into a snuff handkerchief – all made a most disagreeable impression, and they cringed whenever he came near.

For all that, they learned to recite Shelley's 'Ode to a Skylark'; to spell Titicaca and Popocatepetl; that the British Empire was the best of all possible empires; that the French were cowards, the Americans traitors; and that Spaniards burned little Protestant boys on bonfires.

On the other hand they went with pleasure to the classes of Miss Clifton, a buxom woman with milky skin and hair the colour of lemon peel.

Benjamin was her favourite. No one knew how she told the difference; but he was, most certainly, her favourite and, as she bent forward to correct his sums, he would inhale her warm motherly smell and snuggle his head between her velvet bodice and the dangling gold chain of her crucifix. She flushed with pleasure when he brought her a bunch of sweet-williams, and, during elevenses, took the twins to her room and told them they were 'proper little gentlemen'.

Her favouritism did not make them popular. The school bully, a bailiff's son called George Mudge, sensed a challenge to his authority and was always trying to part them.

He made them play football on opposite teams. Yet, in the middle of the game, their eyes would meet, their lips part in pleasure; and they would dribble the ball down the pitch, passing it from one to the other, heedless of all the other players, and the catcalls.

Sometimes, in class, they set down identical answers. They made the same mistake over a verse of 'The Lady of Shalott', and Mr Birds accused them of cheating. Summoning them to the blackboard, he made them down their breeches, flexed his birch, and placed on each of their backsides six symmetrical welts.

'It's not fair,' they whimpered as Mary lulled them to sleep with a story.

'No, my darlings, it isn't fair.' She pinched out the candle, and tiptoed to the door.

Shortly afterwards Mr Birds was dismissed from his post for reasons that were 'not to be talked about'.

★

A fortnight before Christmas, a parcel came from Uncle Eddie in Canada containing the oleograph of the Red Indian.

Having started out as a lumberjack, Amos's brother had fallen on his feet and was now the manager of a trading company at Moose Jaw, Saskatchewan. A photo of himself, in a fur hat and with his foot on a dead grizzly, drove the twins wild with excitement. Mary gave them her copy of Longfellow, and they could soon recite from memory the lives of Hiawatha and Minnehaha.

With the other children they played Comanches and Apaches in the spinney behind the schoolhouse. Lewis took the name of 'Little Raven' and beat out the Comanche war-song on an old tin bucket: it was Benjamin's duty to guard the Apache wigwams. Both crossed their hearts and hoped to die and swore to be enemies for ever.

One lunch-break, however, George Mudge, the Apache Chief, found the pair having a powwow in the brambles, and barked out, 'Traitor!'

He summoned his henchmen, who tried to haul Benjamin off for 'nettle-torture' but found Lewis blocking their path. In the fight that followed, the Apaches ran off, leaving their chief to the mercy of the twins, who twisted his arm and pushed his face in the mud.

'We skinned him alive,' crowed Benjamin, as they stormed into the kitchen.

'Did you?' sighed Mary, disgusted at the sight of their clothes.

But this time, Amos was delighted: 'That's my boys! Show me where ye hit him! Ouch! Aye! Proper little fighters both! Again now! Aye! Aye! An' ye twisted his arm? Ouch! That's a way to git him . . . !'

*

A photo, taken at the hay-making of 1909, shows a happy, smiling group in front of a horse-drawn cart. Amos has a scythe slung over his shoulder. Old Sam is in his moleskin waistcoat. Mary, in a gingham dress, is holding a hay-rake. And the children – together with young Jim the Rock, who had come to earn a few pennies – are all sitting cross-legged on the ground.

The twins are as yet indistinguishable: but years later, Lewis recalled it was he who held the sheepdog, while Benjamin tried to stop his sister wriggling – in vain, for Rebecca appears in the picture as a whitish blur.

Later that summer Amos broke in a couple of mountain ponies, and the boys went riding round the countryside, often as far as the Lurkenhope lumber-mill.

This was a red-brick building standing on a strip of level ground between the mill-race and the wall of a gorge. The slates had blown off the roof; ferns grew out of the gutters; but the waterwheel still turned the saw-bench and, outside the door, there were mounds of resinous sawdust and stacks of yellow planks.

The twins liked to watch Bobbie Fifield, the sawyer, as he guided the tree-trunks on to the whining blade. But the real attraction was his daughter, Rosie, an impish girl of ten with an insolent way of tossing her head of blonde curls. Her mother dressed her in cherry-red frocks and told her she was 'pretty as a picture'.

Rosie took them to secret hideouts in the wood. No one could fool her into mistaking which twin was which. She preferred to be with Lewis, and would sidle up and purr sweet nonsense in his ear.

Pulling off the petals of a daisy, she would call out, 'He loves me! He loves me not! He loves me! He loves me not!' – always reserving the final petal for 'He loves me not!'

'But I do love you, Rosie!'

'Prove it!'

'How?'

'Walk through those nettles and I'll let you kiss my hand.' One afternoon, she cupped her hands around his ear and whispered, 'I know where there's an evening primrose. Let's leave Benjamin behind.'

'Let's,' he said.

She threaded her way through the hazels and they came into a sunlit clearing. Then she unhooked her dress and let it fall round her waist.

'You may touch them,' she said.

Gingerly, Lewis pressed two fingers against her left nipple – then she darted off again, a flash of red and gold, seen and half-seen through the flickering leaves.

'Catch me!' she called. 'Catch me! You can't catch me!' Lewis ran, and stumbled over a root, and picked himself up, and ran on:

'Rosie!'

'Rosie!'

'Rosie!'

His shouts echoed through the wood. He saw her. He lost her. He stumbled again and fell flat. A stitch burned in his side and, from far below, Benjamin's plaintive wailing reined him back.

'She's a pig,' said Benjamin, later, narrowing his eyes in wounded love.

'She's not a pig. Pigs are nice.'

'Well, she's a toad.'

The twins had their own hideout, in the dingle below Craig-y-Fedw – a hollow hidden among rowans and birches, where water whispered over a rock and there was a bank of grass cropped close by sheep.

They made a dam of turf and branches and, on the hot days, would pile their clothes on the bank and slide into the icy pool. The brown water washed over their narrow white bodies, and clusters of scarlet rowanberries were reflected on the surface.

They were lying on the grass to dry, without a word between them, only the currents that ebbed and flowed through their touching ankles. Suddenly the branches behind them parted, and they sat up:

'I can see you.'

It was Rosie Fifield.

They grabbed their clothes but she ran off, and the last they saw of her was the head of blonde curls hurtling downhill through the fern fronds.

'She'll tell,' said Lewis.

'She won't dare.'

'She will,' he said, gloomily. 'She's a toad.'

Thirteen

After the harvest festival, the seagulls flew inland and Jim Watkins the Rock came to work as a farm boy at The Vision.

He was a thin wiry boy with unusually strong hands and ears that stuck out under his cap, like dock-leaves. He was fourteen. He had the moustache of a fourteen-year-old, and a lot of blackheads on his nose. He was glad to get work away from home, and he had just been baptized.

Amos taught him to handle a plough. It worried Mary that the horses were so big and Jim was so very small, but he soon learned to turn at the hedgerow and draw a straight furrow down the field. Though he was very smart for his age, he was a laggard when it came to cleaning tack, and Amos called him a 'lazy runt'.

He slept in the hay-loft, on a bed of straw.

Amos said, 'I slept in the loft when I were a lad, and that's where he sleeps.'

Jim's favourite pastime was catching moles – 'oonts' as he called them in Radnor dialect (molehills are 'oontitumps') – and when the twins left, smartened up for school, he'd lean over the gate and leer, 'Ya! Ha! Slick as oonts, ain't they?'

He took the twins on scavenging expeditions.

One Saturday, they had gone to gather chestnuts in Lurkenhope Park when a whip hissed in the grey air and Miss Nancy Bickerton rode up on a black hunter. They hid behind a tree-trunk, and peered around. She rode so close they saw the mesh of her hairnet over her golden bun. Then the mist closed over the horse's haunches, and all they found was a pile of steaming dung in the withered grass.

Benjamin often wondered why Jim smelled so nasty and finally plucked up courage to say, 'Trouble with you is you stink.'

'Be not I as stinks,' said Jim, adding mysteriously, 'another!' He led the twins up the loft ladder, rummaged in the straw and took hold of a sack with something wriggling inside. He untied the string and a little pink nose popped out.

'Me ferret,' he said.

They promised to keep the ferret a secret and, at half-term, when Amos and Mary were at market, all three stole off to net a warren at Lower Brechfa. By the time they had caught three rabbits, they were far too excited to notice the black clouds roiling over the hill. The storm broke, and pelted hailstones. Soaked and shivering, the boys ran home and sat by the fireside.

'Idiots!' said Mary when she came in and saw their wet clothes. She dosed them with gruel and Dover's powders, and packed them off to bed.

Around midnight, she lit a candle and crept into the children's room. Little Rebecca was asleep with a doll on her pillow and thumb in mouth. In the bigger bed, the boys were snoring in perfect time.

'Are the youngsters fine?' Amos rolled over, as she climbed back in beside him.

'Fine,' she said. 'They're all fine.'

But in the morning Benjamin looked feverish and complained of pains in his chest.

By evening the pains were worse. Next day, he had convulsions and coughed up bits of hard, rusty-coloured mucus. Pale as a communion wafer, and with hectic spots on his cheekbones, he lay on the lumpy bed, listening only for the swish of his mother's skirt, or the tread of his twin on the stair: it was the first time the two had slept apart.

Dr Bulmer came and diagnosed pneumonia.

For two weeks Mary hardly left the bedside. She ladled liquorice and elderberry down his throat and, at the least sign of a rally, she fed him spoonfuls of egg-custard and slips of buttered toast.

He would cry out, 'When am I going to die, Mama?'

'I'll tell you when,' she'd say. 'And it'll be a long while yet.'

'Yes, Mama,' he'd murmur, and drift off to sleep.

Sometimes, Old Sam came up and pleaded to be allowed to die instead.

Then, without warning, on December 1st, Benjamin sat up and said he was very, very hungry. By Christmas he had come back to life – though not without a change in his personality.

'Oh, we know Benjamin,' the neighbours would say. 'The one as looks so poor.' For his shoulders had slumped, his ribs stuck out like a concertina, and there were dark rings under his eyes. He fainted twice in church. He was obsessed by death.

With the warmer weather he would tour the hedgerows, picking up dead birds and animals to give them a Christian burial. He made a miniature cemetery on the far side of the cabbage patch, and marked each grave with a cross of twigs.

He preferred now not to walk beside Lewis, but one step behind; to tread in his footsteps, to breathe the air that he had breathed. On days when he was too sick for school he would lie on Lewis's half of the mattress, laying his head on the imprint left by Lewis on the pillow.

One drizzly morning, the house was unusually quiet and, when Mary heard the creak of a floorboard overhead, she went upstairs. Opening the door of her bedroom, she saw her favourite son, up to his armpits in her green velvet skirt, her wedding hat half-covering his face.

'Psst! For Heaven's sake,' she whispered. 'Don't let your father see you!' She had heard the sound of hobnails on the kitchen floor. 'Take them off! Quickly now!' – and with a sponge and water, she washed off the smell of cologne.

'Promise you'll never do that again.'

'I promise,' he said, and asked if he could bake a cake for Lewis's tea.

He creamed the butter, beat the eggs, sifted the flour, and watched the brown crust rise. Then, after filling the two layers with raspberry jam, he dusted the top with icing sugar and, when Lewis came back ravenous from school, he carried it, proudly, to the table.

He held his breath as Lewis took the first mouthful. 'It's good,' said Lewis. 'It's a very good cake.'

Mary saw in Benjamin's illness the chance of giving him a better education, and decided to tutor him herself. They read Shakespeare and Dickens; and since she had a little Latin, she borrowed a grammar and dictionary from the vicar and a few of the easier texts – Caesar and Tacitus, Cicero and Virgil – although the Odes of Horace were beyond them.

When Amos tried to object she cut him short: 'Come now: surely you can allow one bookworm in the family?' But he shrugged and said, 'No good'll come of it.' Education as such, he did not mind. What annoyed him was the thought of his sons growing up with educated accents, and wanting to leave the farm.

To keep the peace, Mary often scolded her pupil: 'Benjamin, go at once and help your father!' Secretly, she swelled with pride when, without looking up, he'd say, 'Mama, please! Can't you see I'm reading?' It came as a wonderful surprise when the vicar tested his knowledge and said, 'I do believe we have a scholar on our hands.'

None of them, however, had bargained for Lewis's reaction. He sulked, skimped his jobs; and once, in the small hours of the morning, Mary heard a noise in the kitchen and found him, red-eyed by candlelight, trying to extract the sense from one of his brother's books. Worse, the twins began to bicker over money.

They kept their savings in a pottery pig. And though there was no question but that the coins in its belly belonged to both of them, when Lewis wanted to break the pig open, Benjamin shook his head.

A few months earlier, at the start of a football match, Lewis had confided his pocket-money into his brother's safekeeping – the game was too rough for the invalid – and from then on, it was Benjamin who controlled his money; Benjamin who refused to let him buy a water-pistol; who seldom let him spend so much as a farthing.

Then, unexpectedly, Lewis found a interest in aviation.

To her science class, Miss Clifton had explained the flight of Monsieur Blériot across the English Channel, but from her drawing on the blackboard the twins pictured his monoplane as a kind of mechanical dragonfly.

One Monday, in June of 1910, a boy called Alfie Bufton came back from the weekend with a sensational piece of news: on the Saturday, his parents had taken him to an air-display at the Worcester and Hereford Agricultural Show, where not only has he seen a Blériot monoplane, he had seen one crash.

All week, Lewis waited impatiently for the next issue of the *Hereford Times*, but was forbidden to open its pages until his father had read them first. This Amos did, aloud, after supper: it seemed an age before he came to the crash.

The aviator's first attempt had been a fiasco. The machine rose a few feet, and sank to the ground. The crowds scoffed and clamoured for their money back – whereupon the aviator, a Captain Diabolo, harangued the police to clear the course and took off a second time. Again the machine rose, higher this time; then it veered to the right and crash-landed not far from the Flower Tent.

'The propeller,' Amos continued, with dramatic pauses, 'capable of 2,700 revolutions per minute, dealt blows to the right and left.' Several spectators had been wounded, and a Mrs Pitt of Hindlip had died of her injuries in the Worcester Infirmary.

'Remarkable to state' – he pitched his voice an octave lower – 'about three-quarters of an hour after the disaster, a swan flew low across the showground. His graceful flight seemed to reduce the aviator's unfortunate attempts to mockery.'

Another week had to pass before Lewis was allowed to snip out the article – with its spindly line engraving – and paste it in his scrapbook, a scrapbook that would, eventually, be devoted to air disasters; that went on growing, volume by volume, until the months before his death; and if anyone mentioned the Comet crashes of the Fifties, or the Jumbo collision in the Canaries, he would shake his head and murmur, darkly, 'But I remember the Worcester Catastrophe.'

The other memorable event of 1910 was their trip to the seaside.

Fourteen

All spring and summer, Benjamin continued to cough green phlegm and, when he coughed a few streaks of blood, Dr Bulmer recommended a change of air.

The Reverend Tuke had a sister with a house at St David's in Pembrokeshire. And since the time had come for his annual sketching holiday, he asked if he could take his two young friends along.

Amos bridled when Mary broached the subject: 'I know your kind. All fancy talk and holidays by the seaside!'

'So?' she said. 'I suppose you want your son to catch consumption.'

'Hm!' He scratched the creases of his neck.

'Well then?'

On August 5th, Mr Fogarty the curate drove the party down to the train at Rhulen. The station had been given a coat of fresh brown paint and between each pillar of the platform hung a wire basket planted with trailing geraniums. The station-master was having a spot of bother with a drunk.

The man was a Welshman who had not paid his fare on the incoming train. He had taken a swipe at the porter. The porter had socked him on the jaw, and he now lay, face down on the paving, in a torn tweed coat. Blood leaked from his mouth. His watch-glass had shattered; and the jeering spectators ground the splinters under their boot-heels.

The porter put his mouth to the drunk's ear and bellowed, 'Get up, Taffy!'

'Atcha! A-atch!' the injured man grunted.

'Mama, why are they hurting him?' Benjamin piped up, as he peered through the circle of shiny brown gaiters.

The drunk attempted to stand, only to crumple again at the knees; and this time, two porters grabbed him under the armpits and heaved him to his feet. His face was grey. His pupils rolled back into his skull, and the whites of his eyes were red.

'But what's he done?' Benjamin insisted.

'What I done?' the man croaked. 'H'ain't done nought!' and, opening his maw, he let fly a string of obscenities.

The crowd recoiled. Someone shouted, 'Call a constable!' The porter socked his face again, and a fresh flow gushed down his chin.

'Dirty Saxons,' Benjamin shrilled. 'Dirty Sax——' but Mary clamped her hand over his mouth and hissed, 'One squeak out of you and you're going home.'

She dragged the twins to the end of the platform where they could watch the engine stop. It was a hot day and the sky was a very dark shade of blue. The railway tracks glittered as they rounded the edge of the pine wood. It was the first time they had ridden in a train.

'But I want to know what he done,' Benjamin jumped up and down.

'Sshh, will you?' And at that moment, the signal went down – clonk! – and the train came steaming round the bend. The engine had red wheels and the piston moved in and out, slower and slower, till it came to a panting halt.

Mary and Mr Fogarty helped the clergyman hump the bags into the compartment. The whistle blew, the door slammed and the twins stood at the window, waving. Mary waved a handkerchief, smiling and crying of Benjamin's bravery.

The train passed along winding valleys with whitewashed farms on the hills. They watched the telegraph wires dancing up and down the window, crossing and criss-crossing, and then whizzing over the roof. Stations went by, tunnels, bridges, churches, gas-works and aqueducts. The seats in the compartment reminded them of the texture of bullrushes. They saw a heron low over a river.

Because they were running late, they missed the connection at Carmarthen, and missed the last omnibus from Haverfordwest to St David's. Fortunately, the vicar found a farmer who offered to take them in his waggonette.

It was dark as they came over the crest of Keeston Hill. One of the traces slipped and, while the driver climbed down to hitch it up, the twins stood and stared at St Bride's Bay.

A soft seawind brushed their faces. The full moon scintillated on the black water. A fishing boat glided by, on bat-wings, and vanished. They heard the wash of waves on the beach, and a bell-buoy moaning. Two lighthouses, one on Skomer, the other on Ramsay Island, flashed their beams. The streets of St David's were deserted as the waggonette rumbled over the cobbles, past the Cathedral, and halted by a big white gate.

For the first few days, the twins were in awe of the ladies who lived there, and of the 'artistic' style of the house.

Miss Catharine Tuke was the artist – a pretty, brittle woman with a fringe of cloud-grey hair, who drifted from room to room in a flowery kimono, and was rarely seen to smile. Her eyes were the colour of her Russian Blue cat; and in her studio she had made an arrangement of driftwood and sea-holly.

Miss Catharine spent her winters in the Bay of Naples where she painted a great many views of Vesuvius, and scenes from classical mythology. In summer, she painted seascapes and copied the Old Masters. Sometimes, in the middle of a meal, she'd say, 'Ah!' and slip away to work on a picture. The canvas that fascinated Benjamin showed a beautiful young man, naked against a blue sky, pierced through and through with arrows, and smiling.

Miss Catharine's companion was called Miss Adela Hart.

She was a much larger, sorrowful lady, with a very nervous temperament. She spent most of her day in the kitchen, cooking the dishes she had learned in Italy. She always wore the same heliotrope costume that was halfway between a dress and a shawl. She wore a necklace of amber beads and she cried a lot.

She cried in the kitchen and she cried at mealtimes. She kept snivelling into a lace handkerchief and calling her friend 'Beloved!' or 'My Pussy!' or 'Poppens!' – and Miss Catharine would frown, as if to say, 'Not in front of visitors!' But that only made it worse; for then she broke into a real flood: 'I can't help it,' she'd cry. 'I can't!' And Miss Catharine would purse her lips and say, 'Please go to your room.'

'Why does she call her Pussy?' Benjamin asked the vicar.

'I don't know.'

'Miss Hart should be called Pussy. She's got whiskers.'

'Don't be unkind about Miss Hart.'

'She hates us.'

'She doesn't hate you. She's not used to having little boys in the house.'

'Well, I wouldn't like anyone to call me Pussy.'

'No one's going to call you Pussy,' said Lewis.

They were walking along a white road to the sea. There were whitecaps in the bay and the golden ears of barley swished this way and that way, in the wind. The clergyman clung to his panama and easel. Benjamin carried the paintbox, and Lewis, dragging the handle of the shrimp-net behind him, left a trail in the dust like a grass-snake's.

On reaching the cove, the old man set up the easel and the twins scampered off to play in rock-pools.

They caught shrimps and blennies, poked their fingers into sea-anemones, and stroked the sea-grass that felt like slimy fleece. One by one, the swells flopped on to the pebbly beach, where some lobstermen were caulking their boat.

At low tide, oyster-catchers flew in, needling for shellfish with beaks of flame. Stranded by the entrance was the hulk of a clipper-bowed schooner, her timbers festooned with seaweed and encrusted with mussels and barnacles.

The twins made friends with one of the lobstermen, who lived in a white-roofed cottage, and had once been a member of her crew.

As a young man, he had sailed on the Cape Horners. He had seen the Giant Patagonians and the girls of Tahiti. Listening to his stories, Lewis's jaw would drop with wonder, and he would go off alone to daydream.

He pictured himself on the crow's-nest of a full-rigged ship, scanning the horizon for a palm-fringed shore. Or he would lie among the sea-pinks, stretching his eye to the skerries where seagulls wandered like patches of sunlight, while green rollers thumped on to the rocks below, and sent up curtains of spray.

On a calm day, the old sailor took them mackerel-fishing in his lugger. They sailed out beyond the Guillemot Rock; and no sooner had they let down the spinner than they felt a buzz on the line and saw a glint of silver in the wake. The sailor's fingers were blooded when he came to take the fish off the hook.

By mid-morning, the bilges were full of fish – flapping, flouncing, iridescent in their death-agony: their scarlet gills reminded the boys of the carnations in Mr Earnshaw's greenhouse. Miss Hart cooked the mackerel for supper; and from then on, they were all good friends.

On the day of their departure, the sailor gave them a ship-in-a-bottle with yardarms made of matchsticks and sails from a handkerchief. And when the train drew into Rhulen Station, Benjamin raced down the platform shouting: 'Look-what-we've-got! A ship-in-a-bottle!'

Mary could hardly believe that this smiling sunburned boy was the sick son she had sent away. Neither she nor Amos took much notice of Lewis, who came up with the shrimp-net and said, quietly and emphatically, 'When I grow up, I'm going to be a sailor.'

Fifteen

The autumn was cruel. On Guy Fawkes' Day, Mary gazed at the gloomy yellow light over the hill and said, 'It looks like snow.'

'Too early for snow yet,' said Amos; but it was snow.

The snow fell in the night, and melted, leaving long white smears on the screes. Then it fell again, a heavy fall this time; and though they dug a great many sheep from the drifts, the ravens had a feast when it thawed.

And Sam was sick.

At first, there was something the matter with his eyes. He woke with a crust of discharge over his eyelids and Mary had to bathe them open with warm water. His mind began to wander. He kept repeating the same story, about a girl in the cider-house in Rosgoch, and how he had hidden a horn cup in a niche beside the fireplace.

'I'd like that cup,' he said.

'I'm sure it's still there,' she said. 'And one day we'll go and find it.'

It was towards the end of November that they started losing chickens.

Lewis had a pet pullet that would peck the grains of corn

from his hand; but one morning, on opening the hatch of the hen-house, he found that she had vanished. A week later, Mary counted six birds missing. Two more went in the night. She searched for clues and found, neither blood nor feathers, but the imprint of a boy's boot in the mud.

'Oh dear,' she sighed, as she wiped the eggs and arranged them in the egg-rack, 'I'm afraid we've got a human fox.' But she kept her suspicions from Amos until she had proof. He was already in a very ugly mood.

After the snowfall, he had driven half the flock off the mountain and set them to graze the oat-stubble. A strip of thicket, choked with brambles and riddled with badger sets, ran along the top of the oatfield; and on the far side there was a ragged hedge, which was the boundary between The Vision and The Rock. One afternoon, Mary went to pick sloes and came back with the news that Watkins's sheep had broken through and were in among their own.

Infuriated, less by the loss of feed than the risk of scab – for Watkins seldom bothered to dip – Amos sorted out the strays and told young Jim to drive them back along the lane.

'Be a good lad,' he said. 'Get your father to keep his beasts in.'

A week went by, and the sheep broke through again. But this time, when Amos inspected the thicket, he saw from the fresh white cuts that someone had hacked a passage through.

'That settles it,' he said.

He took an axe and two billhooks and, calling the twins, set off to pleach the hedge himself.

The ground was hard. The sky was blue. Strewn over the creamy stubble were heaps of orange mangolds, half-eaten, and the grimy white sheep clustered round them. A smokescreen of old man's beard stretched away over the brambles. They had hardly felled the first thornbush when Watkins himself came limping down the pasture with a shotgun in his hand.

Tongue-tied with rage, he stood with his back to the raking sunlight, his forefinger quivering round the trigger-guard.

'Get ye away, Amos Jones.' He had broken the silence. 'That land belongs to we' – and he launched into a tirade of abuse.

No, Amos answered. The land belonged to the Estate, and he had a map to prove it.

'No. No,' Watkins shouted. 'The land belongs to we.'

They went on shouting but Amos saw the dangers of provoking him further. He calmed him down, and the two men agreed to meet in Rhulen at the Red Dragon on market day.

In the tap-room of the Red Dragon it was a little too hot. Amos sat away from the fire, peering through dirty net curtains on to the street. The barman swabbed down the counter. A pair of horse-dealers in high spirits were swigging at their tankards, and shooting gobs of spit on to the sawdust-covered floor: from another table came the clack of dominoes and the noise of boozy laughter. Outside, the sky was grey and grainy, and it was freezing hard. The clock showed Watkins twenty minutes late. A hard black hat moved up and down the street, in front of the tap-room window.

'I'll give him ten more minutes.' Amos looked again at the clock.

Seven minutes later, the door swung open and Watkins pushed his way into the room. He nodded with the spiritually uplifted air of a man at a prayer-meeting. He did not take off the hat, or sit down.

'What's yours?' asked Amos.

'Nothing,' said Watkins, folding his arms and sucking in his cheeks so the skin over his cheekbones shone.

Amos pulled from his pocket a copy of his lease to The Vision. The beer glass had made a wet ring on the table. He wiped it with his sleeve before spreading out the map. His fingernail came to rest on a little pink tongue marked '1/2 acre'.

'There!' he said. 'Look!'

In law, plainly, the patch of scrubland belonged to the Lurkenhope Estate.

Watkins screwed up his eyes at the maze of lines, letters and numbers. The air whistled through his teeth. His whole frame shook as he scrunched up the map, and chucked it, across the room, into the grate.

'Stop him!' Amos shouted; but by the time he had rescued the singeing paper, Watkins had bolted through the door. That evening, young Jim, too, was missing.

Next morning, after foddering, Amos changed into his Sunday suit and called on the Bickertons' agent. The agent heard him out, resting his jowls on his fists and, occasionally, raising an eyebrow. The integrity of the Estate had been called into question: it was appropriate to act.

Four men were sent to build a wall between the two farms, and a police constable went to Craig-y-Fedw, warning the Watkinses not to touch a stone of it.

Every year at The Vision, the week before Christmas was set aside for 'feathering' ducks and geese.

Amos wrung their necks and tied them up, one after the other, by their webs to a beam in the barn. By evening the place was like a snowstorm. Little Rebecca went about sneezing as she stuffed the down into a sack. Lewis singed the carcasses with a taper; and Benjamin showed not a trace of squeamishness when it came to drawing the guts.

They stored the dressed birds in the dairy, which was said to be rat-proof. Amos lined the waggon with straw, and then sent everyone to bed – to be up at four in time to catch the Birmingham buyers.

The night was cloudless and the moonlight kept Mary awake. Some time after midnight, she thought she heard an animal in the yard. She tiptoed to the window, and peered out. The larches trailed their black hair over the moon. The figure of a small boy flitted into the shadow of the cowshed. A latch grated. The dogs did not bark.

'So,' she breathed. 'The fox.'

She woke her husband, who put on a coat and caught Jim in the dairy with five geese already in his sack. The carthorses whinnied at the sound of the screaming.

'I hope you didn't hurt him too much,' Mary said, as Amos climbed into bed.

'Dirty thieves!' he said, and rolled over.

It was starting to snow again, in Rhulen, at dusk on Christmas Eve. Outside the butcher's in Broad Street, strings of hares, turkeys and pheasants were swinging in the gusts. Snowflakes sparkled on wreaths of holly and ivy; and as the shoppers passed under the glare of the gaslights, a door would fling open, a band of brighter light fall across the pavement, and a cheerful voice call out, 'And a Merry Christmas to you! Come in for a glass of grog!'

A children's choir was singing carols: the snowflakes hissed as they hit their hurricane lamp.

'Look!' Benjamin nudged his mother. 'Mrs Watkins!'

Aggie Watkins was walking down the street, in a hat of black ribbons and a brown plaid shawl. Under her arm she carried a basket of eggs:

'Fresh eggs! Fresh eggs!'

Mary set down her own basket and walked towards her with a serious smile:

'Aggie, I am sorry about Jim, but——'

She jerked herself back as a stream of saliva shot from the old woman's mouth, and landed on the hem of her skirt.

'Fresh eggs! Fresh eggs!' Aggie's raucous voice increased in volume. She hobbled round the clock and back again: 'Fresh eggs! Fresh eggs!' A man stopped her, but she rolled her eyes glassily at the gaslights: 'Fresh eggs! Fresh eggs!' And when the Hereford buyer blocked her path – 'Come on, Mother Watkins! It's Christmas! What'll I give you for the basket?' – she raised her arm in fury, as if he meant to steal her baby: 'Fresh eggs! Fresh eggs!' Then the snow flurries closed around her, and the night.

'Poor thing,' said Mary. She had climbed into the dog-cart and was spreading a rug over the children. 'I'm afraid she's a little touched.'

Sixteen

Three years later, with a big bruise over her left eye, Mary wrote to her sister in Cheltenham stating her reasons for leaving Amos Jones.

She did not make excuses. Nor did she ask for sympathy. She simply asked for shelter till she found herself a job. Yet, as she wrote, her tears made blotches on the notepaper, and she told herself that her marriage had not been doomed; that it could have worked; that they had both been in love and loved each other still; and that all of their troubles had begun with the fire.

Around eleven o'clock on the night of the 2nd of October 1911, Amos had put away his carving chisels and was watching his wife sew the final stitches of a sampler, when Lewis ran downstairs shouting, 'Fire! There's a fire!'

Parting the curtains, they saw a red glow above the line of the cowshed roof. At the same moment, a column of sparks and flame shot upwards into the darkness.

'It's the ricks,' said Amos, and rushed outside.

He had two ricks on a patch of level ground between the buildings and the orchard.

The wind blew from the east and fanned the blaze. Wisps of

burning hay flew up into the smokecloud, and fell. Frightened by the glare and the crackle, the animals panicked. The bull bellowed; horses stomped in their stalls; and the pigeons, pink in the flamelight, flew round and round in erratic circles.

Mary worked the pump-handle; and the twins carried the slopping pails to their father who was up a ladder, desperately trying to douse the thatch of the second rick. But the burning hay fell thicker and thicker, and that rick, too, was soon a crucible of flame.

The fire was seen for miles, and by the time Dai Morgan came up with his farm-servant, the sides of both ricks had caved in.

'Get out of my sight,' Amos snarled. He also shook off Mary as she tried to take his arm.

At dawn, a pall of grey smoke hung over the buildings, and Amos was nowhere to be seen. Stifled by the fumes, she called out fearfully, 'Amos? Amos? Answer me! Where are you?' – and found him, black in the face and beaten, slumped in the muck, against the pigsty wall.

'Do come inside,' she said. 'You must sleep now. There's nothing you can do.' He gritted his teeth and said, 'I'll kill him.'

Obviously, he believed it was arson. Obviously, he believed that Watkins was the arsonist. But Mr Hudson, the constable in charge of the case, was a bland, pink-faced fellow, who did not like interfering in a neighbour's quarrel. He suggested that the hay had been damp.

'Delayed combustion, most likely,' he said, doffing his cap and cocking his leg over his bicycle.

'I'll give him delayed combustion!' Amos reeled indoors, tramping mud over the kitchen floor. A teacup whizzed past

Mary's head, smashed a pane of the china-cabinet and she knew that there were bad times on the way.

His hair fell out in handfuls. His cheeks became streaked with livid veins; and the blue eyes, once friendly, sank in their sockets and peered, as if down a tunnel, at a hostile world outside.

He never washed and seldom shaved – though that, in itself, was a relief; for when he whetted his razor, a look of such viciousness passed over his face that Mary held her breath and backed towards the door.

In bed, he used her roughly. To stifle her groans, he rammed his hand over her mouth. The boys, in their room along the landing, could hear her struggles and clung to one another.

He beat them for the smallest misdemeanour. He even beat them for speaking in a classy accent. They learned to rephrase their thoughts in the dialect of Radnorshire.

He only seemed to care, now, for his daughter – a wilful, mean-eyed child whose idea of fun was to pull the legs off daddy-long-legs. She had a head of flaming hair that licked downwards. He would dandle her on his knee and croon, 'You're the one as loves me. Ain't ye? Ain't ye?' And Rebecca, who sensed Mary's lack of affection, would glare at her mother and brothers as if they were tribal enemies.

Little by little, the war with The Rock flourished into a ritual of raid and counter-raid: to call in the law was beneath the dignity of either belligerent. Nor was there any premeditated pattern; but a flayed lamb here, a dead calf there, or a gander dangling from a tree – all served as reminders that the feud continued.

Mary had long grown used to her husband's rages that

came and went with the seasons. She even welcomed them, like thunder, because after the thunder, their old love had the habit of returning.

In other years, they had an unspoken pact: that the storm would pass by Easter. All through Holy Week she would watch him struggling with his demons. On Holy Saturday, they would go out walking in the woods and come back with a basket of primroses and violets to make a floral cross for the altar of Lurkenhope Church.

After supper, she would spread the flowers on the table, and, setting aside the violets for the letters INRI, she would thread the stems of the primroses into a frame of copper wire. He would be standing behind her, caressing the nape of her neck. Then, with the final letter finished, he would lift her in his arms and carry her to bed.

But that year – the year of 'the fire' – he did not go out walking. He did not eat his supper. And when, anxiously, she laid out the primroses, he attacked them, beating them as if they were flies, and crushing them to a greenish pulp.

She gave a strangled cry and ran out into the night.

That was the summer when the hay rotted and the sheep went unshorn.

Amos prevented Mary from seeing the few friends she had. He hit her for putting a second pinch of tea in the pot. He forbade her to set foot in the Albion Drapery, in case she squandered money on embroidery silks. And when news came of the Reverend Tuke's death – from pneumonia, after falling in a salmon-pool – he stopped her sending flowers to the funeral.

'He was my friend,' she said.

'He was a heathen,' he said.

'I shall leave you,' she said, but had nowhere else to go – and her other friend, Sam, was dying.

All spring, he had complained of 'gatherings' down his left side, and was too weak to move from his garret. He lay under the greasy quilt, gaping at the cobwebs, or drifting off to sleep. Once when Benjamin came up with his food on a tray, he said:

'I'd like my cup. Be a good lad! Run over to Rosgoch and get her to give you the cup.'

By June, the pain of living was more than he could bear. He suffered for Mary and, in a lucid interval, tried to reason with his son.

'Mind your own business,' said Amos. 'You stupid old fool!'

One market day, when they were alone in the house, Sam persuaded his daughter-in-law to pay a call on Aggie Watkins:

'Tell her goodbye from me! She's a good old girl. A nice tidy person as never meant no harm.'

Mary slipped on a pair of galoshes and squelched her way across the boggy pasture. The wind moved over the field. The grassheads flashed like shoals of minnows, and there were purple orchids and heads of red sorrel. A pair of plovers flew off, screaming, and the mother alighted by some reeds and stretched her 'broken' wing. Mary said a silent prayer as she untied the gate into Craig-y-Fedw.

The dogs howled and Aggie Watkins came to the door. Her face registered no emotion, and no expression. Bending forward, she unleashed a black mongrel tied up beside the water-butt.

'Git,' she said.

The dog crouched and bared its gums but, when Mary

turned for the gate, it bounded forward and sank its teeth into her hand.

Amos saw the bandage and guessed the cause. He shrugged and said, 'Serves you right!'

By Sunday the wound had turned septic. On Monday she complained of a swollen gland in her armpit. Grudgingly, he offered to drive her to the evening surgery – along with little Rebecca, who had a sore throat.

The twins came back from school to find their father greasing the hubs of the trap. Mary, pale but smiling, was sitting in the kitchen with her arm in a sling.

'We've been waiting for you,' she said. 'Don't worry. Do your homework and keep an eye on Grandpa.'

By sunset, the twins were speechless with grief, and Old Sam had been two hours dead.

At five in the afternoon, the boys were scribbling their sums at the kitchen table when a creak on the landing made them stop. Their grandfather was groping his way down the stairs.

'Sshh!' said Benjamin, tugging his brother by the sleeve.

'He should be in bed,' Lewis said.

'Sshh!' he repeated, and dragged him into the back kitchen. The old man hobbled across the kitchen and went outside. There was a high windy sky, and the mares'-tails seemed to dance with the larches. He was wearing his wedding-best – a frock coat and trousers, and shiny patent leather pumps. A red handkerchief, knotted round his neck, made him young again – and he carried the fiddle and bow.

The twins peeped round the curtains.

'He's got to go back to bed,' Lewis whispered.

'Quiet!' hissed Benjamin. 'He's going to play.'

A harsh croak burst from the ancient instrument. But the

second note was sweeter, and the successive notes were sweeter still. His head was up. His chin stuck truculently out over the sound-box; and his feet shuffled over the flagstones in perfect time.

Then he coughed and the music stopped. One tread at a time, he heaved himself up the stairs. He coughed again, and again, and after that there was silence.

The boys found him stretched out on the quilt with his hands folded over the fiddle. His face, drained of colour, wore a look of amused condescension. A bumble-bee, trapped inside the window, was buzzing and bouncing against the pane.

'Don't cry, my darlings!' Mary stretched her good arm around them as they blubbed out the news. 'Please don't cry. He had to die some time. And it was a wonderful way to die.'

Amos spared no expense on the funeral and ordered a brass-bound coffin from Lloyd's of Presteigne.

The hearse was drawn by a pair of glistening black horses and, on all four corners of the roof, there were black urns full of yellow roses. The mourners walked behind, picking their steps through the puddles and cart-ruts. Mary wore a collar of jet droplets that she had inherited from an aunt.

Mr Earnshaw had sent a wreath of arums to lay on the lid of the coffin. But when the pall-bearers set it down in the chancel, there were mounds of other wreaths to heap around it.

Most of these were sent by people who were strangers to Mary, but who certainly knew Old Sam. She hardly recognized a soul. She looked round the church, wondering who, in Heaven's name, were all those old biddies snivelling into their handkerchiefs. Surely, she thought, he can't have had that many flames?

Amos stood Rebecca on the pew so she could see what was going on.

'"Death be not proud . . ."' The new vicar began his address; and though the words were beautiful, though the vicar's voice was resonant and pleasant, Mary's mind kept wandering to the two boys sitting beside her.

How tall they'd grown! They'll soon have to shave, she thought. But how thin and tired they were! How tiring it was to come home from school, and then be put to work on the farm! And how awkward they looked in those threadbare suits! If only she had money, she'd buy them nice new suits! And boots! It was so unfair to make them go about in boots two sizes too small! Unfair, too, not to let them go again to the seaside! They'd been so well and happy last summer. And there now, Benjamin coughing again! She must knit him another muffler for the winter, but where would she get the wool?

'"Ashes to ashes, dust to dust . . ."' The clods thumped on to the coffin-lid. She handed the sexton a sovereign and walked away with Amos to the lych-gate, where they stood and bade farewell to the mourners.

'Thank you for coming,' she said. 'Thank you . . . No. He died quite peacefully . . . It was a mercy . . . Yes, Mrs Williams, the Lord be praised! No. We shan't be coming this year. So much to do . . .' – nodding, sighing, smiling, and shaking hands with all these kind commiserating people, one after the other till her fingers ached.

And afterwards, at home, when she had taken out her hatpins and her hat lay like a slug on the kitchen table, she turned to Amos with a look of heartfelt longing, but he turned his back and sneered, 'I suppose you never had a father of your own.'

Seventeen

That October, a new visitor made his appearance at The Vision.

Mr Owen Gomer Davies was a Congregational Minister who had recently removed from Bala to Rhulen and had taken charge of the Chapel at Maesyfelin. He lived with his sister, at Number 3, Jubilee Terrace, and had a bird-bath in his garden, and a yucca.

He was a bulky man, with unpleasantly white skin, a roll of fat round his collar, and facial features set in the form of a Greek cross. His sharp mouth grew even sharper if he happened to smile. His handshake was frigid, and he had a melodious singing voice.

One of his first acts, on coming into the county, had been to quarrel with Tom Watkins over the price of a coffin. That alone was enough to recommend him to Amos – though to Mary he was a grotesque.

His views on the Bible were childlike. The doctrine of Transubstantiation was far too abstruse for his literal mind; and from the sanctimonious gesture with which he dropped a saccharin tablet into his teacup, she suspected him of a weakness for sticky cakes.

One teatime, he solemnly set his fists on the table and announced that Hell was 'hotter than Egylypt or Jamaico!' – and Mary, who had hardly smiled all week, had to cover her face with a napkin.

She provoked him by wearing an uncommon amount of jewellery. 'Ah!' he said. 'The sin of Jezebel!'

He made a point of wincing whenever she opened her mouth, as if her English accent alone condemned her to Eternal Damnation. He seemed intent on weaning away her husband – and Amos was easily led.

The feud with Watkins had preyed on his mind. He had called on God for guidance. Here, at last, a man of God was willing to take his side. He read, with furious concentration, the mounds of pamphlets that the preacher deposited on the tea-table. He left the Church of England, and took the twins away from school. He made Benjamin sleep apart from his brother, in the hay-loft; and when he caught the boy sneaking up the ladder with the ship-in-the-bottle, he confiscated it.

Ten hours, twelve hours, the twins had to work all day till they collapsed, except of course on Sundays when the family did nothing but worship.

The Chapel at Maesyfelin was one of the oldest Non-Conformist chapels in the country.

A long stone building, devoid of decoration but for a sundial over the door, it lay between the stream and the lane, encircled by a windbreak of Portuguese laurel. Alongside was the Chapel Hall, a corrugated structure painted green.

Inside, the walls of the chapel were whitewashed. There were oak box-pews and plain oak benches, and on the pulpit were written the names of all the former ministers – the

Parrys, the Williamses, the Vaughans and Joneses – going back to the days of the Commonwealth. At the east end stood the communion table carved with the date of 1682.

In India, Mary had watched the ways of Non-Conformist missionaries, and for her the word 'Chapel' represented all that was harsh and cramped and intolerant. Yet she masked her feelings and consented to go. Mr Gomer Davies was so blatant a fraud, surely it was best to let him go on bamboozling Amos, who would, one day, come to his senses? She sent a note to the vicar explaining her absence. 'A passing phase,' she added as a postscript; for she was incapable of taking it seriously.

How to keep a straight face as Mrs Reuben Jones pounded out the hymns of William Williams on the wheezy harmonium? Or at the warbling voices and wobbly feather hats? Or the men – sensible farmers all week – now sweating and swaying and hooting 'Hallelujah!' and 'Amen!' and 'Yea, Lord! Yea!' And when, in the middle of the 150th Psalm, Mrs Griffiths Cwm Cringlyn reached for her handbag and pulled out a tambourine, again Mary had to close her eyes and suppress the temptation to giggle.

And surely the sermons were absolute rubbish?

One Sunday, Mr Gomer Davies enumerated all the animals aboard the Ark and at evening service he excelled himself. He stationed five lighted candles on the rim of the pulpit so that, when he pointed his finger at the congregation, five separate shadows of his forearm were reflected onto the ceiling. Then, in a low, liturgical voice, he began, 'I see your sins as cats' eyes in the night . . .'

For all that, there came a time when it shamed her to think that she had mocked these austere ceremonies; times when the Holy Word seemed to set the walls a-tremble; and one particular time when a visiting preacher overwhelmed her with his eloquence:

'He is a Black Lamb, my beloved lamb, black as a raven and chief among the thousand. My beloved is a White Lamb, a ruddy lamb and chief among the ten thousand. He is a Red Lamb. Who is this that cometh out of Edom, his garments red, from Bozrah? Is this not a Wonderful Lamb, my brethren? O my brethren, strive to lay hold of this lamb! Strive! Strive to lay hold of a limb of this lamb . . . !'

After the sermon, the preacher called the worshippers to communion. They sat on benches, the husbands facing the wives. Along the length of the table stretched a runner of freshly laundered linen.

The preacher cut the loaf into chunks, blessed them and passed them round on a pewter plate. Then he blessed the wine in a pewter cup. Mary took the cup from her neighbour and, as her lips touched the rim, she knew, in a flash of revelation, this *was* the Lord's Feast; this *was* the Upper Room; and all the great cathedrals were built not so much for the glory of God as the vanity of Man; and Popes and bishops were Caesars and princes; and if afterwards, anyone reproached her for deserting the Church of England, she stooped her head and said, simply, 'The Chapel gives me great comfort.'

But Amos went on raving and ranting and suffering from migraines and insomnia. Never – even among fakirs and flagellants – had Mary encountered such fanaticism. In the evenings, straining his eyes in the lamplight, he would comb the Bible for vindication of his rights. He read the Book of Job: ' "My bones are pierced in me in the night season: and my sinews take no rest . . ." '

He threatened to move away, to buy a farm in Carmarthen-shire, in the heart of Wales. But his bank account was empty, and his thirst for vengeance rooted him to the spot.

In March of 1912, he caught Watkins in the act of hacking down a gate. There was a fight: he staggered home with a gash above his temple. A week later, the postman found the Watkinses' mule by the laneside, still breathing, with a pile of intestines spilling out on to the grass. On April Fool's Day, Amos woke to find his favourite dog dead on the muck-heap; and he broke down and blubbed like a baby.

Mary saw no end to the misery. She looked at herself in the mirror, at a face more grey and cracked than the mirror's pitted surface. She wanted to die, but knew she had to live for the twins. To distract herself, she read the novels she had loved as a girl – hiding them from Amos, who, in his present mood, would burn them. One wintry afternoon, drowsy from the fire, she dozed off with a copy of *Wuthering Heights* open on her lap. He came in, woke her roughly, and slammed the corner of the binding into her eye.

She jumped to her feet. She had had enough. Her fear had gone and she was strong again. She stiffened her back and said, 'You silly fool!'

He stood by the piano, shaking all over, with his lip hanging loose – and then he was gone.

There was one course open to her now – her sister in Cheltenham! Her sister who had a house and an income! From her writing-case she removed two sheets of notepaper. 'Nothing', she concluded the final paragraph, 'can be lonelier than the loneliness of marriage . . .'

Before breakfast next morning, Amos trundled the milk-churn from the dairy and saw her hand the envelope to the postman. He seemed to know each line of the letter. He tried to be pleasant to the twins, but they returned his advances with a steely stare.

As her black eye subsided and turned a yellowish purple, Mary felt more and more elated. The daffodils were in flower. She began to forgive him and, from his guilty glances, she knew he accepted her conditions. She resisted the temptation to gloat. The letter came from Cheltenham. He was terribly nervous as he watched her slit it open.

Her eyes danced over the spinsterish handwriting, and she threw back her head and laughed:

' . . . Father always said you were headstrong and impulsive . . . No one can say I didn't warn you . . . But wedlock is wedlock . . . a binding sacrament . . . and you must stick to your husband through thick and thin . . .'

She said, 'I'm not even going to tell you what's in it.' She blew him a kiss. Her lips trembled with tenderness as the letter flared up in the fire.

Eighteen

Six months later, Benjamin had shot up in height, and was three inches taller than Lewis.

First, he grew a wispy black moustache and the fuzz spread over his cheeks and chin. Then his whole face came up in pimples and he was not a pretty sight. He was ashamed and embarrassed to be so much bigger than his brother.

And Lewis was jealous – jealous of the broken voice, jealous even of the pimples, and worried he might never grow as tall. They avoided each other's eyes, and the meals went by in silence. On the morning of Benjamin's first shave, Lewis stamped out of the house.

Mary fetched a dressing mirror and set a basin of warm water on the kitchen table. Amos whetted the razor on its leather strop and showed him how to hold it. But Benjamin was so nervous, and his hand was so unsteady, that when he wiped away the lather, his face was covered with bleeding cuts.

Ten days later, he shaved again, alone.

Often, in the past, if either twin caught sight of himself – in a mirror, in a window, or even on the surface of water – he mistook his own reflection for his other half. So now, when

Benjamin poised his razor at the ready and glanced up at the glass, he had the sensation of slitting Lewis's throat.

After that, he stubbornly refused to shave until Lewis had grown as tall, and grown a beard. Mary watched her sons and sensed that, one day, they would both slide back into the old, familiar pattern of dependence. In the meantime, Lewis was flirting with girls; and because he was limber and attractive, the girls egged him on.

He flirted with Rosie Fifield. They exchanged a breathless kiss behind a haystack and held hands for twenty minutes at a choral evening. One moonless night, strolling along the lane to Lurkenhope, he passed some girls in white dresses searching the hedgerow for glow-worms. He heard Rosie's laughter, rippling clear and cold in the darkness. He slipped his hand around her satin sash, and she slapped him:

'Get ye away, Lewis Jones! And take your big nose out of my face!'

Benjamin loved his mother and his brother, and he did not like girls. Whenever Lewis left the room, his eyes would linger in the doorway, and his irises cloud to a denser shade of grey: when Lewis came back, his pupils glistened.

They never went back to school. They worked on the farm, and providing they worked in tandem they could do the work of four. Left alone – to dig potatoes or pulp the swedes – Benjamin's energy began to fail, and he would wheeze and cough and feel faint. Their father saw this and, with a farmer's eye to efficiency, he knew it was useless to part them: it took the twins another ten years to work out a division of labour.

Lewis still dreamed of faraway voyages but his interest had shifted to airships. And when a picture of a Zeppelin appeared in the newspaper – or the mention of Count Zeppelin's name – he would cut out the article and paste it in his scrapbook.

Benjamin said that Zeppelins looked like cucumbers.

He never thought of abroad. He wanted to live with Lewis for ever and ever; to eat the same food; wear the same clothes; share a bed; and swing an axe in the same trajectory. There were four gates leading into The Vision; and, for him, they were the Four Gates of Paradise.

He loved the sheep, and the open air made him strong again. His eye was quick to spot a case of pulpy kidney or a prolapsed uterus. At lambing time he would walk round the flock with a crook on his arm, checking the ewes' teats to make sure the milk was flowing.

He was also very religious.

Crossing the pasture one evening, he watched the swallows glinting low over the dandelion clocks, and the sheep standing out against the sunset, each one ringed with an aureole of gold – and understood why the Lamb of God should have a halo.

He would spend long hours patterning his ideas of sin and retribution into a vast theological system that would, one day, save the world. Then, when the fine print tired his eyes – both the twins were a little astygmatic – he would pore over Amos's colour print of 'The Broad and Narrow Path'.

This was a gift from Mr Gomer Davies, and hung beside the fireplace in its frame of gothic niches.

On the left side, ladies and gentlemen were strolling in groups towards 'The Way of Perdition'. Flanking the gate were statues of Venus and the Drunken Bacchus; and, beyond them, there were more smart people – drinking, dancing, gambling, going to theatres, pawning their property and taking trains on Sundays.

Higher up the road, the same sort of people were seen robbing, murdering, enslaving and going to war. And finally, hovering over some blazing battlements – which looked a bit like Windsor Castle – the Devil's Attendants weighed the souls of sinners.

The right side of the picture was 'The Way of Salvation'; and here the buildings were, unmistakably, Welsh. In fact, the Chapel, the Sunday School and the Deaconesses' Institution – all with high-pitched gables and slate roofs – reminded Benjamin of an illustrated brochure for Llandrindod Wells.

Only the humbler classes were to be seen on this narrow and difficult road, performing any number of pious acts, until they, too, trudged up a mountainside that looked exactly like the Black Hill. And there, on the summit, was the City of New Jerusalem, and the Lamb of Zion, and the choirs of trumpeting angels . . . !

This was the image that haunted Benjamin's imagination. And he believed, seriously, that the Road to Hell was the road to Hereford, whereas the Road to Heaven led up to the Radnor Hills.

Nineteen

Then the war came.

For years, the tradesmen in Rhulen had said there was going to be war with Germany, though nobody knew what war would mean. There had been no real war since Waterloo, and everyone agreed that with railways and modern guns this war would either be very terrible, or over very quickly.

On the 7th of August 1914, Amos Jones and his sons were scything thistles when a man called over the hedge that the Germans had marched into Belgium, and rejected England's ultimatum. A recruiting office, he said, had opened in the Town Hall. About twenty local lads had joined.

'More fool them,' Amos shrugged, and glared downhill into Herefordshire.

All three went on with their scything, but the boys looked very jittery when they came in for supper.

Mary had been pickling beetroot, and her apron was streaked with purple stains.

'Don't worry,' she said. 'You're far too young to fight. Besides, it'll probably be over by Christmas.'

Winter came, and there was no end to the war. Mr Gomer Davies started preaching patriotic sermons and, one Friday, sent word to The Vision, bidding them to a lantern lecture, at five o'clock, in the Congregation Hall.

The sky was deepening from crimson to gunmetal. Two limousines were parked in the lane; and a crowd of farm boys, all in their Sunday best, were chatting to the chauffeurs or peering through the windows at the fur rugs and leather upholstery. The boys had never seen such automobiles at close quarters. In a nearby shed, an electric generator was purring.

Mr Gomer Davies stood in the vestibule, welcoming all comers with a handshake and muddy smile. The war, he said, was a Crusade for Christ.

Inside the Hall, a coke stove was burning and the windows had misted up. A line of electric bulbs spread a film of yellow light over the planked and varnished walls. There were plenty of Union Jacks strung up, and a picture of Lord Kitchener.

The magic lantern stood in the middle of the aisle. A white sheet had been tacked up to serve as a screen; and a khaki-clad Major, one arm in a sling, was confiding his box of glass slides to the lady projectionist.

Veiled in cigar smoke, the principal speaker, Colonel Bickerton, had already taken his seat on the stage and was having a jaw with a Boer War veteran. He extended his game leg to the audience. A silk hat sat on the green baize table-cloth, beside a water-carafe and a tumbler.

Various ministers of God – all of whom had sunk their differences in a blaze of patriotism – went up to pay their respects to the squire, and show concern for his comfort.

'No, I'm quite comfortable, thank you.' The Colonel enunciated every syllable to perfection. 'Thank you for looking after me so well. Pretty good turn-out, I see. Most encouraging, what?'

The hall was full. Lads with fresh, weatherbeaten faces crammed the benches or elbowed forward to get a better look at the Bickertons' daughter, Miss Isobel – a brunette with moist red lips and moist hazel eyes, who sat below the platform, composed and smiling, in a silver fox-fur cape. From her dainty hat there spurted a grey-pink glycerined ostrich plume. At her elbow crouched a young man with carroty hair and mouth agape.

It was Jim the Rock.

The Joneses took their seats on a bench at the back. Mary could feel her husband, tense and angry beside her. She was afraid he was going to make a scene.

The vicar of Rhulen opened the session by proposing a vote of thanks to Mr Gomer Davies for the use of the Hall, and electricity.

Rumbles of 'Hear! Hear!' sounded round the room. He went on to sketch the origins of the war.

Few of the hill-farmers understood why the murder of an Archduke in the Balkans should have triggered off the invasion of Belgium; but when the vicar spoke of the 'peril to our belovèd Empire' people began to sit up.

'There can be no rest,' he raised his voice, 'until this cancer has been ripped out of European society. The Germans will squeal like every bully when cornered. But there must be no compromise, no shaking hands with the devil. It is useless to moralize with an alligator. Kill it!'

The audience clapped and the clergyman sat down.

Next in turn was the Major, who had been wounded, he said, at Mons. He began with a joke about 'making the Rhine whine' – whereupon the Colonel perked up and said, 'Never cared for Rhine wines myself. Too fruity, what?'

The Major then lifted his swagger stick.

'Lights!' he called, and the lights went off.

One by one, a sequence of blurred images flashed across the screen – of Tommies in camp, Tommies on parade, Tommies on the cross-Channel ferry; Tommies in a French café; Tommies in trenches; Tommies fixing bayonets, and Tommies 'going over the top'. Some of the slides were so fuzzy it was hard to tell which was the shadow of Miss Isobel's plume, and which were shell-bursts.

The last slide showed an absurd goggle-eyed visage with crows' wings on its upper lip and a whole golden eagle on its helmet.

'That', said the Major, 'is your enemy – Kaiser Wilhelm II of Germany.'

There were shouts of 'String 'im up' and 'Shoot 'im to bloody bits!' – and the Major, also, sat down.

Colonel Bickerton then eased himself to his feet and apologized for the indisposition of his wife.

His own son, he said, was fighting in Flanders. And after the stirring scenes they'd just witnessed, he hoped there'd be few shirkers in the district.

'When this war is over,' he said, 'there will be two classes of persons in this country. There will be those who were qualified to join the Armed Forces and refrained from doing so . . .'

'Shame!' shrilled a woman in a blue hat.

'I'm the Number One!' a young man shouted and stuck up his hand.

But the Colonel raised his cufflinks to the crowd, and the crowd fell silent:

' . . . and there will be those who were so qualified and

came forward to do their duty to their King, their country . . .
and their womenfolk . . .'

'Yes! Yes!' Again the hands arose with fluid grace and,
again, the crowd fell silent:

'The last-mentioned class, I need not add, will be the
aristocracy of this country – indeed, the only true aristocracy
of this country – who, in the evening of their days, will have
the consolation of knowing that they have done what
England expects of every man: namely, to do his duty . . .'

'What about Wales?' A sing-song voice sounded to the
right of Miss Bickerton; but Jim was drowned in the general
hullabaloo.

Volunteers rushed forward to press their names on the
Major. There were shouts of 'Hip! Hip! Hurrah!' Other voices
broke into song, 'For they are jolly good fellows . . .' The
woman in the blue hat slapped her son over the face,
shrieking, 'Oh, yes, you will!' – and a look of childlike
serenity had descended on the Colonel.

He continued, in thrilling tones: 'Now when Lord
Kitchener says he needs you, he means YOU. For each one
of you brave young fellows is unique and indispensable. A
few moments ago, I heard a voice on my left calling, "What
about Wales?"'

Suddenly, you could hear a pin drop.

'Believe you me, that cry, "What about Wales?" is a cry that
goes straight to my heart. For in my veins Welsh blood and
English blood course in equal quantities. And that . . . that is
why my daughter and I have brought two automobiles here
with us this evening. Those of you who wish to enlist in our
beloved Herefordshire Regiment may drive with me . . . But
those of you, loyal Welshmen, who would prefer to join that

other, most gallant regiment, the South Wales Borderers, may go with my daughter and Major Llewellyn-Smythe to Brecon . . .'

This was how Jim the Rock went to war – for the sake of leaving home, and for a lady with moist red lips and moist hazel-coloured eyes.

Twenty

In India, Mary had once seen the Lancers riding to the Frontier; and a bugle-call sent tingles up her spine. She believed in the Allied Cause. She believed in Victory, and in answer to Mrs Bickerton's 'appeal for knitted garments' she and Rebecca spent their spare time knitting gloves and balaclavas for the boys at the Front.

Amos hated the war and would have no truck with it.

He hid his horses from the Remount Officers. He ignored an order from the Ministry to plant wheat on a north-facing slope. It was a matter of pride, both as a man and as a Welshman, to stop his sons from fighting for the English.

He read into the Bible a confirmation of his views. Surely the war was God's visitation on the Cities of the Plain? Surely all the things you read in the papers – the shelling, the bombs, the U-boats and mustard gas – were they not the instruments of His Vengeance? Perhaps the Kaiser was another Nebuchadnezzar? Perhaps there'd be a Seventy Year Captivity for Englishmen? And perhaps there'd be a remnant who'd be spared – a remnant such as the Rechabites, who drank no wine, neither lived in cities, nor bowed before false idols, but obeyed the Living God?

He expounded these opinions to Mr Gomer Davies, who stared at him as if he were mad and accused him of being a traitor. He, in turn, accused the minister of glossing over the Sixth Commandment and discontinued his attendance at Chapel.

In January of 1916 – after the Conscription Act became law – he learned that a Rechabite Friendly Society held regular meetings in Rhulen, and so came into contact with Conscientious Objectors.

He took the twins to their sessions in a draughty loft over a cobbler's shop in South Street.

Most of the members were artisans or manual labourers, but there was a gentleman among them – a lanky young fellow with a big Adam's apple, who dressed in shabby tweeds and rewrote the minutes in elevated prose.

The Rechabites held that tea was a sinful stimulant: so refreshments were limited to a blackcurrant cordial and a plate of thin arrowroot biscuits. One by one, the speakers professed their faith in a peaceable world and pronounced on the fate of their comrades. Many were under sentence of court martial or in jail. And one of their number, a quarryman, had led a hunger strike in the Hereford Detention Barracks, when the sergeants tried to make him handle the regimental rum supply. He had died, from pneumonia, after forcible feeding. A mixture of milk and cocoa, syringed up his nostrils, had filtered down into his lungs.

'Poor Tom!' the cobbler said, and called for three minutes' silence.

The company stood – an arc of bald heads bowed in a pool of lamplight. Then all linked hands and sang a song, the words of which they knew, but not the tune:

Nation with nation, land with land,
Unarmed shall live as comrades free;
In every heart and brain shall throb
The pulse of one fraternity.

At first, Mary found it hard to reconcile her husband's violent temperament with his pacifism: after news of the Somme, she conceded he might be right.

Twice a week, she walked down to Lurkenhope to cook a meal for Betty Palmer, a poor widow, who had lost her only son in the battle, and lost the will to eat. Then, in May of 1917, she patched up her quarrel with Aggie Watkins.

She saw a lonely figure in black, dragging her feet round the market booths, drying her tears on her sleeve.

'It must be Jim,' she cried out loud.

Aggie's face was blotchy from crying, and her bonnet was awry. A light rain was falling and the street vendors were covering their wares, and taking shelter under the arches of the Town Hall.

'It be Jim,' Aggie sobbed. ''Im were in France and workin' with mules. An' now comes this card as says 'im's done for.'

She poked her arthritic fingers into her basket of eggs, pulled out a crumpled card, and passed it to Mary.

It was one of the Standard Field Service Postcards that front-line soldiers were allowed to send home after a battle.

Mary frowned as she tried to puzzle it out, and then relaxed into a smile.

'But he's not dead, Aggie. He's fine. Look! That's what the cross means. It says, "I'm quite well."'

A spasm shook the old woman's face. Glowering with disbelief, she grabbed the card. But when she saw Mary's

121

open arms, and the tears in her eyes, she dropped her basket, and the two women flung their arms round each other's necks, and kissed.

'Now look what you've done,' Mary said, pointing to the egg-yolks smeared over the shiny wet cobbles.

'Eggs!' said Mrs Watkins, disdainfully.

'And look!' said Mary, recovering the card. 'It's got an address for parcels. Let's send him a cake!'

That afternoon, she baked a big fruitcake, full of raisins and nuts and glacé cherries. She wrote the name 'JIM THE ROCK' in blanched almonds on the crust, and left it on the table for Amos to see.

He shrugged and said, 'I'd like a cake like that.' A day or so later, he passed Tom Watkins in the lane. They nodded – and a truce was assumed to exist.

But the news from the Great War was worse than ever.

In cottage kitchens, mothers sat helplessly waiting for the postman's knock. When the letter came from the King, a black-bordered card would appear in one of the windows. In a cottage along the lane to Rhulen, Mary saw two cards fixed in front of the net curtains. After Passchendaele, a third card joined them.

'I can't bear it,' she choked, clutching Amos by the sleeve as they drove by. 'Not all three of them!' The twins would be eighteen in August, and liable to serve. All winter, she had the same recurring dream – of Benjamin standing under an apple-tree, with a red hole through his forehead, and a reproachful smile.

On the 21st of February – a date Mary shuddered to remember – Mr Arkwright, the Rhulen solicitor, drove up to The Vision in his motor. He was one of the five members of the local Military Service Tribunal. A dapper little man with arctic eyes and sandy waxed moustachios, he wore a grey Homburg and a grey serge topcoat; and on the passenger seat sat his red setter bitch.

He began by demanding why, in the name of God, the twins hadn't registered for their National Identity Cards. Did they, or did they not, realize they had broken the law? Then, taking great care not to muddy his spats or shoes, he jotted down particulars of the land, the numbers of stock, and the buildings, and wound up by pronouncing, with the solemnity of a judge passing sentence, that The Vision was too small a farm to warrant exemption for more than one son.

'Of course,' he added, 'none of us likes taking lads off the land. Food shortages and all that! But the law's the law!'

'Them be twins,' stammered Amos.

'I know they're twins. My dear good man, we can't start making exceptions . . .'

'Them'll die apart . . .'

'If you please! Healthy boys like them! Never heard such nonsense! . . . Maudie! . . . Maudie!' The red setter was barking at a rabbit-hole in the hedge. She lolloped back to her master, and sat down again in the passenger seat. Mr Arkwright revved the engine and released the handbrake. The tyres cracked the ice-puddles as the car slewed off down the yard.

'Tinpot tyrant!' Amos raised his fist, standing alone in a cloud of blue exhaust.

Twenty-one

Next market day, Amos approached the bailiff of a big farm near Rhydspence, who was said to be short of hands. The man agreed to take on Lewis as a ploughman, and sponsor him when his case came up before the Tribunal.

Benjamin almost fainted at the news.

'Don't worry,' Mary tried to console him. 'He'll be back when the war's over. Besides, it's only ten miles away, and he's bound to come and see us on Sundays.'

'You don't understand,' he said.

Lewis put on a brave face when the time came to leave. He tied a few clothes in a bundle, kissed his mother and brother, and jumped into the trap beside Amos. The wind ripped at Benjamin's coat-sleeves as he watched them disappearing down the lane.

He began to pine.

Though he ate his food, the thought of Lewis eating different food, off different plates, at a different table, made him sadder and sadder and he soon grew thin and weak. At nights, he would reach out to touch his brother, but his hand came to rest on a cold unrumpled pillow. He gave up washing for fear of reminding himself that – at that same moment – Lewis might be sharing someone else's towel.

'Do cheer up,' Mary said. She could see the separation was more than he could bear.

He revisited the places where they had played as children. Sometimes, he called the sheepdog, 'Mott! Mott! Come on, let's find the master! Where's he? Where's he?' And the dog would jump up and wag his tail, and they would clamber up the screes of the Black Hill, until the Wye came into view – all a-glitter in the winter sunshine – and the fresh brown plough around Rhydspence where Lewis might be ploughing.

At other times, he went alone to the dingle and watched the peaty water sluicing through their old bathing pool. Everywhere, he kept seeing Lewis's face – in a cattle-trough, in the milk-pail, even in puddles of liquid dung.

He hated Lewis for leaving and suspected him of stealing his soul. One day, staring into the shaving mirror, he watched his face grow fainter and fainter, as if the glass were eating his reflection until he vanished altogether in a crystalline mist.

This was the first time he thought of killing himself.

Lewis used to arrive for Sunday lunch, pink in the face after a ten-mile hike across country, his leggings coated with mud and his breeches with dead burrs.

He kept them all amused with stories of life on a big farm. He liked his job. He liked to tinker with the new-fangled machinery, and had driven a tractor. He liked looking after the pedigree Herefords. He liked the bailiff, who instructed him in the mysteries of the stud-book; and he had made friends with one of the dairy-maids. He loathed the Irish stock-man, who was a 'bloody drunken savage.'

One Wednesday, towards the end of April, the bailiff sent him by train to Hereford, along with some lots of store-cattle, which were due to be sold at auction. Since the lots came up at eleven, the rest of the day was free.

It was a very gloomy day and the clouds brushed low over the Cathedral tower. Lines of grey sleet smacked on to the pavements and rattled on the oilcloth hoods of the horse-cabs. In High Town, the poor cab-horses stood in line beside the swollen gutter; and under a green-painted canopy, some cabbies were warming their hands over a brazier.

'Come on in, laddie!' one of them beckoned, and Lewis joined them.

A military vehicle drove by, and a pair of sergeants strutted past in mackintosh capes.

'Bitter day for a funeral,' said a man with a cheesy complexion.

'Bitter,' agreed another.

'And what age are you, laddie?' the first man went on, rattling a poker in the coals.

'Seventeen,' said Lewis.

'And your birth-date?'

'August.'

'Watch it, laddie! Watch it, or they'll have you, for sure.'

Lewis fidgeted on the bench. When the sleet let up, he sauntered through the maze of lanes behind Watkins's Brewery. He stood in the entrance of a cooper's shop and saw the brand-new barrels amid heaps of yellow shavings. From another street, he heard a brass band playing, and walked towards it.

Outside the Green Dragon Hotel a knot of bystanders had gathered to watch the funeral procession go by.

The dead man was a Colonel of the Herefords, who had died of war wounds. The Guard of Honour marched with eyes fastened on the tips of their naked sword blades. The drummer wore a leopard skin. The march was the 'Dead March' in Saul.

The wheels of the gun-carriage grated on the macadam and the coffin, draped in a Union Jack, passed across the level-lidded gaze of the ladies. Four black automobiles followed, with the widow, the Lord Mayor and the mourners. Jackdaws spewed from the belfry as the bells began to toll. A woman in a fox-fur grabbed Lewis's arm and clamoured, shrilly:

'And you, young man, aren't you ashamed to be seen in civvies?'

He nipped off down an alley in the direction of the market.

An aroma of coffee beans caused him to halt before a bow-fronted window. On the shelves sat little wicker baskets heaped with conical mounds of tea: the names on the labels – Darjeeling, Keemun, Lapsang Souchong, Oolong – carried him away to a mysterious east. The coffees were on the lower shelves, and in each warm brown bean he saw the warm brown lips of a negress.

He was daydreaming of rattan huts and lazy seas, when a butcher's cart rolled by; the carter yelled, 'Watch it, mate!' and chutes of muddy water flew up and dirtied his breeches.

In Eign Street, he paused to admire a cap of houndstooth tweed displayed in the window of a Messrs Parberry and Williams, Gentlemen's Hosiers.

Mr Parberry himself stood in the doorway, a pendulous man with strands of oily black hair coiled around his skull.

'Come on in, my boy!' he said in a fluty voice. 'Costs you nothing to look round. And what takes your fancy this fine spring morning?'

'The cap,' said Lewis.

The shop smelled of oilskins and kerosene. Mr Parberry removed the cap from the window, fingered the label, priced it at five shillings and sixpence, and added, 'I'll knock the sixpence off!'

Lewis ran his thumbnail over the milled edges of the florins in his pocket. He had just been paid his wages. He had a pound's-worth of silver.

Mr Parberry cocked the cap on Lewis's head and turned him to face the pier-glass. It was the right size. It was a very smart cap.

'I'll take two of them,' Lewis said. 'One for my brother.'

'Good for you!' said Mr Parberry, and ordered his assistant to fetch down an oval hatbox. He spread the caps on the counter, but no two were identical; and when Lewis insisted, 'No, I must have two the same,' the man lost his temper and spluttered, 'Get out, you young whippersnapper! Get out and stop wasting my time!'

At one o'clock, Lewis looked in at the City and County Dining-Room to give himself a feed. The waitress said she'd have a table in a jiffy and told him to wait five minutes. From the menu-board, he chose a steak-and-kidney pudding, and a jam roly-poly for afters.

Stubble-jowled farmers were gorging great quantities of suet and black pudding; and a gentleman chaffed the waitress for failing to serve him. From time to time, the clatter of plates broke through the hubbub, and a volley of curses was heard through the kitchen hatch. Whiffs of frying-fat and tobacco filled the room. A tabby cat slipped in and out among the customers' legs and, on the floor, there were patches of beer-sodden sawdust.

The slatternly waitress came back, grinned, set her hands on her hips, said, 'Come on, pretty boy!' – and Lewis took to his heels.

He purchased a pasty from a street-vendor and, feeling very low, took shelter in the entrance of a ladies' fashion-house.

Models in tea-gowns stared with blue glass eyes on to the rainy street, and there was a picture of Clemenceau beside the King and Queen.

He was about to bite into the pasty when he started to shiver. He watched his fingertips, whitening. He knew his brother was in danger, and ran for the station.

The train for Rhulen was standing at Platform One.

It was hot and airless in the compartment, and the windows had misted up. His teeth went on chattering. He could feel the goose-pimples rubbing against his shirt.

A girl with glowing cheeks stepped in, set down her basket and sat in the far corner. She took off her homespun shawl and hat, and laid them on the seat. The afternoon was very dark. The lights were lit. The train moved off with a whistle and a jerk.

He wiped his sleeve over the misted window and looked out at the telegraph poles that flashed, one after the other, across the rosy reflection of the girl.

'You've got a fever,' she said.

'No,' he said. He did not turn round. 'My brother's freezing.'

He wiped the window again. The furrows of a ploughed field went whizzing by, like the spokes of a wheel. He saw the Cefn Hill plantation, and the Black Hill covered with snow. He was waiting with the door open, poised to jump, as the train pulled in to Rhulen.

'Can I help?' the girl called after him.

'No,' he called back, and raced down the platform.

It was after four by the time he reached The Vision and Rebecca was alone in the kitchen, distractedly darning a sock.

'Them've gone out looking for Benjamin,' she said.

'And I know where him do be,' Lewis said.

He went to the porch and changed his wet cape for a dry one. He pulled a sou'wester over his face and walked out into the snow.

Around eleven that morning, Amos had looked towards the west and said, 'I don't like the look of them clouds. Better get the ewes off the hill.'

It was late in the lambing season and the ewes and early lambs were on the mountain. For ten days the weather had been lovely. The thrushes were nesting, and the birches in the dingle were dusted with green. No one had expected any more snow.

'No,' Amos repeated. 'I don't like the look of it.'

He had a chill on his chest, and his legs and back were stiff. Mary fetched his boots and gaiters and noticed, all of a sudden, that he was old. He bent down to tie his laces. Something cricked in his spine, and he sank back into the chair.

'I'll go,' said Benjamin.

'Quickly now!' his father said. 'Before it comes to snow.'

Benjamin whistled for the dog and walked over the fields to Cock-a-loftie. From there he took the steeper path up the escarpment. He reached the rim, and a raven flew off a thornbush, croaking.

Then the cloud came down and the sheep, when he could see them, were like little packs of vapour – and then it began to snow.

The snow fell in thick woolly flakes. The wind got up and blew drifts across the track. He saw something dark close by: it was the dog shaking the snow off his back. Icy trickles ran down his neck, and he realized his cap was gone. His hands were in his pockets but he could not feel them. His feet felt so heavy it was hardly worth bothering to take the next step – and, just then, the snow changed colour.

The snow was not white any more, but a creamy golden rose. It was not cold any more. The tussocks of reed were not sharp, but soft and downy. And all he wanted now was to lie down in this nice, warm comfortable snow, and sleep.

His knees began to weaken, and he heard his brother bellowing in his ear:

'You've got to go on. You mustn't stop. I'll die if you go to sleep.'

So he went on, dragging one foot after the other, back to the rocks along the cliff edge. And that really was the place to curl up, out of the wind, with the dog, and sleep.

It was white when he woke, and it took him some time to realize that the whiteness was not snow, but bed-linen. Lewis was by the bedside, and the sharp spring sunlight streamed through the window.

'How do you feel?' he said.

'You left me,' said Benjamin.

Twenty-two

Benjamin's right hand was frostbitten. For a while, he seemed likely to lose a finger or two; and until he recovered, Lewis stayed at his side. He was a week away from work. Then, when he did go back to Rhydspence, the bailiff lost his temper, said his farm was not some institution for shirkers, and sacked him.

Ashamed and footsore, Lewis reached home at suppertime, took his place at table, and rested his head in his hands.

'I am sorry, Father,' he said, after coming to the end of his story.

'Hm!' Amos replaced the cover of the cheese-dish.

Twenty minutes went by, silent but for the chink of cutlery and the ticking of the grandfather clock.

'You're not to blame,' he said, and reached for his tobacco-pouch. He rose from the table, put his hand on the boy's shoulder, and then went to sit by the fire.

For the whole of the following week he fretted about the Tribunal, blaming himself, blaming Lewis, and wondering what to do next. Finally, he decided to confide in Mr Arkwright.

The solicitor was very reticent about his origins but was known to have lived in Chester before buying the Rhulen practice in 1912. His manner was unbending towards the 'lower orders', although he blossomed in the presence of a squire. He lived with his ailing wife in a mock-Tudor villa called 'The Cedars' and prided himself on a lawn free of dandelions. There were those who said there was 'something fishy about the fellow'.

A brass plaque, engraved with his name in Roman capitals, gleamed outside his office at Number 14, Broad Street.

The articled clerk showed Amos upstairs into a room of knobbly beige wallpaper, where there were stacks of black tin deed boxes and a bookcase crammed with *Law Society Annuals*. The carpet had a pattern of blue flowers, and on the grey slate mantelpiece sat a carriage clock.

Without attempting to stir from his desk, the solicitor leaned back in his leather chair, tugging at his pipe, while Amos, red in the face and flustered, explained how his sons were not two persons, but one.

'Quite so!' Mr Arkwright stroked his chin. After hearing the story of the snowstorm, he started to his feet and slapped his visitor across the back.

'Don't give it another thought!' he said. 'A simple matter! I'll arrange it with my colleagues.

'We're not ogres, you know,' he went on, extending a cold dry hand to Amos, and ushered him on to the street.

It was glorious summery weather on the day of the Tribunal; and four of its five members were in a rip-roaring mood. The morning papers carried news of the Allied 'breakthrough' in France. Major Gattie, the Military Representative, called for a 'dashed good luncheon to celebrate'. Mr Evenjobb, an agricultural merchant, agreed. The vicar agreed; and Mr Arkwright confessed to feeling 'pretty peckish' himself.

So the members treated themselves to a tip-top luncheon at the Red Dragon, downed three bottles of claret, drowsily took their places in the Committee Room of the Town Hall, and waited for their Chairman, Colonel Bickerton.

The room reeked of Jeyes Fluid and was so hot and airless that even the flies stopped droning round the skylight. Mr Evenjobb nodded off. The Reverend Pile felt exhilarated by notions of youth and sacrifice, while the conscripts who hoped for exemption sat outside in a gloomy green corridor on benches, with a police constable guarding them.

The Colonel arrived a little late from his own luncheon party at Lurkenhope. Flushed in the face, and with a rosebud in his buttonhole, he was in no mood to grant any further exemptions, having, at the previous session, exempted two of his hunt servants, and his valet.

'This Tribunal must be fair,' he opened the proceedings. 'The agricultural needs of the community must be taken into account. Yet there is a great and barbarous enemy which must be destroyed. And to destroy it, the Army needs men!'

'Seconded,' said Major Gattie, scrutinizing his fingernails. The first to be called was Tom Philips, a shepherd lad from Mousecastle, who mumbled about his sick mother and no one to look after the sheep.

'Speak up, my boy,' the Colonel interrupted. 'Can't hear one word of what you're saying.'

But Tom still couldn't make himself understood and the Colonel lost his patience. 'Report to Hereford Barracks within five days.'

'Yessir!' he said.

The panel next heard the case of a pallid youth who loudly affirmed he was a Socialist and a Quaker. Nothing, he said, could force him to reconcile military discipline with his conscience.

'In which case,' said the Colonel, 'I strongly advise you to go to bed early and get up early and your conscience will soon cease to trouble you. Case dismissed. Report to Hereford Barracks within five days.'

The twins had hoped the Colonel would smile: he had known them, after all, since they were three. His face was a blank when they appeared in the doorway.

'One at a time, gentlemen! One at a time! You, on the left, kindly step forward, please. The other gentleman should retire!'

The floorboards creaked as Lewis approached the panel. He had hardly opened his mouth when Mr Arkwright rose and whispered in the Colonel's ear. The Colonel nodded, 'Ah!' and with an air of benediction, said, 'Exemption granted! Next please!'

But when Benjamin edged into the room, Major Gattie eyed him up and down and drawled, 'We need that man!'

Later, Benjamin recalled only the drift of what followed. But he did remember the vicar leaning forward to ask whether, or not, he believed in the sanctity of the Allied Cause. And he remembered hearing his own voice reply, 'Do you believe in God?'

The vicar's head shot up like a startled hen.

'What gross impertinence! Do you realize I'm a clergyman?'

'Then do you believe in the Sixth Commandment?'

'The Sixth Commandment?'

' "Thou shalt not kill!" '

'Damned cheek, what?' Major Gattie lifted an eyebrow.

'Damnable cheek!' echoed Mr Arkwright. And even Mr

Evenjobb stirred from his torpor, as the Colonel pronounced the standard formula:

'This Tribunal, having carefully considered your case, finds itself unable to grant exemption from service in His Majesty's Armed Forces. Report to Hereford Barracks within five days!'

Mary was heating beeswax to seal some jars of blackcurrant jam. The smell of boiling fruit filled the kitchen. She heard the clip of hooves in the yard. She gave a start at the sight of Lewis's blotchy face, and knew what had happened to his brother.

'I shall go, Mama,' said Benjamin, calmly. 'The war's as good as over now.'

'I don't believe it,' she said.

The evening was muggy and airless. Clouds of midges spiralled around a couple of heifers. They heard the flop of cowpats and the burbling of geese in the orchard. The sheepdog slunk up the path with his tail between his legs. All the flowers in the garden – the gaillardias, the fuchsias, the roses – were purple or yellow or red. It never occurred to Mary that Benjamin would come back alive.

She believed that Amos had sacrificed their weaker son, her favourite son. She believed Mr Arkwright had offered him a choice. He had chosen Lewis, the twin who would survive on his own.

Amos hung his cap in the porch. He tried to stammer excuses, but she spun round and screamed, 'Don't lie to me, you brute!'

She wanted to hit him, to spit in his face. He stared across the darkening room, dumbfounded by her fury.

She took a taper to light the lamp. The wick flared up:

then, as she replaced the green glass shade, a band of light fell across the frame of her wedding photograph. She jerked it off its hook, dashed it to the floor, and disappeared upstairs.

Amos crouched.

The frame had split, the glass shattered, and the mount was bent, but the photo itself was unharmed. He swept up the slivers of glass into a dustpan. Then he picked up the frame and began to fit the pieces together.

Without undressing, Mary spent a sleepless night on Old Sam's palliasse, and the clouds passed over the moon. By breakfast-time, she had shut herself in the dairy – anywhere to avoid another confrontation. Benjamin found her aimlessly cranking the butter-churn.

'Don't be hard on Papa,' he said, touching her sleeve. 'It wasn't his fault. It was my fault, really.'

She went on turning the handle and said, 'You know nothing about it.'

Lewis offered to substitute himself. No one, he said, would ever know the difference.

'No,' said Benjamin. 'I'll go on my own.'

He was very brave and packed up his things, methodically, in a canvas bag. On the morning of his departure, he blinked into the rising sun and said, 'I'll stay till they come and get me.'

Amos made plans to hide both sons, in a secret place, high up in the Radnor Forest; but Mary scoffed and said, 'I suppose you've never heard of bloodhounds.'

On September 2nd, Police Constables Crimp and Bannister drove up to The Vision and made a big show of searching the barn. They hardly hid their disappointment when Benjamin walked from the house, pale, but with the suggestion of a smile, and bared his wrists to the handcuffs.

After a night in the cells, he appeared before the Rhulen magistrate, who 'deemed' him to be a soldier, and fined him £2 for failing to report for duty. A Non-Commissioned Officer then took him by train to Hereford.

At The Vision, they waited for news, and there was none. A month later, certain warning signals told Lewis that the Army had given up trying to train his brother, and was using force.

From the ache in his coccyx, Lewis knew when the N.C.O.s were frog-marching Benjamin round the parade-ground; from the pain in his wrists, when they lashed him to the bed-frame; from a patch of eczema on his chest, when they rubbed his nipples with caustic. One morning, Lewis's nose began to bleed and went on bleeding till sundown: that was the day when they stood Benjamin in a boxing ring and slammed straight-lefts into his face.

Then, one drizzly November morning, the war was over. The Kaiser and his crew had 'gone down like ninepins'. The World was Safe for Democracy.

On the streets of Hereford, Scotsmen played bagpipes, the jam factory sounded its hooter, railway engines whistled, and Welshmen roamed about playing mouth-organs or chanting 'Land of Our Fathers'. A soldier, deaf and dumb since the Dardanelles, saw the Union Jack floating above the newspaper office and recovered his speech, though not his hearing.

In the Cathedral, the Bishop, in a cope of cloth-of-gold, read the First Lesson from the altar: ' "I will sing unto the Lord, for he hath triumphed gloriously: the horse and his rider hath he thrown into the sea . . ." '

In faraway London, the King came out on to the balcony

of Buckingham Palace, accompanied by Queen Mary in a sable coat.

Meanwhile, Benjamin Jones lay gasping for air in the sickbay of the Hereford Detention Barracks.

He had Spanish influenza.

Outside the gate, Lewis Jones clamoured to be let in. A sentry with a bayonet kept him back.

Twenty-three

For three months after his 'dishonourable discharge' Benjamin refused to leave the farm. He slept late, stayed indoors, and did a few odd jobs around the house. There were sharp lines across his forehead, and dark rings under his eyes. His face was screwed up with a tic. He seemed to have slipped back into childhood, and only wanted to bake cakes for his brother – or to read.

Mary heaved a sigh at the sight of him slumped, unshaven, on the settle: 'Couldn't you go outside and help them today? It's a lovely day, and they're lambing, you know.'

'I know that, Mother.'

'You used to love the lambing.'

'Yes.'

'Please, please, don't sit there doing nothing.'

'Please, Mother, I'm reading,' – but he was only reading the advertisements of the *Hereford Times*.

Mary blamed herself for his moods. She felt guilty for allowing him to be taken, guiltier by far for the day of his return.

The morning had been foggy, and the train from Hereford was late. Icicles hung in a frieze from the canopy, and the melting drops smacked on the flagstones. She had been standing beside the station-master, wrapped in a winter coat, her hands in a fur muff. When the train pulled in, the last two carriages were hidden from view, in the fog. Doors opened and slammed shut. The passengers – grey shapes looming up the platform – handed in their tickets and filed out through the gate. Eager and smiling, she pulled her right hand from the muff, ready to fling it around Benjamin's neck. Then Lewis dashed up to a gaunt, crop-haired man, who was dragging a kitbag by its cord.

She called out, 'That's not Benj——' It was Benjamin. He had heard her. She threw herself towards him: 'Oh, my poor darling!'

He wanted to forget – willed himself to forget – the Detention Barracks: but even the squeak of bed-springs reminded him of the dormitory; even Amos's hobnails, of the corporal who came to 'get him' at reveille.

To avoid showing his face in public, he stayed behind while the others went to Chapel. Only on Good Friday did Mary persuade him to come: he sat between her and Lewis, neither singing a note nor raising his eyes above the pew in front.

Fortunately, Mr Gomer Davies had gone back to Bala; and the new minister, a Mr Owen Nantlys Williams, was a far nicer person, who came from the Rhymney Valley, and held pacifist views. As soon as the meeting was over, he took Benjamin by the arm and led him round the back of the building.

'From what they tell me,' he said, 'you're a very brave young man. An example to all of us! But you have to forgive them now. They'd no idea what they were doing.'

Spring came. The apples were matted with blossom. Benjamin went for walks, and began to look better. Then, one evening, Mary slipped out to pick a sprig of parsley and found him, spreadeagled by some nettles, banging his head against the wall.

At first, she thought he was having an epileptic fit. She crouched down and saw his eyes and tongue were normal. Crooning softly, she cradled his head in her lap:

'Tell me! Tell me what's the matter! You can tell your mother everything.'

He picked himself up, shook the dirt from his clothes and said, 'It's nothing.'

'Nothing?' she pleaded, but he turned his back and walked away.

For some time she had noticed his look of resentment when his brother came in from the fields. After supper, she made Lewis carry a meat-dish to the back-kitchen, and rounded on him, sharply: 'You're going to tell me what's the matter with Benjamin.'

'I don't know,' he faltered.

So that's it, she thought. A girl!

Amos had rented the grass-keep of two adjoining fields and, after deciding to increase his head of beef cattle, sent Lewis to inspect a Hereford bull, at stud on a farm near Glan Ithon.

On the way home, Lewis took a short cut through Lurkenhope Park. He skirted the lake and then entered the gorge that leads to the mill. The sky was hazy and the beeches were bursting into leaf. Above the path was the grotto, reeking of bats, where – so the story went – a forbear of the Bickertons paid a hermit to gaze at a skull.

Below, the river splashed against the boulders in midstream, and big trout lazily flicked their fins in the deep green pools. Pigeons cooed, and he could hear the *toc-toc* of a woodpecker.

In places, the winter floods had washed away the path: he had to watch his footing. Twigs and dead branches had caught in the bushes along the bank. He climbed a bluff. On the downward slope some lilies-of-the-valley pushed up through a carpet of moss. He sat down and peered past the branches at the river.

Upstream was a thicket of ash-saplings, leafless as yet, and beneath them a carpet of bluebells, wild garlic, and a wood-spurge with sharp green flowers.

Suddenly, above the sound of the rushing water he heard a woman's voice, singing. It was a young voice, and the song was slow and sad. A girl in grey was walking downstream through the bluebells. He froze until she started to climb the bluff. Her head had reached the level of his feet when he called out, 'Rosie!'

'Oh Lord, how you scared me!' Breathlessly, she took a seat beside him. He spread out his jacket to cover the damp moss. He was wearing black braces and a striped wool shirt.

'I was walking to work,' she said, her face contracting with sorrow: already he knew of her two tragic years.

Her mother had died of tuberculosis in the winter of '17. Her brother had died, from fever, in Egypt. Then, as the war was ending, Bobbie Fifield had been taken by the Spanish flu. On hearing that she was homeless, Mrs Bickerton gave her a job as a chambermaid. But the big house scared her: there was a lion on the landing. The other servants made her life a misery, and the butler had tried to corner her in the pantry.

Mrs B. wasn't too bad, she said. She was a lady. But the Colonel was a real rough one . . . and that Mrs Nancy! So awfully upset about losing her husband. Never stopped picking. Pick, pick, pick! And her dogs! Something dreadful! Yap, yap, yap!

She chattered on, her eyes sparkling with all the old malice as the sun went down and the ash-trees hung their shadows over the river.

And Mr Reginald! She couldn't think what to do about Mr Reggie. Couldn't think which way to look! Lost his leg in the war . . . but that didn't stop him! Not even at breakfast! She'd bring in his breakfast tray and he'd try and drag her down on to the bed—'Sshh!' Lewis put his finger to his lips. A pair of mallard had landed below them. The drake was mounting the duck in an eddy under a rock. He had a lovely sheeny green head.

'Oo-ooh! He's a beauty!' She clapped her hands, scaring the birds, which took off and flew upriver.

She reminded him of the games they had played here as children.

He grinned: 'Remember the time you caught us by the pool?'

She jerked her head back with a throaty laugh: 'Remember the evening primrose?'

'We could find another one, Rosie!'

She stared for a second into his taut, puzzled face: 'We couldn't.' She squeezed his hand. 'Not yet, we couldn't.'

She stood and flicked a dead leaf from the hem of her skirt. She gave him a rendezvous for Friday. Then she brushed her cheek against his, and left.

After that, they would meet once a week outside the grotto, and go for long walks in the woods.

Benjamin watched his brother's comings and goings, said nothing, and knew all.

In the middle of July, Lewis and Rosie arranged to meet in Rhulen for the National Peace Celebrations: there was to be a Thanksgiving Service in the parish church, and sports in Lurkenhope Park.

'You don't have to come,' Lewis said, as he adjusted his tie in a mirror.

'I'm coming,' said Benjamin.

Twenty-four

The morning of the celebrations began in brilliant sunshine. From the early hours, the townspeople had been scrubbing their doorsteps, polishing their doorknockers and festooning their windows with bunting. By nine, Mr Arkwright, the moving spirit behind the festivities, could be seen, bird-necked in a double starched collar, bustling hither and thither to make sure things were going to plan. To every stranger, he touched the brim of his Homburg, and wished him a happy holiday.

Under his 'all-seeing eye', the façade of the Town Hall had been tastefully adorned with trophies and bannerets. Only the week before, he had hit on the idea of planting a patriotic display of salvias, lobelias and little dorrit around the base of the municipal clock; and if the result looked a bit scraggy, his colleague Mr Evenjobb declared it a 'stroke of genius'.

At the far end of Broad Street – on the site set aside for the War Memorial – stood a plain wood cross, its base half hidden under a mound of Flanders poppies. A glazed case contained a parchment scroll, illuminated with the names of the 'gallant thirty-two' who had made the 'Supreme Sacrifice'.

The service had ended before the Jones twins reached the church. A band of ex-servicemen was playing a selection from 'The Maid of the Mountains', and the triumphal procession to Lurkenhope was gradually gathering coherence.

The Bickertons and their entourage had already left by car.

In an 'act of spontaneous generosity' – the words were Mr Arkwright's – they had 'thrown open their gates and hearts to the public', and were providing a sit-down luncheon for the returning heroes, for their wives and sweethearts, and for parishioners over the age of seventy.

All comers, however, were welcome at the soup-kitchen: the Sports and Carnival Pageant were scheduled to start at three.

All morning, farmers and their families had been pouring into town. Demobbed soldiers peacocked about with girls on their arms and medals on their chests. Certain 'females of the flapper species' – again, the words were Mr Arkwright's – were 'garbed in indecorous dress'. The farm wives were in flowery hats, little girls in Kate Greenaway bonnets, and their brothers in sailor-suits and tams.

The grown men were drabber; but here and there, a panama or stripy blazer broke the monotony of black jackets and hard hats.

The twins had put on identical blue serge suits.

Outside the chemist's some urchins were blowing their peashooters at a Belgian refugee: 'Mercy Bow Coop, Mon Sewer! Bon Jewer, Mon Sewer!'

'Zey sink zey can laffe.' The man shook his fist. 'Bott soon zey vill be khryeeng!'

Benjamin doubted the wisdom of appearing in public, and tried to slink out of sight – in vain, for Lewis kept elbowing forward, looking high and low for Rosie Fifield. Both brothers tried to hide when P.C. Crimp detached himself from the crowd and bore down on them:

'Ha! Ha! The Jones twins!' he boomed, mopping the sweat from his brow and clamping his hand on Lewis's shoulder: 'Now which one of you two is Benjamin?'

'I am,' said Lewis.

'Don't think you can get away from me, young feller-me-lad!' the policeman chortled on, pressing the boy to his silver buttons. 'Glad to see you looking so fit and hearty! No hard feelings, eh? Bunch o' bloomin' hooligans in Hereford!'

Nearby, Mr Arkwright was deep in conversation with a W.A.A.C. officer, an imposing woman in khaki who was voicing a complaint about the order of the procession: 'No, Mr Arkwright! I'm not trying to do *down* the Red Cross nurses. I'm simply insisting on the unity of the Armed Forces . . .'

'See those two?' the solicitor interrupted. 'Shirkers! Wonder they dare show their faces! Some people certainly have a bit of gall . . . !'

'No,' she took no notice. 'Either my girls march *behind* the Army boys or in *front* of them . . . But they must march together!'

'Quite so!' he nodded dubiously. 'But our patron, Mrs Bickerton, as head of Rhulen Red Cross——'

'Mr Arkwright, you've missed the point. I——'

'Excuse me!' He had caught sight of an old soldier propped up on crutches against the churchyard wall. 'The Survivor of Rorke's Drift!' he murmured. 'Excuse me one moment. One must pay one's respects . . .'

The Survivor, Sergeant-Major Gosling, V.C., was a favourite

local character who always took the air on such occasions, in the scarlet dress uniform of the South Wales Borderers.

Mr Arkwright threaded his way towards the veteran, lowered his moustache to his ear, and mouthed some platitude about 'The Field of Flanders'.

'Eh?'

'I said, "The Field of Flanders".'

'Aye, and fancy giving them a field to fight in!'

'Silly old fool,' he muttered under his breath, and slipped away behind the W.A.A.C. officer.

Meanwhile, Lewis Jones was asking anyone and everyone, 'Have you seen Rosie Fifield?' She was nowhere to be found. Once, he thought he saw her on a sailor's arm, but the girl who turned round was Cissie Pantall the Beeches.

'If you please, Mr Jones,' she said in a shocked tone, while his eye came to rest on the bulldog jowls of her companion. At twenty past twelve, Mr Arkwright blew three blasts on his whistle, the crowd cheered, and the procession set off along the low road to Lurkenhope.

At its head marched the choristers, the scouts and guides, and the inmates of the Working Boys' Home. Next in line were the firemen, the railway workers, Land Girls with hoes over their shoulders, and munitions girls with heads bound up, pirate-fashion, in the Union Jack. A small delegation had been sent by the Society of Oddfellows, while the leader of the Red Cross bore a needlework banner of Nurse Edith Cavell, and her dog. The W.A.A.C.s followed – having assumed, after a vitriolic squabble, their rightful place in the parade. Then came the brass band, and then the Glorious Warriors.

An open charabanc brought up the rear, its seats crammed

with pensioners and war-wounded, a dozen of whom, in sky blue suits and scarlet ties, were waving their crutches at the crowd. Some wore patches over their eyes. Some were missing eyebrows or eyelids; others, arms or legs. The spectators surged behind the vehicle as it puttered down Castle Street.

They had come abreast of the Bickerton Memorial when someone shouted in Mr Arkwright's ear, 'Where's the Bombardier?'

'Oh my God, whatever next?' he exploded. 'They've forgotten the Bombardier!'

The words were hardly off his lips when two schoolboys in tasselled caps were seen racing in the direction of the church. Two minutes later, they were racing back, pushing at breakneck speed a wheeled basket-chair containing a hunched-up figure in uniform.

'Make way for the Bombardier!' one of them shouted.

'Make way for the Bombardier!' – and the crowd parted for the Rhulen hero, who had rescued his commanding officer at Passchendaele. The Military Medal was pinned to his tunic.

'Hurrah for the Bombardier!'

His lips were purple and his ashen face stretched taut as a drumskin. Some children showered him with confetti and his eyes revolved in terror.

'Hrrh! Hrrh!' A spongy rattle sounded in his throat, as he tried to slither down the basket-chair.

'Poor ol' boy!' Benjamin heard someone say. 'Still thinks there's a bloody war on.'

Shortly after one, the leaders of the procession sighted the stone lion over the North Lodge of the Castle.

Mrs Bickerton had planned to hold the luncheon in the dining-room. Faced with a revolt from the butler, she had it transferred to the disused indoor dressage-school: as a wartime economy, the Colonel had given up breeding Arabs.

She had also planned to be present, with her family and house-party, but the guest-of-honour, Brigadier Vernon-Murray, had to drive back to Umberslade that evening; and he, for one, wasn't wasting his whole day on the hoi polloi.

All the same, it was a right royal feed.

Two trestle tables, glistening with white damask, ran the entire length of the structure; and at each place setting there was a bouquet of sweet-peas, as well as a saucer of chocolates and Elvas plums for the sweet of tooth. Dimpled tankards were stuck with celery; there were mayonnaises, jars of pickle, bottles of ketchup and, every yard or so, a pyramid of oranges and apples. A third table, bent under the weight of the buffet – round which a score of willing helpers were waiting to carve, or serve. A pair of hams wore neat paper frills around their shins. There were rolls of spiced beef, a cold roast turkey, polonies, brawns, pork pies and three Wye salmon, each one resting on its bed of lettuce hearts, with a glissando of cucumber slices running down its side.

A pot of calf's-foot jelly had been set aside for the Bombardier.

Along the back wall hung portraits of Arab stallions – Hassan, Mokhtar, Mahmud and Omar – once the pride of the Lurkenhope Stud. Above them hung a banner reading 'THANK YOU BOYS' in red.

Girls with jugs of ale and cider kept the heroes' glasses topped to the brim; and the sound of laughter carried as far as the lake.

Lewis and Benjamin helped themselves to a bowl of mulligatawny at the soup-kitchen, and sauntered round the shrubbery, stopping, now and then, to talk to picnickers. The weather was turning chilly. Women shivered under their shawls, and eyed the inky clouds heaped up over the Black Hill.

Lewis spotted one of the gardeners and asked if he'd seen Rosie Fifield.

'Rosie?' The man scratched his scalp. 'She'd be serving lunch, I expect.'

Lewis led the way back to the dressage-school, and pushed through the crush of people who were thronging the double doors. The speeches were about to begin. The port decanters were emptying fast.

At his place at the centre of the table, Mr Arkwright had already toasted the Bickerton family in *absentia* and was about to embark on his oration.

'Now that the sword is returned to the scabbard,' he began, 'I wonder how many of us recall those sunny summer days of 1914 when a cloud no bigger than a man's hand appeared on the political sky of Europe –'

At the word 'cloud' a few faces tilted upward to the skylight, through which the sun had been pouring but a minute before.

'A cloud which grew to rain death and destruction upon well nigh the whole continent of Europe, nay, upon the four corners of the globe . . .'

'I'm going home,' Benjamin nudged his brother.

An N.C.O. – one of his torturers from the Hereford Barracks – sat leering at him loutishly through a cloud of cigar smoke.

Lewis whispered, 'Not yet!' and Mr Arkwright raised his voice to a tremulous baritone:

'An immense military power rose in its might, and forgetting its sworn word to respect the frontiers of weaker nations, tore through the country of Belgium . . .'

'Where's old Belgey?' a voice called out.

' . . . burned its cities, towns, villages, martyred its gallant inhabitants . . .'

'Not him they didn't!' – and someone shoved forward the Refugee, who stood and gaped blearily from under his beret.

'Good old Belgey!'

'But the Huns never reckoned with the sense of justice and honour which are the attributes of the British people . . . and the might of British righteousness tipped the scales against them . . .'

The N. C. O.'s eyes had narrowed to a pair of dangerous slits.

'I'm going,' said Benjamin, edging back towards the door.

The speaker raked his throat and continued: 'This is no place for a mere civilian to trace the course of events. No need to speak of those glorious few, the Expeditionary Force, who pitted themselves against so vile a foe, for whom the meaning of life was the study of death . . .'

Mr Arkwright looked over his spectacles to assure himself that his listeners had caught the full flavour of his *bon mot*. The rows of blank faces assured him they had not. He looked down again at his notes:

'No need to speak of the clarion call of Lord Kitchener – for men and yet more men . . .'

A serving-girl, in grey, was standing close to Lewis with a jug of cider in her hand. He asked if she'd seen Rosie Fifield.

'Not all morning,' she whispered back. 'She's probably off with Mr Reggie.'

'Oh!'

'No need to record the disappointments, the months that lengthened into years, and still no chink was found in the enemy's armour . . .'

'Hear! Hear!' said the N.C.O.

'Everyone in this room will recall how the demon of warfare swallowed up our most promising manhood, and still the monster flourished . . .'

The last remark obviously tickled the N.C.O.'s fancy. He shook with laughter, bared his gums, and went on staring at Benjamin. A clap of thunder shook the building. Raindrops pocked on the skylight, and the picnickers pressed forward through the doors, pushing the twins to within feet of the speaker.

Undeterred by the storm, Mr Arkwright carried on: 'Men and more men was the cry, and meanwhile submarine piracy threatened with starvation those whose lot it was to remain at home . . .'

'Not 'im it didn't,' muttered a woman nearby, who must have known, at first hand, of the solicitor's black-market peccadillo.

'Sshh!' – and the woman fell silent; for he appeared to be moving towards the final coda: 'So at last, righteousness and justice prevailed and, with God's help, a treacherous and inhuman foe was laid low.'

The rain slammed on the roof. He raised his hands to acknowledge the clapping; but he had not finished: 'In that glorious consummation, all those present have played an honourable part. Or should I say,' he added, removing his glasses and fixing a steely stare on the twins, 'almost all of those present?'

In a flash, Benjamin saw what was afoot and, clawing his brother's wrist, began to squirm towards the door. Mr Arkwright watched them go and then turned to the tricky topic of contributions to the War Memorial Fund.

The twins stood under the cedar of Lebanon, alone, in the rain.

'We didn't ought to have come,' said Benjamin.

They sheltered until the rain blew over. Benjamin still wanted to leave, but Lewis lingered on and, in the end, they stayed for the Carnival Pageant.

For four days, Mr Arkwright and his committee had 'moved heaven and earth' to prepare the ground for the afternoon's events. Hurdles had been erected, white lines drawn on the grass, and, in front of the finishing-post, a canvas awning covered the podium to shield the notabilities from sun or shower. Garden seats had been reserved for the heroes and pensioners: the others had to sit where they could.

The sun shone fitfully through a confused mass of cloud. In the far corner of the field, beside a stand of wellingtonias, the entrants for the Carnival were putting the finishing touches to their floats. Mr Arkwright looked anxiously from his watch to the cloud, and to the gate of the Italian garden.

'I do wish they'd come,' he fretted, wondering what on earth was detaining the Bickertons.

To occupy himself, he darted about, blew his whistle, escorted the pensioners and made a show of pushing the Bombardier's wheel-chair into the place of honour.

At last, the gate swung open and the luncheon party

emerged through a gap in the topiary like a parade of prize beasts at a show.

The crowd parted for Mrs Bickerton, who walked ahead of the others in her Red Cross uniform. On seeing the Jones twins, she stopped: 'Do give your mother my love. I wish she'd come and see me.'

Her husband limped along on the arm of Lady Vernon-Murray, an ample woman from whose hat a bird-of-paradise plume curled downwards and tickled the corner of her mouth. A frock of fog-blue voile framed her ankles, and she looked extremely cross. The Brigadier, an immense purple-faced presence, appeared to be trapped in a web of polished brown leather straps. Members of the local gentry followed; and, lastly, in magenta, came the Bickerton war-widow, Mrs Nancy. A young man from London was with her.

She was halfway to the podium when she paused and frowned: 'Re-ggie! Re-ggie!' she called with a stammer. 'N-now whe-ere's he gone? He was here a se-econd ago.'

'Coming!' a voice called back from behind the topiary peacocks, and a youngish man, in a blazer and whites, appeared in the open, on crutches. His left leg was off at the knee.

At his side, conspicuous as a magpie against the evergreens, was a girl in a maid's uniform, with white flounces on her shoulders.

It was Rosie Fifield.

'I told you,' Benjamin said, and Lewis began to tremble.

The twins moved towards the podium where Mr Arkwright, as Master of Ceremonies, had the privilege of escorting the guests-of-honour to their seats.

'I hope we shall be amused,' said Lady Vernon-Murray, as he slid a cane-seated chair beneath her haunches.

'Surely yes, my lady!' he replied. 'We have a pot-pourri of entertainment on the programme.'

'Well, it's dashed cold,' she said, sourly.

Reggie had chosen a chair on the far left of the platform, and Rosie was standing beneath him. He tickled her vertebrae with the toe of his shoe.

'Ladies and gentlemen,' Mr Arkwright succeeded in silencing the crowd. 'Permit me to introduce our illustrious guests – the Hero of Vimy Ridge, and his lady . . .'

'Gosh, it's perishing,' said her ladyship, as the Brigadier acknowledged the cheers.

He was preparing to open his mouth when two stable-lads rushed forward carrying effigies of the Kaiser and Prince Ruprecht, gagged and bound to a pair of kitchen chairs. On top of the Kaiser's helmet was a stuffed canary, smeared with gold paint.

The Brigadier glared, with mock ferocity, at the foe.

'Ladies and gentlemen,' he began, 'soldiers of the King, and you two miserable specimens of humanity, whom we shall soon have the pleasure of consigning to the bonfire . . .'

Another round of cheers went up.

'Now sewiously sewiously . . .' The Brigadier raised a hand as if passing to serious matters. 'This is a memowable day. A day that will go down in the annals of our history . . .'

'I thought we said we weren't having speeches.' Mrs Bickerton turned coldly to the solicitor.

'Unfortunately, there are people here today who may think they can't wejoice with us because they've lost a dear one. Well, my message to them is this. Wejoice with the west of us now the whole thing's over. And wemember that your husbands or fathers, bwothers or sweethearts have all died in a good cause . . .'

This time the applause was fainter. Mrs Bickerton bit her lip and stared at the mountain. Her face was white as her nurse's cap.

'I . . . I . . .' The Brigadier was warming to his theme. 'I can count myself one of the lucky ones. I was at Vimmy. I was at Wipers. And I was at Passiondale. I witnessed appalling gas-shelling . . .'

All eyes turned to the five gas victims, who sat lined up on a bench, coughing and wheezing like an exhibition for the horrors of war.

'Our conditions were absolutely filthy. One went for days without a change of clothes, nay, weeks without so much as a bath. Our casualties, especially among the gunners, were quite dweadful . . .'

'I can't bear it,' murmured Mrs Bickerton, and shielded her face with her hand.

'I often think back to the time I was wounded and in hospital. We'd been thwough an absolute bloodbath near Weemes. But we happened to have a chap in the wegiment . . . turned out to be something of a poet. Well, he jotted down a few lines, and I'd like to wepeat them to you. At the time, anyway, they were a gweat comfort to me:

> 'If I should die, think only this of me:
> That there's some corner of a foweign field
> That is fowever England.'

'Poor Rupert,' Mrs Bickerton leaned across to her husband. 'He'd turn in his grave.'

'Christ, this man's a bore!'

'How can we shut him up?'

'And what of the future for our belovèd country?' The Brigadier had changed tack. 'Or should I say our belovèd county? Our cwying need is not just to feed the people of these islands, but to export bloodstock to our partners overseas. Now I have seen Heweford cattle in evewy part of the globe. Indeed, whewever you will find the white man, there you will find the white-faced bweed. I know you must all feel twemendously pwoud of the Lurkenhope Hewefords . . .'

'Be damned if they are,' said the Colonel, reddening.

'But it's always been a mystewy to me, why, when one looks wound the countwyside, one sees so many infewior animals . . . half-bweeds . . . diseased . . . deformed . . .'

The war-wounded, already in agony from the hard benches, began to look frayed and fidgety.

'The only way forward is to eliminate second-wate animals for good and all. Now in the Argentine and Austwalia . . .'

Mrs Bickerton glanced about helplessly; and, in the end, it was Mr Arkwright who saved the day. It was time for the Carnival Procession. Another storm, the colour of black grapes, was brewing over the mountain.

Plucking up courage, he whispered in Lady Vernon-Murray's ear. She nodded, tugged her husband by the coat-tails and said, 'Henry! Time's up!'

'What, m'dear?'

'Time's up!'

So he hurriedly bid his audience adieu, hoped to meet them all ''ere long on the hunting field', and sat down.

The next item on the agenda was the presentation, by her ladyship, of a silver cigarette-case to 'each and every man returned from these wars'. Loud acclamations greeted her as she descended the steps. She held out the Bombardier's, and a clawlike hand shot out from the basket-chair, and grabbed it.

'Hrrh! Hrrh!' came the same spongy rattle.

'Oh, it's too cruel,' breathed Mrs Bickerton.

'Ladies and gentlemen,' Mr Arkwright called through the megaphone. 'We now come to the principal attraction of the afternoon: the judging of the Carnival floats. I give you Number One . . .' He consulted his programme. 'The Lurkenhope Stable Boys, who have chosen as their theme . . . "The Battle of Om-dur-man"!'

A team of white-fronted shires came into view hauling a hay-waggon, on which was a *tableau-vivant* with Lord Kitchener surrounded by potted palms and half a dozen lads, some with leopard-skins round their tummies, some in underpants, and all smeared head to toe with soot, waving spears or assegais, yelling, or beating a tom-tom.

The spectators yelled back, chucked paper darts, and the Survivor of Rorke's Drift shook his crutch: 'Lemme get me mits on 'em Sambos,' he shrieked, as the cart drew off.

Cart Number Two arrived with 'Robin Hood and his Merrie Men'. Next came 'The Dominions' with Miss Bessel of Frogend as Britannia and, fourthly, 'The Working Boys' Pierrot Troupe'.

The boys sang to the accompaniment of a ragtime piano, and when they rhymed the words 'German sausage' with 'abdominal passage', there was a hushed and horrified silence – except for the cackles of Reggie Bickerton, who laughed and laughed and hardly seemed able to stop. Rosie hid her own sniggers by burying her face in her apron.

Meanwhile, Lewis Jones was edging towards her. He whistled to attract her attention and she stared straight through him, smiling.

The last float but one, showing 'The Death of Prince Llewellyn', roused a clique of Welsh Nationalists to song.

'Enough, gentlemen!' shouted Mr Arkwright. 'Enough is enough. Thank you!' Then a burst of hurrah-ing brought everyone to their feet.

The men whistled. Women craned their necks and offered tender-hearted comments: 'Isn't she lovely? . . . Lovely! . . . Oh! And do look at the little angels! . . . The little darlings! . . . Aren't they sweet? . . . Oh, it's Cis . . . Do look! It's our Cissie . . . Oh! Oh! Isn't she bee-yewtiful?'

'Miss Cissie Pantall the Beeches,' Mr Arkwright continued in a tone of rapture, 'who has deigned to honour us with her presence – as "Peace". Ladies and gentlemen! I give you . . . "Peace"!'

Fluid folds of white calico covered the floor and sides of the cart. Laurel swags hung down over the wheel-hubs and on all four corners there were pots of arum lilies.

A choir of angels formed a ring around the throne, and on it sat a big blonde girl in a snowy tunic. She held a wicker cage containing a white fantailed pigeon. Her hair fell like a fleece on to her shoulders, and her teeth were chattering with cold.

The ladies looked up at the chutes of rain already tumbling over the Black Hill, and cast around for the nearest umbrella.

'Let's be going,' said Benjamin.

After a brief conference with Lady Vernon-Murray, Mr Arkwright hastily announced the foregone conclusion: Miss Pantall the Beeches was the winner. Her proud father then led his horse-team round in a circle, so that Cissie could step on to the podium and collect her trophy.

Frightened by the applause and approach of thunder, the Dove of Peace panicked and shredded its wings against the bars of the cage. Feathers flew, fluttered in the wind, and fell near Rosie Fifield's feet. She stooped and picked up two of them. Flushed in the face and smiling, she stood provocatively in front of Lewis Jones.

'Fancy you showing up!' she said. 'I've got a present for you.' And she handed him one of the feathers.

'Thank you very much,' he said, with a puzzled smile. He took the feather before his brother could stop him: he had never even heard of 'white-feathering'.

'Shirkers!' she jeered. And Reggie Bickerton laughed; and the group of soldiers round her also burst out laughing. The N.C.O. was with them. Lewis dropped the feather, and the rain began to fall.

'The Sports will be postponed,' the solicitor called through the megaphone as the crowd broke ranks and ran for the trees.

Lewis and Benjamin crouched under some rhododendrons, and the water ran in trickles down their necks. When the rain let up, they stole away towards the edge of the shrubbery and out onto the carriage drive. Four or five Army louts were blocking their paths. All of them were wet through, and tipsy.

"Ad it soft in 'Ereford, didn't ya, mate?' The N.C.O. swung a fist at Lewis, and he ducked.

'Run!' he yelled, and the twins ran back to the bushes. But the path was slippery; Lewis tripped on a root, and fell full-length in the mud. The N.C.O. fell on top of him and twisted his arm.

Another soldier shouted, 'Wipe their bloody snouts in the muck!' And Benjamin booted him behind the knees and toppled him. Then all his world was wheeling, and the next thing he heard was a sneering voice, 'Aw! Leave 'em to stew!'

Then they were alone again, with swollen eyes and the taste of blood on their lips.

That night, climbing the crest of Cefn Hill, they saw a bonfire blazing on Croft Ambrey, another on the Clee and far off, faintly, a dull glow over the Malverns – blazing as they had blazed at the time of the Armada.

The Bombardier did not survive the celebrations. While clearing up the mess in the Park, an estate worker found him in the wheeled basket-chair. No one had remembered him in the rush for shelter. He had ceased to breathe. The man was amazed by the strength of his grip as he prised his fingers from the silver cigarette-case.

Twenty-five

Jim the Rock spent the Great Day at a military hospital on Southampton Water.

Serving as a muleteer with the South Wales Borderers, he had survived the First and Second Battles of Ypres, and then the Somme. He came through the war without a scratch until, in the final week, two lumps of shrapnel caught him behind the kneecaps. Septicaemia set in and, for a time, the doctors considered amputation.

When at last he came home after the long months of therapy, he was still very shaky on his pins; his face was pitted with black specks, and he was inclined to snap.

Jim had loved his mules, treated them for ophthalmia and mange, and dragged them from the mud when they fell in up to their fetlocks. He had never shot a wounded mule unless there was no hope of saving him.

The sight of dead mules had distressed him far more than the sight of dead men. 'I see'd 'em,' he'd say in the pub. 'All along the road and stinkin' summut 'orrible. Poor ol' boys what never did no 'arm.'

He had hated it most when the mules got gassed. In one gas attack, he survived when the whole of his mule-train died – and that made him extremely angry. Marching up to his lieutenant, he saluted sullenly and blurted out, 'If I can 'ave me gas mask, why can't me mules?'

This piece of logic so impressed the lieutenant that he sent a report to the general, who, instead of ignoring it, sent back a note of commendation.

By 1918, most British units had equipped their horses and mules with gas-masks, whereas the Germans went on losing supplies; and though no military historian would credit Jim the Rock with the invention of the equine mask, he persisted in the illusion that it was he who had won the war.

So whenever it came to another round – at the Red Dragon in Rhulen, the Bannut Tree in Lurkenhope, or the Shepherd's Rest at Upper Brechfa – he'd stare defiantly at his fellow-drinkers: 'Aw, stand us another pint. I won the war, I did!' And when they jeered back, 'Get ye off, y'old scalliwamp,' he'd fish in his pocket for the general's letter, or the photo of himself and a pair of mules – all three of them in their gas-masks.

Jim's sister Ethel was immeasurably proud of him and his shining medals, and said he needed a 'good long rest'.

She had grown into a strong, big-boned woman who stamped around in an ex-Army greatcoat and stared at the world from under her mossy eyebrows. 'Never you mind,' she'd say, if Jim gave up on a job. 'I'll a-finish it myself.' And when he rode off to the pub, a placid smile would spread across her face. 'That Jim!' she'd say. 'He be wonderful fond of scenery.'

Aggie also doted on Jim and looked on him as one arisen from the grave. But Tom the Coffin – by now a craggy, matt-bearded old man with a luminous stare – had resented the lad for volunteering, and doubly resented his return. At the sight of the war-hero sunning himself, he'd yell in a hoarse and terrible voice: 'I've warned you. I've warned you. This is your last chance. Get yourself to work or I'll clout you. I'll knobble you, you good-for-nothing lump! I'll moil your fat face . . .'

One evening, he accused Jim of stealing a snaffle-bit and beat his cheeks like a tambourine – whereupon Aggie glowered and said, 'That's it. I've had enough.'

At suppertime, her husband found that the bolts had been drawn against him. He banged and banged, but the door was solid oak, and he went away nursing his knuckles. Around midnight, they heard a terrifying whinny from the beast-house. In the morning he was gone, and Jim's mare lay dead with a nail through her skull.

The next news of the old man, he was living in the Ithon Valley with a farmer's widow, whom he'd gotten with child. People said he'd 'fixed the devil's stare' on her when he went to deliver her husband's coffin.

Without the money from the coffins, Aggie no longer had enough to keep a 'nice house' and, after scouring round for other sources of income, hit on the idea of boarding unwanted children.

The first of her 'rescues' was a baby girl called Sarah, whose mother, the miller's wife at Brynarian, had been seduced by a seasonal shearer. The miller had refused to rear the child under his own roof, but offered £2 a week for her upkeep.

This arrangement brought in Aggie a clear profit of £1 and, on the strength of it, she took in two more illegitimates –

Brenda and Lizzie – and, in this way, maintained her standards. The tea-caddy was full. They ate pickled lamb once a week. She bought a new white linen table-cloth, and a tin of pineapple chunks sat proudly on the Sunday tea-table.

As for Jim, he lorded it over his female brood, shirked work, and would sit on the hillside playing his penny-whistle to the whinchats and wheatears.

He hated to see any creature in pain; and if he found a rabbit in a snare, or a gull with a broken wing, he'd carry it home and bind the wound with a bandage, or the wing with a splint of twigs. Sometimes, there'd be several birds and animals festering in boxes by the fire; and when one of them died, he'd say, 'Poor ol' boy! An' I dug a hole an' put 'im in the ground.'

For years he went on harping about the war, and had the habit of slipping down to The Vision to hector the Jones twins.

They were scything one sunset in their shirtsleeves, when Jim limped up and launched into his usual harangue: 'An' them tanks I'm a-tellin' yer! Baroom! ... Baroom!' The twins went on scything, stooping occasionally to whet their blades and, when a fly blew into Benjamin's mouth, he spat it out: 'Aagh! Them pithering flies!'

Of Jim they took no notice and he ended up losing his temper: 'An' you? You'd a-lasted a fraction of a second in that war. An' you'd a farm to fight for! An' I . . . I'd only me own skin to save!'

Since the day of the peace celebrations, the twins' world had contracted to a few square miles, bounded on one side by

Maesyfelin Chapel and on the other by the Black Hill: both
Rhulen and Lurkenhope now lay on enemy soil.

Deliberately, as if reaching back to the innocence of early
childhood, they turned away from the modern age; and
though the neighbours invested in new farm machinery,
they persuaded their father not to waste his money.

They shovelled muck on to the fields. They broadcast seed
from a basketwork 'lip'. They used the old binder, the old
single-furrow plough, and even did their threshing with a
flail. Yet, as Amos was forced to admit, the hedges had never
been neater, the grass greener, the animals healthier. The
farm even made money. He had only to set foot in the bank
for the manager to slip round the counter, and shake his
hand.

Lewis's only extravagance was a subscription to the *News
of the World*, and after lunch on Sundays, he would riffle
through its pages in case there was an air-crash to paste in
his scrapbook.

'Really,' Mary pretended to protest. 'What a morbid
imagination you have!' Already, though they were only twenty-
two, her sons were behaving like crabby old bachelors. But
her daughter gave her greater concern.

For years, Rebecca had basked in her father's infatuation:
nowadays they seldom spoke. She would steal off to Rhulen
and come back with cigarette smoke on her breath and rouge
rubbed off around her lips. She raided Amos's cash-box. He
called her a 'harlot' and Mary despaired of reconciling them.

To get her out of the house, she found the girl a job as a
sales assistant at the old Albion Drapery, which, in a flush of
post-war francophilia, had changed its name to 'Paris
House'. Rebecca lodged in an attic above the shop and came

home at weekends. One Saturday afternoon, as the twins were washing out the milk-churns, they heard the shouts and screams of a dreadful row in the kitchen.

Rebecca had confessed to being pregnant – and worse: the man was an Irish navvy, a Catholic, who worked on the railway. She left the house with a bleeding lip and fifteen gold sovereigns in her purse, astonishing everyone with her sly smile and the coolness of her behaviour.

'And that's all she'll ever have from me,' Amos thundered.

They never heard from her again. From an address in Cardiff she sent her old employer a postcard with news of a baby girl. Mary took a train-journey to see her grandchild, but the landlady said the couple had emigrated to America, and slammed the door in her face.

And Amos never recovered from her disappearance. He kept crying out 'Rebecca!' in his sleep. An attack of shingles maddened him to the point of frenzy. Then, to add to his troubles, the rent went up.

The Bickertons were in financial trouble.

Their Trustees had lost a fortune in Russian bonds. Their stud-farming experiments had failed to repay the investment. The sale of Old Masters was a disappointment and, when the Colonel's lawyers broached the subject of avoiding death-duties, he flared up: 'Don't speak to me about death-duties! I'm not dead yet!'

A circular letter from his new agent warned all tenants to expect substantial rises in the coming year – an awkward time for Amos, who was hoping to buy some land.

Even at his angriest, Amos assumed that both the twins would marry, and continue to farm; and since The Vision could never support two families, they needed extra land.

For years he had had his eye on The Tump – a smallholding of thirty-three acres, set in a circle of beeches, on high ground half a mile from the Rhulen lane. The owner was an old recluse – a defrocked priest, so they said – who lived alone in scholarly squalor until one snowy morning Ethel the Rock saw no smoke from his chimney and found him spreadeagled in his garden, with a Christmas rose in his hand.

On making enquiries, Amos was told the place would be sold at auction. Then, one Thursday evening, he took Lewis aside and said sourly:

'Your old friend, Rosie Fifield, moved herself into The Tump.'

Twenty-six

While working at Lurkenhope, one of Rosie's duties had been to carry the bathwater upstairs to Reggie Bickerton's bedroom.

This place, to which few people were ever admitted, was situated in the West Tower, and was a perfect bachelor's den. The walls were hung with deep-blue paper. The tapestry curtains and bed-hangings were worked in green with a design of heraldic beasts. There were chintz-covered chairs and ottomans; the carpet was Persian and in front of the fireplace lay a polar-bearskin rug. On the mantelpiece was an ormolu clock, flanked with figures of Castor and Pollux. Most of the paintings were of oriental subjects, bazaars, mosques, camel caravans and women in latticed rooms. His Eton photographs showed groups of young athletes with imperturbable smiles; and the evening sun filtering through roundels of stained glass, shed flecks of blood-red light over the frames.

Rosie would spread out the bath-mat, drape a towel over a chair, and lay out the soap and sponge. Then, after plunging a thermometer into the water – to be sure of not scalding the young master's stump – she tried to slip away without his calling her back.

Most evenings, he'd be lying on the ottoman loosely wrapped in a yellow silk dressing-gown, sometimes pretending to read or jotting down notes with his serviceable hand. He watched her every movement from the corner of his eye.

'Thank you Rosie,' he'd say, as she turned the door-handle. 'Er . . . Er . . . Rosie!'

'Yes, sir!' She would stand, almost to attention, with the door half-open.

'No! Forget it! It's of no importance!' – and, as the door closed behind her, he would reach for his crutch.

One evening, stripped to the waist, he asked her to help him into the water.

'I can't,' she gasped, and rushed for the safety of the passage.

In 1914, Reggie had gone to war with a head full of chivalric notions of duty to caste and country. He had come home a cripple, with a receding hairline, three fingers missing from his right hand, and the watery eyes of a secret drinker. At first, he made light of his injuries with upper-class stoicism. By 1919, the first wave of sympathy had worn off, and he had become 'a case'.

His fiancée had married his best friend. Other friends found the Welsh Border too far from London for frequent visits. His favourite sister, Isobel, had married and gone to India. And he was left in this huge gloomy house, alone with his squabbling parents and the sad, stuttering Nancy, who showered him with unwanted affection.

He tried his hand at writing a novel about his wartime experiences. The strain of composition tired him: after twenty minutes of left-handed scribbling, he would be staring out of the window – at the lawn, the rain and the hill.

He longed to live in a tropical country and he longed for a tumbler of whisky.

One May weekend, the house was full of guests and Rosie was mouthing her supper in the Servant's Hall, when the bell of Bedroom Three began to ring: she had already seen to his bathwater.

She knocked.

'Come in.'

He was on the ottoman, half-dressed for dinner, trying with his wounded hand to press a gold stud through his shirtfront:

'Here, Rosie? I wonder if you could do these for me?'

Her thumb felt for the back of the stud, but just as it went 'pop' through the starched-up hole, he caught her off balance and pulled her on top of him.

She struggled, shook him off and backed away. A rush of crimson coloured her neck, and she stammered, 'I didn't mean to.'

'But I did, Rosie,' and he protested his love.

He had teased her before. She said it was mean of him to make fun of her.

'But I'm not making fun of you,' he said, in real despair.

She saw he was serious and went out slamming the door.

All through Sunday, she pretended to be sick. On the Monday, when the house-party was over, he apologized with the full force of his charm.

He made her laugh by describing the private lives of all the guests. He spoke of travelling to the Mediterranean, and the Isles of Greece. He gave her novels, which she read by candlelight. She admired the clock above the mantelpiece:

'They're the Heavenly Twins,' he said. 'Take it. It's a present. Anything here can be yours.'

She held him at bay another week. He suspected a rival. Maddened by her resistance, he proposed to her.

'Oh!'

Calmly and slowly, she walked towards the leaded window and looked out over the topiary, and the woods behind. A peacock squawked. In her imagination, she saw the butler bringing in her breakfast-tray; and in the deepening evening, she slipped between the sheets.

Thereafter, they established a regular pattern of deception. She felt humiliated by having to leave him at five, before the house began to wake. When the whispering started they had to be even more careful. One night, she had to hide in the wardrobe while Nancy lectured him to lay off:

'Re-eally, Re-eggie!' she protested. 'It's the s-s-candal of the village!'

Rosie pressed him to tell his parents. He promised to do so once the peace celebrations were over. Another month went by. He came to his senses when she missed her first period.

'I shall tell them,' he said. 'Tomorrow, after breakfast.'

Three days later, his mother had left for the South of France, and he said, 'Please, please, please, please will you give me a little more time?'

The leaves were yellowing in the park, and sportsmen came from London to stay in the house. On the second Saturday of pheasant shooting, the butler ordered her to take a picnic to the Colonel's party over by Tanhouse Wood. A groom was driving her and the hampers back across the park. She saw a blue motor speeding towards the West Lodge.

Reggie had packed his bags and was off, abroad.

She did not cry. She did not break down. She was not even greatly surprised. By creeping off like a coward, he had confirmed her opinion of men. On her bed, she found a letter and tore it to contemptuous shreds. A second letter advised her to visit a Mr Arkwright, Solicitor, in Rhulen.

She went. The offer was for five hundred pounds.

'Make it six,' she said, returning to Mr Arkwright an even icier stare.

'Six,' he agreed. 'And not a penny more!' She walked away with the cheque.

That winter, she took lodgings at a dairy farm and paid her way by making cheeses. When her boy was born, she left him with a wet-nurse and went out to work.

She had always suffered from bronchial troubles, and loved the clean air of the mountains. One summer evening with the swifts whooshing low over her head, she was rambling back along the ridge from the Eagle Stone, and stopped to talk to an old man resting by a hump of reddish rock.

He told her the names of the surrounding bluffs: she asked him the name of the rocks they were sitting on.

'Bickerton's Knob,' he said, perplexed by the hoots of derisive laughter with which she greeted his reply.

The old recluse was lame and stiff. He pointed to his cottage, far below in its ring of beech trees. She escorted him down the slope, then sat with him till dark while he recited his poems. She took to fetching his groceries. He died two winters later, and she was able to buy his property.

She bought a small flock of sheep, and a pony, and taking her son, she shut herself off from the world. She burned the poet's rubbish, but saved his papers and his books. Her only protection was a squeaky door, and a dog.

One day, Lewis Jones went chasing after a runaway ram. He came to a stream in a copse of hazels, where the water combed over a rock, and there were piles of bleached bones brought down by the winter flood. Peering through the leaves, he saw Rosie Fifield, in a blue dress, sitting on the far side of the gully. Her washing was laid out to dry on the gorsebushes, and she was buried in a book. A little boy ran up to her, and held a buttercup under her chin.

'Please, Billy!' she stroked his hair. 'No more now!' – and the child settled down to make a daisy-chain.

Lewis watched them for ten minutes, frozen as you would watch a vixen playing with her cubs. Then he went back to the house.

Twenty-seven

On boxing day of 1924, the hounds met at Fiddler's Elbow and began drawing the coverts of Cefn Wood. Around eleven-thirty, Colonel Bickerton was thrown from his hunter and kicked in the spine by an oncoming horse. The schoolchildren were given a holiday for the funeral. In the pub, the drinkers toasted the old squire's memory, and said, 'It's the way he'd have wanted to go.'

His widow came for three days, and went back to Grasse.

Having quarrelled with the rest of her family, she had chosen to live in France, painting and gardening in a small Provençal house. Mrs Nancy lived on at Lurkenhope, 'holding the fort' for Reggie, who was away, on his coffee plantation, in Kenya. Most of the servants were given their notice. In July, Amos Jones heard a rumour that the hillfarms would be sold to pay the death-duties.

This was the moment for which he had waited all his life.

He called on the land-agent, who confirmed, in confidence, that all tenants of ten or more years' standing would be offered their farms at a 'fair valuation'.

'And what would a fair valuation be?'

'For The Vision? Hard to say exactly! Somewhere between two and three thousand, I expect.'

Amos next called in on the bank-manager, who foresaw no difficulty in securing a loan.

The prospect of owning his own farm made him feel young again. He seemed to forget his daughter. He looked over the land with the new eyes of love, dreamed of buying modern machinery, and delivered moralistic sermons on the decline of the gentry.

The Hand of God, he said, had delivered the land unto him and his seed; and when he spoke of 'seed', the twins both blushed and looked at the floor. One day, during the grouse season, he hid among the larches and watched Mrs Nancy striding up the pasture with a party of guns and beaters.

'And next year,' he shouted down the supper-table, 'next year, if they so much as show their fat faces in my field, I'll see them off . . . I'll set the dogs on them . . .'

'Good heavens!' said Mary, as she set down a dish of shepherd's pie. 'What did they ever do to you?'

Autumn slipped by. Then, towards the end of October, two valuers came from Hereford and asked to be shown the fields and the buildings.

'And what do you two gentlemen think the place might be worth?' Amos asked, deferentially opening the door of their saloon.

The older man rubbed his chin: 'Around three thousand on the open market. But I'd keep that figure dark if I were you.'

'Open market? But it's not to be sold on the open market.'

'I dare say you're right,' the valuer shrugged, and pulled the self-starter.

Amos suspected that something was wrong. But never, in

On the Black Hill

his wilder moments of anxiety, was he prepared for the announcement in the *Hereford Times*: that the farms were to be sold, at public auction, on a date six weeks hence, at the Red Dragon in Rhulen. Apprehensive of the new Labour Government, and alert to new legislation that might go against the landlord, the Lurkenhope Trustees had opted to go for the last farthing, and were forcing their tenants to compete with outside buyers.

Haines of Red Daren called a meeting in the hall at Maesyfelin where, one after the other, the tenants protested against 'this monstrously underhand behaviour', and promised to disrupt the sale.

The sale went ahead as planned.

It was sleeting on the big day. Mary put on a warm grey woollen dress, her winter coat, and the hat she wore for funerals. As she took her umbrella, she turned to the twins and said, 'Please, do come! Your father needs you. Today, he needs you more than ever.'

They shook their heads and said, 'No, Mother! We'd not go to town.'

The Banqueting Hall of the Red Dragon had been cleared of tables, and the manager, alarmed for his parquet floor, was hovering in the entrance on the look-out for hobnail boots. The auctioneer's clerk was setting slips of paper on the chairs reserved for bidders. Nodding to friends and acquaintances, Mary sat down in the third row, while Amos went to join the other tenants, who – Welshmen to a man – stood in a ring with waterproofs over their arms, speaking in low murmurs as they tried to agree on a strategy.

The ringleader was Haines of Red Daren, now a gaunt,

179

stringy man in his fifties with a squashed-up nose, a mop of greyish curls and crooked teeth. He had recently lost his wife.

'Right!' he said. 'If anyone bids against a tenant, I shall kick him from this room with my own boot.'

The room was filling up, with both bidders and spectators. Then a youngish, frowsy-looking woman came in wearing a rain-drenched hat of green feathers. On her arm was old Tom Watkins the Coffin.

Amos broke from the circle to greet his former enemy, but Watkins turned his back and glared at a hunting print.

At twenty past two, Mr Arkwright, the vendors' solicitor, appeared as if dressed for a shooting-party, in chequered tweed plus-fours. He, too, had recently lost his wife; but when David Powell-Davies went up to commiserate 'on behalf of all members of the Farmers' Union', the solicitor returned a withering smile:

'A sad business to be sure! But a mercy! Believe me, Mr Powell-Davies! A great mercy!'

Mrs Arkwright had spent her last year in and out of the Mid Wales Insane Asylum. The widower walked away to engage the auctioneer in conversation.

The auctioneer was a Mr Whitaker, a tall, bland, sandy-haired man with a high complexion and oyster-coloured eyes. He was dressed in the uniform of the professional classes – a black jacket and striped trousers – and his Adam's apple jerked up and down in the V of his winged collar.

At half-past two precisely, he mounted the rostrum and announced, 'By Order of the Trustees of Lurkenhope Estates, the sale of fifteen farms, five parcels of accommodation land, and two hundred acres of mature forest.'

'Shall I not die in the farm I were born in?' A deep voice, resonant with irony, sounded from the rear of the room.

'Of course you shall,' said Mr Whitaker, pleasantly. 'By making the appropriate bid! I do assure you, sir, the reserves are low. Are we ready to begin then? Lot One . . . Lower Pen-Lan Court . . .'

'No, sir!' It was Haines of Red Daren. 'We are not ready to begin. We are ready to put an end to this nonsense. Is it right to put up property of this kind without giving the tenants a chance to buy?'

Mr Whitaker turned from the muttering crowd to Mr Arkwright: they had been warned in advance to expect a disturbance. He laid down his ivory gavel and addressed the chandelier:

'All this, gentlemen, is a little late in the day. But I will say the following: as farmers you advocate open markets for selling your stock. Yet you come here expecting a closed market against your landlord.'

'Is there government control of the price of land?' It was Haines again, his sing-song voice rising in anger. 'There is government control of the price of stock.'

'Hear! Hear!' – and the Welshmen started clapping, slowly.

'Sir!' Mr Whitaker's mouth quivered and turned down at the corners. 'This is a sale by public auction. It is not a political meeting.'

'It'll turn political soon enough.' Haines waved a fist in the air. 'You Englishmen! You think you've had troubles enough in Ireland. I can tell you, there's a room full of Welshmen to make trouble enough right here.'

'Sir!' The gavel sounded, *rat-tat-tat!* 'This is not the time or place to discuss imperial questions. There is one question before us, gentlemen! Do we, or do we not, wish this sale to proceed?'

From all sides came cries of 'No!' . . . 'Yes!' . . . 'Chuck the bugger out!' . . . 'Bloody Bolshevik!' . . . 'God Save the King!' – while the core of Welshmen joined hands and sang in chorus, *Hen Wlad Fy Nhadau*, 'O Land of My Fathers'.

Rat-tat-tat-tat-tat-tat-tat!

'Unfortunately, I cannot compliment you on your singing, gentlemen!' The auctioneer paled. 'I shall say one thing more. If this disturbance continues, the lots will be withdrawn and offered for sale by private treaty in a single block.'

'Bluffer! . . . Chuck him out! . . .' But the shouts carried little conviction and soon petered off into silence.

Mr Whitaker folded his arms and gloated over the effectiveness of his threat. In the shadows, David Powell-Davies was remonstrating with Haines of Red Daren.

'All right! All right!' Haines raked his fingernails down his pitted cheeks. 'But if I catch any man, woman or dog bidding against a tenant, I'll boot him——'

'Very well, then.' The auctioneer surveyed the lines of tense, self-centred faces. 'The gentleman has given us permission to proceed. Lot One, then . . . Lower Pen-Lan Court . . . Five hundred pounds, am I bid?' – and within twenty-five minutes he had sold off the land, woodland, and fourteen farms, every one of them to their tenants.

Dai Morgan gave £2,500 for The Bailey. Gillifaenog went to Evan Bevan for £2,000 only, but the land was poor. The Griffithses had to pay £3,050 for Cwm Cringlyn; and Haines bought Red Daren for a full £400 below the estimate.

That certainly perked him up. He circulated round his

cronies, pumping their hands and promising a round of drinks at opening time.

'Lot Fifteen . . .

'This is it,' breathed Mary. Amos was trembling, and she slipped her grey-gloved hand over his.

'Lot Fifteen, The Vision Farm. House and outbuildings, with a hundred and twenty acres and grazing rights on the Black Hill . . . What am I bid? Five hundred pounds? . . . Five hundred it is! Your bid, sir! . . . At five hundred . . . !'

Amos pushed his bids against the reserve: it was like pushing a cart uphill. He clenched his fists. His breath came in sharp bursts.

At £2,750, he glanced up and saw the gavel poised to fall.

'Your bid, sir!' said Mr Whitaker; and Amos felt that he had reached a sunny summit and the clouds had all dispersed. Mary's hand lay over his relaxing knuckles, and his mind flashed back to that first evening, together in the overgrown farmyard.

'Very well, then,' Mr Whitaker was winding up the sale. 'Sold to the tenant for two thousand, seven hun——'

'Three thousand!'

The voice fell like a pole-axe on the base of Amos's skull.

Chairs squeaked as the spectators turned to stare at the unexpected bidder. Amos knew the bidder, but would not turn round.

'At three thousand,' Mr Whitaker beamed with pleasure. 'The bid is at the back of the room at three thousand.'

'Three thousand one hundred,' Amos choked.

'And five hundred!'

The bidder was Watkins the Coffin.

'And six at the front!'

And where was Red Daren now, Amos wondered. Where was his boot now? He felt, with each bid, that he was going to burst. He felt he was fighting for air, that each hundred was his final breath, but the cold voice behind him continued.

Now he opened his eyes and saw the complacent, coaxing smile on the auctioneer's face.

'Yours at the back,' the voice was saying. 'Sold to the bidder at the back for five thousand two hundred pounds. Have you all done? Against you, sir!'

Mr Whitaker was enjoying himself. You could tell he was enjoying himself by the way he moistened his lower lip with the tip of his tongue.

'Five thousand three hundred!' said Amos, his eyes agape in a trance-like stare.

The auctioneer caught the bids in his mouth, like flowers flying.

'Near me, at five thousand three hundred!'

'Stop!' Mary's fingers clawed at her husband's shirt-cuff. 'He's mad,' she hissed. 'You've got to stop!'

'Thank you, sir! Five thousand four hundred at the back!'

'And five,' Amos barked.

'Near me again, at five thousand five hundred!' Again, Mr Whitaker stretched his gaze beyond the chandelier – and blinked. A look of perplexity passed over his face. The second bidder had bolted for the door. People were leaving their seats and putting on their coats.

'Very well, then!' He raised his voice above the crinkle of oilskins. 'Sold to the tenant for five thousand five hundred pounds!' – and the gavel descended with an onanistic thud.

Twenty-eight

It was sleeting again next afternoon as Mary drove the dog-cart on her way to the solicitor. The fields were full of sodden sheep, and there were sheets of muddy water in the lane. Amos had taken to his bed.

The clerk showed her into the office, where a coal fire was blazing.

'Thank you, I'd prefer to stand here a moment,' she said, warming her hands while she collected her thoughts.

Mr Arkwright came in and rearranged some papers on his desk: 'Dear lady, how good of you to call in so soon!' he said, and went on to discuss the deposit and exchange of contracts: 'We'll soon have the matter sewn up.'

'I haven't come to speak of the contract,' she said, 'but the unfair price at the sale.'

'Unfair, madam?' The monocle popped out of his eye-socket and swung to and fro on its black silk ribbon. 'In what way unfair? It was a public auction.'

'It was a private vendetta.'

The steam spiralled up from her skirt as she explained the feud between her husband and Watkins the Coffin.

The solicitor toyed with his paper-knife, adjusted his

cravat-pin, leafed through a journal; then he rang for his secretary and asked, very pointedly, for 'one cup of tea'.

'Yes, Mrs Jones, I am listening,' he said, as Mary came to the end of her tale. 'Is there anything more you wish to tell me?'

'I was hoping . . . I was wondering . . . if the Trustees would agree to reduce the price . . .'

'Reduce the price? What a suggestion!'

'Is there no way——?'

'None!'

'No hope of——?'

'Hope, madam? I call it sheer effrontery!'

She stiffened her backbone and curled her lip: 'You won't get that price from anyone else, you know!'

'I beg your pardon, madam. On the contrary! Mr Watkins came to see me this very morning. Only too willing to place his deposit if the purchaser defaults!'

'I don't believe you,' she said.

'Don't,' he said, and pointed to the door. 'You have twenty-eight days in which to decide.'

A pity, he thought, as he listened to her footsteps on the linoleum. She must have been a handsome woman once: and she had caught him lying! But then she had – had she not? – betrayed her class. He was twitching nervously when the secretary fetched in the tea.

The evening clouds were darker than the hill. Great flocks of starlings flew low over Cefn Wood, expanding and condensing in arcs and ellipses, then sweeping in a whirlwind and settling on the branches. On ahead, Mary saw the lights of her home, but hardly dared advance towards it.

The twins came out, unharnessed the pony and wheeled the cart into its shed.

'How's Father?' she said, shivering.

'Acting strange.'

All day, he had called on God to smite him for the sin of pride.

'And what can I tell him now?' she said, crouching on a footstool by the grate. Benjamin fetched her a mug of cocoa. She closed her eyes to the blaze and seemed to see the lines of red corpuscles streaming over her eyelids.

'What can we, any of us, do?' she addressed the flames; and the flames, to her amazement, answered back.

She stood up. She went to the piano and opened the marquetry box in which she kept her correspondence. Within seconds, she had fished out Mrs Bickerton's Christmas card from last year. Under the signature was an address, near Grasse.

The twins ate their supper and went off to bed. A gale blew over the roof and, in the bedroom, she could hear Amos groaning. The flames crackled, the nib scratched. She wrote letter after letter, crumpling them up until she achieved the right effect. Then she stamped the envelope and left it for the postman.

She waited a week, two weeks, twenty days. The twenty-first day was a bright chilly morning, and she told herself not to run out to the postman, but to wait for the postman's knock.

The letter had come.

As she slit it open, something yellow, the colour of a baby chick, bounced out on to the hearthrug. She held her breath as her eyes raced over Mrs Bickerton's confident scrawl:

'Poor you! What an ordeal! I do so agree . . . some people

are absolutely mad! Thank heavens, I still have *some* clout with the Trustees! And I should think so too! . . . Wonderful invention, the telephone . . . Got through to London in ten minutes flat! . . . Sir Vivian most understanding . . . Couldn't remember offhand what the reserve on The Vision was . . . Under three thousand, he thought . . . But whatever it was, you can certainly have it for that!'

Mary raised her eyes to Amos and a tear dropped on to the notepaper. She went on reading aloud:

' . . . Garden lovely! . . . Mimosa time . . . and almond blossom . . . Heaven! Love you to come down if you can get away . . . Ask that awful Arkwright to get you the ticket . . .'

Suddenly, she was terribly embarrassed. She looked again at Amos.

'Big of them!' he snarled. 'Very very big of them!' – and he stamped out on to the porch.

She picked up the thing that had fallen from the letter. It was a flowerhead of mimosa, squashed but still fluffy. She held it to her nostril and inhaled the smell of the South.

One year, in the late Eighties, she and her mother had met the missionary's ship when it docked in Naples. Together they had travelled through a Mediterranean spring.

She remembered the sea, the olives blown white in the wind, and the scents of thyme and cistus after rain. She remembered lupins and poppies in the fields above Posilippo. She remembered warmth and ease in her body, under the sun. And what would she give now, for a new life, in the sun? To shrivel and die in the sun? Yet this letter, the letter she had prayed for, was it not also a sentence to stay, trapped for ever and ever, for the rest of her existence, in this gloomy house below the hill?

And Amos? If he could have smiled, or been grateful, or even understanding! Instead of which, he banged and stamped and broke crockery, and cursed the bloody English, and the Bickertons in particular. He even threatened to burn the place down.

And finally, when the Trustees' letter came – offering The Vision for £2,700 – all the years of brewed-up resentment burst into the open:

It had been her connections that got them the lease. Her money that stocked the farm. Her furniture furnished the house. Because of her, his daughter had run off with the Irishman. It was her fault that his sons were idiots. And now, when everything'd gone to whinders, it was her class and her clever clever letter that had saved all that he, Amos Jones – man, farmer, Welshman – had worked for, saved for, ruined his health for – and now did not want!

Did she hear that? DID–NOT–WANT! No! Not at that price! Nor at any price! And what did he want? He knew what he wanted! His daughter! Rebecca! He wanted her. Back. Back home! And the husband! Bloody Irishman! Couldn't be worse than them two halfwits! And he'd find them! And bring her back! Bring 'em both back! Back! Back! Back!—

—'I know . . . I know . . .' Mary stood behind him, cradling his head in her hands. He had collapsed onto the rocking-chair, and was shaking with sobs.

'We'll find her,' she said. 'Somehow we'll find her. Even if we have to go to America, we'll somehow get her back.'

'Why did I put her out?' he whimpered.

He clung to Mary as a frightened child clings to a doll, but to his question she could find no answer.

Twenty-nine

Spring had dusted the larches. The cream was coming thick and yellowy in the cream-separator when a call from Benjamin made Mary drop the handle and rush for the kitchen. Amos lay stretched out on the hearthrug, mouth open and fish-eyes gaping at the rafters.

He had had a stroke. He had just passed his fifty-fifth birthday, and had been bending to tie a bootlace. On the table there was a mug of primroses.

Dr Galbraith, the jovial young Irishman who had taken over the practice, congratulated his patient on having the 'strength of an ox' and said he'd have him on his feet in no time. Then, taking Mary aside, he warned her to expect a second attack.

Yet despite one paralysed arm, Amos recovered sufficiently to hobble round the yard, wave his stick, curse the twins and get in the way of the horses. He was very hard to handle when his thoughts harked back to Rebecca.

'Well, 'ave you found her?' he'd snap each time the postman brought a letter.

'Not yet,' Mary'd say, 'but we'll keep on trying.'

She knew the Irishman's name was Moynihan, and wrote

letters to the police, to the Home Office, and to his old employers on the railway. She advertised in the Dublin newspapers. She even wrote without success to the immigration authorities in America.

The couple had vanished.

That autumn, she announced with an air of finality, 'There's nothing more we can do.'

From then on, since neither twin went out, and even Benjamin had lost the habit of handling money, it was she who ruled The Vision; she who kept the accounts; she who decided what to plant. She was a shrewd judge of business and a shrewd judge of men, knowing when to buy and when to sell; when to placate the stock-dealers and when to send them packing.

'Phew!' a man was heard to complain after she'd struck some ferocious bargain. 'That Mother Jones is the stingiest woman on the hill.'

The remark was passed back to her, and it gave her great pleasure.

To avoid any question of paying death-duties, she put the deeds of The Vision in the twins' joint name. Her triumphant stare was enough to send Mr Arkwright scuttling down the street. She hooted with laughter at the news of the solicitor's arrest – for murder.

'Murder, Mother?'

'Murder!'

At first, Mrs Arkwright was thought to have died from nephritis and the effects of insanity. Then a rival solicitor, Mr Vavasour Hughes, asked the widower certain embarrassing questions about a client's will. At a tea-party designed to dispel his doubts, Mr Arkwright pressed him to eat a bloater paste sandwich, from which he nearly died in the night. A fortnight later Mr Hughes received a box of chocolates 'from an admirer'; and again he nearly died. He reported his suspicions to the police, who found that each chocolate had been syringed with arsenic. They put two and two together, and ordered the dead woman to be exhumed from Rhulen churchyard.

Dr Galbraith professed himself shocked by the result of the forensic tests: 'I knew she was martyr to indigestion,' he said, 'but I never expected this.'

To avail himself of her capital, Mr Arkwright had laced his wife's Benger's Food with arsenic purchased for the persecution of dandelions. He was convicted in Hereford and hanged in Gloucester.

'They've hanged old Arkwright,' Lewis waved the *News of the World* in his father's face.

'Eh?' Amos was now very deaf.

'I said, they've hanged old Arkwright,' he bellowed.

'An' 'e should a-been hanged at birth,' he said, decisively, bubbles of saliva dribbling down his chin.

Mary watched for signs of the second stroke; but it was not a stroke that killed him.

Olwen and Daisy were The Vision's two heavy brood-mares, and they foaled alternate years.

Lewis loved them dearly, saw whole worlds in their gleaming flanks, and liked to scrub them, comb them, polish their brasses, and fluff the white 'feathering' out around their hoofs.

A mare came on heat around the end of May, and waited for the visit of the stallion – a magnificent animal called

Spanker who made a tour of the hill-farms with his master, Merlin Evans.

This Merlin was a wiry, tow-haired fellow with a pitted triangular face and a set of brown broken teeth. Around his neck he wore a number of ladies' chiffon scarves – until they rotted off – and a single gold hoop through his earlobe. He astonished the twins with his tales of conquest. They had only to mention some saintly, Chapel-going woman and he would grin: ''Ad her in the dingle over by Pantglas,' or ''Ad her standing up in the beast-house.'

Some nights he slept behind a haystack, others between linen sheets. People said he had sired a good few more offspring than Spanker: in fact there were farmers who, with an eye to fresh blood in the family, made a point of leaving their wives alone in the house.

Every year, before Christmas, he took a week's holiday in the capital; and once, when Lewis paid him twenty-five shillings for the stallion's services, Merlin spread the coins in his palm: 'Them'll get me one woman in London,' he said, 'and five in Abergavenny!'

In the spring of '26 a girl delayed him in Rosgoch, and he arrived at The Vision a week late.

Shreds of cloud hung motionless in the sky. The hills were silvery in the sunlight, the hedges white with hawthorn, and the buttercups spread a film of gold over the fields. The paddock was thick with bleating sheep. A cuckoo called. Sparrows chattered, and house-martins sliced the air. The two mares stood in their stalls, their muzzles in their oat-bags, kicking because of the flies.

Lewis and Benjamin were expecting the shearers at any moment.

All morning, they had been lashing the pens, boiling the tar-pot, oiling rusty shears, and taking the greasy oak shearing-benches down from the hayloft.

Indoors, Mary made lemon barley water for the men's refreshment. Amos was taking a nap, when a sharp voice sounded by the gate: 'Giddy-up then! Here comes the old lecher!'

The clatter of horseshoes woke the invalid. He went out to see what was going on.

The sun was very bright, and it dazzled him. He didn't seem to see the mares.

Nor did the twins see him as he limped into the strip of shadow between the stalls and the stallion. Nor did he hear Merlin Evans bawling, 'Watch it, yer old fool!'

It was too late.

Olwen had kicked. The hoof caught him under the chin, and the sparrows went on chattering.

Thirty

From the moment he set foot on the staircase, Mr Vines the undertaker registered an expression of doubt. The doubts increased as he cast a professional eye on the gap between the newel-post and the passage wall. He took a tape-measure to the corpse, and descended to the kitchen.

'He's a big man,' he said. 'We'll have to coffin him down here, I suppose.'

'I suppose so,' said Mary. A black crêpe handkerchief was tucked into her sleeve, in readiness for the tears that would not come.

In the afternoon, she scrubbed the kitchen floor and, sprinkling some bed-sheets with lavender-water, tacked them to the picture rail, so that they hung in folds over the frames. She fetched a branch or two of laurel from the garden, and made a frieze from the shining leaves.

The weather continued hot and muggy: the twins went on with the shearing. Five of the neighbours had come to help, clipping all day in competition for the prize of a costrel of cider.

'I'll put my money on Benjamin,' said old Dai Morgan, as Benjamin dragged another ewe from the pen. He was five beasts ahead of Lewis. He had strong, agile hands, and was a wonderful shearer.

The sheep lay quietly under the shears, and endured the torture. Then, creamy white again – though some with bloody cuts about their udders – they bounded out into the paddock, jumping in the air, as if over an imaginary fence, or simply to be free. None of the shearers spoke of the dead man.

Two boys – Reuben Jones's grandsons – rolled up the fleeces, teased the neck-wool into cords, and tied them. Now and again, Mary appeared in the doorway, in a long green dress, with a jug of the lemon barley water.

'You must be terribly thirsty,' she smiled, cutting short their efforts to commiserate.

When Mr Vines drove up at four, the twins downed tools and carried the coffin in through the porch. Their hands were greasy and their overalls shiny black from the lanolin. They wrapped their father in a sheet and fetched him down the staircase. They laid him on the kitchen table, and left the undertaker to his business.

Mary went for a walk, alone, over the fields to Cock-a-loftie. She watched a kestrel quivering under a curdled sky. Around sunset, like crows at the lambing season, women in black came to pay their last respects, and kiss the corpse.

The coffin lay open on the table. Candles stood on either side, and their light flickered up through the bacon-rack and made a grid of shadow with the rafters. Mary, also, had changed into black. Some of the women were crying:

'He was a fine man.'

'He was a good man.'

'The Lord have mercy!'

'God be with him!'

'God have mercy on his soul!'

The coffin was lined with wadding and domett. To conceal the contusions on his chin, a white scarf had been wrapped around the lower half of his face, but the mourners saw the wisps of reddish hair poking out of his nostrils. The room smelled of lavender and lilac. Mary was unable to cry.

'Yes,' she replied. 'He was a good man.'

She showed her guests into the parlour and served each one a glass of mulled ale with lemon peel. This, she recalled, was custom in the valleys.

'Yes,' she nodded. 'There are no friends like old friends.'

The twins stood silently against the kitchen wall, eyeing the people who were eyeing their father.

Mary went into Rhulen and bought for the funeral a black velvet skirt, a black straw hat, and a black blouse with a collarette of accordion-pleated chiffon. She was still in the bedroom, dressing, as the hearse drew up to the gate. The kitchen was full of people. The pall-bearers shouldered the coffin; but she continued to gaze at her reflection in the pier-glass, slowly swivelling her head and surveying her profile. Her cheeks were like crumpled rose-petals beneath the chenille-spot veil.

She held up through the service and the committal. She walked from the grave without a final look – and within a week she gave way to despair.

First, she blamed herself for Amos's stroke. Then she assumed those aspects of his character which had once annoyed her most. She lost her appetite for the least of luxuries. She bought no clothes. She lost her sense of humour, no longer laughing at the little absurdities that had lightened her existence; and she even remembered his mother, old Hannah, with affection.

She carried her devotion to the point of eccentricity.

She patched his jacket and darned his socks, laid a fourth place for supper and would heap his plate with food. His pipe, his tobacco-pouch, his spectacles, his Bible – all were set out in their familiar places; also his box of chisels in case he wanted to carve.

They held conversations three times a week – not through table-turning or the techniques of spiritism, but from the simpler belief that the dead were alive and would answer if called.

She would take no decision without his assent.

One November night, when a field belonging to Lower Brechfa was coming up for sale, she parted the curtains and whispered into the darkness. Then, turning to face her sons, she said, 'Lord knows where we'll find the money, but Father says we should buy.'

On the other hand, when Lewis wanted a new McCormick binder – he no longer held to his hatred of machinery – she tightened her lips, and said, 'Definitely not!'

Then, havering, she said, 'Yes!'

Then she said, 'Father says, "No!"'

Then she said, 'Yes!' again; but by that time, Lewis was so confused he let the matter drop, and they didn't buy a binder till after the Second World War.

Nothing – not even a teacup – was replaced; and the house began to look like a museum.

The twins never ventured out, rather from force of habit now than fear of the outside world. Then, during the summer of '27, there was a very disagreeable incident.

Thirty-one

Two years after Jim the Rock came home from the war, his sister Ethel gave birth to a boy. His name was Alfie, and he grew up simple. Who the father was, Ethel wasn't saying; but because the lad had Jim's carroty hair and cauliflower ears, unkind people used to say, 'Brother and sister! What can you expect? Small wonder the kid's a halfwit!' – which was quite unfair, because Jim and Ethel were not blood-relations.

Alfie was a troublesome child. He was always stripping off his clothes and playing naked in the beast-house, and sometimes he went missing for days. Ethel shrugged at these absences, and said, 'He be bound to show up sooner or later.' One summer evening, Benjamin Jones found him frolicking on the hill and, having a childish streak himself, the two of them went on playing till sundown.

But the boy had only one true friend and that was a clock.

The clock – its glass always filthy from peatsmoke – had a white enamel dial and Roman numerals, and lived in a wooden case on the wall above the fireplace.

As soon as he was tall enough, Alfie would climb a chair, stand on tiptoe, open the tiny trap-door and peer at the pendulum swinging to and fro, tick-tock . . . tick-tock . . . Then he would crouch by the grate, as if his icy eyes could quench the embers, clicking his tongue, tick-tock . . . tick-tock . . . and nodding his head in time.

He thought the clock was alive. He would come home with presents for the clock – a pretty pebble perhaps, a piece of moss, a bird's egg or a dead fieldmouse. He longed to make the clock say something other than tick-tock . . . He fiddled with the hands and the pendulum. He tried to wind it up and, in the end, he broke it.

Leaving the case behind on the wall, Jim took the mechanism to Rhulen. The clock-repairer examined it – it was a fine eighteenth-century model – and offered him £5. Jim left the shop whistling happily on his way to the pub, but little Alfie was heartbroken.

He missed his friend, screamed, searched the barn and buildings, and butted his blazing head against the whitewashed wall. Then, convinced the clock was dead, he vanished.

Ethel made no special effort to find him and, even three days later, merely grumbled that Alfie'd 'gone the devil knows where.'

Below Craig-y-Fedw there was a boggy pool, hidden among hazels, where Benjamin went picking watercress for tea. Some bluebottles were buzzing around a clump of kingcups. He saw a pair of legs poking out of the mud, and ran back home to fetch Lewis.

By the time the police came on the scene, Ethel the Rock had thrown a fit of hysterics, and was moaning and wailing that Benjamin was the murderer.

'I knew it,' she bawled. 'I knew he was that kind!' – and poured forth a rigmarole of how Benjamin took the boy on lonely walks.

Benjamin was dumbstruck: the presence of policemen carried him back to the terrible days of 1918. Escorted to The Vision for questioning, he hung his head and was unable to return a single coherent answer.

As usual, it was Mary who saved the day: 'Officer, don't you see it's a complete fabrication. Poor Miss Watkins! She's a little bit out of her mind.'

The interview ended with the policemen doffing their helmets and offering apologies. At the inquest, the coroner returned a verdict of 'death by misadventure'; but relations between The Vision and The Rock were sour again.

Thirty-two

As Amos's widow, Mary wanted at least one daughter-in-law and a brood of grandchildren. As the mother of twins, she wanted to keep both sons for herself, and in her daydreams made a mental picture of the scene at her death.

She would be lying, a withered husk with wisps of silver hair on the pillow, and her hands stretched out over a patchwork quilt. The room would be filled with sunshine and birdsong; a breeze would stir the curtains, and the twins be standing, symmetrically, on either side of the bed. A beautiful picture – and one she knew to be a sin!

There were times when she chided Benjamin, 'What is all this nonsense about not going out? Why can't you find a nice young lady?' But Benjamin's mouth would tighten, his lower lids quiver, and she knew he would never get married. At other times, wilfully displaying the perverse side of her character, she took Lewis by the elbow and made him promise never, never to marry unless Benjamin married too.

'I promise,' he said, slumping his head like a man receiving a prison sentence; for he wanted a woman badly.

All through one winter, he became very jumpy and argumentative, would snap at his brother and refuse to eat.

Mary feared a repetition of Amos's black moods and, in May, she made a momentous decision: both the boys were going to the Rhulen Fair.

'No.' She shot a piercing look at Benjamin. 'I won't hear any excuses.'

'Yes, Mama,' he said, lifelessly.

She packed them a picnic lunch and waved goodbye from the porch.

'Mind you pick the pretty ones!' she called out. 'And don't come back till dark!'

She strolled into the orchard and gazed across the valley at the two ponies, one cantering round in circles, the other ambling at a trot, until they vanished over the skyline.

'Well, at least we've got them out of the house.' She scratched Lewis's sheepdog behind his ear, and the dog wagged his tail and nuzzled his head against her skirt. Then she went indoors to read a book.

She had lately discovered the novels of Thomas Hardy, and she wanted to read them all. How well she knew the life he described – the smell of Tess's milking-parlour; Tess's torments, in bed and in the beetfield. She, too, could whittle hurdles, plant pine saplings, or thatch a hayrick – and if the old unmechanized ways were gone from Wessex, time had stood still, here, on the Radnor Hills.

'Think of The Rock,' she told herself. 'Nothing's changed there since the Dark Ages.'

She was reading *The Mayor of Casterbridge*. She liked it less than *The Woodlanders*, which she had read the week before, and Hardy's 'coincidences' had begun to grate on her nerves. She read three more chapters; then, letting the book fall into her lap, she allowed herself to slide into a reverie of certain nights and mornings – in the bedroom with Amos. And suddenly, he came to her – with his flaming hair and the light streaming out round his shoulders. And she knew she must have slept because the sun had come round to the west and sunbeams were pouring past the geraniums, in between her legs.

'At my age!' she smiled, shaking herself awake – and heard the sound of horses in the yard.

The twins were standing by the gate, Benjamin puffed into a state of exalted indignation, while Lewis looked over his shoulder as if searching for somewhere to hide.

'Whatever's the matter?' she burst out laughing. 'Were there no young ladies at the fair?'

'It was terrible,' said Benjamin.

'Terrible?'

'Terrible!'

Skirts, since the twins were last in Rhulen, had risen not above the ankle, but above the knee.

At eleven that morning, they had stopped on the hilltop and looked down over the town. Already the fair was in full swing. They heard the hum of the crowd, the whine of Wurlitzer organs, and the odd snarl or bellow from the beasts in the menagerie. In Broad Street alone, Lewis counted eleven merry-go-rounds. There was a Ferris-wheel in the marketplace, and a little Tower of Babel, which was a helter-skelter.

For the last time, Benjamin begged his brother to turn back.

'Mother'd never know,' he said.

'I'd tell her,' said Lewis, and kicked his pony.

Twenty minutes later, he was wandering round the fairground like a man possessed.

Farmlads strolled the streets in gangs of seven or eight, puffing at cigarettes, ogling the girls, or daring one another to spar with 'The Champ' – a Negro boxer in red satin shorts. Gipsy fortune-tellers offered lilies-of-the-valley, or your fortune. Ping . . . ping sounded from the shooting galleries. An exhibition of freaks showed the 'smallest mare and foal in the world', and one of its larger women.

By noon, Lewis had ridden an elephant, flown in a 'Chairoplane', drunk the milk of a coconut, licked a lollipop, and was looking for other amusements.

As for Benjamin, all he saw were legs – bare legs, legs in silk stockings, legs in fish-net stockings – kicking, dancing, prancing, and reminding him of his one and only visit to an abattoir and the kicks of the sheep in their death throes.

Around one o'clock, Lewis paused outside the 'Theatre de Paris' where four can-can girls, encased in raspberry velvet, were doing a come-on act, while, behind painted draperies, a Mamzelle Delilah performed the 'Dance of the Seven Veils' to an audience of heavy-breathing farmers.

Lewis felt for the sixpence in his pocket, and a hand clamped around his wrist. He turned to meet his brother's flinty stare:

'You'll not go in there!'

'Just you try and stop me!'

'Won't I just?' Benjamin sidestepped across his brother's path, and the sixpence slid back down into his pocket.

Half an hour later, Lewis's gaiety had left him. He moped around the booths looking desolate. Benjamin dogged him, a few paces behind.

A beatific vision had been offered – offered for the price of a drink – and Lewis had turned aside. But why? Why? Why? He asked the question a hundred times, until it dawned on him that he was not just afraid of hurting Benjamin: he was afraid of him.

At a hoop-la stand, he almost accosted a girl in flamingo straining every fibre of her torso to land her hoop over a five pound note. He saw his brother glaring through a stack of tea-sets and goldfish bowls; and his courage failed.

'Let's go home,' said Benjamin.

'To hell with you,' Lewis said, and was on the point of relenting when two girls accosted him.

'Want a cigarette?' asked the elder one, poking her stubby fingers in her handbag.

'Thank you very much,' said Lewis.

The girls were sisters. One wore a green frock, the other a tunic of mauve jersey with an orange sash around her bottom. Their cheeks were rouged, their hair shingled, and their nostrils were cavernous. They winked at one another with insolent pale blue eyes, and even Lewis saw that skimpy hemlines looked absurd on their short, heavy-breasted bodies.

He tried to shake them off: they clung on.

Benjamin watched from a distance as his brother treated them to lemonade and brandy-snaps. Then, realizing they were no competition, he joined the group. The girls burst into fits at the thought of walking out with twins.

'What a lark!' said the mauve one.

'Let's go on the Wall of Death!' said the green one.

A huge cylindrical drum stood beside its steam-engine at the top end of Castle Street. Lewis paid the grimy youth at the ticket kiosk; and all four stepped inside.

Several other passengers were waiting for the start. The youth shouted, 'Stand against the wall!' The door slammed and the drum began to spin faster and faster on its axis. The floor rose, pushing the passengers upward till their heads were almost level with the rim. When the floor fell again, they were stranded, pinned by centrifugal force, in attitudes of the Crucifixion.

Benjamin felt his eyeballs being squashed back into his skull. For three endless minutes, the agony continued. Then, as the drum slowed up, the girls slithered down and their frocks concertina-ed above their hips, so that gaps of bare flesh showed between their stockings and suspender-belts.

Benjamin staggered on to the street and vomited into the gutter.

'I've had enough,' he spluttered, and mopped his chin. 'I'm off.'

'Spoil-sport!' squealed the girl in green. 'He's only putting it on.' The sisters linked their arms around Lewis's and tried to march him up the street. He did shake them off, and turned on his heels and followed the tweed cap through the crowd in the direction of the ponies.

That night, on the staircase, Mary brushed her cheek against Benjamin's and, with a sly smile, thanked him for bringing his brother home.

Thirty-three

She bought them Hercules bicycles for their thirty-first birthday and encouraged them to take an interest in local antiquities. At first, they went for short rides on Sundays. Then, moved by the spirit of adventure, they extended their range to take in the castles of the Border Barons.

At Snodhill they ripped the ivy off a wall, and uncovered an arrow-slit. At Urishay they mistook a rusty pannikin for 'something mediaeval'. At Clifford they pictured the Fair Rosamond, lovelorn in a wimple; and when they went to Painscastle, Benjamin thrust his hand down a rabbit-hole and pulled out a fragment of iridescent glass.

'A goblet?' suggested Lewis.

'A bottle,' Benjamin corrected.

He borrowed books from the Rhulen Lending Library and read aloud, in condensed versions, the chronicles of Froissart, Giraldus Cambrensis and Adam of Usk. Suddenly, the world of the Crusading Knights became more real than their own. Benjamin vowed himself to chastity; Lewis to the memory of a fair damsel.

They laughed – and laying their bikes behind a hedge, went off to laze beside a stream.

They imagined battering-rams, portcullises, crucibles of boiling pitch and bloated bodies floating in a moat. Hearing of the Welsh archers at Crécy, Lewis stripped a yew branch, hardened it with fire, strung it with gut and fletched some arrows with goose feathers.

The second arrow whizzed across the orchard and pierced a chicken through the neck.

'A mistake,' he said.

'Too dangerous,' said Benjamin, who, meanwhile, had unearthed a most interesting document.

A monk of Abbey Cwmhir relates that the bones of Bishop Cadwallader lie in a golden coffin beside St Cynog's Well at Glascoed.

'And where be that?' Lewis asked. He had read about the Tomb of Tutankhamun in the *News of the World*.

'There!' said Benjamin, placing his thumbnail under some Gothic lettering on the Ordnance Survey Map. The place was eight miles from Rhulen, off the road to Llandrindod.

After Chapel next Sunday, Mr Nantlys Williams saw the twins' bicycles propped against the palings, and a spade lashed to Lewis's crossbar. He chided them gently for labouring on the Lord's Day, and Lewis blushed as he bent down to fix his cycle-clip.

At Glascoed, they found the Holy Water gurgling from a mossy cleft, then dribbling away among some burdocks. It was a shady spot. There were cowpats in the mud, and horseflies buzzing round them. A boy in braces saw the two strange men and took to his heels.

'Where do we dig?' Lewis asked.

'Yonder!' said Benjamin, pointing to a hummock of earth half-hidden by nettles.

The soil was black and glutinous and wriggling with earthworms. Lewis dug for half an hour and then handed his brother a piece of porous bone.

'Cow!' said Benjamin.

'Bull!' said Lewis, only to be interrupted by a strident voice shouting across the fields: 'I tell you to get from here!'

The boy in braces had come back with his father, a farmer who was fuming on the far side of the bushes. The twins saw a shotgun. Remembering Watkins the Coffin, they crept out, sheepishly, into the sunshine.

'And I'll be keeping the spade,' the farmer added.

'Yes, sir!' said Lewis, and dropped it. 'Thank you, sir!' – and they mounted their bikes, and rode off.

Forswearing gold as the root of all evil, they turned their attention to the early Celtic saints.

Benjamin read, in a learned paper by the Rector of Cascob, that these 'spiritual athletes' had retreated into the mountains to be at one with Nature and the Lord. St David himself had settled in the Honddhu Valley, in 'a mean shelter covered with moss and leaves' – and there were several other sites within cycling distance.

At Moccas, they found the place where St Dubricius saw a white sow suckling her litter. And when they went to Llanfrynach, Benjamin teased his brother about the woman who tried to tempt the saint with 'wolfsbane and other lustful ingredients'.

'I'll thank you for keeping your mouth shut,' Lewis said.

In Llanveynoe Church, carved on a Saxon stone, they saw a sturdy youth suspended from the Tree: the church's patron, St Beuno, had once cursed a man for refusing to cook a fox.

'Fox wouldn't pass my mouth neither,' said Lewis, pulling a face.

They considered taking up the life of anchorites – an ivy bower, a babbling brook, a diet of berries and wild leek and, for music, the chatter of blackbirds. Or perhaps they'd be Holy Martyrs, clinging to the Host while hordes of marauding Danes looted, burned and raped? It was the year of the Slump. Perhaps there was going to be a revolution?

One August afternoon, pedalling as fast as they could go beside the Wye, they were 'buzzed' by an airplane.

Lewis braked and stopped in the middle of the road.

The crash of the R 101 had given a tremendous boost to his scrapbook, although his true loves, now, were the lady aviators. Lady Heath . . . Lady Bailey . . . Amy Johnson . . . The Duchess of Bedford: he could string off their names as if saying his prayers. His favourite, of course, was Amelia Earhart.

The plane was a Tiger Moth, with a silver fuselage. It circled a second time and the pilot dipped, and waved.

Lewis waved back, passionately, in case it was one of his ladies; and when the plane zoomed low on its third circuit, the figure in the cockpit flicked back her goggles, and showed her tanned and smiling face. The plane was so close that Lewis swore he saw her lipstick. Then she soared her machine, back into the eye of the sun.

Over supper, Lewis said that he, too, would like to fly. 'Hm!' Benjamin grunted.

He was far more concerned about their next-door neighbour than the likelihood of Lewis flying.

Thirty-four

The farmhouse at Lower Brechfa lay in a very windy position and the pine-trees around it slanted sideways. Its owner, Gladys Musker, was a strong meaty woman, with glossy cheeks and tobacco-coloured eyes. A widow of ten years' standing, she somehow managed to keep a tidy house and support her daughter, Lily Annie, and her mother, Mrs Yapp.

Mrs Yapp was an irritable old scrounger, more or less crippled with rheumatism.

One day, soon after the Joneses bought her field, Lewis was pleaching a hedge between the two properties when Mrs Musker came out and watched him hammering in the stakes. Her defiant gaze unnerved him. She heaved a sigh and said, 'Life's all moil and toil, isn't it?' and asked if he'd come and rehang a gate. At tea, he polished off six mince-pies, and she put him on her list of possible husbands.

At suppertime, he happened to mention that Mrs Musker was an excellent pastrycook, and Benjamin shot an anxious glance at his mother.

Lewis warmed to Mrs Musker, and she was certainly very friendly to him. He stacked her straw, slaughtered her porker, and one day she came running over the fields, out of breath:

'For the love of God, Lewis Jones. Come and help me with the cow! She gone down like the Devil kicked her!'

The cow had colic, but he succeeded in coaxing her to her feet.

Sometimes, Mrs Musker tried to show him upstairs into the bedroom; but he never went that far, preferring to sit in her nice fuggy kitchen and listen to her stories.

Lily Annie had a pet fox cub that answered to the name of Ben and lived in a wire-netting cage. Ben ate kitchen scraps and was so tame she could handle him like a dolly. Once, when he escaped, she ran down the dingle, calling, 'Bennie! Bennie!' – and he bounded out of the brambles and curled in a ball at her feet.

Ben became quite a local celebrity, and even Mrs Nancy the Castle came to see him.

'But he's very choosy, you know,' crowed Mrs Yapp. 'He don't take to every Tom, Dick or Harry! Mrs Nancy brought the Bishop of Hereford a while back, and Our Bennie jumped up on the mantelpiece and done his business. It was an awful foxy smell, I can tell you.'

Unlike her mother, Mrs Musker was an uncomplicated soul, who enjoyed having a man about the place; and if a man did her a favour, she'd give a favour in return. Among her callers were Haines of Red Daren and Jim the Rock – Haines because he gave her tiddling lambs, and Jim because he gave her a good long laugh.

Lewis hated the idea of her seeing these two and she was plainly disappointed in him. Some days, she was all smiles: at other times, she'd say, 'Oh, it's you again! Why don't you sit and have a chat with mother?' But Lewis was bored by Mrs Yapp, who only wished to talk about money.

One morning, having strolled over to Lower Brechfa, he saw the fox's skin nailed to some barnsiding and Haines's grey cob tethered to the gate. He left, and did not see Mrs Musker again till February, when he met her in the lane. Draped around her neck there was a red fox-fur.

'Yes,' she said, clicking her tongue. 'It's poor old Ben. He bit into Lily Annie's hand, and Mr Haines says that's the way to get lock-jaw, so we had him shot. I cured him myself with saltpetre. And fancy! I only fetched him from the furrier's Thursday.'

She added, smiling silkily, that she was alone in the house.

He waited two days and then trudged through the snowdrifts to Lower Brechfa. The pines were black against a crystalline sky, and the rays of the setting sun seemed to rise, not fall, as if toward the apex of a pyramid. He blew through his hands to warm them. He had made up his mind to have her.

The cottage was windowless on the north side. Icicles hung from the gutter, and a drop of cold water trickled down his neck. Coming round the end of the house, he saw the grey horse and heard the groans of love in the bedroom. The dog barked, and he ran. He was halfway across the field when Haines's voice came bawling after him.

Four months later, the postman confided in Benjamin that Mrs Musker was expecting Haines's baby.

She was ashamed to show herself in Chapel, so she stayed at home, cursing the lot of women and waiting for Mr Haines to do the proper thing.

This he did not. He said his two sons, Harry and Jack, had set their teeth against the marriage, and offered to pay her.

Indignantly, she refused. But the neighbours, instead of despising her, overwhelmed her with sympathy and kindness.

Old Ruth Morgan offered to act as midwife. Miss Parkinson, the harmonium player, brought a lovely gloxinia, and Mr Nantlys Williams himself said a prayer at the bedside.

'Don't fret, my child,' he consoled her. 'It is the woman's part to be fruitful.'

She held her head high the day she drove to Rhulen to register the birth of her daughter.

'Margaret Beatrice Musker,' she printed the capitals when the clerk handed her the form, and when Haines came knocking on the door to see his daughter, she shooed him away. A week later she relented and allowed him to hold her for half an hour. After that, he behaved like a man possessed.

He wanted to have her baptized Doris Mary, after his mother, but Mrs Musker said, 'Her name is Margaret Beatrice.' He offered wads of pound notes: she threw them in his face. She cuffed him when he tried to make love to her. He begged her, pleaded on his knees for her to marry him.

'Too late!' she said, and locked him out for good.

He would mooch round the yard, uttering threats and curses. He threatened to kidnap the baby, and she threatened him with the police. He had a terrible temper. Years earlier, he and his brother had slogged at one another with bare fists, for three whole days, until the brother slunk away and disappeared. Somewhere in his family there was said to be a 'touch of the tarbrush'.

Mrs Musker was frightened to leave the house. On a page of almanac, she scribbled a note to Lewis Jones and gave it to the postman to deliver.

Lewis went; but when he came to the gate, Haines was lurking by the beast-house with a lurcher straining on a leash.

Haines yelled, 'Get yer dirty interfering nose from here!' The dog slavered, and Lewis headed for home. All afternoon he wondered whether to call the police but, in the end, thought better of it.

A gale blew in the night. The old pine creaked; windows rattled, and twigs flew against their bedroom window. Around twelve Benjamin heard someone on the door. He thought it was Haines and woke his brother.

The hammering went on and above the shrieking wind, they heard a woman's voice calling, 'Murder! There's been a murder!'

'God in Heaven!' Lewis jumped out of bed. 'It's Mrs Yapp.'

They led her into the kitchen. The embers were still whispering in the grate. For a while she sat babbling, 'Murder! . . . Murder!' Then she pulled herself together and said, grimly, 'He done hi'self as well.'

Lewis lit a hurricane lamp and loaded his shotgun.

'Please,' said Mary – she was on the staircase in a dressing-gown – 'please, I beg of you, be careful!' The twins followed Mrs Yapp into the darkness.

At Lower Brechfa, the kitchen window had been broken. Dimly, in the lamplight, they saw the body of Mrs Musker, her brown homespun dress spread round her, hunched over the rocking-cradle, in the centre of a blackish pool. Lily Annie crouched in the far corner cradling a dark object, which was the baby – alive.

At nine o'clock, Mrs Yapp had gone, as she usually went, to answer Haines's knock; but instead of waiting on the doorstep, he had slipped round the house, smashed his gunstock through the window, and fired both barrels, point-blank, at his lover.

She, in her final flash of instinct, threw herself over the cradle, and so saved the child. The shot sprayed Lily Annie's hands; and she hid with her grandmother in a cupboard under the stair. Half an hour later, they heard two further shots, and after that there was silence. Mrs Yapp had waited two hours more before she went for help.

'Swine!' Lewis said, and went outside with the lamp.

He found Haines's body in the blood-spattered Brussels sprouts. The gun was at his side, and his head was off. He had tied a length of twine around the triggers, passed it round the stock, put the barrel in his mouth, and pulled.

'Swine!' he kicked the corpse, once, twice, but checked himself before blaspheming the dead three times.

The inquest was held in the hall at Maesyfelin. Almost everyone was sobbing. Everyone was in black except for Mrs Yapp, who arrived dry-eyed in a hat of crimson plush with a pink chiffon sea-anemone that waved its tentacles when she nodded.

The Coroner addressed her in a sad, sepulchral voice: 'Did the Chapel folk forsake your daughter in the hour of her distress?'

'No,' said Mrs Yapp. 'Some of them come up to the house and was very nice to her.'

'Then all honour to this little Bethel which did not forsake her!'

He had intended to pass a verdict of 'wilful murder followed by suicide', but when Jack Haines read his father's final note, he changed his mind to 'manslaughter in a sudden transport of passion'.

The inquest adjourned and the mourners trooped out for

the funeral. There was a sharp wind. After the service, Lily Annie followed her mother's coffin to the grave. Her wounded hands were wrapped in a flapping black shawl, and she carried a wreath of daffodils to lay on the mound of red soil.

Mr Nantlys Williams bade all present stay for the second committal, which took place in the far corner of the churchyard. On Haines's coffin there was a single wreath – of laurel leaves with a card affixed: 'To dearest Papa, from H & J.'

Mrs Yapp ransacked the house for anything of value and went with Lily Annie to live at her sister's in Leominster. She refused to spend 'one single penny' on her daughter's memory: so it was left to Lewis Jones to buy the funerary monument. He chose a rustic stone cross carved with a single snowdrop and a legend reading, 'Peace! Perfect Peace!'

Every month or so, he forked the gravel free of weeds. He planted a clump of daffodils to flower each year in the month of her death; and though he never, ever pardoned himself, he was able to enjoy some consolation.

Thirty-five

Before leaving the district, Mrs Yapp let it be known she had no intention of harbouring the 'child of such a union'; and without telling his mother or twin, Lewis offered to raise her at The Vision.

'I'll think about it,' the old woman said.

He heard nothing further until the postman told him that Little Meg had been parked at The Rock. He ran over to Lower Brechfa, where Mrs Yapp and Lily Annie were piling their possessions on a cart. The Rock, he protested, was no place to bring up a baby.

'It's where she belongs,' the old woman retorted tartly: letting it be known that, to her way of thinking, Jim, not Haines, had been the father.

'I see.' Lewis hung his head, and sadly walked home to tea.

He was right: The Rock was no fit place for any baby. Old Aggie, her face a web of grimy wrinkles, was too frail for housework except to jab a poker at the fire. Jim was too idle to sweep the chimney and, on windy days, the smoke blew back into the room, and they could hardly see across it. The three adopted girls – Sarah, Brennie and Lizzie – padded about with smarting eyes and snivelling colds. Everyone itched with lice. Ethel was the only one who worked.

To feed her hungry mouths, she would slip out after dark and snaffle what she could from other farms – a duckling, perhaps, or a tame rabbit. Her thefts from The Vision were unnoticed until the morning Benjamin opened the door of the meal-shed, and a dog shot past his legs and raced up the fields to Craig-y-Fedw. The dog was Ethel's. She had raided the corn-bin: he wanted to call the police.

'No,' Mary restrained him. 'We shall do nothing about it.'

Because of his reverence for animal life, Jim never sent a single beast for slaughter and his flock became more and more decrepit. The oldest animal, a wall-eyed ewe called Dolly, was over twenty years old. Others were barren, or missing their back teeth, and in winter they died from lack of feed. After the snowmelt, Jim would collect the carcasses and dig a communal grave – with the result that, over the years, the farmyard became one big cemetery.

Once when Ethel was at the end of her tether, she ordered him to sell five ewes in Rhulen; but on the outskirts of town, he heard the bleats of other sheep, lost the will to continue and drove his 'girlies' home.

At the end of an auction, he would hang round the sales clerks, and if there was some clapped-out nag that nobody wanted – not even the knacker – he'd step forward and stroke her muzzle: 'Aye, I'll give her a home. All she needs is a bit o' feedin' up.'

Dressed like a scarecrow, he would drive his cart through the neighbouring valleys, picking up bits of scrap metal and cast-off machinery, but instead of trying to turn a profit, he turned The Rock into a fortress.

At the outbreak of Hitler's war the house and outbuildings were encircled with a stockade of rusty hayrakes and ploughshares; mangles, bedsteads and cartwheels, and harrows with their teeth pointing outward.

His other mania was to collect stuffed birds and animals and, eventually, the attic was crammed so full of moth-eaten taxidermy that the girls had no place to sleep.

One morning as Mary Jones was listening to the nine-o'clock news, she looked up and saw Lizzie Watkins pressing her nose against the kitchen window. The girl's hair was lank and greasy. A skimpy floral dress hung from her wasted body, and her teeth were chattering with cold.

'It's Little Meg,' she blurted out, wiping her nose with her forefinger. 'She's dying.'

Mary put on her winter coat and walked out into the wind. For the past week she had not been feeling well. It was the time of the equinoctial gales, and the heather was purple on the hill. As they approached Craig-y-Fedw, Jim came out and cursed the yelping sheep-dogs: 'Atcha! Yer buggers!' She ducked her head to clear the lintel, and entered the murky room.

Aggie was feebly fanning the fire. Ethel sat on the box-bed with her legs apart; and Little Meg, half-covered with Jim's jacket, gaped at the rafters with brilliant blue-green eyes. Her cheeks were inflamed. A tinny cough rattled in her throat. She had a fever and was gasping for breath.

'She's got bronchitis,' said Mary, adding in an expert tone: 'You'll have to get her out of this smoke, or it'll turn to pneumoma.'

'You take her,' Jim said.

She looked him square in the eyes. They were the same as

the eyes of the child. She saw he was pleading and knew that he really was the father.

'Of course I will,' she smiled. 'Let Lizzie come with me and we'll soon make her better.'

She prepared a eucalyptus inhaler and, even after the first few gulps, Meg began to breathe more freely. She spooned some cream of wheat between her lips, and camomile as a sedative. She showed Lizzie how to sponge her with water, and so keep the fever down. All night they kept vigil, holding her warm and upright by the fire. Now and then, Mary sewed a few black stars on to her patchwork quilt. By morning, the crisis had passed.

Long afterwards, when Lewis cast his mind over his mother's last years, one particular image remained in his memory: the sight of her sewing the patchwork quilt.

She had begun the work on threshing day. He remembered coming indoors for a drink and shaking the chaff-dust from his clothes and hair. Her best black skirt lay like a shroud on the kitchen table. He remembered her look of alarm in case the dust disfigured the velvet.

'I shall only go to one funeral now,' she had said. 'And that will be my own.'

Her scissors sliced the skirt into strips. Next, she cut into the dresses of gaily-coloured calico – all reeking of camphor after forty years in a trunk. Then she stitched together the two halves of her life – the early days in India, and her days on the Black Hill.

She had said, 'It will be something to remember me by.'

The quilt was ready by Christmas. Some time before that, though, Lewis had stood behind her chair and noticed, for the first time, her shortness of breath and the solid blue veins on her hands. She had seemed far younger than seventy-two, partly on account of her unlined face, partly because of her hair which grew, if anything, browner with the years. He had realized then that the triangle – of son, mother and son – would shortly cease to be.

'Yes,' she had said, wearily. 'I have a heart.'

For some time, the household had been troubled and divided.

Lewis suspected both his mother and brother of conspiring against him: the fact that he was womanless was all a part of their plan. He resented the way they kept him in ignorance of the farm's finances. Surely he too should have his say? He insisted on checking the accounts; but as he puzzled over the columns of credits and debits, Mary would brush his cheek with her sleeve and murmur softly, 'You've no head for figures, that's all. It's nothing to be ashamed of. So why not leave it to Benjamin?'

He resented, too, their stinginess, which seemed to him unjust. If ever he asked for a new piece of machinery, she would wring her hands and say, 'I'd love to give it to you. We're broke, I'm afraid. It'll have to wait till next year now.' Yet they always had enough money when it came to buying land.

She and Benjamin bought land with a passion, as if with each new acre they could push back the frontier of the hostile world. But extra land meant extra work; and when Lewis suggested replacing the horses with a tractor, they gasped.

'A tractor?' said Benjamin. 'You must be cracked.'

He was terribly angry when both came back from the lawyer's in Rhulen and announced that they had bought Lower Brechfa.

'Bought what?'

'Lower Brechfa.'

Three years had passed since Mrs Musker's death and her smallholding had gone to ruin. Docks and thistles had invaded the pasture. The yard was a sea of nettles. Slates were missing from the roof and, in the bedroom, there was a barn-owl nesting.

'Farm it yourself,' Lewis snapped. 'It's a sin to take a dead-woman's land. I'll not set foot on the place.'

In the end he relented – as he always relented – though not before he had sinned on his own. He drank in pubs and went out of his way to befriend some new people who had settled in the neighbourhood.

At Rhulen market, he had found himself standing within a few feet of a strange, long-legged woman, with scarlet lips and nails, and sunglasses set in wedges of white bakelite. On her arm was a large wicker basket. A younger man was with her and, when he let fall a couple of eggs, she pushed the sunglasses up on to her forehead and drawled in a gravelly voice, 'Darling, don't be so hopeless . . .'

Thirty-six

Joy and Nigel Lambert were an artist's wife and an artist, who had rented a cottage at Gillifaenog.

The artist had once had a successful exhibition in London and was soon to be seen, with paintbox and easel, sketching the effects of cloud and sunshine on the hill. His wreath of fair curls must once have been 'angelic', and already he was running to fat.

The Lamberts shared a conspiracy of gin, but not a bed. They had kicked around the Mediterranean for five years, and had come back to England in the belief that there was going to be a war. Both lived in terror of being considered middle class.

Because of their fondness for peasants – the 'Earlies' as they called them – they drank three nights a week at the Shepherd's Rest, where Nigel impressed the locals with his stories of the Spanish Civil War. On wet nights, he would sweep into the bar wearing a thick wool cape with a brown smear down the front. This, he said, was the blood of a Republican soldier, who had died in his arms. But Joy was bored by his stories, having heard them all before: 'Did you really, duckie?' she'd chip in 'God! It must have been ghastly!'

As long as she was decorating her house, Joy was too busy to pay much attention to her neighbours: if she did take in the Jones twins, they were 'two boys living with their mum.'

She had always been famous for her taste, and her ability to 'make do' on a shoestring. She would add a touch of blue to the whitewash of one wall, and a dash of ochre to the other. Instead of a dining-table, she used an old paper-hanger's trestle. The curtains were made of wadding, the sofa covered in horse-blankets, and the cushions in saddler's plaid. She loathed 'amusing' objects on principle. She owned one work of art, a Picasso etching, and she banished Nigel's paintings to the studio-barn.

One day, looking round the room, she said, 'What this room needs is one . . . good . . . chair!' And she must have cast her eye over hundreds of rush-seated cottage chairs before finding the *one*, beautifully battered example at The Rock.

Nigel had been sketching there all day, and she went up to fetch him: her foot was hardly through the door before she whispered, 'God! There's my chair! Ask the old girl how much she wants for it!'

On another occasion, calling in at The Vision to buy some of Mary's farm-butter, she spotted an old brawn jar poking out of the rubbish dump: 'Gosh! What a pot!' she cried, fingering the crackled grey glaze.

'Well, you can have it if you can use it,' said Lewis, doubtfully.

'I need it for flowers.' She grinned. 'Wild flowers! Hate garden flowers,' she added, sweeping her arm contemptuously over Benjamin's pansies and wallflowers.

A month later, Lewis passed her in the lane with a foxglove in either hand, one of them freakishly pale:

'Now, Mr Jones, I need your advice. Which one would you choose?'

'Thank you very much,' said Lewis, completely nonplussed.

'No! Which one d'you like best?'

'That one.'

'Quite right,' she said, chucking the darker one over the hedge. 'The other was awful.'

She asked him to call in, and he went, astonished to find her, in pink sailor pants and a red headscarf, hacking down a lilac bush and dragging the branches onto a bonfire.

'Don't you absolutely loathe lilac?' she said, the smoke billowing round her legs.

'I can't say I've given much thought to it myself.'

'I have,' she said. 'Smell's made me sick as a dog all week.'

Later in the afternoon, when Nigel came in for his mug of tea, she said, 'Know something? I've rather taken a shine to Lewis Jones.'

'Oh?' he said. 'Which one's that?'

'Really, darling! You *are* unobservant!'

She next met Lewis, on the day of the sheep drive, in the bar of the Shepherd's Rest.

From seven in the morning, farmers on horseback had been clearing the hill, and the bleating white mass was now safe in Evan Bevan's paddock, waiting to be sorted after lunch.

The day was hot, the hills hazy, and the thornbushes looked like little bits of fluff.

Nigel, in a boisterous mood, insisted on buying drinks all round. Lewis was leaning on his elbows with his back to the sill. The net curtains ballooned around his shoulders. His hair was glossy black, parted in the centre, with a fleck or two of grey. He blinked through his steel-rimmed glasses, smiling occasionally as he tried to follow Nigel's story.

Joy glanced up from her gin. She liked his strong white teeth. She liked the way his belt bunched up his corduroys. She liked his big hand around the dimples of the tankard. She had caught him looking at the lipstick on the rim of her glass.

'OK. You prude!' she thought. She stubbed out a cigarette and came to two conclusions: (a) that Lewis Jones was a virgin; (b) that this was going to be a long operation.

Halfway through the shearing, Nigel walked up to The Vision and asked if he could make some drawings of the men at work.

'I'd not be the one to stop you,' said Benjamin, pleasantly.

It was cool and dark in the shearing shed. Flies were spinning round the dusty sunbeams that fell through the chinks in the roof. All afternoon, the artist sat crouched against a hay-bale with the sketch-pad on his knees. At sunset, when the cider keg came out, he followed Benjamin to the fowl-house and said he had something to discuss.

He wanted to make a set of twelve etchings to illustrate 'The Sheep Farmer's Year'. He had a poet friend in London who, he was sure, would write a sonnet for every month. Would he, Mr Jones, consent to pose as the model?

Benjamin frowned. Instinctively, he mistrusted anyone 'from off'. He knew what a sonnet was, but wasn't so sure about an etching.

He shook his head: 'We're busy just now. I couldn't see my way to sparing the time.'

'It wouldn't take time!' Nigel cut him short. 'You'd go on with your work, and I'd just follow and make drawings.'

'Well,' Benjamin stroked his chin apprehensively. 'That's all right then, isn't it?'

During the summer and autumn of '38, Nigel sketched Benjamin Jones – with his dogs, with his crook, with his castrating knife, on the hill, in the valley, or with a sheep slung over his shoulder like an Ancient Greek statue.

On the damp days, he wore his Spanish cape and carried a brandy flask in his pocket. He always bragged a bit when he drank; and it was a relief to have, as an audience, someone who knew nothing of Spain and couldn't check the details of his stories.

And there were things in the stories that reminded Benjamin of his weeks in the Detention Barracks – things the guards made him do; dirty, shameful things; things he had never told Lewis, which now he could get off his chest.

'Yes, they often do that,' Nigel said, eyeing him up and down, and then looking at the ground.

Both the Lamberts grated on Mary's nerves. She knew they were dangerous and tried to warn her sons that these strangers were only playing games. She despised Nigel for lacing his plummy voice with working-class slang. To Benjamin she said, 'He's such a wet:' to Lewis, 'I can't think why you like that woman. All that make-up! She looks like a parrot!'

Every week or so, Mrs Lambert hired Lewis to take her riding. And one misty evening, when they were out on the hill, Nigel appeared at The Vision with news that he'd be leaving next day for London.

'How long'll you be gone?' asked Benjamin.

'Can't say,' the artist answered. 'It all depends on Joy; but we're bound to be back for the lambing.'

'Better be!' Benjamin grumbled, and went on cranking the beet-pulper.

At two that afternoon, Joy had gulped down a quick snack, swallowed three cups of strong black coffee, and was pacing up and down outside her cottage, waiting for Lewis Jones.

'He's late! Damn and blast him!' She whisked her riding-crop at a dead thistle.

The valley was lost in the fog. Spider's webs, wavering white with dew, were stretched over the dead grass; and all she could see, down the line of the hedge, were the grey receding shapes of oak trees. Nigel was in his studio, playing Berlioz on the gramophone.

'Hate Berlioz!' she cried out loud when the record came to an end. 'Berlioz, my dear one, is a bore!'

She examined her reflection in the kitchen window – a pair of long, clean-cut legs in beige breeches. She flexed her knees so that they fitted more snugly into the fork. She undid the button of her russet riding-coat. Underneath she wore a pale grey jersey. She felt comfortable and energetic in these clothes. Her face was framed in a white headscarf and, pinned to it, there was a man's pork-pie.

She smoothed her lipstick with her little finger. 'God! I'm too old for this kind of caper,' she murmured, and heard the ponies thudding over the turf.

'Late!' she grinned.

'Very sorry, mam!' said Lewis, smiling shyly from under his hat-brim. 'I had a spot of bother with my brother. Him was none too keen on it. Says as we might get lost in the fog, like.'

'Well, you're not afraid of getting lost?'

'No, mam!'

'So there! Besides, it'll be sunny on the tops. Just you wait!'

He handed her the reins of the grey. She cocked her leg and swung into the saddle. She led and he followed. They trotted along the track to Upper Brechfa.

The hawthorns made a tunnel over their heads; the branches ripped against her hat, and showered her with crystal drops.

'Hope to God the pins stay in,' she said and kicked the horse into a canter.

They passed the Shepherd's Rest and stopped at the gate that leads on to the mountain. She opened the latch with her riding-crop. When she closed it behind him, he said, 'Thank you very much.'

The path was muddy and the gorse brushed their boots. She leaned forwards, rubbing herself against the pommel. The damp mountain air filled her lungs. They saw a buzzard. On ahead it was already looking lighter.

Coming to a clump of larches, she cried, 'Look! What did I tell you? The sun!' The golden hair of the larches shone out against a milky blue sky.

Then they cantered on into the sunlight with the clouds spread out below, on and on, for miles it seemed, until she reined in her pony at the edge of a gully. In a hollow, out of the wind, there were three Scots pines.

She dismounted and walked towards them, dribbling a pine-cone over the close-cropped turf.

'I love Scots pines,' she said. 'And when I'm very very old I'd like to look like one. Know what I mean?'

He was breathing beside her, hot under his mackintosh. She clawed at the bark, a flake of which came away in her hand. An earwig scuttled for safety. Judging that the moment had come, she transferred her lacquered fingers from the tree-trunk to his face.

It was dark when she pushed through the door of the cottage, and Nigel was drowsing by the fire. She banged her riding-crop on the table. There were moss-stains on her breeches: 'You lost the bet, duckie. You owe me a bottle of Gordon's.'

'You had him?'

'Under an ancient pine! Very romantic! Rather damp!'

From the moment Lewis crossed the threshold, Mary knew exactly what had happened.

He was walking differently. His eyes roamed the room like a stranger's. He stared at her, as if she too were a stranger. With trembling hands, she served a giblet pie. The silver spoon glinted. A wisp of steam curled up. He went on staring as though he'd never sat at supper in his life.

She toyed with her food, but could not bring herself to eat it. She sat waiting for Benjamin to explode.

He pretended to notice nothing. He cut a sliver of bread and began mopping the juices off his plate. Then his voice rasped out: 'What's that you got on your cheek?'

'Nothing,' Lewis faltered, fumbling for a napkin to wipe away the lipstick, but Benjamin had nipped round the table and rammed his face up close.

Lewis panicked. His right fist smashed into his brother's teeth, and he ran from the house.

Thirty-seven

He went away, to work on a pig farm near Weobley in Herefordshire. Two months later, drawn irresistibly in the direction of home, he got a job in Rhulen, as a porter for an agricultural merchant. He bunked on the premises and spoke to no one. The farmers who came into the offices were astonished by the blankness of his stare.

Because he sent no word to his mother, she arranged, one afternoon, for a neighbour to give her a lift into town.

A sharp wind was whistling down Castle Street. Her eyes watered; and the shops, the housefronts and pedestrians dissolved into a greyish blur. Holding her hat, she pushed her steps along the pavement and then turned left, out of the wind, into Horseshoe Yard. Outside the merchant's a cart was being loaded with meal-sacks.

Another sack came out through the double doors.

She gave a start at the sight of the bony, sunken-eyed man in dirty dungarees. His hair had gone grey. Around one wrist there was a vicious purple scar.

'What's that?' she asked when they were alone.

'If thy right hand offend thee . . .' he murmured.

She gasped, covered her mouth – and breathed out, 'Thank heaven for that!'

She slipped her arm into his, and they walked towards the river and out along the bridge. The Wye was in spate. A heron stood in the shallows and, on the far bank, a fisherman was casting for salmon. Snow lay on the tops of the Radnor Hills. With their backs to the wind they watched floodwater sluicing past the piles.

'No.' She was quivering all over. 'You can't come home yet. It's terrible to see your brother in such a state.'

Benjamin's love for Lewis was murderous.

Spring came. The celandines made stars in the hedgerows. It still seemed that Benjamin's anger would never die down. To take her mind off her misery, Mary wore herself out with housework; she darned every moth-hole she could find in the blankets; she knitted socks for both her sons; she stocked the store-cupboard and cleaned the dirt from hidden crevices – as though these were preparations before leaving on a journey. Then, when she could work no more, she would collapse into the rocking chair and listen to the beating of her heart.

Images of India kept passing before her eyes. She saw a shimmering flood-plain, and a white dome afloat in the haze. Men in turbans were bearing a cloth-bound bundle to the shore. There were fires smouldering, and kitehawks spiralling above. A boat glided by downstream.

'The river! The river!' she whispered, and shook herself out of her reverie.

One day in the first week of September, she woke with flatulence and indigestion. She fried a few rashers of bacon for Benjamin's breakfast but lacked the strength to fork them from the skillet. A pain gripped her chest. He had carried her to the bedroom before the attack.

He jumped on his bike, rode to the call-box at Maesyfelin, and phoned for the doctor.

At six that evening, Lewis came in from delivering a load of cow-cake. In the office the clerk was glued to the wireless, listening to the latest news from Poland. He glanced up and told him to call the surgery.

'Your mother's had a coronary,' Dr Galbraith told him. 'Looks like a bad one to me. I've given her morphine and she's hanging on. But I'd get up there quick as you can.'

Benjamin was kneeling on the far side of the bed. The evening sunlight raked in through the larches, and touched the black frame of the Holman Hunt engraving. She was sweating. Her skin was yellowish, and her gaze fixed intently on the doorknob. The name of Lewis rustled on her lips. Her hands lay motionless on the black velvet stars.

A motor sounded in the lane.

'He's come,' said Benjamin. From the dormer window, he watched his brother paying off the taxi.

'He's come,' she repeated. And when her head dropped sideways on the pillow, Benjamin was holding her right hand, and Lewis her left.

In the morning they hung black crêpe over the beehives to tell the bees that she had gone.

The night after the funeral was the night of their weekly bath.

Benjamin boiled the copper in the back-kitchen, and spread a cloth over the hearthrug. They took turns to soap each other's backs, and scrub them with a loofah. Their favourite sheepdog crouched beside the tub, his head on his forepaws, and the flamelight fluttering in his eyes. Lewis rubbed himself dry and saw, laid out on the table, two of their father's unbleached white calico nightshirts.

They put them on.

Benjamin had lit the lamp in their parents' room. He said, 'Give us a hand with the sheets.'

From the chest of drawers they unfolded a pair of fresh linen sheets. Grains of lavender fell at Lewis's feet. They made the bed and smoothed down the patchwork quilt. Benjamin plumped up the pillows; and a feather, that had worked its way through the ticking, floated upwards in the lamplight.

They climbed into bed.

'Goodnight now!'

'Goodnight!'

United at last by the memory of their mother, they forgot that all of Europe was in flames.

Thirty-eight

The war washed over them without disturbing their solitude.

Now and then, the drone of an enemy bomber, or some niggling wartime restriction, reminded them of the fighting beyond the Malvern Hills. But the Battle of Britain was too big for Lewis's scrapbook. An invasion scare – of German parachutists on the Brecon Beacons – was a false alarm. And when, one November night, Benjamin saw a red glow on the horizon and the sky lit up with incendiary flares – it was the Coventry Raid – he said, 'And a good job t'isn't we!' – and went back to bed.

Lewis thought of joining the Home Guard but Benjamin dissuaded him from doing so.

In Chapel, the twins sat side by side in their parents' pew. Before each meeting they spent an hour or so, lost in silent meditation by the grave. Some Sundays, especially if there was a Bible-class beforehand, Little Meg the Rock came with one of her foster-sisters; and the sight of her, an angular waif in a moth-eaten beret, revived in Lewis memories of lost love, and sadness.

One blustery morning, she came in, blue with cold, clutching at a bunch of snowdrops. The preacher had the habit of reciting the first verse of a hymn, and then making one of the children repeat it line by line. After announcing Hymn Number Three – William Cowper's 'Praise for the Fountain Opened' – his finger fell on Meg:

> *There is a fountain fill'd with blood*
> *Drawn from Emmanuel's veins*
> *And sinners plunged beneath that flood*
> *Lose all their guilty stains.*

Tightening her grip on the snowdrops, Meg struggled through the first line, but the effort of 'Emmanuel's veins' choked her to silence. The crushed flowers fell at her feet, and she started sucking her thumb.

The schoolteacher said there was 'nothing to be done with the child'. Yet, though Meg neither read nor wrote nor did the simplest sums, she could mimic the voice of any animal or bird; and she embroidered white lawn handkerchiefs with garlands of flowers and leaves.

'Yes,' the teacher confided in Lewis, 'Meg's a handy little needlewoman. I believe it was Miss Fifield as taught her the art' – adding, for the sake of gossip, that young Billy Fifield was a pilot in the R.A.F., and that Rosie was alone at The Tump, laid up with bronchitis.

After lunch, Lewis packed a basket of provisions and filled a can of milk from the dairy. A pewter sun hung low over the Black Hill. The milk sloshed against the lid as he walked. The beeches were grey behind the cottage, and rooks flew off, their wingtips glinting like flakes of ice. There were Christmas roses flowering in the garden.

It was twenty-four years since they had met.

Rosie shuffled to the door in a man's overcoat. Her eyes were blue as ever, but her cheeks were hollow and her hair was grey. Her jaw dropped when she saw the tall greying stranger on the doorstep.

'I heard you was poorly,' he said. 'So I brought you some things.'

'So it's Lewis Jones,' she wheezed. 'Come on in and warm yourself.'

The room was cramped and dingy, and the whitewash flaking from the wall. On a ledge over the fireplace were tea-canisters and her clock of the Heavenly Twins. A chromolithograph hung on the back wall – of a blonde girl picking a posy along a woodland path. Slung over an armchair was a needlework sampler, half completed. A tortoiseshell butterfly, awoken by the sunlight, flapped against the window, although its wings were trapped in a dusty cobweb. The floor was strewn with books. On the table were some jars of pickled onions – which were all she had to eat.

She unpacked the basket, greedily examining the honey and biscuits, the brawn and bacon, spreading them out without a word of thanks.

'Sit down and I'll make you a cup of tea,' she said, and went to the scullery to rinse the teacups.

He looked at the picture and remembered their walks along the river.

She took a bellows to sharpen up the fire, and as the flames licked the sooty underside of the kettle, her coat fell open revealing a pink flannelette nightie slipping off her shoulder. He asked about Little Meg.

Her face lit up: 'She's a good girl. Honest as the day! Not

like them others and all their thieving! Ooh! It makes my blood boil the way they treat her. Her as never harmed a living thing. I've seen her in the garden here, and the finches feeding out of her hand.'

The tea was scalding hot. He sipped it, uneasily, in silence.

'He's dead, isn't he?' Her voice was sharp and accusing. He paused before taking another sip, and said, 'I'm very sorry to hear it.'

'What's it to you?'

'In an aeroplane, was it?'

'Not him!' she snapped. 'I don't mean my Billy. I mean the father!'

'Bickerton?'

'Aye, Bickerton!'

'Well, him's dead for sure,' he answered. 'In Africky, as I did hear it. It was the drink as killed him.'

'And a good job!' she said.

Before leaving, he foddered her sheep which had gone a whole week without hay. He took the milk-can and promised to come back on Thursday.

She clutched his hand and breathed, 'Till Thursday then?'

She watched him from the bedroom window walking away along the line of hawthorns, with the sunlight passing through his legs. Five times, she wiped the condensation from the pane until the black speck vanished from view.

'It's no good,' she said out loud. 'I hate men – all of them!'

On the Thursday, her bronchitis was better and though she was able to talk more freely, only one topic held her attention: Lurkenhope Castle, which had just been requisitioned for American troops.

★

The place had lain empty for five years.

Reggie Bickerton had died, of D.T.s in Kenya, in the year that his coffee plantation failed. The Estate had passed to a distant cousin, who had had to pay a second round of death-duties. Isobel, too, had died, in India; and Nancy had moved into a flat above the stables – which, so her father said, were better built than the house. And there she lived, alone with her pugs, fretting about her mother who was interned in the South of France.

She gave a dinner-party for some black G.I.s and people said the strangest things.

Apart from the Negro boxer at the Rhulen Fair, the twins had never set eyes on a black man. Now, hardly a day passed without their meeting these tall dark strangers, sauntering round the lanes in twos and threes.

Benjamin pretended to be shocked by the stories coming out of the Castle. Could it be true they ripped up the floorboards and burned them in the grate?

'Ooh!' he rubbed his hands. 'It be hot where them do come from.'

One frosty evening, walking home from Maesyfelin, he was hailed by a nattily turned-out giant:

'Hi, feller! I'm Chuck!'

'I'm not so bad myself,' said Benjamin, shyly.

The man's expression was grave. He stopped to talk, and spoke of the war and the horrors of Nazism. But when Benjamin asked what it was like to live 'in Africky', he creased with laughter, and clung to his stomach as if he were never going to stop. Then he disappeared into the darkness, flashing a broad white grin over the turned-up collar of his greatcoat.

Another memorable occasion was the day when troops from the Dominions staged a mock-assault on Bickerton's Knob.

The twins came back from drenching some calves at Lower Brechfa to find the farmyard swarming with 'darkies', some in lopsided hats, some with their heads 'wrapped in towels' – they were Gurkhas and Sikhs – all 'chittering away like monkeys and scaring off the fowls'.

But the big event of the war was the crashed plane.

The pilot of an Avro Anson, flying home from a reconnaissance, misjudged the height of the Black Hill and pancaked into the bluff above Craig-y-Fedw. A survivor limped down the escarpment and roused Jim the Rock, who went up with the search-party and found the pilot dead.

'I see'd 'im,' Jim said afterwards. 'Froze to death, like, an' 'is face split open an' all 'angin' down.'

The Home Guard sealed off the area, and removed seven cartloads of wreckage from the site.

Lewis was very disappointed that Jim had seen the crash and he had not. All he found, strewn over the heather, were some shreds of canvas and a strip of aluminium with a bolt through it. He stuffed these into his pockets, and kept them as souvenirs.

Meanwhile, Benjamin had taken advantage of a depressed market to add a farm of sixty acres to the list of their possessions.

The Pant lay half a mile down the valley, and had two big arable fields on either side of the brook. Ploughed and planted, these yielded an excellent crop of potatoes; and to help with the harvest, the man from the Ministry assigned the twins a German prisoner-of-war.

His name was Manfred Kluge. He was a beefy, pink-cheeked fellow from a country district of Baden-Württemburg, whose father, the village woodman, had flogged him sadistically, and whose mother was dead. Drafted into the Army, he had served in the Afrika Korps: his capture at El Alamein was one of the few strokes of fortune he had known.

The twins never tired of listening to his stories:

'I have seen the Führer with my eyes, Ja! I am in Sieg-maringen. Ja! . . . And many peoples! Verrymanypeoples! Ja! "Heil Hitler!" . . . "Heil Hitler!" Ja? . . . Ja? And I say "Fool!" LOUD!! And this man next me in crowd . . . Verrybigman. RED-FACE-BIG-MAN . . . Ja? He say me, "You say, Fool!" And I say him, "Ja, very fool!" And he hit! Ja? And other peoples all hit! Ja? And I run away . . . ! Ha! Ha! Ha!'

Manfred was a hard worker. At the end of the day, there were sweat-rings under the armpits of his uniform; and with the indulgence of doting parents, the twins gave him other clothes to wear about the house. A third cap in the porch, a third pair of boots, a third place at table – all helped remind them that life had not entirely passed them by.

He wolfed his food and was always ready with a show of affection as long as there was a square meal in sight. He was neat in his personal habits, and slept in the attic in Old Sam's room. Every Thursday, he had to report to barracks. The twins dreaded Thursdays in case he was transferred elsewhere.

Because he had a special talent for poultry, they allowed Manfred to breed his own flock of geese and keep the proceeds as pocket money. He loved his geese, and they could be heard burbling to each other in the orchard: 'Komm, mein Lieseli! Komm . . . schon! Komm zu Vati!'

Then, one lovely spring morning, the war came to an end with a bold headline in the *Radnorshire Gazette*:

51½lb SALMON 'GRASSED' AT COLEMAN'S POOL

Brigadier tells of 3-hour struggle with titanic fish

For readers who wished to keep abreast of international events, there was a shorter column on the far side of the page:

'Allies enter Berlin – Hitler dead in Bunker – Mussolini killed by Partisans.'

As for Manfred, he was equally indifferent to the Fall of Germany, though he brightened up, a few months later, on seeing in the *News of the World* a photo of the mushroom cloud above Nagasaki:

'Is good, Ja?'

'No.' Benjamin shook his head. 'It's terrible.'

'*Nein, nein!* Is good! Japan finish! War finish!'

That night, the twins had an identical nightmare: that their bed-curtains had caught fire, their hair was on fire, and their heads burned down to smouldering stumps.

Manfred showed no signs of wanting to go home when the first batches of prisoners were repatriated. He spoke of settling in the district, with a wife and a poultry-farm; and the twins encouraged him to stay.

Unfortunately, he had a very weak head for liquor. Once the wartime restrictions were lifted, he struck up a drinking friendship with Jim the Rock. He would stagger home at all hours, and the twins would find him, next morning, dead drunk in the straw. Benjamin suspected him of messing with one of the Watkins girls, and wondered whether they ought to get rid of him.

One summer afternoon, they heard the gander honking and hissing and Manfred gabbling away in German.

Coming out through the porch, they saw in the farmyard a middle-aged woman in brown corduroy trousers and a blue aertex shirt. She held a map in her hand. Her face lit up as she turned to face them:

'So!' she exclaimed. 'Tvinss!'

Thirty-nine

A tall statuesque woman, with slanting grey eyes and golden braids like hawsers, Lotte Zons had left Vienna not a month too soon. Her father, a surgeon, had been too ill to travel, her sister blind to the danger. She had arrived at Victoria Station with a domestic science diploma in her handbag; in the spring of 1939, to come as a servant was the only sure way of getting into England.

Her love of England, deriving as it did from English literature, had mixed in her memory with hikes in the Vorarlberg, gentians, the scent of pines, and the pages of Jane Austen blinding her in the alpine sunlight.

She moved with the ample grace of ladies in the age before Sarajevo. Her life in wartime London had been grimmer than anything she had known.

First, she was interned. Then, because of her training as a psychotherapist, she got a job treating air-raid victims at a clinic in Swiss Cottage. Her salary scarcely paid the rent of a cheerless room. Her strength ebbed away on a diet of corned beef and packet potato. A solitary gas-ring was her only means of cooking.

Sometimes, she met other Jewish refugees in a Hampstead

café; but the nusstorte was uneatable, the backbiting made her even more miserable, and she would grope her way home through the foggy, blacked-out streets.

As long as the war went on, she allowed herself the luxury of hope. Now, with victory, hope had gone. No word came from Vienna. After seeing the pictures of Belsen, she broke down completely.

The head of the clinic suggested she take a holiday.

'I could do,' she said, doubtfully, 'but where will I find some mountains?'

She took a train to Hereford, and the bus to Rhulen. For days she lost herself along leafy lanes unchanged since the time of Queen Elizabeth. A pint of draught cider went to her head. She read Shakespeare in ivy-covered churchyards.

On her last day, feeling so much stronger, she climbed the summit of the Black Hill.

'Aah!' she sighed in English. 'Here at last von can breeze . . . !'

She happened to walk back through The Vision yard and overheard Manfred talking, in German, to his geese.

Lewis shook hands with the visitor and said, 'Please to come on in.' After tea, she jotted down Benjamin's recipe for Welsh cakes, and he offered to show her the house.

He opened the door of the bedroom without a trace of embarrassment. Her eyebrow arched at the sight of their lace-trimmed pillow-cases: 'So you loved your mother very much?'

Benjamin lowered his head.

Before leaving, she asked if they would welcome her again.

'If you would come,' he said; for something in her manner had reminded him of Mary.

★

In the following year, she came at the end of September at the wheel of a small grey coupé. She asked for 'my young friend Manfred' and Benjamin frowned: 'We had to put him over the door, like.'

Manfred had got Lizzie the Rock into trouble. He had, however, done the 'gentlemanly thing' and married her, thus securing his right to remain in Britain. The couple had gone to Kington to work on a poultry farm.

Lotte took the twins on motoring expeditions round the countryside.

They visited megalithic tombs, crumbling abbeys, and a church with a Holy Thorn. They walked along a stretch of Offa's Dike and climbed Caer Cradoc, where Caractacus made his stand against the Romans.

Their interest in antiquities revived. Against the chill autumn winds, she wore a plum cord jacket with big patch pockets and padded shoulders. She recorded their comments in a buckram-bound notebook.

She seemed to have absorbed the entire contents of the lending library. There was something terrifying about her grasp of local history; and at times she could be quite tigerish.

On a trip to Painscastle, they met an elderly man in plus-fours, an amateur antiquary who was measuring the moat. He mentioned in passing that Owen Glendower had defended the castle in 1400.

'Qvite hrongg!' she contradicted. The battle was at Pilleth, not Painscastle – in 1401, not 1400. The man looked flustered, excused himself, and fled.

Lewis laughed: 'Oooh! She do have her head screwed on!' – and Benjamin agreed.

She had taken a room in a bed-and-breakfast place in

Rhulen, and showed no sign of wanting to return to London. Little by little, she broke through their shyness. She earned her place as the third person in their lives and ended up extracting their most intimate secrets.

Not that she made a secret of her interest in them! She told them that, before the war in Vienna, she had made a study of twins who had never separated. Now, she would like to continue it.

Twins, she said, play a role in most mythologies. The Greek pair, Castor and Pollux, were the sons of Zeus and a swan, and had both popped out of the same egg:

'Like you two!'

'Fancy!' They sat up.

She went on to explain the difference between one-egg and two-egg twins; why some are identical and others not. It was a very windy night and gusts of smoke blew back down the chimney. They clutched their heads as they tried to make sense of her dizzying display of polysyllables, but her words seemed to drift towards the borderland of nonsense: ' . . . psychoanalysis . . . questionnaires . . . problems of heredity and environment . . .' What did it all mean? At one point, Benjamin got up and asked her to write the word 'monozygotic' on a scrap of paper. This he folded and slipped in his waistcoat pocket.

She wound up by saying that many identical twins were inseparable – even in death.

'Ah!' sighed Benjamin in a dreamy voice. 'That's as I always felt.'

She clasped her hands, leaned forward in the lamplight, and asked if they would answer a full range of questions.

'I'd not be the one to stop you,' he said.

Lewis sat upright on the settle and stared into the fire. He did not want to answer questions. He seemed to hear his mother saying, 'Beware of this foreign woman!' But in the end, to please Benjamin, he relented.

Lotte followed the twins on their daily round. Neither was accustomed to making confessions; but her warm understanding and harsh guttural accent struck a proper balance of proximity and distance. She had soon compiled a sizeable dossier.

At first, Benjamin gave her the impression of being a biblical fundamentalist.

She asked, 'Then how do you imagine Hell-fire?'

'Something like London, I expect.' He screwed up his nose and sniggered. Only when she probed a little further did she discover that his concept of the life-to-come – whether in Heaven or in Hell – was a blank and hopeless void. How could you believe in an immortal soul, when your own soul, if you had one, was the image of your brother across the breakfast table?

'Then why do you go to Chapel?'

'Because of Mother!'

Both twins said they hated being mistaken for one another. Both recalled mistaking their own reflection for their other half: 'And once,' Lewis added, 'I mistook my own echo.' But when she steered her enquiry in the direction of the bedroom, she drew an identical, innocent blank.

She noticed it was Benjamin who poured the tea, while Lewis cut the loaf; Lewis who fed the dogs, and Benjamin the fowls. She asked how they divided their labour, and each replied, 'I reckon we done it atween we.'

Lewis remembered how, at school, he had given all his

money to Benjamin and ever since, the idea of owning sixpence – let alone a chequebook – was unthinkable.

One afternoon, Lotte found him in the cowshed, in a long brown work-coat, pitching the straw on to a cart. He was red in the face, and bothered. Skilfully timing her question, she asked if he was angry with Benjamin.

'Bloomin' mad!' he said: Benjamin had gone into Rhulen and was buying another field.

There wasn't any sense in it, he said. Not without a man to work it! And Benjamin was far too tight to pay a man a wage! They should buy a tractor! That's what they should do!

'Catch him buying a tractor!' he muttered angrily. 'Sometimes I think I'd be better off on my own.'

Her melancholic gaze met his. He rested his pitchfork, and the anger died in him:

How he'd loved Benjamin! Loved him more than anything in the world. No one could deny that! But he'd always felt left out . . . 'Pushed out, you might say . . .'

He paused: 'I was the strong one and him was a poor mimmockin' thing. But him was always the smarter. Had more grounding, see? And Mother loved him for it!'

'Go on!' she said. He was close to tears.

'Aye, and that's the worry! Sometimes, I lie awake and wonder what'd happen if him weren't there. If him'd gone off . . . was dead even. Then I'd have had my own life, like? Had kids?'

'I know, I know,' she said, quietly. 'But our lives are not so simple.'

On her last Sunday Lotte drove the twins to Bacton to see the memorial to Dame Blanche Parry, a maid of Queen Elizabeth's bed-chamber.

The churchyard was choked with willow-herb. Fallen yew-berries made little red scabs along the path to the porch. The memorial had columns and a Roman arch and stood at the far end of the chancel. On the right sat a white marble effigy of the Queen herself – a jewel-encrusted manikin weighted under a chain of Tudor roses. Dame Blanche knelt beside her, in profile. Her face was drawn but beautiful, and in her hand she held a prayer book. She wore a ruff, and below it there hung a pectoral cross on a ribbon.

The church was chilly: Benjamin was bored. He sat outside in the car, while Lotte copied the inscription in her notebook:

> . . . *So that my tyme I thus did passe awaye*
> *A maede in courte and never no man's wyffe*
> *Sworne of Quene Ellsbeths bedd chamber*
> *Alwaye with the maedn Quene*
> *A maede did ende my lyffe.*

She completed the line. The pencil fell from her hand and bounced from the altar-carpet on to the flagstone floor. For suddenly all the loneliness of her life came back to stifle her – the narrow spinster's bed, the guilt of leaving Austria, and the bitterness of the squabbles in the clinic.

Lewis stooped to recover the pencil; and he too recalled the misery of his first loves, and the fiasco of the third. He squeezed her hand and pressed it to his lips.

She withdrew it gently.

'No,' she said. 'It would not be correct.'

After high-tea, she took Benjamin aside and told him, in no uncertain terms, that he was going to buy Lewis a tractor.

Forty

Aggie Watkins died during the terrible winter of '47. She was over ninety years of age. The snow had drifted over the roof, and she died in darkness.

Jim had run out of hay. The cows kept everyone awake with their bellowing. The dogs whimpered, and the cats nipped in and out with hunger-swollen eyes. Seven of his ponies were missing on the hill.

He shoved his mother into a sack, and laid her, frozen stiff on the woodpile, out of reach of the dogs, but not the cats or rats. Three weeks later, when the thaw set in, he and Ethel lashed her to a makeshift sled and hauled her down to Lurkenhope for burial. The sexton was staggered at the state of the corpse.

Jim found his ponies a few days later, all seven together, in a cleft among some rocks. They had died on their feet, in a circle, their muzzles pointing inwards like the spokes of a wheel. He wanted to dig a grave for them, but Ethel made him stay and help with the house.

A big bulge had appeared in the gable-end, and the whole wall seemed likely to collapse. Some rafters had given way under the weight of snow. The icy water had seeped through

Jim's stuffed animals, and poured from the attic into the kitchen. And though he kept on saying, 'I'll get me a few tile an' fix 'em up like new,' all he ever did was spread a leaky tarpaulin over the roof.

When the spring came, he tried to buttress the wall with stones and railway-sleepers, but so undermined the foundations that it caved in completely. Next winter, no one lived in the east end of the house, and no one had to; for all the Watkins girls, except Little Meg, had left.

Lizzie, married to Manfred, pretended The Rock did not exist. Brennie had gone off with 'some kind o' darkie', a G. I., of whom nothing was heard until a postcard arrived from California. Then, at the May Fair in Rhulen, Sarah met a haulage contractor, who took her to live with him on his smallholding behind the Begwyns.

Sarah was a big-boned, blowzy young woman, with a tangle of black hair and a very unpredictable temper. Her one great fear was of lapsing into poverty; and this sometimes made her seem callous and grasping. Unlike Lizzie, however, she kept her eye on The Rock and made it her business to see they never starved.

In 1952, after another storm had made the kitchen uninhabitable, Ethel abandoned it to the hens and ducks and piled all the furniture into the one remaining room.

This place now looked like a junk-dealer's shed. Behind the curving settle was an oak chest, on top of which stood a tallboy and a stack of cardboard boxes. Strewn over the tables were an assortment of pots, pans, mugs, jamjars, dirty plates, and usually a bucket of fowl-mash. All three occupants slept in the box-bed. The perishable food was stored in baskets that dangled from the roofbeams. Heaped up on the mantelpiece was every kind of object – from shaving bowls to sheep-shears – rusty, worm-eaten, smeared with candle-grease and speckled with the excrement of flies.

A file of headless lead soldiers marched along the windowsill.

As the wall-plaster crumbled, Jim tacked up sheets of newspaper and roofing felt.

'Aye,' he'd say optimistically, 'I be makin' it wind-proof, like.'

The smoke from the chimney covered everything with a film of brown resin. In time, the walls were so sticky that if a picture took his fancy – a postcard from California, the label off a tin of Hawaiian pineapple, or the legs of Rita Hayworth – all he had to do was slap it up – and there it stuck!

If a stranger came near, he would reach for his ancient muzzle-loader – without the shot or powder to charge it – and when the Tax Inspector came asking for a 'Mr James Watkins', Jim poked his head over the stockade and shook his head: "Aven't see'd 'im in a good while. 'Im be gone to France! Fightin' the Germins, as I did 'ear it.'

Despite her attacks of emphysema, Ethel would walk into town on market day, striding briskly down the middle of the lane, always in the same dirty orange tweed coat, and a pair of shopping-bags slung at either end of a horse girth round her neck.

One day, on the crest of Cefn Hill, Lewis Jones drove up behind on his new tractor, whereupon she waved him to a halt, and nipped up on to the footplate.

From then on, she timed her departure to coincide with his. She never said a word of thanks for the lift, and would jump down at the War Memorial. The morning she spent scavenging round the stalls. Around noon, she called in at Prothero's Grocery.

Knowing her to be light-fingered, Mr Prothero winked at his assistant, as if to say, 'Keep an eye on the old girl, will you?' A kindly, shiny-faced man, bald as a Dutch cheese, he would always let her lift a can of sardines or cocoa. But if she overstepped the mark and took, say, a large tin of ham, he would slip round the counter, and block the door:

'Come along, Miss Watkins! What have we got in the bag this morning? That one shouldn't be there, should it now?' – and Ethel would stare stiffly out of the window.

This went on year after year until Mr Prothero retired and sold his business. He told the new owners they should pardon her peccadilloes; yet the first time Ethel stole a can of Ideal Milk, they worked themselves into a fever of righteous indignation and called the police.

The next time it was a £5 fine: after that, six weeks in Hereford jail.

She was never the same again. People saw her moving through the market like a sleepwalker, stooping now and then to pick up an empty cigarette packet and stuff it in her bag.

One drizzly November night, the passengers waiting for the last bus saw a figure slumped in the corner of the shelter. The bus drew up and a man called, 'Wake up! Wake up! You'll miss the bus.' He shook her, and she was dead.

Meg was nineteen at the time, a nice compact little person with dimpled cheeks and eyes that seemed to outglare the sun.

She woke at dawn and worked all day, never leaving The Rock unless to gather whimberries on the hill. Sometimes, a hiker saw her tiny figure rattling a bucket on the edge of the pond, and a file of white ducks waddling towards her. She would bolt for the house if anyone came near.

She never took off her clothes or her hat.

The hat, a grey felt cloche, had with age and greasy fingers come to resemble a cowpat. Her two pairs of breeches – a brown pair over a beige – had ripped around the knees, leaving the lace-up parts as leggings, while the rest flapped, in panels, from her waist. She wore five or six green jerseys at a time, all so riddled with holes that patches of her skin showed through. And when one jersey rotted away, she would keep the wool and use it to mend the others with hundreds of tiny green bows.

The sight of Meg in these clothes made Sarah feel very vexed. She brought her blouses and cardigans and windcheaters: but Meg only wore green jumpers and only if they were falling off her back.

On one of Sarah's visits, she found Jim squelching up to his ankles in the ooze:

'An' 'ow's you?' he grunted. 'An' what d'yer want anyway? Why can't yer leave us alone?'

'I come to see Meg, not you!' she snapped, and he limped off, cursing her under his breath. A week earlier, Meg had been complaining of pains in her abdomen.

Pushing past the hens, Sarah found Meg squatting by the fireside, listlessly fanning the embers in the grate. Her face was twisted with pain, and there were sores up her arms.

'You're coming with me,' Sarah said. 'I'm taking you to the doctor.'

Meg shuddered, swayed back and forth, and began to drone a repetitive dirge:

'No, Sarah, I'd not go from here. Very kind of you, Sarah,

but I'd never go from here. Jim and me, we been together, like. We done the work together, like. Aye, and the foddering and the feeding and lived our lives together. And the poor ducks'd starve if I'd be gone. Aye, and the chicks'd starve. An' that poor ol' pullet in the box there! Her was all a-dying and I took her back to life. But her'd die if I'd be gone. And the birdies in the dingle, them'd die if I dinna feed them. And the cat? You canna say what'd happen to the cat if I'd be gone . . .'

Sarah tried to argue. The doctor, she said, was only three miles away, in Rhulen: 'Don't be daft! You can see his house from the hill. I'll take you down to surgery and bring you straight back.'

But Meg had slipped her fingers under her hat-brim and, covering her face with both palms, said, 'No, Sarah, I'd never go from here.'

A week later, she was in Hereford Hospital.

At dawn on the Friday Sarah was woken with a reverse-charge call from the phone-box at Maesyfelin. It was Jim the Rock, from whose incoherent sputterings she gathered that Meg was sick, if not actually dying.

The fields around Craig-y-Fedw were frozen hard: so she was able to drive her van to the gate. The house and buildings were blanketed with fog. The dogs howled and tried to burst from their shelters. Jim was in the doorway, hopping up and down like a wounded bird.

'How is she?' Sarah asked.

'Bad,' he said.

In the front room the hens were still drowsing on their perches. Meg lay on the floor, eyes closed, amid the droppings. She was moaning quietly. They rolled her on to a plank and carried her to the van.

Halfway down the hill, the thought of taking Meg to the doctor in such a state made Sarah feel dreadfully ashamed. So instead of driving directly to Rhulen, she took the patient home, where, with soap, hot water and a decent coat, she made her look a little more presentable. By the time they reached the surgery, Meg was delirious.

A young doctor came out and climbed into the back of the van. 'Peritonitis.' He spat the word through his teeth and shouted to his secretary to call for an ambulance. He was very offensive to Sarah for not having brought her in sooner.

Later, Meg had only the haziest recollection of her weeks in hospital. The metal beds, the medicines, the bandages, the bright lights, lifts, trolleys and trays of shining implements were things so removed from her experience that she dismissed them as the fragments of a nightmare. Nor did the doctors tell her they had taken out her womb. All she did remember was what she was told: 'Run down! That's as 'em says I was and that's as I was. Run down! But them didna say the harf of it what buggered me.'

Forty-one

The first tractor to arrive at The Vision was a Fordson Major. Its body was blue, its wheels were orange, and it had the name 'Fordson' written in raised orange letters down the sides of the radiator.

Lewis loved his tractor, thought of her as a woman, and wanted to give her a woman's name. He toyed with 'Maudie', then 'Maggie', then 'Annie'; but none of these names suited her personality, and she ended up with no name at all.

To begin with, she was extremely difficult to handle. She gave him a bad fright by slewing sideways into a ditch; and when he mistook her clutch for the brake-pedal, she landed him in the hedge. Yet once he had her under control, he thought of entering a ploughing competition.

He liked nothing better than to hear her firing on all eight cylinders, purring in neutral, or growling uphill with the plough behind.

Her engine, too, was perplexing as a woman's anatomy! He was forever checking her plugs, fiddling with her carburettor, poking his grease gun into her nipples, and fretting about her general state of health.

At the slightest splutter, he would reach for the

maintenance manual and read aloud from the list of possible ailments: 'Wrongly set choke-valve . . . mixture too rich . . . defective leads . . . dirt in the float chamber' – while his brother pulled a face as though he were listening to obscenities.

Again and again, Benjamin groused over the cost of running the tractor and kept saying darkly, 'We'll have to go back to horses.' Having paid for a plough, a seed-drill and a link-box, there seemed no end to the number and cost of her accessories. Why did Lewis need a potato-spinner? What was the point of buying a baler? Or a muck-spreader? Where would it ever end?

Lewis shrugged off his brother's outbursts and left it to the accountant to explain that, far from being ruined, they were rich.

In 1953, they had a nasty brush with the Inland Revenue. They hadn't paid one penny of taxes since Mary's death. And though the inspector treated them leniently, he insisted they take professional advice.

The young man who came to audit their books had the pimply and undernourished complexion of someone living in digs: yet even he was astonished by their frugality. They had clothes to last their lifetime; and since the grocery bill, the vet, and the agricultural merchant were all paid by cheque, they hardly ever handled cash.

'And what shall we put down to incidentals?' asked the accountant.

'Like money in our pockets?' said Benjamin.

'Pocket money, if you like!'

'About twenty pound?'

'A week?'

'Oh no, no . . . Twenty'd see us through the year.'

When the young man tried to explain the desirability of running at a loss, Benjamin puckered his forehead and said, 'That can't be right.'

By 1957, a large taxable profit had piled up in The Vision's farm account; and the accountant, too, had 'filled out'. A beer-stomach bulged over the belt of his cavalry twills. A hacking-jacket, yellow socks and chukka boots completed his outfit; and he kept foul-mouthing a Mr Nasser.

He thumped his fist on the table: 'Either you spend £5,000 on farm machinery, or you give it as a present to the Government!'

'I suppose we'd better buy another tractor,' said Benjamin.

Lewis pored over prospectuses and decided on an International Harvester. He cleared a stable in which to house her and chose a fine dry afternoon to drive her up from Rhulen.

She was not the kind of tractor one used. He would scrub her tyres, flick her with a duster, and drive her along the lane for an occasional airing; but for years he kept her, idly enshrined in the stable, under padlock and key. From time to time, he would peep through a chink in the door, feasting his eyes over her scarlet paintwork like a little boy peeping into a brothel.

The Fifties were years of spectacular air-crashes: two Comets tumbling from the sky, thirty spectators killed at the Farnborough Air Display. Benjamin had a hernia, The Vision was hitched up to mains electricity, and one by one the older generation fell ill and died. Hardly a month went by without a funeral service in Chapel and when old Mrs Bickerton died in the South of France – at the age of ninety-two she had drowned herself in her swimming-pool – there was a lovely memorial service in the parish church and Mrs Nancy the Castle gave a sit-down lunch for all the old tenants and estate workers.

The Castle itself lay crumbling into ruins until, one August evening, a schoolboy sneaked in to shoot rats with a bow-and-arrow, dropped a lighted cigarette butt, and the place went up in flames. Then in April of 1959, Lewis had his cycling accident.

He had been riding to Maesyfelin with a bunch of wallflowers to lay on the graves. The afternoon was bitterly cold. The buckle of his overcoat worked loose; the belt caught in the front spokes – and over the handlebars he went! A plastic surgeon rebuilt his nose in Hereford Hospital and, for ever after, he was always a little deaf in one ear.

The day of their sixtieth birthday was almost a day of mourning.

Each time they tore a page from the calendar, they had forebodings of a miserable old age. They would turn to the wall of family photos – row on row of smiling faces, all of them dead or gone. How was it possible, they wondered, that they had come to be alone?

Their wrangles were over. They were inseparable now as they had been before Benjamin's childhood illness. But surely, somewhere, there was a cousin they could trust? What was the point of owning land, or tractors, if the one thing you lacked was an heir?

They looked at the picture of the Red Indian and thought of Uncle Eddie. Perhaps he had grandsons? But they would be in Canada and would never come back. They even considered their old friend Manfred's son, a pale-eyed lad who sometimes came to visit.

Manfred had started up his own poultry farm, in some Nissen huts put up for Polish refugees, and despite his thick guttural accent, he was now 'more English than the English'. He had changed his name by deed poll from Kluge to Clegg. He wore green tweed suits, rarely missed a point-to-point, and was Chairman of the local Conservative Association.

Proudly, he drove the twins to see his establishment; but the wire cages, the smell of chicken-shit and fish-meal, and the birds' raw, featherless necks so nauseated Benjamin that he preferred not to go there again.

In December 1965, the calendar showed a picture of the Norfolk Broads under ice. Then on the 11th – a date the twins would never forget – a rusty Ford van drove into the yard, and a woman in gumboots got out and introduced herself as a Mrs Redpath.

Forty-two

She had auburn hair going grey, and hazel eyes, and delicate rose-pink cheeks unusual in a woman of her age. For at least a minute she stood beside the garden gate, nervously fumbling with the latch. Then she said she had something of importance to discuss.

'Come on in now!' Lewis beckoned. 'And you'll have a cup of tea.'

She apologized for the mud on her boots.

'No harm in a bit of mud,' he said pleasantly.

She said, 'No bread-and-butter, thank you!' but accepted a slice of fruitcake, cutting it into neat little strips and placing each one, daintily, on the tip of her tongue. Now and then, she glanced round the room, and wondered out loud how the twins found time to dust 'all those curios'. She spoke of her husband, who worked for the Water Board. She spoke of the clement weather and the cost of Christmas shopping. 'Yes,' she replied to Benjamin, 'I could manage another cup.' She took a further four lumps of sugar and began to tell her story:

All her life, she had believed that her mother was the widow of a carpenter, who had to take in lodgers and had made her childhood a misery. Then last June, as the old woman lay dying, she had learned she was illegitimate, a foundling. Her real mother, a girl from a farm on the Black Hill, had left her to board in 1924 and gone overseas with an Irishman.

'Rebecca's baby,' murmured Lewis, and his teaspoon tinkled on the saucer.

'Aye,' breathed Mrs Redpath, summoning an emotional sigh. 'My mother was Rebecca Jones.'

She had checked her birth-certificate, checked the parish register – and here she was, their long-lost niece!

Lewis blinked at the handsome workaday woman before him, and saw, in her every gesture, a resemblance to his mother. Benjamin kept quiet. In the harsh shadow cast by the naked light bulb, he had noticed her unamiable mouth.

'Just you wait till you see my little Kevin!' She reached for a knife and cut herself another slice of cake. 'He's the spitting image of you both.'

She wanted to bring Kevin to The Vision the very next day, but Benjamin was none too keen: 'No. No. We'll come up and see him some time.'

All through the following week the twins were once again at loggerheads.

Lewis believed that Kevin Redpath had been sent as a gift from Providence. Benjamin suspected – even if the story were true, even if he was their great-nephew – that Mrs Redpath was bent on their money, and no good would come of it.

On the 17th, a Christmas card – of Santa Claus and a reindeer-sleigh – came 'With Seasons Greetings from Mr and Mrs Redpath, and Kevin!!' Tea was again on the table when she reappeared and asked if she could drive them, that very evening, to the nativity play at Llanfechan, where her son was playing Father Joseph himself.

'Aye, I'd come with you,' said Lewis, on impulse. And taking a kettle off the hob, he nodded to his brother and went upstairs to shave and dress. Left alone in the kitchen, Benjamin felt himself covered with embarrassment. Then he, too, followed upstairs to the bedroom.

It was dark when they came to leave. The sky was clear and the stars revolved like little wheels of fire. A hoar-frost blanketed the hedgerows and floury shapes rose up in the glare of the headlights. The van skidded on a bend, but Mrs Redpath was a careful driver. Benjamin sat slumped in the back, on a sack stuffed with straw, gritting his teeth until she drew up outside the Chapel Hall. She hurried off to make sure Kevin was dressed.

Inside, it was freezing. A pair of paraffin stoves did nothing to heat the benches at the back. A draught whined in under the door, and the floorboards reeked of disinfectant. The audience sat muffled in scarves and overcoats. The preacher, a missionary returned from Africa, shook hands with each member of his flock.

Drawn across the stage was a curtain consisting of three grey ex-Army blankets, peppered with moth-holes.

Mrs Redpath rejoined her uncles. The lights were switched off, except for the light onstage. From behind the curtain they heard the whispering of children.

The schoolteacher slipped through the curtain and sat down at the piano-stool. Her knitted hat was the same puce pink as the azalea on the piano; and as her fingers hammered the keyboard, the hat bobbed up and down, and the petals of the azalea quivered.

'Carol Number One,' she announced. ' "O Little Town of Bethlehem" – which will be sung by the children only.'

After the opening bars, the sound of faltering trebles drifted over the curtain; and through the moth-holes, the twins saw flashes of sparkling silver, which were the tinsel haloes of the angels.

The carol ended; and a blonde girl came out front, shivering in a white nightie. In her diadem there was a silver-paper star.

'I am the star of Bethlehem . . .' Her teeth chattered. ''Tis ten thousand years since God put a great star in the sky. I am that star . . .'

She finished the prologue. Then the curtain jerked back with the noise of squeaky pulleys to reveal the Virgin Mary, in blue, on a red rubber kneeler, scrubbing the floor of her house in Nazareth. The Angel Gabriel stood beside her.

'I am the Angel Gabriel,' he said in a suffocated voice. 'And I have come to tell you that you are going to have a baby.'

'Oh!' said the Virgin Mary, blushing crimson. 'Thank you very much, sir!' But the Angel fluffed the next line, and Mary fluffed the one after, and they both stood helplessly in the middle of the stage.

The teacher tried to prompt them. Then, seeing that no amount of prompting could rescue the scene, she called out, 'Curtain!' and asked all present to sing 'Once in Royal David's City'.

Everyone knew the words without having to open their hymnals. And when the curtain drew back again, everyone guffawed at the two-piece donkey that kicked and bucked and neighed and nodded his papier-mâché head. Two scene-shifters carried in a bale of straw, and a manger for feeding calves.

'That's my Kevin!' whispered Mrs Redpath, nudging Benjamin in the ribs.

A little boy had come onstage in a green tartan dressing-gown. Wound round his head was an orange towel. He had a black beard gummed to his chin.

The twins sat up and craned their necks; but instead of facing the audience, Father Joseph shied away and spoke his lines to the backdrop: 'Can't you find us a room, sir! My wife's going to have a baby at any minute.'

'I ain't got a room in the place,' replied Reuben the innkeeper. 'The whole town's chock-a-block with folks as come to pay their taxes. Blame the Roman Government, not me!

'I got this stable, though,' he went on, pointing to the manger. 'You can sleep in there if you want to.'

'Oh, thanks very much, sir!' said the Virgin, brightly. 'It'll do very nicely for humble folks like us.'

She started rearranging the straw. Joseph still stood facing the backdrop. He raised his right arm stiffly to the sky.

'Mary!' he shouted, suddenly plucking up courage. 'I can see something up there! Looks like a cross to me!'

'A cross? Ugh! Don't mention that word. It reminds me of Caesar Augustus!'

Through the double thickness of their corduroys, Lewis could feel his brother's kneecap, shaking: for Father Joseph had spun round, and was smiling in their direction.

'Yes,' said the Virgin Mary towards the end of the final scene. 'I think it's the loveliest baby I ever set eyes on.'

As for the Jones twins, they, too, were in Bethlehem. But it was not the plastic doll that they saw. Nor the innkeeper, nor the shepherds. Nor the papier-mâché donkey, nor the living sheep that nibbled at the straw. Nor Melchior with his box of chocolates. Nor Kaspar with his bottle of shampoo. Nor Black Balthazar with his crown of red cellophane and a ginger jar. Nor the Cherubim and Seraphim, nor Gabriel, nor the Virgin Mary herself. All they saw was an oval face with grave eyes and a fringe of black hair beneath a wash-towel turban. And – when the choir of angels started singing, 'We will rock you, rock you, ro-ock you . . .' they rocked their heads in time and tears dripped on to their watch-chains.

After the performance, the minister took some snapshots with a flash. The twins waited outside the Chapel where the mothers were changing their children.

'Kevin! . . . Kevin!' came a shrill voice. 'If you don't come here, I'll slap your bottom . . . !'

Forty-three

He was a nice boy, lively and affectionate, who liked his Uncle Benjamin's fruitcake and loved to ride with Uncle Lewis on the tractor.

In the school holidays, his mother sent him to stay for weeks on end: they came to dread, as much as he did, the first day of term.

Perched on the tractor mudguard, he would watch the plough-share bite into the stubble, and the herring-gulls shrieking and swooping over the fresh-turned furrow. He saw lambs being born, potatoes harvested, a cow calving and, one morning, there was a foal in the field.

The twins said all this, one day, would be his.

They fussed over him like a little prince, waited on him at table, learned never to serve cheese or beetroot and, in the attic, found a humming-top that whined like a contented bee. Wilfully retracing the steps of their own childhood, they even thought of taking him to the seaside.

Some nights, his eyelids heavy with sleep, he'd rest his head in his hands and yawn, 'Please, please will you carry me?' So they carried him upstairs to their old bedroom, and undressed him; and put on his pyjamas, and tiptoed out with the night-light burning.

In a patch of garden, he planted lettuces, radishes and carrots, and a row of sweet-peas. He liked listening to the zinging sound of seeds in their packets, but saw no point in sowing biennials.

'Two years,' he'd moan. 'That's far too long to wait!'

With a bucket slung over his arm, he went off scouring the hedges for anything that took his fancy – toads, snails, furry caterpillars – and once he came home with a shrew. When his tadpoles grew into baby frogs, he built a frog-castle, on a rock in the middle of an old stone trough.

About this time, the farmer below Cwm Cringlyn started a pony-trekking centre; and in the summer months, up to fifty boys and girls might trot through The Vision on their way to the hill. Often, they forgot to shut the gates; churned the pasture into a mud-pie; and Kevin wrote a sign reading 'Trespassers will be Prosecuted'.

One afternoon, Lewis was scything nettles by the pig-sties and saw him racing across the field.

'Uncle! Uncle!' he shouted, breathlessly. 'I seen a very funny person.'

He dragged Lewis by the hand, and together they walked to the edge of the dingle.

'Sshh!' Kevin raised a finger to his lips. Then, parting the leaves, he pointed at something through the undergrowth. 'Look!' he whispered.

Lewis looked and saw nothing.

The sun filtered through the hazels, spattering the stream-bank with varied light. The stream tinkled. Croziers of young bracken curled up through the cow-parsley.

Woodpigeons cooed. A jay chattered nearby, and lots of smaller birds were chirping and twittering around a mossy tree-stump.

The jay glided off its perch and hopped onto the stump. The small birds scattered. The stump moved.

It was Meg the Rock.

'Sshh!' Kevin pointed again. She had brushed off the jay and the other birds were coming back to feed from her hand.

Her skin was plastered with reddish mud. Her breeches were the colour of mud. Her hat *was* a rotting stump. And the tattered green jerseys, tacked one to the other, were the mosses, and creepers, and ferns.

They watched her for a little while, and then they walked away.

'Isn't she lovely?' said Kevin, knee-deep in the ox-eye daisies.

'Yes,' his uncle said.

At the start of the Christmas holidays, Kevin said he wanted to give the 'Bird Lady' a present. He bought an iced chocolate cake with his own pocket-money; and because Thursday was Jim's day at market, he and Lewis chose a Thursday to take it to The Rock.

Slaty clouds were tumbling over the hill as they picked their way through the defences. The wind was whipping the surface of the pond. Meg was indoors, up to her elbows in a bucket of dog-feed. She cringed at the arrival of visitors.

'I brought you a cake,' Kevin stammered, and screwed up his nose at the stench.

Lowering her eyes, she said, 'Aye, and thank you very much!' and then slipped outside with the bucket.

They heard her yelling, 'Quiet, y'old buggers!' And when she came back in, she said, 'Them dogs is wild as hawks.'

She transferred her gaze from the cake to the boy, and her face lit up: 'And will I boil you people a kettle for tea?'

'Yes.'

She split some sticks with a hacker, and set them alight. No one had come to tea for years. Dimly, she remembered the day Miss Fifield showed her how to lay the table. She flitted round the room with the agility of a dancer and, taking a cracked cup here, a chipped plate there, laid three places each with a knife and fork. She put a pinch of tea in the pot, and pierced a can of condensed milk. She wiped the breadknife on her breeches, cut three hefty slices of cake, and threw the crumbs to a pair of bantams.

'Poor ol' boys!' she said. 'Them was buggered by the cold, but I be feedin' 'em up in the house.'

The shyness had left her. She said that Sarah had taken Jim to Hereford to sell some ducks: 'That's as 'em says!' She rested her hands on her hips. 'But them won't get no moneys 'cos them gulls is old. Let 'em live, that's what I say! Let 'em live! Let 'em rabbits live! And 'em hares live! Let 'em stoats go on a-playin'! Aye, and 'em foxes, I won't harm 'em. Let all God's creatures live . . . !'

She clasped both hands around her cup, and her head swayed to and fro. Her cheeks crinkled with merriment when Lewis mentioned the pony-trekkers:

'Aye, I see'd 'em,' she said. 'Drunk as zowls, and howlin' and hollerin' and fallin' dead drunk off their horses.'

Kevin, horrified by the squalor, was itching to go.

'And I'll cut you another slice?' she asked.

'No, thanks,' he said.

She cut a second, larger slice for herself, and swallowed it. She did not throw the crumbs to the bantams, but mopped them up with her fingers and put them in her mouth. Then she licked her finger tips, one by one, and burped, and slapped her stomach.

'We'll be off now,' said Lewis.

Her eyelids drooped. In a dispirited voice she said, 'And what'll I owe you for the cake?'

'It's a present,' said Kevin.

'But you'll take it along with you?' She put the remains of the cake back in its box and, sadly, shut the lid: 'I wouldn't want Jim to catch me with a cake.'

Outside in the yard, Lewis helped her heave a tarpaulin off some hay-bales. The trapped rainwater sluiced over and splashed down Kevin's wellingtons. On the roof of the barn, a loose tin sheet was rattling in the wind. All of a sudden, a gust lifted it in the air, and it flew, like a monstrous bird, in their direction, and landed with a clatter on the scrap-heap.

Kevin threw himself flat on the mud.

'Bloomin' gale,' said Meg. 'Blaowin' 'em zincs about!'

The boy clung to his uncle's arm as they walked away across the hummocky field. He was filthy and whimpering with fright. The clouds were breaking and patches of blue flew low over their heads. One by one, the dogs stopped barking. They looked back and saw Meg, by the willows, calling in her ducklings. Her voice was carried in the wind: 'Wid! Wid! Come on then! Wid! Wid! . . .'

'Do you think he'll beat her?' the boy asked.

'I don't know,' said Lewis

'He must be a very nasty man.'

'Jim's not so bad.'

'I don't ever want to go there again.'

Forty-four

Kevin grew up far faster than either of his uncles thought possible. One summer, he was singing with the trebles. The next – or so it seemed – he was the long-haired daredevil riding a bronco at the Lurkenhope Show.

When he was twelve, the twins made out their will in his favour. Owen Lloyd the lawyer pointed out the advantage of giving Vision Farms to Kevin in their lifetime. Far be it from him, he said, to influence them in any way: but providing they lived another five years, their estate would escape paying death-duties.

'Nothing to pay?' Benjamin perked up, thrusting his face across the lawyer's desk.

'Nothing but the Stamp Duty,' said Mr Lloyd.

To Benjamin, at least, the idea of doing down the Government was irresistible. And besides, in his eyes, Kevin could do no wrong. His faults, if he had them, were Lewis's faults – and that made them all the more lovable!

Naturally, Mr Lloyd continued, Kevin would be legally bound to provide for their old age, especially, he added in an undertone, 'if either of you two gentlemen fell ill . . .'

Benjamin glanced round at Lewis, who nodded.

'That settles it, then,' Benjamin said, and instructed the lawyer to draw up the deed of gift. Kevin would inherit the property at the age of twenty-one – by which time the twins would be eighty.

No sooner were the documents signed than his mother, Mrs Redpath, began to plague them. As long as the inheritance had been in doubt, she had kept her distance and minded her manners. Suddenly, overnight, she changed her tactics. She acted as though the farm was her birthright – almost as though the twins had swindled her out of it. She importuned them for money, rummaged in their drawers, and made jibes about them sharing a bed.

She said, 'Fancy trying to cook on that old range! Small wonder the food tastes of soot! There are such things as electric stoves, you know! . . . And those stone floors, I ask you? In this day and age! So unhygienic! What that floor needs is a damp course and some nice vinyl tiling.'

One Sunday, simply for the sake of disrupting lunch, she announced that her mother was alive and well, a wealthy widow in California.

Benjamin dropped his fork, then shook his head.

'I doubt it,' he said. 'She'd have wrote if she was living' – whereupon Mrs Redpath burst into a flood of crocodile tears. No one had ever loved her. No one had wanted her. She had always been pushed out, passed over.

In an effort to console her, Lewis unfolded the green baize of the silver box, and gave her Rebecca's christening spoon. Her eyes narrowed. She demanded harshly, 'What else you got of Mother's?'

Leading her to the attic, the twins unlocked a trunk and spread out all that remained of the little girl's belongings. A sunbeam, falling through the skylight, played over the tartan coat, the pairs of white silk stockings, the buttoned boots, a tam with a pompom, and some lace-trimmed blouses.

Moved to silence, the twins stared at these sad, crumpled relics and recalled those other Sundays, long ago, when they all drove to Matins in the dog-cart. Then, without so much as a by-your-leave, Mrs Redpath wrapped the lot in a bundle, and left.

Kevin, too, had begun to disappoint them.

He was charming: he even charmed a motor-bike out of Benjamin. But he was incurably lazy, and attempted to hide his laziness under a patter of technical jargon. He pooh-poohed the twins' farming methods, and worried them silly with his talk of silage and foetus-implantation.

He was supposed to put in two days' work at The Vision and three at a local polytechnic. In practice, he did neither. He would turn up from time to time, in sunglasses and a denim jacket decorated with studs and a death's head mask. A transistor radio dangled from his wrist. He had a snake tattooed on his arm, and he had bad friends.

In the spring of '73, a young American couple called Johnny and Leila bought the old farmhouse at Gillyfaenog in which to set up a 'community'. They had private means. Already their health-food shop in Castle Street was the talk of the town; and when Lewis Jones inspected it, he said it looked 'a bit like a meal-shed'.

Some members of the commune wore loose orange robes, and shaved their heads. Others wore pigtails and Victorian costume. They kept a herd of white goats; played the guitar and flute; and were sometimes to be seen in their orchard, cross-legged in a circle, saying and doing nothing, with their eyes half-closed. It was Mrs Owen Morgan who put around the rumour that the Hippies slept together 'like pigs'.

That August, Johnny built a strange scarlet tower in the vegetable garden, from which hung ribbon-like banners, printed with pink flowers and intertwined with black lettering. These, according to Mrs Morgan, were the symbols of the cult. Indian, she thought it was.

'Something to do with the Pope, then?' said Lewis. He hadn't heard her above the noise of the tractor.

They were standing outside the Chapel at Maesyfelin.

'No,' she shouted. 'That's Italian.'

'Oh!' he nodded.

A week later he gave a lift to a red-bearded giant, dressed in a homespun jerkin, with his feet bound up in sackcloth: his beliefs, he said, forbade him the use of leather.

Lewis dropped him at the gate, and asked about the letters on the flag. The young man bowed, raised his hands in prayer, and chanted very slowly: 'OM MANI PADME HUM' – which he translated equally slowly, 'Hail, Jewel in the Lotus! Hum!'

'Thank you very much,' said Lewis, touching his hat-brim and engaging the gear-shift.

After this encounter the twins revised their opinion of the Hippies, and Benjamin suggested they were 'taking some kind of rest'. All the same, he wished young Kevin wouldn't mess around with them. Halfway through a greenish sunset, the boy had tottered up the garden path, reeled into the kitchen with a glazed and faraway look and dumped his yellow crash-helmet on the rocking chair.

'Been drinking?' said Benjamin.

'No, Uncle,' he grinned. 'I been eating mushrooms.'

Forty-five

In their seventies, the twins found a new, unexpected friend in Nancy, the last of the Bickertons, who now lived at the old Rectory in Lurkenhope.

Arthritic, myopic and with scant control of the foot-pedals, she had somehow persuaded the licensing officer that she was fit to drive her 'rattletrap Sunbeam', and was forever going off on trips. She had known about The Vision all her life, and now expressed a wish to see it. She came once, and then again and again, always unheralded, at teatime, with an offering of rock cakes, and her five spluttering pugs.

The gentry bored her. Besides, she shared with the Jones twins certain memories of the happier days before the First World War. She said The Vision was the prettiest farmhouse she'd ever set eyes on, and that if Mrs Redpath gave 'one iota of trouble', they should show her the door.

She pressed them to come to the Rectory, which they hadn't seen since the death of the Reverend Tuke: it took them weeks of hesitation before they consented to go.

They found her halfway down the herbaceous border, in a pink smock and raffia hat, yanking at some convolvulus that threatened to smother the phlox.

Lewis coughed.

'Oh, there you are!' She turned to face them: she had long ago lost her stammer.

The two old gentlemen were standing, side by side on the lawn, nervously fingering their hats.

'Oh, I *am* glad you came!' she said, and took them on a tour of the garden.

A thick layer of make-up covered the blotches on her face; and a pair of ivory bangles flew up and down her wasted arm and clacked as they hit her hand.

'That!' she gestured to a cloud of white blossom. 'That's *crambe cordifolium!*'

She kept apologizing for the chaos: 'One can no more find a gardener than the Holy Grail!'

The pillars of the pergola had fallen; the rock garden was a mound of weeds; the rhododendrons were leggy or dying, and the rest of the clergyman's shrubbery had 'gone back to jungle'. On the door of the potting-shed, the twins found a horse-shoe they had nailed up there for luck.

A breeze blew clouds of thistledown across the lily pond. They stood on the margin and watched the goldfish moving under the lily-fronds, lost in a reverie of Miss Nancy being rowed across the lake by her brother. Then the housekeeper called them in for tea.

They passed through the French windows into a sea of memorabilia.

By temperament, Nancy was incapable of throwing anything away, and had crammed into her eight rooms of vicarage the relics from fifty-two rooms of castle.

On one wall of the drawing-room hung a moth-eaten tapestry, of Tobit; on another, a vast canvas of Noah's Ark and Mount Ararat, its treacly surface bubbling with welts of bitumen. There were 'gothick' cupboards, a bust of Napoleon, half a suit of armour, an elephant's foot, and any number of other big-game trophies. Potted pelargoniums shed their yellowing leaves over the piles of pamphlets and *Country Lifes*. A budgie clawed at the bars of its cage; demijohns of home-made wine were busy fermenting under the console, while, dotted here and there over the carpet, were the urine stains of generations of incontinent pugs.

The tea things came rattling in on a trolley.

'China or Indian?'

'Mother lived in India,' said Benjamin, abstractedly.

'Then you must meet my niece, Philippa! Was born in India! Adores it! Goes there all the time! I mean the tea!'

'Thank you,' he said. So to be on the safe side, she poured them two cups of Indian with milk.

At six, they moved out on to the terrace. She served them elderberry wine, and they sat reminiscing of the old times. The twins reminded her of Mr Earnshaw's peaches.

'Now he', she said, 'really *was* a gardener! Wouldn't like it nowadays, would he?'

The wine loosened Lewis's tongue. Flushed in the face, he confessed how, as boys, they had hidden behind a tree-trunk and watched her ride past.

'Really,' she sighed, 'if only I'd known . . .'

'Aye,' Benjamin chuckled. 'And you should have heard what this one told Mother!'

'Tell me!' She gave Lewis a square look.

'No. No,' he said, smiling sheepishly. 'No. I couldn't.'

'He said,' said Benjamin, ' "When I grow up, I'm going to marry Miss Bickerton." '

'So?' She gave a throaty laugh. 'He has grown up. What are we waiting for?'

They sat in silence. House-martins chattered under the eaves. Bees were humming round the night-scented stocks. Sadly, she spoke of her brother, Reggie:

'We were all sorry for him. The leg, you remember? But he was a bad lot, really. Should have married the girl. She'd have been the making of him. And it was all my fault, you know?'

Often over the years, she had tried to make amends to Rosie, but the door of the cottage always slammed in her face.

There was another silence. The setting sun made a rim of gold around the ilex.

'My God!' she murmured. 'The guts of that woman!'

Only the week before, she had sat and watched her from the car – a bent, pigeon-toed figure in a knitted hat, knocking at the vicarage door to collect her weekly envelope of two five-pound notes. Only Nancy and the vicar knew where the envelope came from: she daren't increase the sum in case Rosie suspected.

'You must come again.' Nancy clutched each twin by the hand. 'It's been such fun. Now promise me you'll come!'

'And you'll come to us again?' said Benjamin.

'Oh but I will! I'll come next Sunday! And I'll bring my niece, Philippa! And you can have a good long natter about India.'

The tea-party for Philippa Townsend was a tremendous success.

Benjamin went to endless pains, meticulously followed his mother's recipe for cherry cake, and when he lifted the lid of the willow-pattern dish, the guest-of-honour clapped her hands and said, 'Gosh! Cinnamon toast!'

When the table was cleared, Lewis unwrapped Mary's Indian sketchbook, and Philippa turned its pages and called out the names of the subjects: 'That's Benares! There's Sarnath! . . . Do look! It's the Holi Festival. Look at all the lovely red powder! . . . Oh, what a beautiful punkah-wallah!'

She was a short and very courageous woman with laugh wrinkles at the edge of her slaty eyes, and silver hair cut in a fringe. She spent several months of each year riding alone round India on a bicycle. She turned the last page but one and stared, thunderstruck, at a watercolour of a pagoda-like structure, standing among some conifers with the Himalayas stacked up behind.

'I don't believe it,' she shouted at the top of her voice. 'I thought I was the only white woman to see that temple.' But Mary Latimer had seen it in the Nineties.

Philippa told them she was writing a book about English lady travellers of the nineteenth century. She asked if she could have the picture copied to use as an illustration.

'You can,' said Benjamin, who insisted on her taking it away.

Three weeks later, the sketchbook came back by registered mail. In the same parcel was a lovely colour-plate book, entitled *Splendours of the Raj*; and though neither of the twins was quite sure what they were looking at, it became one of the treasures of the household.

Every month or so, the Radnor Antiquarians held meetings in the Village Hall at Lurkenhope; and whenever there was a lantern-slide lecture, Nancy took her 'two favourite boyfriends' along. In the course of the year, they listened to a variety of topics – 'Early English Fonts in Herefordshire', 'The Pilgrimage to Santiago' – and when Philippa Townsend gave a talk on travellers in India, she told the audience of the 'fascinating sketchbook' at The Vision, while the twins sat beaming in the front row with identical red polyanthuses in their buttonholes.

Afterwards, refreshments were served at the back of the Hall and Lewis found himself being manoeuvred into a corner by a fleshy man in a purple-striped shirt. The man spoke very rapidly, slurring his words through a set of discoloured teeth, his eyes darting shiftily to and fro. He dipped his ginger-nut into his coffee, and sucked it.

Then he slipped Lewis a card on which was written, 'Vernon Cole – Pendragon Antiques, Ross-on-Wye,' and asked if he could pay them a call.

'Aye,' Lewis answered, assuming 'Antiques' and 'Antiquarian' were the same. 'We'd be pleased for you to come.'

Mr Cole came the very next day in a Volkswagen van.

It was drizzling and the hill was lost in cloud. The dogs kicked up a shindy as the stranger picked his way through the toffee-coloured puddles. Lewis and Benjamin were mucking out the cowshed, and resented the interruption; yet, out of politeness, they stuck their dung-forks in the steaming pile, and asked him to come indoors.

The antique dealer was entirely at his ease. He eyed the room up and down; turned a saucer over, and said, 'Doulton;' peered at the 'Red Indian' to make sure it was only a print; and wondered whether, by chance, they had any Apostle spoons.

Half an hour later, smearing strawberry jam over his bread-and-butter, he asked if they'd ever heard of Nostradamus:

'Never heard of the prophet Nostradamus? Well, I'm darned!'

Nostradamus, he went on, lived centuries ago, in France; yet he got Hitler 'spot on': his Antichrist was probably Colonel Gaddafi; and he'd predicted the End of the World for 1980.

'1980?' asked Benjamin.

'1980.'

The twins stared at the tea-things with crestfallen faces.

Mr Cole then rounded off his monologue, walked up to the piano, laid his hands on Mary's writing cabinet, and said, 'It's terrible!'

'Terrible?'

'Beautiful marquetry, like that! It's a sacrilege.'

The veneer on the lid had buckled and cracked, and one or two bits were missing.

'I mean, it's got to be repaired,' he continued. 'I've got just the man for it.'

The twins hated letting the cabinet leave the farm, but to think they'd neglected a relic of Mary's made them even more miserable.

'I'll tell you what,' he pattered on. 'I'll take it with me, and show him. And if he hasn't come in a week, I'll bring it straight back.'

He removed from his pocket a receipt-pad on which he scribbled something illegible:

'What . . . er . . . what figure shall we say then? Hundred quid? . . . Hundred and twenty! Better be on the safe side! Here, sign this, would you?'

Lewis signed. Benjamin signed. The man ripped off the bottom copy; grabbed his 'find'; bade them a very good afternoon, and left.

After two sleepless nights, the twins decided to send

Kevin to recover the cabinet. Instead, a cheque – for £125 – arrived with the postman.

They felt dizzy and had to sit down.

Kevin borrowed a car and offered to drive them to Ross, but their courage failed. Nancy Bickerton offered to 'box the man's ears' but she was eighty-five. And when they called in on Lloyd the lawyer, he took the receipt, deciphered the words, 'One antique Sheraton writing-cabinet. For sale or return' – and shook his head.

He did, however, send a stiff solicitor's letter, but from Mr Cole's solicitor got a far stiffer letter by return: his client's professional integrity was being impugned, and he would sue.

There was nothing to be done.

Embittered and violated, the twins retreated back into their shells. To have lost the cabinet through theft or fire, that they could have borne. To have lost it through their own stupidity, to a man they had invited, who had sat at Mary's table and drunk from her teacups – the thought of it preyed on their minds and made them ill.

Benjamin had an attack of bronchitis. Lewis, with an infection in his inner ear, took even longer to recover – if, indeed, he was ever the same again.

From then on, they lived in dread of being robbed. They barricaded the door at night; and Lewis bought a box of cartridges to set beside the old twelve-bore. One stormy night in December, they heard someone thumping on the door. They lay motionless under the bedclothes until the banging died down. At dawn next morning they found Meg the Rock asleep among the wellingtons inside the porch.

She was numb with cold. They led her to the firestool, and she sat with her hands on her cheeks, her legs ajar.

'And Jim's gone!' It was she who broke the silence.

'Aye,' she went on in a low monotone. 'His legs was all mossified and his hands was red as fire. And I put him a-bed and he slept. And I was woke in the night, and the dogs was yelpin', and Jim was out-a-bed, on the floor, like, and his head was all a-blooded where he fell. But him was livin' and talkin', mind, and I put him back up.

' "Well, cheerio!" he says. "Feed 'em!" he says. "Feed 'em yowes! An' chuck 'em a bit o' hay if you got any! Feed 'em! Fodder 'em! And give 'em ponies a bit o' cake if you got some o' that. An' don't let Sarah sell 'em! Them'll be all right with a bit o' feedin' . . .

' "An' tell 'em Jonesies there's plums up at Cock-a-loftie! Tell 'em to pick some plums! I see'd 'em . . . Beautiful yeller plums! An' the sun's up! The sun's a-shinin'! I see'd 'im! The sun's all a-shinin' through the plums . . ."

'That's what him said – as you was to 'ave some plums. And I felt his feet, and them was cold. And I felt him up, and him was all cold. And the dogs was a-howlin' and a-yowlin' and a-yowlpin' and a-rattlin' at the che-ains . . . and that's as I knew Jim was gone . . . !'

Forty-six

An hour after Jim's funeral, the four principal mourners had wedged themselves in the Smoke Room of the Red Dragon, ordered soup and cottage pies, and were thawing out. The day was raw and drizzly. Their shoes were soaked from standing in the slush-covered graveyard. Manfred and Lizzie were dressed in shades of black and grey; Sarah wore slacks and a blue nylon parka; and Frank the haulier, a bulky man in a tweed suit several sizes too small, hung his head with embarrassment and stared at his crotch.

At the bar, a cider-drunk slammed down his tankard, belched and said, 'Aah! The wine o' the West!' A man and a girl were playing a computer game, and its electronic warbling filled the room. Manfred racked his brains to stave off a row between his wife and sister-in-law. He leaned across and asked the players, 'What do you call zis game?'

'Space Invaders,' the girl said glumly, and emptied a packet of peanuts down her throat.

Lizzie pursed her colourless lips and said nothing. But Sarah, her face already flushed from the fire, unzipped her parka and made up her mind to speak.

'Nice onion soup,' she said.

'French onion soup,' said the thinner woman.

There was a silence. A party of climbers came in and dumped their rucksacks in a heap. Frank refused to touch his soup and continued to stare at his crotch. His wife tried once again to make conversation.

She turned to a huge brown trout in a glass case above the mantelpiece, and said, 'I wonder who caught that fish.'

'I wonder,' Lizzie shrugged, and blew at her soupspoon.

The barman's girlfriend came with the cottage pies: 'Yes,' she said in broad Lancashire, 'that trout's quite a talking point. An American caught it in the Rosgoch Reservoir. An airforce-man, he was. He'd have had a Welsh record if he hadn't gutted it. He left it here to be stuffed.'

'Quite some fish!' Manfred nodded.

'It's a hen,' the woman went on. 'You can tell from the shape of the jaw. And a cannibal to boot! Has to be to reach that size! The taxidermist had a terrible time finding eyes big enough.'

'Yes,' said Sarah.

'And where there's one, there's two. That's what the fishermen say.'

'Another hen?' Sarah asked.

'A cock, I should imagine.'

Sarah glanced at her wristwatch and saw that it was almost two. In another half hour they had their appointment with Lloyd the lawyer. She had something else to say and gave a hard look at Lizzie.

'What about Meg?' she said.

'What about her?'

'Where's she going to live?'

'How should I know?'

'She's got to live somewhere.'

'Get her a living van and a few fowls and she'll be perfectly happy.'

'No,' Manfred interrupted, the colour invading his cheeks. 'She not be happy. You take her from The Rock and she go crazy.'

'Well, she can't go on living in that pigsty,' Lizzie snapped.

'Vy not? She live there all her life.'

'Because it's for sale!'

'I beg your pardon?' Sarah swivelled her head – and the quarrel flared out into the open.

Sarah believed The Rock should be hers. For twenty years she had bailed Jim out; and he had promised to leave her the property. Time and again, she'd gripped his arm: 'Now you have been to the lawyer, haven't you?' 'Aye, Sarah,' he used to say, 'I seed Lloyd the lawyer and I done what you said.'

She had counted on selling up the moment he died. Frank's haulage business had been doing badly and, besides, The Rock'd make a 'nice little nest-egg' for her teenage daughter Eileen. She even had a purchaser in mind – a businessman from London who wanted to put up Swedish-style chalets.

Lizzie, for her part, maintained The Rock was her home as much as anyone's, and she was entitled to her fair share. The argument volleyed back and forth – and Sarah became quite weepy and hysterical, prattling on about the sacrifices she'd made, the money she'd spent, the times she'd battled through snowdrifts, the times she'd saved their lives – 'And for what? A kick in the teeth, that's all!'

Then Lizzie and Sarah started screaming and yelling, and though Manfred shouted, 'Pliss! Pliss!' and Frank snarled, 'Aw! Cut it, will you?' the pub lunch almost ended in a fist-fight.

The barman asked them to leave.

Frank paid the bill and they walked up Broad Street, picking their way through the lines of slush till they came to the lawyer's door. Both women blanched when Mr Lloyd lifted his spectacles and said, 'There is no will.' Furthermore, since neither Sarah nor Lizzie nor Meg were Jim's blood relatives, his estate would be passed to the Official Receiver. Meg, Mr Lloyd added, had best claim on the place – for she was the incumbent and had lived there all her life.

So Meg lived on alone at The Rock. She said, 'I can't live for the dead 'uns. I got my own living to do.'

On frosty mornings she sat on an upturned bucket, warming her hands around a mug of tea while the tits and chaffinches perched on her shoulder. When a green woodpecker took some crumbs from her hand, she imagined the bird was a messenger from God and sang His Praises in doggerel all through the day.

After dark, she would huddle over the fire and fry up her bacon and potatoes. Then, when the candle guttered, she curled up on the box-bed with a black cat for company, a coat for a blanket, and a sack stuffed with fern for a pillow.

Having so little to separate the real world from the world of dreams, she imagined it was she who played with the badger cubs; she who soared with the hawks above the hill. One night, she dreamed of being attacked by strange men.

'I heard 'em,' she told Sarah. 'A young 'un and an old. Poonin' on the roof! Aye! And te-akin' off the tiles and comin' down in. So I lit me a candle and I shouted, "Git, yer buggers! I got me a gun in here and I'll blaow yer bloomin' heads off." That's as I said and I ain't heard nothing since!' –

all of which went to confirm Sarah's opinion that Meg was 'losing her marbles'.

Sarah had arranged with Prothero's for Meg's groceries to be delivered to a disused oil-drum by the side of the lane. But this hiding place was soon found by Johnny the Van, a red-eyed rascal who lived in an old fairground waggon nearby. There were weeks when Meg almost fainted from hunger: and the dogs, without meat, howled all day and night.

When the spring came, both Sarah and Lizzie set out to curry favour with Meg. Each would arrive with cakes or a box of chocolates, but Meg saw through their blandishments and said, 'Thank you people very much, and I'll see you again next week.' Sometimes they tried to get her to sign a prepared statement: she simply stared at the pencil as if it were poisoned.

One day Sarah drove up with a trailer to fetch a pony which, so she claimed, was hers. She walked towards the beast-house with a halter, but Meg stood, arms folded, by the door.

'Aye, you can te-ake him,' she said. 'But what are you people going to do about them dogs?'

Jim had left thirteen sheepdogs; and these, cooped up in tin shanties, had grown so mangy and ravenous on a diet of bread and water that they were unsafe to be let off their chains.

'Them poor ol' dogs is mad,' Meg said. 'Them'll 'ave to be shot.'

'We could take 'em to the vet?' Sarah suggested, doubtfully.

'Nay,' Meg answered back. 'I'm not putting them dogs in no death-van! Get that Frank o' yours to come up with his gun, and I'll dig a hole and put 'em in the ground.'

*

The morning of the shooting was damp and misty. Meg gave the dogs their last feed and led them out, two by two, and chained them to a crab-apple in the pasture. At eleven, Frank gulped down a swig of whisky, tightened his cartridge belt, and walked out into the mist, in the direction of the tree.

Meg stopped her ears; Sarah stopped hers; and her daughter Eileen sat in the Land Rover listening to rock music through the headphones of her cassette-player. A whiff of gunpowder drifted downwind. There was one final whimper, one isolated shot; and then Frank came back, out of the mist, haggard and about to vomit.

'An' a good job,' said Meg, slinging a spade across her shoulder. 'Thank you people very much.'

Next morning she saw Lewis Jones driving along the skyline on his red International Harvester. She ran up to the hedge and he switched off the engine.

'So them come and shot the dogs,' she said, catching her breath. 'Poor ol' dogs what done no 'arm. Nor che-ased no sheep nor nobody. But what with them all a-hungered, and with the summer a-comin', and the heat a-comin', and the smell in them coops, and the che-ains'd bite into their necks, like ... Aye! And bloody 'em! And then the flies'd come and lay eggs and there'd be worms in their necks. Poor ol' dogs! And that's why I 'ad 'em shot.'

Her eyes flashed. 'But I'm a-tellin' yer one thing, Mr Jones. It's the people not the dogs as should be punished ...!'

Not long afterwards, Sarah ran into Lizzie outside the chemist's in Rhulen. They agreed to have a coffee in the Hafod Tearoom, each hoping the other would dispel a dreadful rumour: that Meg had a fancy man.

Forty-seven

Theo the tent was his name. He was the red-bearded giant whom Lewis Jones had met in the lane. He was known as 'The Tent' on account of a domed construction made of birch saplings and canvas, and pitched in a paddock on the Black Hill, where he lived alone with a mule called Max, and a donkey to keep Max company.

His real name was Theodoor. He came from a family of hard-nosed Afrikaners, who had a fruit farm in Orange Free State. He had quarrelled with his father over the eviction of some workers, quit South Africa, come to England, and 'dropped out'. At the Free Festival near Glastonbury, he met a group of Buddhists, and became one.

Following the Dharma at the Black Hill Monastery made him calm and happy for the first time in his life. He shouldered all the heavy labour; and he enjoyed the visits of a Tibetan Rinpoche who came, now and then, to give courses in higher meditation.

His appearance sometimes put people off. Only when they realized he was incapable of hurting a fly, did they take advantage of his gentle, trusting nature. He had a little money from his mother, to which the leaders of the commune helped themselves. During one financial crisis, they ordered him to collect his entire annual income from the bank, in cash.

On the way to Rhulen, he stopped by the pine plantation and stretched out on the grass. The sky was cloudless. Harebells rustled. A peacock butterfly winked its eyes on a warm stone – and, suddenly, everything about the monastery disgusted him. The purple walls, the smell of joss-sticks and patchouli, the garish mandalas and simpering images – all seemed so cheap and tawdry; and he realized that, no matter how hard he meditated, or studied the *Bardo Thodol*, he would never come, That Way, to Enlightenment.

He packed his few belongings and went away. Soon afterwards the other Buddhists sold up and left for the United States.

He bought his paddock, on a steep pitch overlooking the Wye, and there he made his tent – or rather his yurt – from a plan in a book on High Asia.

Year in, year out, he roamed the Radnor Hills, played his flute to the curlews, and memorized the tenets of the *Tao Tê Ching*. On rocks, on gate-posts and on tree stumps, he would carve the three-line *haikus* that came into his head.

He remembered, in Africa, seeing the Kalahari Bushmen trekking through the desert, the mothers laughing, with their children on their backs. And he had come to believe that all men were meant to be wanderers, like them, like St Francis; and that by joining the Way of the Universe, you could find the Great Spirit everywhere – in the smell of bracken after rain, the buzz of a bee in the ear of a foxglove, or in the eyes of a mule, looking with love on the blundering movements of his master.

Sometimes, he felt that even his simple shelter was preventing him from following The Way.

One wild March day, standing on the screes above Craig-y-Fedw, he peered down and watched Meg's tiny figure, bent under a load of brushwood.

He decided to pay her a visit, unaware that Meg had already been watching him.

She had watched him winding his way over the mountain in the grey winter rain. She had watched him on the skyline with the clouds piled up behind. She was standing, arms folded in the doorway, as he tethered up the mule. Something told her he was not the kind of stranger to cringe from.

'I was wonderin' when you was a-comin',' she said. 'Tea's in the pot. So come on in and sit down.'

He could hardly see her face across the smoke-filled room.

'I tell you what I done,' she went on. 'I was up with the sun. I foddered the sheep. I gave hay to the horses. Ay! And a bit o' cake to the cows. I fed the fowl. I fetched up a load o' wood. And I was just havin' my cup-o'-tea and thinkin' to muck out the beast-house.'

'I'll help you,' said Theo.

The black cat jumped on to her lap, clawed at her breeches and scratched the bare patches of thigh.

'Ow! Ouch!' she cried. 'And where be you a-goin', little black man? What be you a che-asin', little darkie doll?' — squealing with laughter until the cat calmed down and started purring.

The beast-house had not been cleared for years; the layers of dung had risen four feet above the floor; and the heifers scraped their backs on the roofbeams. Meg and Theo set to work with fork and shovel and, by mid-afternoon, there was a big brown pile in the yard.

She showed not a trace of being tired. Now and then, as she pitched a forkful of muck through the door, the bows on her sweaters came undone. He could see that, underneath, she had a nice tidy body.

He said, 'You're a tough one, Meg.'

' 'Ave to be,' she grinned, and her eyes narrowed down to a pair of Mongolian slits.

Three days later, Theo came back to mend her window and rehang a door. She had found a few coins in Jim's pockets, and insisted on paying him a wage. In fact, whenever he did a job of work, she'd reach for a knotted sock, untie it, and hand him a ten-penny piece.

'Ain't much pie in it for you,' she'd say.

He took each one of these coins as if she were offering a fortune.

He borrowed a set of rods to clean her chimney. Halfway up, the brush snagged on something solid. He pushed, harder, and clods of soot came tumbling into the grate.

Meg chortled with laughter at the sight of his black face and beard: 'And I'd think you was the divil hi'self to look on.'

As long as her gentle giant was around she felt herself safe from Sarah, or Lizzie, or any outside threat. 'I'll not 'ave it,' she'd say. 'I'll not let 'em lay their 'ands on one o' m'chicks.'

If he stayed away a week, she began to look terribly dejected, imagining that 'men from the Ministry' were coming to take her away, or murder her. 'I know it,' she said gloomily. 'It'll be one o' them things in the papers.'

There were times when even Theo thought she was 'seeing things'.

'I see'd a couple o' townees' dogs,' she said. 'Black as sin! Coursin' down the dingle to buggery and che-asin' 'em little lambs! And I'd be gone out and find 'em dead and thinkin' 'em dead o' cold but them was dead o' fright o' the townees' dogs.'

She hated to think that he would, some day, go away.

For hours on end, he used to sit by the fire listening to the harsh and earthy music of her voice. She spoke of the weather, the birds and animals, the stars and phases of the moon. He felt there was something sacred about her rags and, in their honour, composed this poem:

> Five green jerseys
> A thousand holes
> And the Lights of Heaven shining through.

He brought her little luxuries from Rhulen – a chocolate cake or a packet of dates – and, to earn an extra pound or two, he hired himself out as a drystone waller.

One of his first jobs took him to The Vision, where Kevin had backed the tractor into a pigsty.

Kevin was out of favour with his uncles.

He was due to take possession of the farm in a year and a half; yet showed not the least inclination to take up farming.

He mixed with the 'county' set. He drank. He ran up debts; and when the bank manager refused him a loan, he demonstrated his disdain for life by joining a parachute club. Then, to compound the catalogue of his infamies, he got a girl into trouble.

Usually, his grin was so infectious that the twins forgave him everything: this time, he was white with apprehension. The girl, he confessed, was Sarah's daughter Eileen; and Benjamin banned him from the house.

Eileen was a pretty, purse-lipped girl of nineteen with a freckled nose and a head of bouncy russet curls. Her normal expression was a pout; yet, providing she wanted something, she could assume an air of saintlike simplicity. She was mad about horses, won trophies at gymkhanas and, like many horsy people, her financial needs were large.

She first met Kevin at the Lurkenhope Show.

The sight of his trim figure, perfectly balanced astride the bucking pony, brought her flesh out in goose-pimples. She felt a lump in her throat as he collected the prize. On learning that he was rich – or would be – she methodically laid her plans.

A week later, after flirting through a Country-and-Western evening at the Red Dragon, the pair crept into the back of Sarah's Land Rover. Another week went by, and he had promised to marry her.

Warning her to tread warily with his uncles, he brought her to The Vision as a prospective bride, and though her table-manners were excellent, though she studiously admired every knick-knack in the house, and though Lewis thought her 'quite a little piece', it made Benjamin far from happy to think she was one of the Watkinses.

One sweltering day in early September, she scandalized him by driving her car in a bikini, and blowing him a kiss as she passed. In December, on purpose or otherwise, she mistimed the pill.

Benjamin stayed away from the wedding, which, at

Sarah's insistence, was held in an Anglican church. Lewis went alone, and came back from the reception tiddly, saying that even if it had been a 'shotgun wedding' – an expression he'd picked up from a fellow-guest – it was, all the same, a very nice wedding and the bride had looked lovely in white.

The couple went on honeymoon to the Canaries and, when they came back, brown and beautiful, Benjamin relented. She failed to charm him: he was immune to her kind of charm. What did impress him was her common sense, her grasp of money matters, and her promise to calm Kevin down.

The twins agreed to build a bungalow for the youngsters at Lower Brechfa.

In the meantime, Kevin moved in with his parents-in-law – who proceeded to run him off his feet. Either Frank's truck needed a spare part from Hereford, or Sarah's show-jumper had a sprain, or Eileen would have a sudden craving for kippers and send her husband off to the fishmonger.

As a result, in the last weeks of Eileen's pregnancy, Kevin hardly had a moment for The Vision; missed the sheep-drive, the shearing and the hay harvest; and because they were so short-handed, the twins employed Theo to help.

Theo was a magnificent worker, but because he was a strict vegetarian he made a scene whenever they sent an animal for slaughter. He refused to drive a tractor or operate the simplest piece of machinery, and his opinion of the twentieth century made Benjamin feel quite modern.

One day, Lewis questioned the wisdom of living in a tent – whereupon the South African got extremely nettled and said that the God of Israel had lived in a tent; and if a tent was good enough for God, it was good enough for him.

'I expect,' Lewis nodded, doubtfully. 'Israel's a warm climate, isn't it?'

For all their differences, Theo and the twins were devoted to one another and on the first Sunday in August, he asked them over to lunch.

'Thank you very much,' Lewis said.

Coming up to the skyline above Craig-y-Fedw, the two old gentlemen paused to catch their breath and mop their foreheads.

A warm westerly breeze was combing through the grass-stems, skylarks hovered over their heads, and creamy clouds came floating out of Wales. Along the horizon, the hills were layered in lines of hazy blue; and they reflected how little had changed since they walked this way with their grandfather, over seventy years before.

A pair of jet fighters screamed low over the Wye, reminding them of a destructive world beyond. Yet as their weak eyes wandered over the network of fields, plotted and painted red or yellow or green, and the whitewashed farmhouses where their Welsh forbears had lived and died, they found it hard – if not impossible – to believe what Kevin said: that it would all go, any day, in a great big bang.

The gate into Theo's paddock was a mishmash of sticks and wire and string. He was waiting to greet them, in his homespun jerkin and leggings. His hat was crowned with honeysuckle, and he looked like Ancient Man.

Lewis had crammed his pockets with sugar-lumps to give to the mule and donkey.

Theo led the way downhill, past his vegetable patch, to the entrance of the yurt.

'And you live in that?' The twins had spoken in one breath.

'Yes.'

'Fancy!'

They had never seen so strange a structure.

Two tarpaulins, a green one over a black, were lashed over a circular frame of birch branches, and weighted down with stones. A metal chimney poked from the centre: the fire was out.

Out of the wind, Theo's friend, a poet, was boiling water for rice, and some vegetables were sizzling in a pot.

'Come on in,' said Theo.

Squatting down, the twins crept through the entrance hole and were soon sitting, propped up on cushions, on a ragged blue carpet covered with Chinese characters. Pencils of sunlight filtered through the holes in the tarpaulin. A fly droned. It was all very tranquil, and there was a place for everything.

A yurt, Theo tried to explain, was an image of the Universe. On its south side, you kept the 'things of the body' – food, water, tools, clothing; on the north, the 'things of the mind'.

He showed them his celestial globe, his astronomical tables, a sand-glass, some reed pens and a bamboo flute. On a red-painted box sat a gilded statuette. This, he said, was Avalokitesvara, the bodhisattva of Infinite Mercy.

'Funny name,' said Benjamin.

On the sides of the box were some lines of poetry, stencilled on in white.

'What does it say now?' asked Lewis, 'I canna see a thing without my proper specs.'

Theo flicked his feet into the lotus position, half-crossed his eyes, and recited the verse in full:

Who doth ambition shun,
And loves to live i' the sun,
Seeking the food he eats,
And pleas'd with what he gets,
Come hither, come hither, come hither:
> *Here shall he see*
>> *No enemy*
> *But winter and rough weather.*

'Very nice,' Lewis said.

'*As You Like It*,' said Theo.

'I wouldn't like it for winter, either.'

Theo then reached for his bookstand and read his favourite poem. The poet, he said, was a Chinaman who also liked to roam around the mountains. His name was Li Po.

'Li Po,' they repeated, slowly. 'That's all?'

'All.'

Theo said the poem was about two friends who rarely saw one another and, whenever he read it, he remembered a friend in South Africa. There were lots more funny names in the poem and the twins made neither head nor tail of it till he came to the last few lines:

What is the use of talking, and there is no end of talking,
There is no end of things in the heart.
I call in the boy,
Have him sit on his knees here
To seal this,
And send it a thousand miles, thinking.

And when Theo sighed, they sighed, as if they too were separated from somebody by thousands and thousands of miles.

They said the lunch was 'very tasty, thank you!' and, at three o'clock, Theo offered to walk them back to Cock-a-loftie. All three walked, in single file, along the sheep tracks. No one exchanged a word.

At the stile, Benjamin looked at the South African and anxiously bit his lip: 'He won't forget Friday, will he?'

'Kevin?'

Friday was their eightieth birthday.

'No,' Theo smiled from under his hat-brim. 'I know he hasn't forgotten.'

Forty-eight

On Friday the 8th of August, the twins awoke to the sound of music.

Coming to the window in their nightshirts, they parted the lace curtains and peered at the people in the yard. The sun was up. Kevin was strumming at his guitar. Theo played the flute. Eileen, in maternity clothes, was clinging to her Jack Russell terrier, and the mule munched a rose-bush in the garden. Parked outside the barn was a red car.

Over breakfast, Theo gave the twins their present – a pair of Welsh love-spoons, linked with a wooden chain and carved by himself from a single piece of yew. The card read, 'Birthday Greetings from Theo the Tent! May you live three hundred years!'

'Thank you very much,' said Lewis.

Kevin's present had not yet arrived. It would be ready, he said, at ten, and it was an hour's drive away.

Benjamin blinked. 'And where would that be?'

'A surprise,' Kevin grinned at Theo. 'It's a mystery tour.'

'We canna go till we fed the animals.'

'The animals are fed,' he said; and Theo was staying behind to keep an eye of the place.

'Mystery tour' suggested a visit to a stately home; so the twins went upstairs and came down in starched white collars and their best brown suits. They checked their watches with Big Ben, and said they were ready to go.

'Whose is the car?' asked Benjamin, suspiciously.

'Borrowed,' said Kevin.

When Lewis got into the back seat, Eileen's terrier took a nip at his sleeve.

He said, 'Angry little tiddler, ain't he?' – and the car lurched off down the track.

They drove through Rhulen and then up among some stumpy hills where Benjamin pointed out the sign to Bryn-Draenog. He winced every time Kevin came to a corner. Then the hills were less rocky; the oak trees were larger, and there were half-timbered manors painted black and white. In Kington High Street, they got stuck behind a delivery van, but soon they were out among fields of red Hereford cattle; and, every mile or so, they passed the gates of a big red-brick country house.

'Is it Croft Castle we're going?' Benjamin asked.

'Perhaps,' said Kevin.

'Quite a distance, then?'

'Miles and miles,' he said and, half a mile further, turned off the main road. The car bounced down a stretch of bumpy tarmac. The first thing Lewis saw was an orange wind-sock: 'Oh my! It's an aerodrome!'

A black hangar came into view, then some Nissen huts, and then the runway.

Benjamin seemed to shrivel at the sight of it. He looked frail and old, and his lower lip was trembling: 'No. No. I'd not go in a plane.'

'But, Uncle, it's safer than driving a car . . .'

'Aye! With your driving, maybe! No, No . . . I'd never go in a plane.'

The car had scarcely stopped moving before Lewis had hopped out and was standing on the tarmac, stupefied.

Ranked on the grass were about thirty light aircraft – Cessnas mostly, belonging to members of the West Midlands Flying Club. Some were white. Some were brightly coloured. Some had stripes, and all of their wingtips quivered as if they were itching to be airborne.

The wind was freshening. Patches of shadow and sunlight raced one another down the runway. On the control tower, an anemometer whirled its little black cups. On the far side of the airfield was a line of swaying poplars.

'Breezy,' said Kevin, his hair blowing over his eyes.

A young man in jeans and a green bomber jacket shouted, 'Hi, Kev!' and strolled over, dragging his boot-heels across the asphalt.

'I'm your pilot.' He grasped Lewis by the hand. 'Alex Pitt.'

'Thank you very much.'

'Happy birthday!' he said, turning to Benjamin. 'Never too late to take up flying, eh?' Then, pointing to the Nissen huts, he asked them to follow. 'One or two formalities,' he said, 'and we're off!'

'Aye, aye, sir!' said Lewis, thinking that was what you said to a pilot.

The first room was a cafeteria. Above the bar was a wooden propeller from the First World War: the walls were hung with coloured prints of the Battle of Britain. The airfield had once been a parachute-training centre – and still, in a sense, it was.

A party of young men, dressed for a 'drop', were drinking

coffee. And on seeing Kevin, a beefy fellow got to his feet, slapped his hand on his friend's leather jacket, and asked if he was coming too.

'Not today,' Kevin said. 'I'm flying with my uncles.'

The pilot ushered them into the Briefing Room, where Lewis greedily examined the notice-board, the maps marked with airlanes, and a blackboard covered with an instructor's scribbles.

A black labrador then bounded out of the air-controller's office, and rested its paws on Benjamin's trousers. In the animal's appealing stare, he seemed to see a warning not to go. He felt dizzy, and had to sit down.

The pilot put three printed forms on the blue formica table – one . . . two . . . three . . . and asked the passengers to sign.

'Insurance!' he said. 'In case we land in a field and kill some old farmer's cow!'

Benjamin gave a start, and almost dropped the ball point pen.

'Don't you scare my uncles,' Kevin bantered.

'Nothing could scare your uncles,' said the pilot, and Benjamin was aware that he had signed.

Eileen and the terrier waved at the flying party as they walked across the grass towards the Cessna. There was a broad brown stripe down the length of the fuselage, and a much thinner stripe along the wheel-spats. The plane's registration number was G-BCTK.

'TK stands for Tango Kilo,' Alex said. 'That's its name.'

'Funny name,' said Lewis.

Alex then began the external checks, explaining each one in turn. Benjamin stood forlornly by the wingtip, and thought of all the crashes in Lewis's scrapbook.

But Lewis seemed to think he was Mr Lindbergh.

He crouched down. He stood on tiptoe. His eyes were glued to the young man's every movement. He watched how to check the landing gear, to make sure of the flaps and ailerons, and how to test the warning horn that beeped if the plane was about to stall.

He noticed a slight dent in the tail-fin.

'Probably a bird,' said Alex.

'Oh!' said Benjamin.

His face fell even further when the time came to board. He sat in the back seat and, when Kevin fastened his safety-belt, he felt more trapped and miserable than ever.

Lewis sat on the pilot's right, trying to make sense of all the dials and gauges.

'And this one?' he ventured. 'Joystick, I suppose?'

The plane was a trainer and had dual controls.

Alex corrected him: 'We call it the control column nowadays. One for me and one for you if I faint.'

There was a hiccough from the back seat but Benjamin's voice was drowned by the rattle of the propeller. He closed his eyes as the plane taxied out to the holding-point.

'Tango Kilo checks completed,' the pilot radioed. Then, with a touch of throttle, the plane was on the runway.

'Tango Kilo leaving circuit to the west. Estimate return forty-five minutes. Repeat, forty-five minutes.'

'Roger, Tango Kilo,' a voice came back over the intercom.

'We take off at sixty!' Alex bawled into Lewis's ear – and the rattle rose to a roar.

By the time Benjamin opened his eyes again, the plane had climbed to 1,500 feet.

Down below there was a field of mustard in flower. A

greenhouse flashed in the sun. The stream of white dust was a farmer fertilizing a field. Woods went by, a pond coated with duckweed, and a quarry with a team of yellow bulldozers. He thought a black car looked a bit like a beetle.

He still felt a little nauseous, but his fists were no longer clenched. On ahead was the Black Hill and clouds streaming low over the summit. Alex climbed the plane another thousand feet, and warned them to expect a bump or two.

'Turbulence,' he said.

The pines on Cefn Hill were blue-green and black-green in the varied light. The heather was purple. The sheep were the size and shape of maggots, and there were inky pools with rings of reed around them. The plane's shadow moved upon a herd of grazing ponies, which scattered in all directions.

For one terrible moment, the cliffs above Craig-y-Fedw came rushing up to meet them. But Alex veered off and eased down into the valley.

'Look!' cried Lewis. 'It's The Rock!'

And there it was – the rusty stockade, the pool, the broken roof, and Meg's white geese in a panic!

And there, on the left, was The Vision! And there was Theo!

'Aye! It's Theo all right!' Now it was Benjamin's turn to be excited. He pressed his nose against the window and peered down at the tiny brown figure, waving its hat in the orchard, as the plane flew low on its second circuit, and dipped its wings.

Five minutes later, they were out of the hills and Benjamin was definitely enjoying himself.

Alex then glanced over his shoulder at Kevin, who winked. He leaned across to Lewis and shouted, 'It's your turn.'

'My turn?' He frowned.

'To fly.'

Gingerly, Lewis laid his hands on the control column and strained, with his good ear, to catch each word of the instructor. He pulled towards him, and the nose lifted. He pushed, and it fell away. He pressed to the left, and the horizon tilted. Then he straightened up and pressed to the right.

'You're on your own now,' said Alex, calmly, and Lewis made the same manoeuvres, on his own.

And suddenly he felt – even if the engine failed, even if the plane took a nosedive and their souls flew up to Heaven – that all the frustrations of his cramped and frugal life now counted for nothing, because, for ten magnificent minutes, he had done what he wanted to do.

'Try a figure-of-eight,' Alex suggested. 'Down on the left! . . . That's enough! . . . Now straighten up! . . . Now down on the right! . . . Easy does it! . . . Good! . . . Now another big loop and we'll call it a day.'

Not until he had handed back the controls did Lewis realize that he had written the figures eight and zero in the sky.

They were coming in to land. They saw the runway approaching, first as a rectangle, then a trapeze, then as a sawn-off pyramid, as the pilot radioed his 'finals' and the plane touched down.

'Thank you very much,' said Lewis, shyly smiling.

'It was my great pleasure,' Alex said, and helped the twins step down.

He was a professional photographer; and it was only ten days since Kevin had commissioned an aerial photograph of The Vision, in colour.

Mounted and framed, this was the second half of the

twins' birthday present. They unwrapped it in the car park, and gave the young couple each a kiss.

The big question was where to hang it.

Plainly, it belonged on the wall of photographs in the kitchen. But nothing had been added since Amos's death, and the wallpaper, though faded in between the frames, was as fresh as new behind them.

For a whole week, the twins bickered and juggled and lifted uncles and cousins off hooks that had been theirs for sixty years. And finally, just as Lewis had given up and decided to hang it above the piano, with 'The Broad and Narrow Path', it was Benjamin who lit on the solution: that by shifting Uncle Eddie and the grizzly *up* one, and by shifting Hannah and Old Sam *along* one, there was just enough space for it to fit beside their parents' wedding-group.

Forty-nine

The days were drawing in. Swallows chattered on the electric cables, all set for the long journey south. A gale blew in the night and they were gone. Around the time of the first frost, the twins had a call from Mr Isaac Lewis, the minister.

They went so seldom now to Chapel, but the Chapel was on their conscience, and their visitor made them nervous.

He had walked all the way from Rhulen, over Cefn Hill. His trouser bottoms were coated in mud and, though he scraped his soles on the boot scraper, he left a trail on the kitchen floor. A long forelock hung down between his eyebrows. His bulging brown eyes, though glittering with the light of faith, were none the less watering from the wind. He commented on the unseasonable weather: 'Harsh for September, isn't it?'

'Harsh!' agreed Benjamin. 'Like as it's the first day of winter.'

'And the Lord's House deserted,' the minister went on sombrely. 'And the People far from Him . . . Not counting the cost . . . !'

He was a Welsh nationalist of extreme views. But he expressed these views in so allusive a language that few of his listeners had the least idea what he was talking about. It took the twins twenty minutes to realize he was asking them for money.

The finances of Maesyfelin Chapel were in disarray. In June, while repairing some tiles, the roofer had uncovered a patch of dry rot. The pre-war wiring had proved to be a fire hazard, and the interior had been repainted, blue.

The minister was very red in the face, as much from embarrassment as the heat of the fire. He sucked the air in through his teeth, as if his whole life consisted of embarrassing interviews. He spoke of materialism, and of an ungodly age. Gradually, he hinted that Mr Tranter, the contractor, was pressing him for payment.

'And have I not paid fifty pounds from my own pocket? But what is the good of fifty pounds today, I ask you?'

'How much was the bill then?' Benjamin interrupted.

'Five hundred and eighty-six pounds,' he sighed, as if exhausted by prayer.

'And will I make the payment to Mr Tranter directly?'

'To him,' said the minister, too surprised to say anything else.

His eyes followed Benjamin's pen as it wrote out the cheque. This he folded meticulously and slipped into his wallet.

The wind was tossing the larches when he came to leave. He paused by the porch and reminded the twins of the Harvest Festival, at three o'clock on Friday.

'Indeed, a time for thanksgiving!' he said, and turned up the collar of his coat.

Early on Friday morning, Lewis drove his tractor to The Tump and asked Rosie Fifield to join them.

'To thank who for what?' she snapped and banged the door. At half past two Kevin came to collect the twins by car. He was smartly turned out in a new grey suit. Eileen was expecting at any minute, and so stayed at home. Benjamin was limping with a touch of sciatica.

Outside the Chapel, farmers with fresh weatherbeaten faces were quietly moaning about Mrs Thatcher's government. Inside, children in white ankle-socks were playing hide-and-seek among the pews. Young Tom Griffiths was distributing the Harvest Hymn Sheet, and women were arranging their dahlias and chrysanthemums.

Betty Griffiths Cwm Cringlyn – the one they all call 'Fattie' – had baked a loaf in the shape of a wheatsheaf. Heaped on the communion table were apples and pears; pots of honey and chutney; ripe tomatoes and green tomatoes; green grapes and purple grapes; marrows, onions, cabbages and potatoes, and runner beans that were the size of sawblades.

Daisy Prothero brought in a basket labelled 'Fruits of the Field'. There were corn-dollies pinned to the pillars of the aisle, and the pulpit had been wreathed with old man's beard.

The 'other' Joneses came, Miss Sarah showing off as usual in her musquash coat and hat of parma violets. The Evan Bevans had come, Jack Williams the Vron, Sam the Bugle, all the remaining Morgans; and when Jack Haines Red Daren hobbled in on a stick, Lewis got up and shook his hand: it was the first time they had spoken since the murder of Mrs Musker.

There was a sudden silence when Theo came in with Meg.

Aside from her spell in hospital, she had never left Craig-y-Fedw in over thirty years: so her appearance in the world was an event. Shyly, in an overcoat down to her ankles, she took her place beside the giant South African. Shyly, she raised her eyes and, when she saw the rows of smiling faces, she screwed her own face into a smile.

Mr Isaac Lewis, in a suit of goose-shit green, was standing by the door to greet his flock. He had the odd habit of cupping his hands in front of his mouth, and gave the impression of wanting to catch his previous statement and cram it back between his teeth.

Bible in hand, he went up to Theo and asked him to read the Second Lesson – Chapter 21 of the Book of Revelation: 'I suggest you leave out verses 19 and 20. You might have some difficulty with the words.'

'No,' Theo stroked his beard. 'I know the stones of New Jerusalem.'

The first hymn – 'For the Beauty of the Earth' – got off to a shaky start with the singers and harmonium player at variance as to both tempo and tune. Only a few valiant voices struggled on to the end. Then the preacher read a chapter of Ecclesiastes:

' "A time to be born, and a time to die; a time to plant, and a time to pluck up that which is planted . . ." '

Lewis felt the heat of the radiator burning through his trousers. He smelled a whiff of singeing wool, and nudged his brother to move down the bench.

Benjamin stared at the black curls curling over the back of Kevin's collar.

' "A time to get, and a time to lose; a time to keep, and a time to cast away . . ." '

He glanced down at the Harvest Hymn Sheet, on which were printed pictures of the Holy Land – women with sickles, men sowing grain, fishermen by Galilee, and a herd of camels round a well.

He thought of his mother, Mary, remembering that she too had been in Galilee. And of how, next year, when the farm belonged to Kevin, it would be so much easier to slip through the needle's eye, and join her.

' "A time to love, and a time to hate; a time of war, and a time of peace . . ." '

On the back page was a caption reading 'All is Safely Gathered In' and, below it, a photo of some smiling crop-haired boys, with tin mugs in their hands and tents behind.

He read that these were the Palestinian Refugees, and thought how nice it would be to send them a Christmas present – not that they had Christmases over there, but they'd get their present all the same!

Outside, the sky was darkening. A clap of thunder sounded over the hill. Gusts shook the windows, and raindrops pecked against the leaded panes.

'Hymn Number Two,' said the preacher. ' "We plough the fields and scatter the good seed on the land . . ." '

The congregation rose and opened its mouth, but all the thin voices were silenced by one strident voice from the back.

The room was alive with the noise of Meg's singing and, when she came to the line, 'By Him the birds are fed,' a tear fell from Lewis's eyelid, and trickled down the crease of his cheek.

Then it was Theo's turn to hold the audience spellbound:

' "And I saw a new heaven and a new earth: for the first heaven and the first earth were passed away; and there was no more sea. And I John saw the holy city . . ." '

Theo moved through the text, listing the jasper and

jacinth, the chrysoprase and chalcedony, without misplacing a syllable. The people facing the windows saw a rainbow arched over the valley, and a flock of black rooks beneath it.

When it was time for the sermon, the preacher got to his feet and thanked his 'brother in Christ' for so memorable a reading. Never in his experience had the Holy City seemed so real, so palpable. He, for one, had felt that he could reach out and touch it.

But this was not a city you could touch! It was not a city of brick or stone. Not a city like Rome or London or Babylon! Not a city of Canaan, for there was falsity in Canaan! This was the city that Abraham saw from afar, a mirage on the horizon, when he went to dwell in the wilderness, in tents and tabernacles . . .

At the word 'tent' Benjamin thought of Theo. Meanwhile, Mr Lewis had lost all trace of his ineloquence. His arms reached out to the roofbeams.

'Nor', he thundered, 'is it a city for the wealthy! Remember Abraham! Remember how Abraham returned his wealth to the King of Sodom! Remember! Not one thread, not one shoe-latchet would he take from the Kingdom of Sodom . . . !'

He paused for breath, and continued in a less emotional tone:

They had gathered in this humble chapel to thank the Lord for a sufficiency. The Lord had fed them, clothed them, and given the necessities of life. He was not a hard taskmaster. The message of Ecclesiastes was not a hard message. There was a time and a place for everything – a time to have fun, to laugh, to dance, to enjoy the beauty of the earth, these beautiful flowers in their season . . .

Yet they should also remember that wealth was a burden,

that worldly goods would stop them travelling to the City of the Lamb . . .

'For the City we seek is an Abiding City, a place in another country where we must find rest, or be restless for ever. Our life is a bubble. We are born. We float upwards. We are carried hither and thither by the breezes. We glitter in the sunshine. Then, all of a sudden, the bubble bursts and we fall to the earth as specks of moisture. We are as these dahlias, cut down by the first frosts of autumn . . .'

The morning of the 15th of November was bright and freezing hard. There was an inch of ice on the drinking-troughs. On the far side of the valley, twenty bullocks were waiting for their fodder.

After breakfast, Theo helped Lewis hitch the link-box to the International Harvester, and forked some hay-bales on to it. The tractor was slow to start. Lewis was wearing a blue knitted muffler. Another chill had gone to his inner ear, and he had complained of feeling giddy. Theo waved as the tractor lurched down the yard. Then he went indoors and chatted to Benjamin in the back-kitchen.

Benjamin had rolled up his shirtsleeves and was scouring egg-yolk from the plates. In the stone sink, rings of bacon fat had floated to the surface. He was very excited about Kevin's baby boy.

'Aye,' he smiled. 'Him be a perky little fellow.'

He squeezed out the dish-mop and dried his hands. A surge of pain shot through his chest. He fell to the floor.

'It be Lewis,' he croaked, as Theo helped him to a chair.

Theo rushed outside and looked across the valley at the frost-covered field. The oaks made long blue shadows in the slanting sunlight. Fieldfares were calling from the root crops. A pair of duck flew down the brook, and a vapour trail bisected the sky. He could not hear the noise of the tractor.

He could see the hay strewn over the field; but the bullocks had scattered, although one or two were beginning to edge back, in the direction of the hay.

He saw a muddy streak running vertically downhill along the line of the hedge. Below it was something red and black. It was the tractor lying on its side.

Benjamin had come out through the porch, hatless and shaking. 'Wait there!' said Theo, quietly, and ran.

Benjamin followed, limping down the path to the dingle. The tractor had slipped out of gear, and rolled. He heard Theo running on ahead. He heard the splash of water and, through the trees, he heard the seagulls shrieking.

The leaves had fallen from the birches along the brook. Points of frost sparkled on the purple twigs. The grass was stiff, and the water moved easily over the flat brown stones. He stood on the bank, unable to move.

Theo was walking towards him, slowly through the shining birch-trunks. 'You shouldn't see him,' he said. Then he folded his arms around the old man's shoulders, and held him.

Fifty

By the gate into Maesyfelin graveyard there is an old yew-tree whose writhing roots have set the paving slabs askew. Rows of headstones flank the path, some carved with classical lettering, some with gothic, and all of them furred with lichen. The stone is soft, and on those that face the prevailing westerlies, the letters have almost worn away. Soon, no one will read the names of the dead and the tombs themselves will crumble into the soil.

By contrast, the more recent tombs have been cut from stone as hard as the stones of the Pharaohs. Their surfaces are polished by machine. The flowers placed upon them are plastic, and their surrounds are not of gravel, but green glass chips. The newest tomb is a block of shiny black granite, one half with an inscription, the other left blank.

Now and then, a tourist who happens to stray behind the Chapel will see, seated on the edge of the slab, an old hill farmer, in corduroys and gaiters, gazing at his reflection while the clouds pass by above.

Benjamin was so confused and helpless after the accident that he could hardly even button his shirt-front. For fear of upsetting him further, he was forbidden to go near the cemetery, and when Kevin moved his wife and baby into The Vision, he would stare straight through them as if they were strangers.

Last May, Eileen began to whisper that the uncle was 'going ga-ga' and that the proper place for him was the old people's home.

He had watched her sell the furniture piece by piece.

She sold the piano to pay for a washing machine, the four-poster for a new bedroom suite. She redecorated the kitchen in yellow, shoved the family photos into the attic, and replaced them with a picture of Princess Anne on a show-jumper. Most of Mary's linen went to a bring-and-buy sale. The Staffordshire spaniels vanished, then the grandfather clock; and the old iron range lay rusting in the farmyard among the docks and nettles.

One day last August, Benjamin walked from the house and, when he failed to return at nightfall, Kevin had to organize a search.

It was a warm night. They found him next morning, sitting on the tomb and calmly picking his teeth with a grass-stem.

Since then, Maesyfelin has become Benjamin's second home – perhaps his only home. He seems to be quite happy as long as he can spend an hour in the graveyard each day. Some afternoons, Nancy Bickerton sends her car to fetch him over for tea.

Theo has traded his South African passport for a British one, has sold his meadow, and gone off to India where he hopes to climb in the Himalayas.

No decision has been reached about The Rock: so Meg lives on there, alone.

Rosie Fifield, too, continues to live in her cottage. Because she is crippled with arthritis, her rooms have become very squalid, but when the District Health Officer suggested she move to an almshouse, she snapped, 'You'll have to drag me by the feet.'

For her eighty-second birthday her son gave her a pair of ex-Army binoculars and, at weekends, she likes to watch the hang-gliding off the summit of Bickerton's Knob – 'helicoptering' as she calls it – a stream of tiny pin-men, airborne on coloured wings, swooping, soaring in the upthrust, and then spiralling like ash-keys to the ground.

Already this year she has witnessed a fatal accident.

Utz

For Diana Phipps

An hour before dawn on March 7th 1974, Kaspar Joachim Utz died of a second and long-expected stroke, in his apartment at No. 5 Široká Street, overlooking the Old Jewish Cemetery in Prague.

Three days later, at 7.45 a.m., his friend Dr Václav Orlík was standing outside the Church of St Sigismund, awaiting the arrival of the hearse and clutching seven of the ten pink carnations he had hoped to afford at the florist's. He noted with approval the first signs of spring. In a garden across the street, jackdaws with twigs in their beaks were wheeling above the lindens, and now and then a minor avalanche would slide from the pantiled roof of a tenement.

While Orlík waited, he was approached by a man with a curtain of grey hair that fell below the collar of his raincoat.

'Do you play the organ?' the man asked in a catarrhal voice.

'I fear not,' said Orlík.

'Nor do I,' the man said, and shuffled off down a side-street.

At 7.57 a.m., the same man unbolted from inside the immense baroque doors of the Church. Without a nod to Orlík he then climbed into the organ loft and, seating himself amid its choir of giltwood and trumpeting angels, began to play a funeral march composed of the two sonorous chords he had learned the day before: from the organist who was too lazy to stir from bed at this hour and had found, in the janitor, a replacement.

At 8 a.m., the hearse – a Tatra 603 – drew up outside the steps: in order to divert the People's attention from retrograde Christian rituals, the authorities had decreed that all baptisms, weddings and funerals must be over by 8.30. Three of the pall-bearers got out, and helped each other open the rear door.

Utz had planned his own funeral with meticulous care. A blanket of white carnations covered the oak coffin – although he had not foreseen the wreath of Bolshevik vulgarity that had been placed on top: red poinsettias, red gladioli, red satin ribbon and a frieze of shiny laurel leaves. A card offered condolences (to whom?) from the Director of the Rudolfine Museum and his staff.

Orlík added his modest tribute.

A second Tatra brought the three remaining pall-bearers. They had squeezed themselves into the front seat beside the chauffeur while, on the back seat, sat a solitary woman in black, her black veil awash with tears. Since none of the men showed any inclination to help her, she pushed the door open and, shaking with grief, almost fell onto the slushy cobbles.

To relieve the pressure on her bunions the sides of her shoes were slit open.

Recognising her as Utz's faithful servant Marta, Orlík rushed to her assistance – and she, collapsing onto his shoulder, allowed him to escort her. When he attempted to carry her brown leatherette bag, she wrenched it from his grasp.

The bearers – employees of a rubber factory who worked night-shift and doubled for the undertaker by day – had shouldered the coffin and were advancing up the main aisle: to music that reminded Orlík of the tramp of soldiers on parade.

Halfway to the altar the procession met the cleaning woman, who, with soap, water and a scrubbing-brush was scrubbing at the blazon of the Rožmberk family, inlaid into the floor in many-coloured marbles.

The leading bearer asked the woman, most politely, to allow the coffin to pass. She scowled and went on scrubbing.

The bearers had no alternative but to take a left turn between two pews, a right turn up the side aisle, and another right to pass the pulpit. Eventually, they arrived before the altar where a youngish priest, his surplice stained with sacramental wine, was anxiously biting his fingernails.

They set down the coffin with a show of reverence. Then, attracted by the smell of hot bread from a bakery along the street, they strolled off to get breakfast leaving Orlík and the faithful Marta as the only mourners.

The priest mumbled the service at the speed of a patter number and, from time to time, lifted his eyes towards a fresco of the Heavenly Heights. After commending the dead man's soul, they had to wait at least ten minutes before the bearers condescended to return, at 8.26.

At the cemetery, from which the snow had almost melted, the priest, though wrapped in a thick serge overcoat, began to suffer from a fit of shivers. The coffin had hardly been lowered into the earth when he began to shove the moaning Marta, by the shoulderblades, towards the waiting limousine. He declined Orlík's invitation to breakfast at the Hotel Bristol. At the corner of Jungmannova Street he shouted for the chauffeur to stop, and jumped out slamming the door.

It was Utz who had arranged, and paid for, this valedictory breakfast. An acrid smell of disinfectant flowed through the dining-room. Chairs were piled on tables, and more cleaning women were swabbing up the mess from a banquet held the previous evening, in honour of East German and Soviet computer experts. In the far left corner, a table covered in white damask was set for twenty people with a fluted Tokay glass at each place.

Utz had miscalculated. He had counted on at least a handful of his more venal cousins turning up, in case there was anything to be had. He had counted, too, on a delegation from the Museum: if only to arrange the transfer of his porcelains into their grasping hands.

As it was, Marta and Orlík sat alone, side by side, ordering smoked ham, cheese pancakes and wine from the slovenly waiter.

At the far end of the table stood a huge stuffed bear, reared on its hindlegs, mouth agape forepaws outstretched – placed there by some humorous person to remind the clientele of their country's fraternal protector. On its plinth, a brass plaque announced that it had been shot by a Bohemian baron, not in the Tatras or Carpathians, but in the Yukon in 1926. The bear was a grizzly.

After a glass or two of Tokay, Marta had apparently given up grieving for her dead employer. After four glasses, she twisted her mouth into a mocking grin and shouted at the top of her voice: 'To the Bear! . . . To the Bear!'

In the summer of 1967 – a year before the Soviet tanks overran Czechoslovakia – I went to Prague for a week of historical research. The editor of a magazine, knowing of my interest in the Northern Renaissance, had commissioned me to write an article on the Emperor Rudolf II's passion for collecting exotica: a passion which, in his later years, was his only cure for depression.

I intended the article to be a part of a larger work on the psychology – or psychopathology – of the compulsive collector. As it turned out, due to idleness and my ignorance of the languages, this particular foray into Middle European studies came to nothing. I remember the episode as a very enjoyable holiday, at others' expense.

On my way to Czechoslovakia I had stopped at Schloss Ambras, outside Innsbruck, to see the Kunstkammer or 'cabinet of curiosities' assembled by Rudolf's uncle, Archduke Ferdinand of the Tyrol. (Uncle and nephew had a friendly but long-standing quarrel as to who should possess the Hapsburg family narwhal horn, and a Late Roman agate tazza that might or might not be the Holy Grail.)

The Ambras collection, with its Cellini salt-cellar and

Montezuma's headdress of quetzal plumes, had survived intact from the sixteenth to the nineteenth centuries when imperial officials, mindful of the revolutionary mob, removed its more spectacular treasures to Vienna. Rudolf's treasures – his mandragoras, his basilisk, his bezoar stone, his unicorn cup, his gold-mounted coco-de-mer, his homunculus in alcohol, his nails from Noah's ark and the phial of dust from which God created Adam – had long ago vanished from Prague.

All the same, I wanted to see the gloomy palace-fortress, the Hradschin, where this secretive bachelor – who spoke Italian to his mistresses, Spanish to his God, German to his courtiers and Czech, seldom, to his rebellious peasants – would, for weeks on end, neglect the affairs of his Holy and Roman Empire and shut himself away with his astronomers (Tycho Brahé and Kepler were his protégés). Or search with his alchemists for the Philosopher's Stone. Or debate with learned rabbis the mysteries of the Cabbala. Or, as the crises of his reign intensified, imagine himself a hermit in the mountains. Or have his portrait done by Arcimboldo, who painted the Emperor's visage as a mound of fruit and vegetables, with a courgette and aubergine for the neck, and a radish for the Adam's apple.

Knowing no one in Prague, I asked a friend, a historian who specialised in the Iron Curtain countries, if there was anyone he'd recommend me to see.

He replied that Prague was still the most mysterious of European cities, where the supernatural was always a possibility. The Czechs' propensity to 'bend' before superior force was not necessarily a weakness. Rather, their metaphysical view of life encouraged them to look on acts of force as ephemera.

'Of course,' he said, 'I could send you to any number of intellectuals. Poets, painters, film-makers.' Providing I could face an interminable whine about the role of the artist in a totalitarian state, or wished to go to a party that would end in a partouse.

I protested. Surely he was exaggerating?

'No,' he shook his head. 'I don't think so.'

He would be the last to denigrate a man who risked the labour camp for publishing a poem in a foreign journal. But, in his view, the true heroes of this impossible situation were people who wouldn't raise a murmur against the Party or State – yet who seemed to carry the sum of Western Civilisation in their heads.

'With their silence,' he said, 'they inflict a final insult on the State, by pretending it does not exist.'

Where else would one find, as he had, a tram-ticket salesman who was a scholar of the Elizabethan stage? Or a street-sweeper who had written a philosophical commentary on the Anaximander Fragment?

He finished by observing that Marx's vision of an age of infinite leisure had, in one sense, come true. The State, in its efforts to wipe out 'traces of individualism', offered limitless time for the intelligent individual to dream his private and heretical thoughts.

I said my motive for visiting Prague was perhaps more frivolous than his – and I explained my interest in the Emperor Rudolf.

'In that case I'll send you to Utz,' he said. 'Utz is a Rudolf of our time.'

Utz was the owner of a spectacular collection of Meissen porcelain which, through his adroit manoeuvres, had survived the Second World War and the years of Stalinism in Czechoslovakia. By 1967 it numbered over a thousand pieces – all crammed into the tiny two-roomed flat on Široká Street.

The Utzes of Krondorf had been a family of minor Saxon landowners with farms in the Sudetenland, prosperous enough to maintain a town house in Dresden, insufficiently grand to figure on the Almanach de Gotha. Among their ancestors they could point to a Crusading Knight. But better-born Saxons would pronounce their name with an air of bewilderment, even of disgust: 'Utz? Utz? No. It is impossible. Who is this people?'

There were reasons for their scorn. In Grimm's Etymological Wordbook, 'utz' carries any number of negative connotations: 'drunk', 'dimwit', 'card-sharp', 'dealer in dud horses'. 'Heinzen, Kunzen, Utzen oder Butzen', in the dialect of Lower Swabia, is the equivalent of 'Any old Tom, Dick or Harry'.

Utz's father was killed on the Somme in 1916, not before he had redeemed the family honour by winning Germany's highest military decoration 'Pour le Mérite'. His widow, whom he had married to the anguish of his parents – was the daughter of a Czech revivalist historian, and of a Jewish heiress whose fortune came from railway shares.

Kaspar was her only grandchild.

As a boy, he spent a month of each summer at Céske Krížove, a neo-mediaeval castle between Prague and Tábor where this wasted old woman, whose sallow skin refused to wrinkle or hair turn to grey, sat crippled with arthritis in a salon hung with crimson brocade and overvarnished paintings of the Virgin.

A convert to Catholicism, she surrounded herself with unctuous and genuflecting priests who would extol the purity of her faith in the hope of financial rewards. The banks of begonias and cinerarias in her conservatory protected her from a magnificent sweep of the Central Bohemian countryside.

Various neighbours were affronted that a woman of her race should affect the outward forms of aristocratic life: to the extent of peopling her staircase with suits of armour, and of keeping a bear in a walled-off section of the moat. Yet, even before Sarajevo, she had foreseen the rising tide of Socialism in Europe, and, twirling a terrestrial globe as another woman might recite the rosary, she would point a finger to the far-flung places in which she had diversified her investments: a copper-mine in Chile, cotton in Egypt, a cannery in Australia, gold in South Africa.

She rejoiced in the thought that her fortune would go on increasing after her death. Theirs would vanish: in war or revolution; on horses, women and the gaming-tables. In Kaspar, a dark-haired, introspective boy with none of his father's high complexion, she recognised the pallor of the ghetto – and adored him.

It was at Céske Krížove that this precocious child, standing on tiptoe before a vitrine of antique porcelain, found himself bewitched by a figurine of Harlequin that had been modelled by the greatest of Meissen modellers, J.J. Kaendler.

The Harlequin sat on a tree trunk. His taut frame was sheathed in a costume of multi-coloured chevrons. In one hand he waved an oxidised silver tankard; in the other a floppy yellow hat. Over his face there was a leering orange mask.

'I want him,' said Kaspar.

The grandmother blanched. Her impulse was to give him everything he asked for. But this time she said, 'No! One day perhaps. Not now.'

Four years later, to console him for the death of his father, the Harlequin arrived in Dresden in a specially made leather box, in time for a dismal Christmas celebration. Kaspar pivoted the figurine in the flickering candlelight and ran his pudgy fingers, lovingly, over the glaze and brilliant enamels. He had found his vocation: he would devote his life to collecting – 'rescuing' as he came to call it – the porcelains of the Mèissen factory.

He neglected his schoolroom studies, yet studied the history of porcelain manufacture, from its origins in China to its rediscovery in Saxony in the reign of Augustus the Strong. He bought new pieces. He sold off those which were inferior, or cracked. By the age of nineteen he had published in the journal Nunc a lively defence of the Rococo style in porcelain – an art of playful curves from an age when men adored women – against the slur of the pederast Winckelmann: 'Porcelain is almost always made into idiotic puppets.'

Utz spent hours in the museums of Dresden, scrutinising the ranks of Commedia dell' Arte figures that had come from the royal collections. Locked behind glass, they seemed to beckon him into their secret, Lilliputian world – and also to cry for their release. His second publication was entitled 'The Private Collector':

'An object in a museum case', he wrote, 'must suffer the de-natured existence of an animal in the zoo. In any museum the object dies – of suffocation and the public gaze – whereas private ownership confers on the owner the right and the need to touch. As a young child will reach out to handle the thing it names, so the passionate collector, his eye in harmony with his hand, restores to the object the life-giving touch of its maker. The collector's enemy is the museum curator. Ideally, museums should be looted every fifty years, and their collections returned to circulation . . .'

'What', Utz's mother asked the family physician, 'is this mania of Kaspar's for porcelain?'

'A perversion,' he answered. 'Same as any other.'

The sexual career of Augustus the Strong, as recounted by Von Pöllnitz in 'La Saxe Galant', served Utz as an exemplary model. But when, in a Viennese establishment, he aspired to imitate the conquests of that grandiose and insatiable monarch – hoping to discover in Mitzi, Suzi and Liesl the charms of an Aurora, Countess of Königsmark, a Mlle Kessel or any other goddess of the Dresden court – the girls were perplexed by the scientific seriousness of the young man's approach, and collapsed with giggles at the miniscule scale of his equipment.

He left, walking the wet streets alone to his hotel.

He got a warmer welcome from the antiquaires. The sale

of his Sudetenland farms, in 1932, allowed him to spend money freely. The deaths, in quick succession, of his mother and grandmother, allowed him to bid against a Rothschild.

Politically, Utz was neutral. There was a timid side to his character that would tolerate any ideology providing it left him in peace. There was a stubborn side that refused to be bullied. He detested violence, yet welcomed the cataclysms that flung fresh works of art onto the market. 'Wars, pogroms and revolutions', he used to say, 'offer excellent opportunities for the collector.'

The Stock Market Crash had been one such opportunity. Kristallnacht was another. In the same week he hastened to Berlin to buy porcelains, in U.S. dollars, from Jewish connoisseurs who wished to emigrate. At the end of the War he would offer a similar service to aristocrats fleeing from the Soviet Army.

As a citizen of the Reich he accepted the annexation of the Sudetenland, albeit without enthusiasm. The occupation of Prague, however, made him realise that Hitler would soon unleash a European war. He also realised, on the principle that invaders invariably come to grief, that Germany would fail to win.

Acting on this insight, he succeeded in removing thirty-seven crates of porcelain from the family house in Dresden. These arrived at Céske Krížove during the summer of 1939. He did not unpack them.

About a year later, shortly after the Blitzkrieg, he had a visit from his red-headed second cousin, Reinhold: a clever but fundamentally silly character, who, as a student, had sworn that Kropotkin's 'Mutual Aid' was the greatest book ever written; who now expounded his views of racial biology with analogies culled from dog-breeding. An Utz, he insinuated, even if tainted with alien blood, should at once assume the uniform of the Wehrmacht.

At dinner, Utz listened politely while his cousin crowed over the victories in France: but when the man prophesied that Germans would occupy Buckingham Palace before the end of the year, he felt, despite his better judgement, a surge of latent anglophilia.

'I do not believe so,' he heard himself saying. 'You underestimate this people. I know them. I was in England myself.'

'*Also*,' the cousin murmured, and, with a click of the heels, marched out towards his waiting staff-car.

Utz had indeed been to England, to learn English at the age of sixteen. During an autumn and dismal December, he had boarded at Bexhill-on-Sea with his mother's former nanny, Miss Beryl Parkinson, in a house of cats and cuckoo-clocks from which he would gaze at the turgid waves that broke across the pier.

He did learn some English – not much! He also made a short trip to London, and came away with a vivid notion of how an English gentleman behaved, and how he dressed. He returned to Dresden in a racily-cut tweed jacket, and a pair of hand-made brogues.

It was this same brown jacket, a little threadbare, a couple of sizes too small, and with leather patches sewn onto the elbows, that he would wear throughout the War – as an act of faith and defiance – whenever German officers were present.

He wore it, too, his racial purity called into question, during the reign of Reinhard Heydrich, 'The Butcher of Prague': one afternoon, he confounded his interrogators by pulling from its pocket his father's First War decoration. How dare they! he shouted, as he slapped the medal onto the table. How dare they insult the son of a great German soldier?

It was a bold stroke, and it worked. They gave him no further trouble. He lay low at Céske Krížove and, for the first time in his life, took regular exercise: working with his foresters at the saw-mill. On February 16th 1945 news came that the Dresden house was flattened. His love of England vanished forever on hearing the B.B.C. announcer, 'There is no china in Dresden today.' He gave the jacket to a gipsy who had escaped the camps.

A month after the surrender, when Germans and German-supporters were being hounded from their homes – or escorted to the frontier 'in the clothes they stood up in' – Utz succeeded in disavowing his German passport and obtaining Czech nationality. He had a harder time dispelling rumours that he had helped in the activities of Goering's art squad.

The rumours were true. He had collaborated. He had given information: a trickle of information as to the whereabouts of certain works of art – information available to anyone who knew how to use an art library. By doing so, he had been able to protect, even to hide, a number of his Jewish friends: among them the celebrated Hebraist, Zikmund Kraus. What, after all, was the value of a Titian or a Tiepolo if one human life could be saved?

As for the Communists, once he realised the Beneš Government would fall, he began to curry favour with the bosses-to-be. On learning that Klement Gottwald had installed himself in Prague Castle, 'a worker on the throne of the Bohemian kings', Utz's reaction was to give his lands to a farming collective, and his own castle for use as an insane asylum.

These measures gave him time: sufficient at least to evacuate the porcelains, without loss or breakage, before they were requisitioned by the canaille.

His next move was to make a show of taking up Hebrew studies under the guidance of Dr Kraus: these were the years when pictures of Marx and Lenin used to hang in Israeli kibbutzes. He got a poorly paid job, as a cataloguer in the National Library. He installed himself in an inconspicuous flat in Židovské Město: its previous inhabitant having vanished in the Heydrichiada.

Twice a week he went loyally to watch a Soviet film.

When his friend Dr Orlík suggested they both flee to the West, Utz pointed to the ranks of Meissen figurine, six deep on the shelves, and said, 'I cannot leave them.'

'How did he get away with it?'

'With what?'

'The porcelain. How did he hang on to it?'

'He did a deal.'

My friend the historian gave me an outline of the facts as he knew them. It seems that the communist authorities – ever ready to assume the veneer of legality – had allowed Utz to keep the collection providing every piece was photographed and numbered. It was also agreed – although never put in writing – that, after his death, the State Museums would get the lot.

Besides, Marxist-Leninism had never got to grips with the concept of the private collection. Trotsky, around the time of the Third International, had made a few offhand comments on the subject. But no one had ever decided if the ownership of a work of art damned its owner in the eyes of the Proletariat. Was the collector a class-enemy? If so, how?

The Revolution, of course, postulated the abolition of private property without ever defining the tenuous borderline between property (which was harmful to society) and household goods (which were not). A painting by a great master might rank as a national treasure, and be liable for confiscation – and there were families in Prague who kept their Picassos and Matisses rolled up between the floor joists. But porcelain? Porcelain could also be classed as crockery. So, providing it wasn't smuggled from the country, it was, in theory, valueless. To start confiscating ceramic statuettes could turn into an administrative nightmare:

'Imagine trying to confiscate an infinite quantity of plaster-of-Paris Lenins . . .'

His face was immediately forgettable. It was a round face, waxy in texture, without a hint of the passions beneath its surface, set with narrow eyes behind steel-framed spectacles: a face so featureless it gave the impression of not being there. Did he have a moustache? I forget. Add a moustache, subtract a moustache: nothing would alter his utterly nondescript appearance. Supposing, then, we add a moustache? A precise, bristly moustache to go with the precise, toy-soldierish gestures that were the only evidence of his Teuton ancestry? He had combed his hair in greasy snakes across his scalp. He wore a suit of striped grey worsted slightly frayed at the cuffs, and had doused himself with Knize Ten cologne.

On reflection, I think I'd better withdraw the moustache. To add a moustache might so overwhelm the face that nothing would linger in the memory but the spectacles and a moustache – with a few drops of paprika-coloured fish-soup adhering to it – across our table at the Restaurant Pstruh.

'Pstruh' is Czech for 'trout' – and trout there were! The cadences of the 'Trout' Quintet flowed methodically through hidden speakers and shoals of trout – pink, freckled, their undersides shimmering in the neon – swam this way and that way in an aquarium which occupied most of one wall.

'You will eat trout,' said Utz.

I had called him on the day of my arrival, but at first he seemed reluctant to see me:

'Ja! Ja! I know it. But it will be difficult . . .'

On the advice of my friend, I had brought from London some packets of his favourite Earl Grey tea. I mentioned these. He relented and asked me to luncheon: on the Thursday, the day before I was due to leave – not, as I had hoped, at his flat, but in a restaurant.

The restaurant, a relic of the Thirties in an arcade of Wenceslas Square, had a machine-age décor of plate-glass, chromium and leather. A model galleon, with sails of billowing parchment, hung from the ceiling. One wondered, glancing at the photo of Comrade Novotný, how a man with so disagreeable a mouth would consent to being photographed at all. The head-waiter, sweltering in the July heat, offered each of us a menu that resembled a mediaeval missal.

We were expecting the arrival of Utz's friend, Dr Orlík, with whom he had lunched here on Thursdays since 1946.

'Orlík,' he told me, 'is an illustrious scientist from our National Museum. He is a palaeontologue. His speciality is the mammoth, but he is also experienced in flies. You will enjoy him. He is full of jokes and charm.'

We did not have long to wait before a gaunt, bearded figure in a shiny double-breasted suit pushed its way through the revolving doors. Orlík removed his beret, revealing a mass of wiry salt-and-pepper hair, and sat down. His hand – rather a crustacean claw than a hand – gave mine a painful nip and moved on to attack the pretzels. His forehead was scoured with deep furrows. I stared with amazement at the see-saw motion of his jaw.

'Ah! Ha!' he leered at me. 'English, he? English-man! Yes. YES! Tell me, is Professor Horsefield still living?'

'Who's Horsefield?' I asked.

'He wrote kind words about my article in the "Journal of Animal Psychology".'

'When was that?'

'1935,' he said. 'Maybe '36.'

'I've never heard of Horsefield.'

'A pity,' said Orlík. 'He was an illustrious scientist.'

He paused to crunch the remaining pretzel. His green eyes glinted with playful malice.

'Normally,' he continued. 'I do not have high regard for your compatriots. You betrayed us at München ... You betrayed us at Yalta . . .'

Utz, alarmed by this dangerous turn to the conversation, interrupted and said, solemnly, 'I cannot believe that animals have souls.'

'How can you say that?' Orlík snapped.

'I say it.'

'I know you say it. I know not how you can say it.'

'I will order,' said Utz, who waved his napkin, like a flag of truce, at the head-waiter. 'I will order trout. "Au bleu", isn't it?'

'Blau,' Orlík bantered.

'Blau yourself.'

Orlík tugged at my sleeve: 'My friend Mr Utz here believes that trout, when it is immersed in boiling water, does not feel more than a tickling. That is not my opinion.'

'There are no trout,' said the head-waiter.

'What can you mean, no trout?' said Utz. 'There are trout. *Many* trout.'

'There is no net.'

'What can you mean, no net? Last week there was a net.'

'Is broken.'

'Broken, I do not believe.'

The head-waiter put a finger to his lips, and whispered, 'These trout are reserved.'

'For them?'

'Them,' he nodded.

Four fat men were eating trout at a nearby table.

'Very well,' said Utz. 'I will eat eels. You also will eat eels?'

'I will,' I said.

'There are no eels,' said the waiter.

'No eels? This is bad. What have you?'

'We have carp.'

'Carp only?'

'Carp.'

'How shall you cook this carp?'

'Many ways,' the waiter gestured to the menu. 'Which way you like.'

The menu was multilingual: in Czech, Russian, German, French and English. But whoever had compiled the English page had mistaken the word 'carp' for 'crap'. Under the heading CRAP DISHES, the list contained 'Crap soup with paprika', 'Stuffed crap', 'Crap cooked in beer', 'Fried crap', 'Crap balls', 'Crap à la juive . . .'

'In England,' I said, 'this fish is called "carp". "Crap" has a different meaning.'

'Oh?' said Dr Orlík. 'What meaning?'

'Faeces,' I said. 'Shit.'

I regretted saying this because Utz looked exceedingly embarrassed. The narrow eyes blinked, as if he hoped he hadn't heard correctly. Orlík's wheezy carapace shook with laughter.

'Ha! Ha!' he jeered. 'Crap à la juive . . . My friend Mr Utz will eat Crap à la juive . . . !'

I was afraid Utz was going to leave, but he rose above his discomfiture and ordered soup and the 'Carpe meunière'. I took the line of least resistance and ordered the same. Orlík clamoured in his loud and crackly voice, 'No. No. I will eat "Crap à la juive" . . . !'

'And to begin?' asked the waiter.

'Nothing,' said Orlík. 'Only the crap!'

I tried to swing the conversation to Utz's collection of porcelain. His reaction was to swivel his neck inside his collar and say, blankly, 'Dr Orlík is also a collector. But his is a collector of flies.'

'Flies?'

'Flies,' assented Orlík.

I began to form a mental picture of his lodgings: the unmade bed, the unemptied ashtrays; the avalanche of yellowing periodicals; the microscope; the killing-jars and, lining the walls, glass-fronted cases containing flies from every corner of the globe, each specimen pierced with a pin. I mentioned some beautiful dragonflies I had seen in Brazil.

'Dragonflies?' Orlík frowned. 'I have not interest. I have only interest for Musca domestica.'

'The common house-fly?'

'That is what it is.'

'Answer me,' Utz interrupted again. 'On which day did God create the fly? Day five? Or Day six?'

'How many times will I tell you?' Orlík clamoured. 'We have one hundred ninety million years of flies. But you will always speak of days!'

'Hard words,' said Utz philosophically.

A fly had landed on the tablecloth and was sopping up some soup that the waiter had let fall from the ladle. With a flick of the wrist Orlík upturned a glass tumbler, and trapped the insect beneath it. He slid the glass to the edge of the table and transferred the fly to the killing-jar he took from his pocket. There was an angry buzzing, then silence.

He flourished a magnifying glass and scrutinised the victim.

'Interesting example,' he said. 'Hatched, I would say, in the kitchen here. I will ask . . .'

'You will not ask,' said Utz.

'I will. I will ask.'

'You will not.'

'And what', I asked, 'brought you and the house-fly together?'

Expelling carp bones through his beard, Orlík described how he had devoted thirty years to studying certain aspects of the woolly mammoth: a labour which had taken him to the tundras of Siberia where mammoths are occasionally found deep-frozen in permafrost. The fruit of these researches – though he was usually too modest to mention it – had culminated in his magisterial paper 'The Mammoth and His Parasites'. But no sooner was it published than he felt the need to study some lowlier creature.

'I chose', he said, 'to study Musca domestica within the Prague Metropolitan area.'

Just as his friend Mr Utz could tell at a glance whether a

piece of Meissen porcelain was made from the white clay of Colditz or the white clay of Erzgebirge, he, Orlík, having examined under a microscope the iridescent membrane of a fly's wing, claimed to know if the insect came from one of the garbage dumps that now encircled the New Garden City.

He confessed to being enchanted by the vitality of the fly. It was fashionable among his fellow entomologists – especially the Party Members – to applaud the behaviour of the social insects: the ants, bees, wasps and other varieties of Hymenoptera which organised themselves into regimented communities.

'But the fly', said Orlík, 'is an anarchist.'

'Sssh!' said Utz. 'You will not say that word!'

'What word?'

'That word.'

'Yes. Yes,' Orlík pitched his voice an octave higher. 'I will say it. The fly is an anarchist. He is an individualist. He is a Don Juan.'

The four fat Party Members, at whom this outburst was directed, were far too busy to notice: they were ogling their second helping of trout whose flesh, at that moment, the waiter was easing off the bone and blue skin.

'I am not from the People,' Orlík said. 'I have noble blood.'

'Oh?' said Utz. 'Which nobility?'

I thought for a moment that lunch was going to end in a slanging match – until I realised that this was another of their well-rehearsed duets. There followed a discussion on the merits (or otherwise) of Kafka, whom Utz revered as a demiurge and Orlík dismissed as a fraud. It was right for his books to be abolished.

'Banned, you mean?' I said. 'Censored?'

'I do not mean,' said Orlík. 'I said abolished.'

'Paf! Paf!' Utz flapped his hand. 'What foolishness is this?'

Orlík's case against Kafka was the doubtful entomological status of the insect in the story 'Metamorphosis'. Again, I thought we were in for trouble. Again, the brouhaha simmered down. We drank a cup of anaemic coffee. Orlík extracted from me my London address, scribbled it on a scrap of paper napkin, rolled it into a pellet, and put it in his pocket.

He intercepted the bill and waved it in Utz's face.

'I will pay,' he announced.

'You will not pay.'

'I will. I must.'

'You will not,' said Utz, who snatched at the paper Orlík held for him to snatch.

Orlík's eyelids dropped in acquiescence.

'Aah!' he nodded gloomily. 'I know it. Mr Utz will pay.'

'And now,' Utz turned to me, 'you will permit me to show you some monuments of our beautiful city.'

Utz and I spent the rest of the afternoon strolling through the thinly peopled streets of Malá Strana, pausing now and then to admire the blistering façade of a merchant's house, or some Baroque or Rococo palace – the Vrtba, the Pálffy, the Lobkovic: he recited their names as though the builders were intimate friends.

In the Church of Our Lady Victorious, the waxen Spanish image of the Christ Child, aureoled in an explosion of gold, seemed less the Blessed Babe of Bethlehem than the vengeful divinity of the Counter-Reformation.

We climbed the length of Neruda Street and walked around the Hradschin: the scene of my futile researches during the previous week. We then sat in an orchard below the Strahov Monastery. A man in his underpants sunned himself on the grass. The fluff of balsam poplars floated by, and settled on our clothes like snowflakes.

'You will see,' said Utz, waving his malacca over the multiplicity of porticoes and cupolas below us. 'This city wears a tragic mask.'

It was also a city of giants: giants in stone, in stucco or marble; naked giants; blackamoor giants; giants dressed as if for a hurricane, not one of them in repose, struggling with some unseen force, or heaving under the weight of architraves.

'The suffering giant', he added without conviction, 'is the emblem of our persecuted people.'

I commented facetiously that a taste for giants was usually a symptom of decline: an age that took the Farnese Hercules for an ideal was bound to end in trouble.

Utz countered with the story of Frederick William of Prussia who had once made a collection of real giants – semi-morons mostly – to swell the ranks of his Potsdam Grenadiers.

He then explained how this weakness for giants had led to one of the most bizarre diplomatic transactions of the eighteenth century: in which Augustus of Saxony chose 127 pieces of Chinese porcelain from the Palace of Charlottenburg, in Berlin, and gave in return 600 giants 'of the required height' collected in the eastern provinces.

'I never liked giants,' he said.

'I once met a man,' I said, 'who was a dealer in dwarfs.'

'Oh?' he blinked. 'Dwarfs, you say?'

'Dwarfs.'

'Where did you meet this man?'

'On a plane to Baghdad. He was going to view a dwarf for a client.'

'A client! This is wonderful!'

'He had two clients,' I said. 'One was an Arab oil sheikh. The other owned hotels in Pakistan.'

'And what did they do with those dwarfs?' Utz tapped me on the knee.

He had paled with excitement and was mopping the sweat from his brow.

'Kept them.' I said. 'The sheikh, if I remember right, liked to sit his favourite dwarf on his forearm and his favourite falcon on the dwarf's forearm.'

'Nothing else?'

'How can one know?'

'You are right,' said Utz. 'These are things one cannot know.'

'Or would want to.'

'And what would cost a dwarf? These days?'

'Who can say? Collecting dwarfs has always been expensive.'

'That's a nice story,' he smiled at me. 'Thank you. I also like dwarfs. But not in the way you think.'

It was now early evening and we were sitting on a slatted seat in the Old Jewish Cemetery. Pigeons were burbling on the roof of the Klausen Synagogue. The sunbeams, falling through sycamores, lit up spirals of midges and landed on the mossy tombstones, which, heaped one upon the other, resembled seaweed-covered rocks at low-tide.

To our right, a party of American Hasids – pale, shortsighted youths in yarmulkes – were laying pebbles on the tomb of the Great Rabbi Loew. They posed for a photograph, with their backs to its scrolling headstone.

Utz told me how the original ghetto – that warren of secret passages and forgotten rooms so vividly described by Meyrink – had been replaced by apartment buildings after the slum clearances of the 1890s. The synagogues, the cemetery and the Old Town Hall were almost the only monuments to survive. These, he said, far from being destroyed by the Nazis, were spared to form a proposed Museum of Jewry, where Aryan tourists of the future would inspect the relics of a people as lost as the Aztecs or Hottentots.

He changed the subject.

'You have heard tell the story of the Golem?'

'I have,' I said. 'The Golem was an artificial man . . . a mechanical man . . . a prototype of the robot. He was a creation of the Rabbi Loew.'

'My friend,' he smiled, 'you know, I think, many things. But you have many things to know.'

The Rabbi Loew had been the undisputed leader of Prague Jewry in the reign of the Emperor Rudolf: never again would the Jews of Middle Europe enjoy such esteem and privilege. He entertained princes and ambassadors, and was entertained by his sovereign in the Hradschin. Many of his writings – among them the homily 'On the Hardening of Pharaoh's Heart' – were absorbed into the teachings of Hasidism. Like any other Cabbalist he believed that every event – past, present and future – was already written down in the Torah.

After his death, the Rabbi was inevitably credited with supernatural powers. There are tales – none dating from his lifetime – of how, with an abracadabra, he moved a castle from the Bohemian countryside to the Prague ghetto. Or told the Emperor to his face that his real father was a Jew. Or trounced the mad Jesuit, Father Thaddeus, and proved the Jews were innocent of blood guilt. Or fashioned Yossel the Golem from the glutinous mud of the River Vltava.

All golem legends derived from an Ancient Jewish belief that any righteous man could create the World by repeating, in an order prescribed by the Cabbala, the letters of the secret name of God. 'Golem' meant 'unformed' or 'uncreated' in Hebrew. Father Adam himself had been 'golem' – an inert mass of clay so vast as to cover the ends of the Earth: that is, until Yahweh shrank him to human scale and breathed into his mouth the power of speech.

'So you see,' said Utz, 'not only was Adam the first human person. He was also the first ceramic sculpture.'

'Are you suggesting your porcelains are alive?'

'I am and I am not,' he said. 'They are alive and they are dead. But if they *were* alive, they would also have to die. Is it not?'

'If you say so.'

'Good. So I say it.'

'Good,' I said. 'Go on about golems.'

One of Utz's favourite golem stories was a mediaeval text discovered by Gershom Scholem: wherein it was written that Jesus Christ ('like *our* friend J. J. Kaendler') used to make model birds from clay – which, once He had uttered the sacred formula, would sing, flap their wings and fly.

A second story ('Oh! What a Jewish story!') told of two hungry rabbis who, having fashioned the figure of a calf, brought it to life – then cut its throat and ate veal for supper.

As for making a golem, a recipe in the Sepher Yetzirah or 'Book of Creation' called for a quantity of untouched mountain soil. This was to be kneaded with fresh spring water and, from it, a human image formed. The maker was required to recite over each of the image's limbs the appropriate alphabetical combination. He then walked around it clockwise a number of times: whereupon the golem stood and lived. Were he to reverse the direction, the creature would revert to clay.

None of the earlier sources say whether or not a golem could speak. But the automaton did have the gift of memory and would obey orders mechanically, without reflection, providing these were given at regular intervals. If not, the golem might run amok.

Golems also gained in stature, inch by inch, every day: yearning, it would seem, to attain the gigantic size of the Cosmic Adam – and so crush their creators and overwhelm the world.

'There was no end', said Utz, 'to the size of golems. Golems were highly dangerous.'

A golem was said to wear a slip of metal known as the 'shem', either across its forehead or under its tongue. The 'shem' was inscribed with the Hebrew word 'emeth', or Truth of God. When a rabbi wished to destroy his golem, he had only to pluck out the opening letter, so that 'emeth' now read 'meth' – which is to say 'death' – and the golem dissolved.

'I see,' I said. 'The "shem" was a kind of battery?'

'It was.'

'Without which the machine wouldn't work?'

'Also.'

'And the Rabbi Leow . . . ?'

'Wanted a servant. He was a good Jewish businessman. He wanted a servant without paying wages.'

'And a servant that wouldn't answer back!'

Yossel was the name of the Rabbi Loew's golem.

On weekdays he did all sorts of menial tasks. He chopped wood, swept the street and the synagogue, and acted as watchdog in case the Jesuits got up to mischief. Yet on the Sabbath – since all God's creatures must rest on the Sabbath – his master would remove the 'shem' and render him lifeless for a day.

One Sabbath the Rabbi forgot to do this, and Yossel went beserk. He pulled down houses, threw rocks, threatened people and tore up trees by the roots. The congregation had already filled the Altneu Synagogue for morning prayers, and was chanting the 92nd Psalm: 'My horn shalt thou exalt like the horn of the unicorn . . .' The Rabbi rushed into the street and snatched the 'shem' from the monster's forehead.

Another version places the 'death', amid old books and prayer-shawls, in the loft of the synagogue.

'Tell me,' I asked, 'would a golem have had Jewish features?'

'Not!' Utz answered with a touch of impatience.

'The golem was always a servant. Servants in Jewish houses were always of the goyim.'

'Would a golem have had Nordic features?'

363

'Yes,' he agreed. 'Giants' features.'

Utz brooded for a while and then arrived at the crux of the discussion:

All these tales suggested that a golem-maker had acquired arcane secrets: yet, in doing so, had transgressed Holy Law. A man-made figure was a blasphemy. A golem, by its presence alone, issued a warning against idolatry – and actively beseeched its own destruction.

'Would you say then', I asked, 'that art-collecting is idolatry?'

'Ja! Ja!' he struck his chest. 'Of course! Of course! That is why we Jews . . . and in this matter I consider myself a Jew . . . are so good at it! Because it is forbidden . . . ! Because it is sinful . . . ! Because it is dangerous . . . !'

'Do your porcelains demand their own death?'

He stroked his chin.

'I do not know. It is a very problematical question.'

The other visitors had left. A black cat had positioned itself on the crest of a tombstone. The guardian told us it was time to leave.

'And now my friend,' said Utz, 'would it amuse you to see my collection of dwarfs?'

An odour of suppurating cabbage leaves seeped from a dustbin in the entrance hall. A rat hopped off as we approached. In an apartment on the second landing, a baby wailed and someone was trying to master one of Dvořák's 'Slavonic Dances' on an out-of-tune piano. On the third landing a woman opened her door to see who was passing: a hysterical face under a heap of auburn curls. She wore a peignoir of magenta peonies, and vehemently slammed the door shut.

'She is mad,' Utz apologised. 'She was a famous soprano.'

On the top floor, he caught his breath, fumbled for his latch-key and ushered me inside. The smell was familiar to me: the stale smell of rooms where works of art are kept, and dusting considered dangerous. In a dingy green kitchenette off the hallway, Utz's servant sat perched on a stool.

She was a solid woman dressed awkwardly in a maid's uniform, with glowing cheeks and sandy hair flecked with grey. Over a black woollen dress there was a frilly white apron and, across her forehead, a fillet of lace. Her legs were encased in black stockings, which had a pair of white 'potatoes' at the knee.

She was expecting us.

In her lap she cradled a dish of emblazoned white porcelain which, I knew from my 'arty' days, was a piece of the celebrated Swan Service made by Kaendler for the Saxon First Minister, Count Brühl. On it she had arranged some slivers of cheese and crackers, Hungarian salami and rounds of pickled cucumber cut in the form of flowers.

She bowed her head deferentially.

'Guten Abend, Herr Baron.'

'Guten Abend, Marta,' he returned her greeting.

We moved into the room. Behind the net curtain, a single north-facing window looked out over the trees of the cemetery.

'I didn't know you were a baron,' I said.

'Yes,' he blushed. 'I am a baron also.'

The room, to my surprise, was decorated in the 'modern style': almost devoid of furniture apart from a daybed, a glass-topped table and a pair of Barcelona chairs upholstered in dark green leather. Utz had 'rescued' these in Moravia, from a house built by Mies van der Rohe.

It was a narrow room, made narrower by the double bank of plate-glass shelves, all of them crammed with porcelain, that reached from floor to ceiling. The shelves were backed with mirror, so that you had the illusion of entering an enfilade of glittering chambers, a 'dream palace' multiplied to infinity, through which human forms flitted like insubstantial shadows.

The carpet was grey. You had to watch your step for fear of tripping over one of the white porcelain sculptures – a pelican, a turkey-cock, a bear, a lynx and a rhino – modelled either by Kaendler or Eberlein for the Japanese Palace in Dresden. All five were scarred with fissures caused by faults in the firing.

Utz waved to some bottles on the table: Scotch, slivovic, and a soda siphon.

'Is it scotch, isn't it?'

'Scotch,' I said.

At the whoosh of the siphon, the maid emerged with her canapés on the Swan Service dish. Her movements seemed so lifeless and mechanical you would have thought that Utz had created a female golem. Yet I detected the suggestion of a superior smile.

'Cheerio!' said Utz, mimicking an English gentleman's accent.

'Your health!' I raised my glass – and took stock of my surroundings.

I am not an expert on Meissen porcelain – although my years of traipsing round art museums have taught me what it is. Nor can I say I like Meissen porcelain. I do, however, admire the boisterous energy of an artist such as Kaendler, at play with a medium which was totally new. And I entirely side with Utz in his feud with Winckelmann – who, in his 'Notes on the Plebeian Taste in Porcelain', would supplant this plebeian vitality with the dead hand of classical perfection.

I am equally fascinated by the way in which 'porcelain sickness' – the Porzellankrankheit of Augustus the Strong – so warped his vision, and that of his ministers, that their delirious schemes for ceramics got confused with real political power. Of Brühl, who would become Director of the Meissen Manufactory, Horace Walpole commented tartly: ' . . . he had prepared nothing but bawbles against a prince (Frederick the Great) that lived in a camp with the frugality of a common soldier . . .'

Utz had chosen each item to reflect the moods and facets of the 'Porcelain Century': the wit, the charm, the gallantry, the love of the exotic, the heartlessness and light-hearted gaiety – before they were swept away by revolution and the tramp of armies.

Arranged along the longer set of shelves were plates, vases, flagons and tureens. There were tea-caddies of polished redware by the 'inventor' of porcelain, Johannes Böttger. There were Böttger tankards with silver-gilt mounts; teapots with 'Watteau' scenes; teapots with eagle-headed spouts and teapots painted with goldfish, after Chinese and Japanese models.

Utz came up behind me, breathing heavily.

'Beautiful, no?'

'Beautiful,' I repeated.

He showed me an excellent example of 'indianische Blumen', and a turquoise bowl painted by Horoldt, with the panel of Augustus enthroned as The Emperor of China.

He showed me the Meissen imitations of K'ang Hsi blue-and-white: the porcelain his hero Augustus had loved so passionately; for which he had emptied his treasury to the dealers of Paris and Amsterdam, causing his Minister of Industry, Graf von Tschirnhaus, to moan, 'China is the bleeding-bowl of Saxony.'

Pride of place, however, was given to a Swan Service tureen: a Rococo fantasy on legs of intertwined fishes, the handles in the form of nereids, the lid heaped high with flowers, shells, swans and a bug-eyed dolphin – which, but for the bravura of its execution, would have been a monstrosity.

I gasped: knowing that the way to endear oneself to an art-collector is to rhapsodise his things.

'Come,' he beckoned me across the room.

I picked my way around the pelican and the rhino and arrived at the second bank of shelves where, in rows of five and six, were assembled a multitude of eighteenth-century figurines, all dazzlingly clothed and coloured.

I saw the characters of the Commedia dell' Arte: Harlequin and Columbine, Brighella and Pantaloon, Scaramouche and Truffaldino; The Doctor with a corkscrew for a beard; The Captain, who, being Spanish, had a jet-black moustache.

Utz reminded me how the Italian players – the real ones! – had been masters of extempore who would decide what to play, and how to play it, a mere five minutes before the curtain rose.

He pointed to the Personification of the Continents: Africa in leopard skin, America in feathers, Asia in a pagoda hat – while a lascivious, broad-bottomed Europa sat astride a white horse.

Next came the ladies of the Court: ladies with frozen smiles and swaying crinolines; their wigs were powdered, their cheeks pocked with beauty spots, and there were black bows tied around their necks. One lady caressed a pug. One kissed a Polish nobleman. Another kissed a Saxon while Harlequin peeped up her skirt. Madame de Pompadour, in a lilac dress scattered with roses, sang the aria from Lully's 'Acis and Galatea' which she had sung in real life, with the Prince de Rohan for a partner, in the Petit Théâtre de Versailles.

The lower orders were represented, each according to his or her occupation: the miner, the rope-maker, the woodcutter, the seamstress, the hairdresser and a fisherman, hopelessly drunk.

Shepherds trilled at their flutes. A Turk puffed a hookah. There were Tartars, Malabars, Circassians and Chinese sages with wispy beards and songbirds perched on their fingers. A party of freemasons scrutinised a globe. A pilgrim bore his staff and scallop-shell, and an endlessly grieving Mater Dolorosa sat next to a disconsolate nun.

'Bravo!' I cried. 'Unbelievable!'

'Now look at these funny fellows!' Utz was stroking the cheek of a grotesque buffoon. 'This one is Court Jester Fröhlich. That one is Postmaster Schmeidl.'

The two clowns used to perform at royal banquets, and keep everyone in stitches all night. Utz thought them as funny in porcelain as they were supposed to have been in real life. Schmeidl, he said, was terrified of mice.

This was why he chose to portray the Court Jester in the act of teasing his friend with a mouse-trap.

'Kaendler', he sniggered, 'was a witty man! A satirical man! He was always choosing persons to laugh at.'

I forced a nervous laugh.

'Now, Sir, if you please, look at this one!'

The model in question showed the soprano, Faustina Bordone, singing in ecstasy while a fox sat playing a spinet. Faustina, he said, had been the 'Callas of her day' and wife of the court composer, Hasse. She also had a lover called Fuchs.

'Fuchs,' said Utz, 'you must know in German means "fox".'

'I do know.'

'That is very amusing? No?'

'Very,' I laughed.

'Good. We agree on that one.'

He let fly an unexpectedly loud cackle, and went on shaking with laughter until Marta returned with her canapés and, with another 'Herr Baron!' silenced him.

The moment her back was turned he re-entered his world of little figures. His face lit up. He grinned, displaying a set of unhealthy pink gums, and showed me his monkey musicians.

'Lovely ones, aren't they?'

'Lovely,' I assented.

The monkeys wore ruffs and powdered wigs and, under the baton of a tyrannical conductor in a blue swallow-tailed coat, were fiddling and scraping, trumpeting, strumming and singing: in mockery of Count Brühl's private orchestra.

'I', Utz boasted, 'am the only private collector to possess the whole set.'

'Good for you!' I said, encouragingly.

Finally, we passed from the monkeys to the rest of the menagerie where there were wagtails, partridges, a bittern, a pair of sparrow-hawks, parrots and parakeets, orioles and roller birds, and peacocks displaying their tail feathers.

I counted a camel, a chamois, an elephant, a crocodile and a Lipizzaner led by a negro. Count Brühl's favourite pug-dog sat curled on a rose-velvet cushion while, on the bottom shelf, like a large albino fish, lay the life-size horse's tail in white porcelain intended – or so Utz said – for an equestrian statue of Augustus to be erected at the Judenhof in Dresden.

He then removed one of his seven figures of Harlequin – the Harlequin his grandmother gave him as a boy – and, turning it upside down, pointed to the 'cross-swords' mark of Meissen, and to an inventory label with a number and letters in code.

This was the label that earmarked the piece for the Museum.

'But those persons', Utz whispered, 'have made a mistake.'

One morning in February of 1952, a rap on the door demanded entry for three unwelcome visitors. They were a curator from the Museum; a photographer and an acne-pitted lout who, as Utz guessed, was a member of the secret police.

For the next two weeks he was a helpless witness while this trio turned the apartment upside down, trampled slush into the carpet, and made an inventory of every object. The curator warned him not to tamper with the labels. If he did so, the collection would be forfeit.

Utz particularly loathed the photographer: a grim, fanatical young woman with an astigmatism, who had worked herself into a fever of indignation. In her view, he had no business keeping treasures that rightfully belonged to the People.

'Really?' he answered. 'By what right? The right of theft, I suppose?'

The policeman told him to hold his tongue – or it would be worse for him.

The photographer converted the room into a makeshift studio, fussing over her plate-camera as though it were a thing beyond price. When Utz accidentally brushed against the lens, she ordered him into the bedroom.

She may have been a competent photographer: but she was so short-sighted, and so clumsy when handling the porcelains that Utz had to sit on the edge of his bed, numbly waiting for the crash. He begged to be allowed to position each piece in front of the camera. He was told it was none of his business.

Finally, when the young woman dropped, and smashed the head off, a figure of Watteau's Gilles, he lost his temper.

'Take it!' he snapped. 'Take it for your horrible museum! I never want to see it again.'

The photographer shrugged. The policeman wobbled his jowls. The curator went into the bathroom and, returning with a length of lavatory paper, wrapped the head and the torso separately, and put them in his pocket.

'This piece', he said, 'will not appear in the inventory.'

'Thank you,' said Utz. 'Thank you for that!'

At last, when they had gone, he gazed miserably at his miniature family. He felt abused and assaulted. He felt like the man who, on returning from a journey, finds his house has been burgled. He summoned up a few vague thoughts of suicide. There wasn't much – was there? – to live for. But no! He wasn't the type. He would never work up the courage. But could he bring himself to leave the collection? Make a clean break? Begin a new life abroad? He still had money in Switzerland, thank God! Who could tell? In Paris or in New York, he might even begin to collect again.

He decided, if he could get out, to go.

During the Gottwald years, the most reliable method of obtaining an exit visa was to apply for foreign travel on the grounds of ill-health. The procedure was to go to your usual physician, and ask him to diagnose an ailment.

'Do you suffer from depression?' Dr Petrasels demanded.

'Constantly,' said Utz. 'I always have.'

'Doubtless a malfunctioning of the liver,' said the doctor, who made no effort to examine him further. 'I advise you to take the cure at Vichy.'

'But surely . . . ?' Utz protested. Czechoslovakia was the land of spas. Surely they'd be suspicious? Surely there were waters for the liver at Marienbad? Or at Carlsbad?

'Far from it,' the doctor assured him. The visa authorities knew all about the waters of Vichy. Vichy was the place for him.

'If you say so,' said Utz, with misgivings.

The official in the visa department glanced at the medical report; mumbled the word 'Vichy' in a disinterested tone, and went to consult the file. A week later, when he returned to the same office, Utz learned he had been given a month's stay abroad. He undertook not to spread malicious propaganda against the People's Republic. The porcelain collection would be considered surety for his good behaviour, and his safe return.

The man insinuated that they had 'ways and means' of finding out where he went in Western Europe, and if he actually turned up at Vichy. Utz was astonished that no one bothered to ask how he would support himself in a foreign country. Was this, he wondered, a trap?

'What can they expect of me?' he asked himself. 'Subsist on air?'

On the eve of his departure, his tickets and passport in order, he took leave of the collection piece by piece. Marta was cooking in the kitchenette. He had ordered dinner for two.

She had spread a fresh damask cloth over the glass-topped table; and as he surveyed the sparkling Swan Service plates, the salt-cellar, the cutlery with chinoiserie handles – he came close to believing in his fantasy: that this *was* the 'porcelain palace', and that he himself was Augustus reincarnate.

Marta, whom he had taught to make a soufflé, asked what time the guest would arrive. He stood up. He straightened his tie. Then, without a hint of condescension, he pressed her calloused hand to his lips.

'This evening, my dear Marta, you are to be the guest.'

She coloured at the neck. She protested. She said she was unworthy, and in the end accepted with delight.

Marta was the child of a village carpenter who lived near Kostelec in Southern Bohemia. His wife's early death, from tuberculosis, drove him to drink, and in a tavern brawl he almost killed a man. Ostracised, accused of the evil eye, he sent his two elder daughters to live with an aunt, and took the youngest along on his travels. He found work as a woodcutter on Utz's estate at Čéske Krížove. When he also died, crushed by a falling tree, the bailiff evicted the girl from their cottage.

She earned a few pennies doing chores for the baker or laundrywoman. Later, to avoid being sent to a workhouse, she went to live on a farm, where she slept on a straw-filled pallet and looked after a flock of geese.

She sang strange, incoherent songs and was thought to be simple: especially when she fell in love with a gander. Children in peasant Europe believed the tales they were told: of werewolves, of stars that were ducks in flight, or the gander who turned into a shining prince.

Marta's gander was a magnificent snow-white bird: the object of terror to foxes, children and dogs. She had reared him as a gosling; and whenever she approached, he would let fly a low contented burble and sidle his neck around her thighs. Some mornings, at first light when no one was about, she would swim with her lover in the lake, and allow him to nibble her long fair hair.

One morning, sometime in the late Thirties, as Utz was driving his Steyr coupé from the castle to catch the early train to Prague, he caught sight of a girl in dripping clothes being hounded down the street by a mob of villagers. He braked the car, and asked her to sit beside him.

'Come with me,' he said kindly.

She cringed, but obeyed. He drove her back to the castle.

A new life opened up for her, in domestic service. She followed her master's movements with an adoring gaze: frequently he had to prevent her from kissing his hand. Four years later, when he had put her in charge of the household, his other retainers, puzzled by the habits of this solitary bachelor, spread rumours that she shared his bed.

The truth was that, in a world of shifting allegiances – and since the death of his grandmother's faithful major-domo – she was the only person he could trust, and, at the same time, use. Only she knew the hay-loft where the Hebrew scholar Dr Kraus – and his Talmuds – was in hiding: she would risk her life to fetch him food. Only she had the key to the cellar where, throughout the War, the porcelains were stored.

Later, in the months after the Communist takeover, when the peasants, still bemused by propaganda, believed that the new ideology allowed them to divide the landlord's property, it was she who stood guard against them. Utz was free to leave the castle with his treasures.

In Prague, she slept in a leaky attic room a few doors down Široká Street. When interrogated about the terms of her employment, she bridled. She was not Mr Utz's employee. She looked after him merely as a friend.

He, by inviting her to share his table, affirmed that the friendship was shared.

Over dinner, he explained the reason for his journey. She dropped her knife and fork, and gasped, 'You're not ill, I hope.'

He calmed her fears, but gave no hint that he might never come back. She should sleep, meanwhile, in the apartment – in his bed if she wished it – and keep the door firmly locked. His friend, Dr Orlík, would look in from time to time, in case there was anything she needed.

The wine went to her head. She became a little flushed. She talked a little too much. For her, it was an evening of perfect happiness.

At breakfast, she came back to make coffee. She helped Utz with his suitcase to the taxi. Then she climbed upstairs, and listened to the beating of the rain.

The customs men were expecting him at the frontier. They frisked him, removed the small change from his pockets and, as experts in the art of irritation, appropriated Marta's picnic. Then, finding nothing in his luggage that could be classed as a work of art, they took his copy of 'The Magic Mountain' and a pair of tortoiseshell hairbrushes.

'I suppose,' he muttered as the green caps moved along the corridor, 'they need those for the Museum also.'

After Nuremberg, the rainclouds lifted and the sun came out. He had nothing now to read and so stared from the window at the telegraph wires, the tarred wood gables of the farmhouses, the orchards, the cows in fields of buttercups, and parties of blond-haired children who clung to the barriers of level-crossings and waved their satchels.

The signal-boxes, he noticed, were pitted with bullet-holes. Across the compartment sat a young married couple.

The girl was turning the leaves of an album of wedding-photos. She was pregnant. She wore a grey smock trimmed with lace. Her bluish legs were unshaven, and her dyed hair dark at the roots.

The boy, Utz was glad to see, was disgusted by her. He

looked very ill-at-ease in his American leather flying-jacket, and shuddered whenever she touched him. He was a swarthy, skinny boy with pouting lips and a head of black curls. His nails were stained with nicotine, and he chain-smoked desperately. Was he an Arab, or something? Or a gipsy? Or Italian? Italian, Utz decided, after hearing him speak. She must have had money, and he had been starving. But what a price to pay!

She began to unpack her hamper and Utz began to have second thoughts. He was ravenous. Had he, perhaps, misjudged her? Perhaps she would offer him a share?

He prepared a grateful smile for when the time came. Then, like a dog at the master's table, he watched her swallow a couple of hard-boiled eggs, a schnitzel, a ham sandwich, half a cold chicken and some rounds of garlic sausage. She swilled these down with a bottle of beer, smacked her lips and continued, absent-mindedly, to stuff slices of pumpernickel between them.

The boy hardly touched his food.

Utz could stand the strain no longer. He had come to a decision. He would ask. He would beg. He opened his mouth to say 'Please' – at which the young man tore off a chicken leg and was in the act of handing it across when the girl, shouting 'No! No! No!', slapped him back, and went on peeling an orange.

The smell of orange rind filled the compartment. Ach! What wouldn't he give for an orange! Even a segment of orange! The oranges one got in Prague, scavenged or stolen from one or other of the embassies, were usually shrivelled and tasteless. But this orange dripped its juice over the monster's fingers.

Utz leaned his head against the leathercloth head-rest and, closing his eyes, remembered Augustus's aphorism: 'The craving for porcelain is like a craving for oranges.'

The girl called for a napkin, and wiped her fingers. A second orange went the way of the first: then a slice of cheese, a slice of Linzetorte, a Nusstorte, a plum cake. Then she poured herself a coffee from a thermos flask.

She belched. She pestered her husband for a show of affection. He whispered in her ear. Again, Utz summoned an ingratiating smile. But, instead of offering him the last ham sandwich, she fixed him with a glutted stare and, lurching to her feet, chucked it from the window.

Utz watched this little drama draw to its inevitable close and mumbled, in German, loud enough for her to hear:

'It could never have happened in Czechoslovakia.'

At Geneva next morning the man from the bank was waiting on the platform: a rendezvous arranged by the Swiss ambassador in Prague, who, in those days, was 'everyone's friend'.

Utz followed the man's preposterous Tyrolean hat to the lavatory, where he took delivery of a thick manilla envelope containing a wad of Swiss francs, and facsimiles of his share certificates.

He had two hours to kill before the train left for Lyon – and Vichy. He couldn't think of anywhere else to go. He checked his bag at the consigne, and went for breakfast at a café opposite the station. But the coffee was weak, the croissants stale, and the cherry jam tasted of chemical preservative.

He glanced at the other tables. The room was crowded with businessmen on their way to work, burying their faces in the financial columns of the newspapers.

'No,' he told himself. 'I am not enjoying this.'

At Vichy the hotel had been redecorated, as if to wipe away the stain of having harboured the Laval administration in its rooms. Utz's own room was furnished with reproduction Louis Seize furniture, painted grey. The carpet was blue, and the walls were baby blue with white trim: the décor of the nursery, of the fresh start. On a commode stood a chipped plaster bust of Marie Antoinette, and there were modern engravings: of other bird-brained eighteenth-century ladies.

'No, no,' Utz repeated. 'I am certainly not enjoying this. The French have lost their taste.'

Nor did he enjoy his meetings with Dr Forestier, a man with papery skin and a mouth full of snobbish indiscretions, who had his consulting room in a Gothic house shrouded by paulownias. Nor the immense cream stucco buildings – 'style pâtissier 1900' – stretched out along the Boulevard des États-Unis where the Gestapo had had its headquarters. Nor the mud baths, the frictions, the facials, the pressure-showers. Nor – judging from the drawn, dyspeptic faces of other sufferers – were these celebrated waters in the least beneficial to the health.

He could take no pleasure from the company of the small,

aged people – 'ex-colons' whose digestion had been wrecked in Africa or Indo-China – clinging to their raffia-covered 'gobletes de cure' and taking slow, careful steps, out of the rain, under the covered walkway that runs beside the Rue du Parc.

He did not appreciate the gerontophile glint of the masseur – 'a very disturbed young man!' – and hoped that perhaps he was too young. Nor did he care for the ladies of the Grand Établissement Thermal: disciplinarian ladies in white coats and gloves who introduced him to the use of 'les instruments de torture' – remedial machines that Kafka *would* have appreciated – so that he found himself being strapped to a saddle and pummelled, gently but firmly in the intestines, with a pair of leather boxing-gloves.

He winced at the sound of English voices. He averted his eyes from the 'mutilés de guerre': men missing an arm or both legs but playing poker, none the less, on white-painted chairs with perforated seats like cullenders. One evening, after dinner, he had to flee from a lady in tourmaline velvet who spoke, in German, of the Aga Khan.

He became abnormally sensitive to people's stares, especially those of solitary men, who, he imagined, were tailing him.

Who, for example, was that youth in the ill-fitting suit? Hadn't he seen him in Prague? Hanging around the foyer of the Hotel Alkron? No. He had not. The youth was a salesman of sanitary equipment.

Utz pottered round the antique shops and found nothing of interest: a few soapstone Buddhas and dubious Empire clocks. A woman tried to sell him Egyptian amulets, and a pack of tarot cards. At a shop that sold lace, he thought of buying a pinafore to take home to Marta.

'But I won't be going home,' he reflected dismally.

'And anyway they'd steal it at the customs.'

He went to the races, and was bored. He was bored at a concert where they played the 'Suite from Finlandia'. He was desperately bored by the 'Spectacle' at the Grand Théâtre du Casino, which began with 'Les Plus Belles Girls de Paris' – all of them English! – and continued with 'Les Hommes en Crystal' – who were a bunch of fairies smeared with silver paint!

In the interval, he reflected on the absurdity of his position. Here he was, another middle-aged, Middle European refugee adrift in an unfriendly world! And worse, the most useless of refugees, an aesthete!

After the interval, he had a change of mood.

The curtain rose on Lucienne Boyer, 'La Dame en Bleu': a compact and rounded woman, approaching fifty yet apparently ageless and wearing a dress of dark blue satin, and a blue rose at the apex of her décolleté. She sang number after number at the microphone. Utz's pupils dilated as he gazed, through opera glasses, at her quivering throat. And when she sang 'Parlez-moi d'amour', he got to his feet and shouted 'Bravo! Bravo! Encore!' – and she gave an encore, four of them. And afterwards, after he had watched her leave the theatre with a younger man, he walked home to the Pavillon Sévigné, over cobbled streets slippery with leaves after a hailstorm, his bald head gleaming in the lamplight, swaying slightly and humming the refrain, 'Je vous aime . . . Je vous aime . . .'

Utz had an idea, derived from Russian novels or his parents' love affair at Marienbad, that a spa-town was a place where the unexpected invariably happened.

Two lonely people, brought thither by the accidents of ill-health or unhappiness, would cross paths on their afternoon walk. Their eyes would meet over a bed of municipal marigolds. Drawn by the natural attraction of opposites, they would sit on the same cast-iron seat, and exchange the first stilted sentences. ('Do you come to Vichy often?' 'No. It's my first visit.' 'And mine!') A rapturous evening would end in one or other of their rooms. Either the affair would end in a sad farewell ('No, my dearest, I beg you. Don't come to the station'). Or, when parting seemed inevitable, they would take the drastic decision that would bind them for the rest of their lives.

Utz had come to Vichy with the romantic notion: that, if the decision had to be taken, he would take it.

He hoped . . . he was sure to find among this crowd of solitaries a tender, middle-aged, preferably vulnerable woman who would love him, not for his looks . . . That, alas, was not possible! . . . He had always been ugly, but he did have other qualities.

There had been occasions in the past when a woman had set her sights on him. On each occasion, when intimacy seemed possible, she had uttered the fatal words, 'Oh, you must see his treasures!' – and a cold draught had killed his affection.

No. Anything was better than to be loved for one's things.

But where was she, this elusive female who would fall into his arms? 'Fall' – that was the operative word! Fall, without having to pursue her. He was tired of pursuing precious objects.

Was she the steel-haired American, widowed or divorced he decided, obviously at Vichy for beauty treatment? Intelligent, of course, but not sympathetic. He mistrusted the acerbic tone with which she ordered her Manhattans from the barman.

Or the soft-voiced creature, Parisian without a doubt, with golden hair and a melting mouth? He saw her first among the morning crowd at the Source des Célestins, moving along the white trellis in a dress of white lace and a hat composed of layers of stiffened chiffon. She had been delicious and would soon be plump. No. Not her. She spent hours in idle chatter in the phone-booth, and came away with a lost look, laughing.

Or the Argentine? 'Grande manguese de viande' – or so the waiter said. Utz had stood behind her baccarat table at the Casino, mesmerised by her scarlet talons; by the carefree gestures with which she manoeuvred her chips over the green baize; by the vein in her neck that bulged over her collar of pearls. Not her either! She was joined by her husband.

And then he saw her, one afternoon, in the lobby: a tall, white-limbed woman in tennis whites, her dark hair plaited in a coif, slipping a cover over her racquet and thanking, in a tone of firm finality, the over-eager pro for his lesson.

Utz heard her conversing in French, although he thought – or was he imagining this? – that he detected a Slavic resonance in her accent. She was not the athletic type: there was an oriental torpor in her movements. She might have been Turkish, this 'femme en forme de violon' with her apple-blossom cheeks, her dimples, her quivering forelip and slanting green eyes. She wasn't beautiful by modern standards: the kind of woman they once bred for the seraglio.

'But she has to be Russian,' he reflected. 'Russian, certainly. With a touch of Tartar?'

She was no longer young, and she seemed very sad.

He spent the rest of the afternoon in a state of feverish excitement, waiting for her to re-emerge from the lift, and attempting to compose a history for her. He imagined the downward spiral of émigré life: the rented apartment in Monaco; later, when the jewels ran out, the lodgings in Paris where her father drove a taxi and played chess after hours. To pay for his medical bills, she had sacrificed herself to the businessman who kept her in a certain style, but also kept a younger mistress. He had taken the mistress to the Riviera and sent his wife, who was childless, to Vichy.

She came downstairs before dinner, still alone, wearing a spotted grey dress and white open-toed shoes. And when Utz saw her little dog, a Sealyham, trailing at her heels, he called to mind the lady in the Chekhov tale and felt for certain the meeting must happen.

He followed her at a distance into the park beside the Allier, stationing himself on a bench which she was almost sure to pass, inhaling the odour of lilac and philadelphus.

'Viens, Maxi! Viens! Viens!' – he heard her calling the dog; and when she came to a choice of forking paths, she chose the path that led towards him.

'Bonsoir, Madame!' Utz smiled, and was about to call 'Maxi!' to the dog. The woman gave a start, and quickened her pace.

He continued to sit, miserably listening to the crunch of her footfalls on the gravel. At dinner, she passed his table and looked the other way.

He saw her again in the morning, in the passenger seat of a silver sports car, her arms around the neck of the man at the wheel.

He asked the concierge who she was and was told she was Belgian.

He turned his attention to food.

On his first day at Vichy he had bought, from a bookshop in the Rue Clemenceau, a 'gastronomic guide' to the region. He had always cared for his stomach, always befriended chefs.

How often, in the war years, especially in moments of terror, did he recollect the pleasures of the table! The day the Gestapo took him for questioning, he had been unable to focus on the abstractions of death or deportation: only on the memory of a particular plate of haricots verts, at a restaurant by a white road in Provence.

Later, during the worst of the winter shortages, the months of cabbage, cabbage, cabbage and potatoes, he comforted himself with the thought that, when sanity returned and the frontiers were open, he would eat once again in France.

He studied the guide with the fastidious dedication he usually reserved for porcelain-hunting: where to find the best 'quenelles aux écrevisses', the best 'cervelas trufflé' or a 'poulet à la vessie'. Or the desserts – the 'bourriouls', 'bougnettes', 'flaugnardes', 'fouasses'. (One could hear the gas in those names!) Or the rare white wine of Château

Grillet, which was said to taste of vine flowers and almonds –
and behave like a capricious young woman.

Putting his new-found knowledge to the test, he reserved
a table at a restaurant beside the Allier.

The day was warm and sunny: sufficiently warm to eat
outside on the terrace, under an awning of green-and-white
striped canvas that flapped lazily in the breeze. There were
three wine glasses set at each place. He watched the reflections
of the poplars z-bending across the river, and the sand-
martins skimming over its surface. On the far bank, fishermen
and their families had spread their picnics on the grass.

The waiters were fussing over a 'prince of gastronomes'
who was paying his annual visit. He had come in after Utz,
flushed crimson in the face and perambulating his stomach
before him. He tucked his napkin inside his collar, and
prepared to plough through an eight-course luncheon.

At last, when the menu came, Utz gave a grateful smile to
the maître d'hôtel.

He ran his eye over the list of specialities. He chose. He
changed his mind. He chose again: an artichoke soup, trout
'Mont Doré' and sucking-pig 'à la lyonnaise'.

'Et comme vin, monsieur?'

'What would you suggest?'

The wine-waiter, taking Utz for an ignoramus, pointed to
two of the more expensive bottles on the list: a Montrachet
and a Clos Margeot.

'No Château Grillet?'

'Non, monsieur.'

'Very well,' Utz acquiesced obediently. 'Whatever you
recommend.'

The meal failed to match his expectations. Not that he

could fault its quality or presentation: but the soup, although exquisite, seemed savourless; the trout was smothered in a sauce of Gruyère cheese, and the sucking-pig was stuffed with something else.

He looked again, enviously, at the picnickers on the opposite shore. A young mother rushed to save her child, who had crawled to the water's edge. He would like to be with them: to share their coarse, home-made pies that surely tasted of something! Or had he lost his own sense of taste?

The bill was larger than he expected. He left in a bad mood. He felt bloated, and a little dizzy.

He had also come to a depressing conclusion: that luxury is only luxurious under adverse conditions.

In the afternoon the clouds came up and it began to rain. He lay down in his room and read some pages of a novel by Gide. His French was inadequate: he lost the thread of the narrative.

He put the book aside, and stared vacantly at the chandelier.

Why, he asked himself, when he had steeled himself to the horrors of war and revolution, should the free world present so frightening an abyss? Why, each time he sank onto the mattress, did he have the sensation of falling, like the elevator, through the floors of the hotel? In Prague he slept soundly. Why did sleep elude him here?

He would lie awake and fret over his finances. In Czechoslovakia he had no finances to speak of: or none that he could lay his hands on. Now, at two and three in the morning, he would spread his share certificates over the bedspread and tot up the figures of his portfolio, searching for a flaw, a mistake; trying to explain why, in a rising stock-market, his fortune in Switzerland had shrunk. Why, with enormous sums invested, were the sums on paper so small? Someone, somewhere was cheating him. Taking advantage while his back was turned! But who? And how?

From the same bookshop he had bought a pocket atlas of the world; and, leafing through its pages, he tried to imagine the country he would like to live in. Or rather, the country that would make him least unhappy.

Switzerland? Italy? France? Three possibilities. None of them inviting. Germany? Never. The break had been final. England? Not after the Dresden raid. The United States? Impossible. The noise would depress him dreadfully. Prague, after all, was a city where you heard the snowflakes falling. Australia? He had never been attracted by the colonies. Argentina? He was too old to tango.

The more he considered the alternatives, the clearer the solution seemed to him. Not that he would be happy in Czechoslovakia. He would be harassed, menaced, insulted. He would have to grovel. He would have to agree with every word they said. He would mouth their meaningless, ungrammatical formulae. He would learn to 'live within the lie'.

But Prague was a city that suited his melancholic temperament. A state of tranquil melancholy was all one could aspire to these days! And for the first time, grudgingly, he felt he could admire his Czech compatriots: not for their decision to vote in a Marxist government . . . Any fool knew by now that Marxism was a winded philosophy! He admired the abstemiousness of their choice.

He continued to stare at the idiotic chandelier, turning over in his mind the most troublesome question of all.

He was desperately homesick, yet hadn't given a thought for the porcelains. He could only think of Marta, alone, in the apartment.

He felt remorse for having left her: the poor darling who adored him; who would lay down her life for him; her passionate heart that beat for him, and him only, concealed under a mask of reserve, of duty and obedience.

He had thought of taking her to the West. But she spoke no language other than Czech, and a few words of German. No. She'd be . . . he groped for the appropriate cliché . . . she'd be a fish out of water.

He remembered the times when, breathless from climbing the stairs, the snowflakes twinkling on her fox fur hat, she would return from a successful deal on the black market. Her capacity for bargaining was prodigious, even with a single dollar bill.

She would stand for hours in a food queue: nothing mattered if the object of her quest would bring him pleasure.

Some days, she filled her shopping-bags with muddy potatoes. No one knew better that the type of policeman who would pry among her purchases was the type to mind muddying his hands. And afterwards, when she had dumped the potatoes in the sink, she would pull from the bottom of the bag a pheasant or a hare that someone had brought in from the country.

Her contacts with the countryside functioned like the bush-telegraph.

'Where did you get those eggs?' he'd ask, as she rushed a golden soufflé to the table.

'A woman brought them,' she would answer vaguely.

She understood, by instinct, why he insisted on the details: the sauce in a sauceboat; the starching of shirt-cuffs; the Sèvres coffee cups on Sunday – for a coffee composed of roasted barley and chicory! – the minor acts of style to demonstrate that he had not given in.

He recognised her attentions as the tokens of her love. He could not bring himself to thank her: nor would she have wanted this.

Their happiest time together was the mushroom season, towards the end of August, after the first late summer cloudbursts. They would catch the early morning train to Tábor; the bus to Čéske Krížove ; and from there, taking care to avoid the big house, take their picnic into the woods.

Mushrooms, he said, were the only reason for revisiting the scenes of his childhood.

He and Marta were like children at play, oblivious of caste or class, as they called to one another through the pine trunks: 'Look what I've found . . . ! Look what I've found . . . !' – a russet-cowled boletus, an edible agaric, or a cluster of chanterelles pushing their orange caps above a carpet of moss.

No one but they and a few woodcutters knew the clearing where, as master of the estate, he had sawn himself a rustic table and seat: from the timbers of a beech tree that had been split by lightning.

They would spread their finds on the table, gills uppermost, discarding those which were spongy or grub-ridden, cleaning off the larger lumps of earth yet leaving the odd pine-needle or a scrap of fern frond.

'Don't clean them too much,' she would scold him. 'A bit of dirt makes them taste much better.'

Then she fried them in butter over a spirit stove, and stirred in a dollop of cream.

One day, on their way back to Prague, they stopped in the town square at Tábor where local mushroom fanciers had set up stalls, under awnings of sackcloth to prevent the sun from shrivelling their treasures.

A hubbub of cheerful voices greeted him. A peasant woman, a white headscarf wrapped low over her weather-beaten face, stood up and cried, 'Look! It's the master come back!' He watched his old doctor, a mushroom fanatic, bartering furiously with a professional mycologist from the university over some very rare specimen. And there was Marianna Palach! – the laundry-woman, wizened to a husk now, who none the less went mushrooming, and had set up shop.

Everyone in the market was laughing, haggling, giving, taking, proving beyond all doubt, whatever the zealots had to say, that the business of trade was one of life's most natural and enjoyable pleasures, no more to be abolished than the act of falling in love . . .

'What am I doing here?' Utz roused himself from his daydream.

He looked at his wristwatch. He was late for dinner. He knotted his tie in front of the bathroom mirror. He trimmed his moustache. (I still cannot be certain if I'm imagining a moustache.) He examined his stubborn little mouth, and said, 'No!'

He was not going to join the flow of exiles. He would not sit complaining in rented rooms. He knew that anti-Communist rhetoric was as deadly as its Communist counterpart. He would not give up his country. Not for them!

He would go back. But he knew that, once he got back, the porcelains would re-exert the power of snobbery. The ladies of the Dresden court could turn their vitreous smiles on Marta, dismissing her to the kitchenette – where she would sit, patiently, in her shabby maid's uniform and black stockings with holes at the knee.

He went down to dinner in the restaurant. At a table nearby, a pair of married couples were engaged in a merciless argument over the merits or otherwise of an 'Alaska', an 'Île flottante' or an 'Omelette norvégienne'. The women had rasping voices. The men were fat and wore rings.

Their menu seemed to consist entirely of desserts: a Mont Blanc, profiteroles, a fruit salad, a tarte Tatin, a raspberry ice with chantilly, a chocolate cake with more chantilly . . .

'This is disgusting,' Utz muttered. 'No. It is impossible I should stay here.'

He rose from the table and told the receptionist he would be leaving on the morning train.

It depressed him, on crossing the Czech frontier, to see the lines of barbed wire and sentry-boxes. But he noted, with a certain relief, that there were no more advertising billboards.

Utz was one of those rare individuals who, throughout the Cold War, persisted in the illusion that the Iron Curtain was essentially flimsy. Because of his investments in the West – and powers of persuasion that mystified both himself and the bureaucrats of Prague – he succeeded in keeping a foot in both camps.

Year after year, he made the ritual pilgrimage to Vichy. By the end of April, his resentment against the regime rose to boiling-point: for its incompetence, nothing more – he considered it common to complain of collectivisation. By April, too, he felt acute claustrophobia, from having spent the winter months in close proximity to the adoring Marta: to say nothing of the boredom, verging on fury, that came from living those months with lifeless porcelain.

Before leaving, he would make a resolution never, ever to return – while at the same time making arrangements for his return – and would set off for Switzerland in the best of spirits.

The journey was always the same: to Geneva, for meetings with his bankers and an antiquaire: on to Vichy, and to Vichy only, to taste the waters, to breathe the fresh air of freedom that rapidly went stale, and order more expensive meals which would disgust him.

He would then bolt for home like a man pursued by demons.

One year, he went to Paris for the week-end: but that completely upset his equilibrium.

These arrangements suited no one except himself. For Marta, his absence was a time of torment, almost of mourning. For the officials who issued his exit visa – men who seriously believed that so incurable a decadent belonged in Vichy, America or some such corrupted place, and who prided themselves on their leniency in letting him go – his return was the act of a madman.

It was equally puzzling to a succession of consuls in the French and Swiss embassies. Accustomed, as they were, to think of Czechoslovakia as a country from which people of Utz's standing fled, in an east-westerly direction, the idea that any normal person might prefer home to exile seemed excessively perverse: an act of ingratitude. Or was there some sinister motive? Was M. Utz a spy?

No. He was not a spy. As he explained to me in the course of our afternoon stroll, Czechoslovakia was a pleasant place to live, providing one had the possibility of leaving. At the same time he admitted, with a self-deprecating smile, that his severe case of Porzellankrankheit prevented him from leaving for good. The collection held him prisoner.

· 'And, of course, it has ruined my life!'

In an unguarded moment he also confessed to a secret cache of Meissen, stored in a numbered safe deposit, in the Union de Banques Suisses in Geneva.

Whenever his share prices rose above a certain level, he siphoned off a sum of money to pay for yet another object: the calculation being that if, over the years, the cache in Geneva approached the quality, not necessarily the quantity, of the collection in Prague, he might once again be tempted to emigrate.

One year – I believe it was 1963 – the New York dealer, Dr Marius Frankfurter, made a special trip to Vichy to offer Utz a piece of porcelain that was quite outside his usual range: a model known as 'The Spaghetti Eater', made not at Meissen, but at the CapodiMonte factory in Naples.

In the same baby blue bedroom, Dr Frankfurter unwrapped the object from its multiple layers of tissue paper and set it on the commode, with the reverence of a priest exhibiting the Host. Utz could hardly help comparing its pearly glaze with the warted epidermis of the dealer. But that was life! The ugliest men loved the most beautiful things.

'So?' said Dr Frankfurter.

'So,' Utz pursed his lips.

The object was adorable. He was not going to say so.

A figure of Pulchinella – the 'Charlie Chaplin' of the Italian Comedy – sat lounging in a kind of invalid chair, wearing a collarette of green lace over a loose linen shirt, and a conical white hat like that of a dancing dervish. At his side, a Neapolitan lad, in a scarlet cap and purple breeches, was feeding him from a chamber pot.

Utz was particularly taken with the coils of spaghetti, poised either to plunge into Pulchinella's mouth – or into one of his cavernous nostrils.

But the price! Even Dr Frankfurter seemed in awe of the price, and could only bring himself to mention it in a whisper.

'Well,' said Utz, after recovering from the initial shock. 'I've never bought a piece of Italian porcelain in my life. How would I know it was genuine?'

'Tschenuin?' Dr Frankfurter spluttered.

Of course it was genuine! And Utz, of course, knew it was genuine. He was simply playing for time.

But the Doctor was aggrieved. He threatened to re-wrap the piece in its tissue: only to relent and reel off a tremendous pedigree of the noble Italian families to whom it had belonged – names that meant no more to Utz than a list of railway stations from Ventimiglia to Bari – until, in a crescendo of name-dropping, he arrived at Queen Maria Amalia herself.

'Oh?' said Utz. 'It belonged to her, did it?'

For he knew – and Dr Frankfurter knew he knew – that, before becoming Queen of Naples, this plain and pox-pitted woman had been a Princess of Saxony, and was the granddaughter of Augustus the Strong.

It was she who, in 1739, had founded the Naples factory, hardly a stone's throw from the Palace, as a project to divert her Germanic energies into something useful.

Utz made his mind up. 'The Spaghetti Eater' would have to be bought: if only to rescue it from Dr Frankfurter's sweaty hands. But he would not give in without a fight!

The Doctor – Doctor in what was a mystery – took the line that he was offering the object as a mark of special friendship. He showed Utz a book in which it was illustrated; a chemical analysis of the paste, and a bill from an auction sale in 1949.

'And the price is a "prix d'ami",' he said, not once but repeatedly. He could sell it in America ten times over. For twice the amount!

His tactic was to pooh-pooh the productions of the Naples factory. The object, he insisted, was not really in his line – although he would like it in the collection 'for the purpose of comparative study'.

The day was overcast and drizzly. He looked from the window at the trees of the Parc de l'Allier. He had counted on being able to knock a third off the price. Dr Frankfurter was obstinate as a mule.

Five times, the dealer stalked off down the corridor with the box under his arm. Five times Utz called him back. Once, they got as far as the lobby, where the other guests were astonished to see two middle-aged gentlemen jabbering in German at the tops of their voices.

Eventually, they struck a deal: out of sheer exhaustion!

There followed a hasty packing of suitcases and a train journey to Geneva – where Utz had promised to withdraw the sum in cash. Neither spoke. Dr Frankfurter was congealed with anxiety that Utz might wriggle out of the bargain. Utz was sunk in gloom that he hadn't gone on bargaining further.

They shook hands, frostily, on the steps of the Union de Banques Suisses.

'So, till next year!' said Dr Frankfurter

'Till next year!' Utz nodded, and turned his back on the taxi.

He returned to the bank, to examine his purchase alone.

He entered the familiar underground corridor where the lines of stainless-steel deposit boxes seemed to stretch away, like railway lines, to vanishing point. Who knew what treasures they contained? Enough to fill a museum, he chuckled. With a lot of expensive junk!

At intervals along the corridor there were tables, lit with anglepoise lamps, where customers could gloat over their possessions. A woman in a red wig sat fingering an emerald bracelet. Beyond her, a Lebanese dealer in antiquities was protesting the authenticity of a corroded bronze animal. His client, an excitable young man in spectacles, denounced it as a fake.

Utz heard the young man say 'Archifaux!' – and trembled.

Perhaps Dr Frankfurter had also sold him a fake? His fingers tore at the tissue-paper. He scrutinised the object with a pocket-magnifying glass – and breathed again.

'Out of the question! It has to be genuine!'

The spaghetti was a marvel. Pulchinella's nose was a marvel. The enamels surpassed in subtlety the colours of Meissen. He had done the right thing. It was cheap. Cheap, when one thought of it. Besides, he adored it! And when the time came to return it to its stainless-steel coffin, he hesitated.

'No,' he told himself. 'I cannot leave it here.'

Thus, when others were bent on smuggling out of Czechoslovakia, in diplomatic bags or a foreign friend's suitcase, any article of value they could lay their hands on – a snuff-box, an ancestral decoration, or a vermeil dessert service, fork by fork – Utz embarked on the opposite course.

'I smuggled it in,' he whispered.

He was standing in the middle of the room, roughly equidistant from the lynx and the turkey-cock. I rose to join him, almost barking my shin on the corner of the Mies van der Rohe table. 'The Spaghetti Eater' stood on the central shelf, to the right of Madame de Pompadour.

'Marta,' Utz called.

The maid came in with a fresh plate of canapés: but the moment she took stock of our position, she withdrew to the kitchenette and, reaching for a couple of aluminium saucepans, began to bang them together like cymbals.

'They cannot hear us now,' he said, standing on tiptoe. He had put his mouth to my ear.

'Are they listening?'

'All the time!' he sniggered. 'There is a microphone in this wall. One in that wall. Another in the ceiling, and I know not where else. They listen, listen, listen to everything. But this everything is too much for them. So they *hear* nothing!'

The saucepans clattered like the noise of a pneumatic drill. From under our feet there was another noise, of a stick or broom-handle being thumped against the ceiling of the apartment below, presumably by the furious soprano.

'Some days,' he continued, 'they call me and say "Utz, what are you doing over there? Breaking porcelains?" "No," I say. "That is Marta cooking supper." One of them, I have to say it, is a very humorous person. We are friends.'

'Friends?'

'Telephone friends. We now learn to like each other. That is correct, no?'

'If you say so.'

'So I say it.'

'Good.'

'Good,' he repeated. 'Now I will ask you questions.'

Bang! . . Bang! . . Bang! . . . Bang! . . . Bang! . . . Bang! . . .

'How much would cost today a Kaendler harlequin in auction sale in London?'

'I've no idea,' I said.

'Really?' he frowned. 'You know porcelains so nicely and you don't know prices.'

'I'd be guessing.'

'Go on,' he giggled. 'Guess it.'

'Ten thousand pounds.'

'Ten thousand? How much that in dollars?'

'Not quite thirty thousand.'

'You are right, sir!' Utz closed his eyes. 'Last one sold twenty-seven thousand dollars. That was in America. Parke-Bernet Galleries. But it was broken as to the hand.'

Bang! . . Bang! . . Bang! . . . Bang! . . . Bang! . . .

'So how much the Augustus Rex vases?'

I cannot recall the size of the figure I mentioned. Certainly,

I thought it high enough to give him pleasure. But he looked dismayed, bit his lip, and said, 'More! More!'

A single vase had fetched more in Paris, at the Hôtel Drouot. This was a complete garniture, without a crack or blemish anywhere.

Little by little, I was drawn into the spirit of the guessing game. I learned, with practice, to come up with the figures he wanted to hear and, in this way, I valued the bittern, the rhino, the Brühl tureen, Fröhlich and Schmeidl, the Pompadour and even 'The Spaghetti Eater'.

We stood for almost an hour. Utz would point to an object on the shelves. Marta would bang her saucepans. I would cup both hands around his ear, stickying my fingers on his brilliantine, and whispering higher and higher prices.

From time to time, he let out a squeal of joy. Finally, he said, 'So how much the whole collection?'

'Millions.'

'Ha! You are right,' said Utz. 'I am a porcelain millionaire.'

The clatter of saucepans died away: to be followed, a few minutes later, by the sound of sizzling fat.

'You will eat with me?' he said.

'I will,' I said. 'Thank you. Do you mind if I use your bathroom?

Utz pretended not to hear.

'Do you mind if I use your bathroom?'

He flinched. His face became contorted with a nervous tic. He fumbled with a cufflink, shot an agonised glance in the direction of the kitchenette – and pulled himself together.

'Ja! Ja! You may do that!' he stuttered, and ushered me, past a double bed, into an immaculate bathroom with a frieze of green-and-lilac jugendstil tiles and a bathtub on which the enamel had worn thin.

I closed the door behind me – and saw an astonishing garment.

Suspended from a hook there was a dressing-gown: but instead of a plaid or a camel-hair dressing-gown, this was a robe of quilted, peach-coloured art silk, with appliqué roses on the shoulders and a collar of matching pink ostrich plumes.

The scenario suggested by this unexpected costume set my imagination into turmoil.

I pulled the lavatory chain. Outside, above the rush and gurgle of the water, I heard Utz and Marta remonstrating, in Czech.

He was waiting to hustle me out of the bedroom. I was not to be hustled.

I paused to admire an eighteenth-century engraving, of a fireworks display at the Zwinger. I saw a photograph of Utz's father. I saw his illustrious decoration on its mount of black velvet. I saw a 'Venetian' blackamoor bed-table and, on it, a book by Schnitzler, and one by Stefan Zweig. I saw a large container of talcum-powder – or was it face-powder? – in front of the dressing-mirror. I saw three other unexpected items: a rosary, a crucifix and a scapular of the Infant of Prague. The frilly lace lampshade had been singed by its electric light bulb. The flounced pink curtains and pink satin eiderdown – both of which had seen better days – gave the room an atmosphere of musty, rather coarse femininity.

I looked at Utz afresh in the light of this discovery. I looked at his shiny scalp. Was there perhaps, hidden under the skirts of the dressing-table, a wig?

He was unable to look me in the eye. Instead, he tinkered with the gramophone and put on a record: a keyboard sonata by the Saxon court composer, Jan Dismas Zelenka.

The maid reappeared and laid two places on the glass-topped table, banging down the knives and forks with a show of bad temper. She turned her back, and returned with a larger Meissen dish on which were arranged some pork chops, sauerkraut and dumplings in gravy.

Utz ate with dulled concentration, pausing now and then

to mouth a little bread, sip a little wine, but scarcely saying a word. He blinked at me: apparently furious with himself for having invited this inquisitive foreigner who had disturbed his peace of mind and might, in the long run, cause trouble.

He cringed whenever the maid showed her face. After helping himself to seconds, he began to relax.

He cut a cube of meat, impaled it, held it in the air, and addressed me, pedantically:

'Each time I see a piece of pork, I must remind myself that "pork" and "porcelain" are the same word.'

'Really?' I said. 'How's that?'

'Really, you don't know it?'

'Really not.'

'So I will explain.'

He reached for one of the shelves and handed me a small white cowrie shell, an ordinary specimen of 'Cypraea moneta'. Did its shape, by any chance, remind me of a pig?

'Why not?'

'Good,' he said. 'We agree on that one also.'

Cowries, he went on, were used as currency in Africa and Asia where they were traded for ivory, gold, slaves or other marketable commodities. Marco Polo called them 'porcelain shells': 'porcella' in Italian was the word for 'little sow'.

He let out a perfect hiccough, probably caused by the sauerkraut.

'I apologise,' he said.

'Don't mention it.'

He then produced, as if from nowhere, a bottle of translucent white porcelain which dated from the epoch of Kublai Khan. He had bought it in Paris before the War. Wouldn't I agree that its glaze resembled that of a cowrie?

'I would.'

'Thank you.'

His next exhibit was the photo of an almost identical bottle in the Treasury of St Mark's: an object which was said to have arrived in Venice in the bags of Marco Polo himself.

'So now you understand about "pork" and "porcelain"?'

'I think so,' I said.

Chinese porcelain, he continued, was one of those legendary substances, like unicorn horn or alchemical gold, from which men hoped to drink the Fountain of Youth. A porcelain cup was said to crack or discolour if poison were poured into it.

Marta cleared the table, served coffee, and opened a box of Carlsbad plums. Utz hiccoughed again and bombarded me with a flood of questions.

Had I been to China? Had I read the letters of Father Matteo Ricci? Or Father d'Entrecolles' description of porcelain manufacture? How serious, really, was my understanding of Chinese porcelain? Under the Sung? The Ming? The Ch'ing?

From the seventeenth century, he said, the Emperors of China had made a colossal impact on the European imagination. They were thought to be very wise and to live to a very great age, dispensing arbitrary, impartial justice according to laws derived from Earth and Heaven. They drank from porcelain. They built pagodas of porcelain. The smooth and lustrous surface of porcelain corresponded to the smooth, unwrinkled surface of themselves. Porcelain was their material – as gold was the material of the Roi Soleil.

'And even today,' Utz added flippantly, 'our Soviet friends are never too poor to pay for gilding.'

'Then would you say', I interrupted, 'that your Augustus's

porcelain-mania was conditioned by legends of the Yellow Emperor?'

'Say it? Of course, I would say it! And not only kings loved porcelain. Philosophers also! Leibniz was crazy for porcelain!'

Leibniz – who had believed this world was the best of all possible worlds – believed that porcelain was its best material.

The maid stood motionless in the hallway, fixing her employer with a hostile stare, as if requiring him to end the interview. He took no notice:

'Now will you look please at these two little persons?'

'These' were a pair of identical statuettes of Augustus the Strong, wreathed as a Roman Emperor and standing like Tweedledum and Tweedledee amid the Dresden ladies. They were not modelled with much sophistication – yet had the concentrated energy of an African fetish.

One was made of red Böttger ware, the so-called 'jasperporcelain'. The other was white.

'Tell me,' said Utz, 'what you know about Böttger.'

'Not much,' I replied. 'He began as an alchemist, and then he invented porcelain.'

'He *may* have invented porcelain. But even that is not so sure.'

I reached for my notebook. He reeled off a synopsis of Böttger's career.

Johannes Böttger is born in 1682, in Schleiz in Thuringia, the son of an official of the Mint. After a childhood in the workshop of his grandfather, a goldsmith, he is apprenticed to a Berlin apothecary by the name of Zorn.

He studies books on alchemy: the Blessed Raymond Lúll, Basilius Valentinus, Paracelsus and Van Helmont's 'Aphorismi Chemici' in which alchemical substances are listed as the Ruby Lion, Black Raven, Green Dragon, and White Lily.

He convinces himself that gold and silver are matured in the bowels of the earth, out of red and white arsenic. One night, his fellow apprentices find him in Zorn's laboratory half-asphyxiated by arsenic fumes.

Among the customers of the pharmacy is a Greek mendicant monk, Lascaris, who is reputed to possess the Red Tincture, or 'Ruby Lion', a grain of which will transmute lead into gold.

The monk falls for the boy.

Böttger obtains a phial of the tincture and performs his first 'successful' transmutation, in the lodgings of a student friend. The second 'successful' experiment takes place in front of Zorn and other sceptical witnesses.

The ladies of Berlin find the young alchemist irresistible. His reputation spreads: to King Frederick William, the 'Giant Lover', who obtains a specimen of the gold from Frau Zorn – and issues a warrant for Böttger's arrest.

Böttger escapes to Wittenberg: a dependency of Augustus the Strong.

In November 1701 the Kings of Prussia and Saxony hold military manoeuvres along their borders. Which of these indigent sovereigns shall possess the goldmaker? Böttger – like a fugitive nuclear physicist – is escorted to Dresden under armed guard.

In the Jungfernbastei, one of several prisons he will occupy over the next thirteen years, he dines off silver plate, keeps a pet monkey and, in a secret laboratory, sets to work on the 'arcanum universale' or Philosopher's Stone.

By 1706 the Saxon Treasury is exhausted: from the cost of the Swedish War and the King's compulsive purchases of Chinese porcelain. Augustus, infuriated by Böttger's failure, threatens to remove him to another laboratory: the torture chamber.

Böttger meets Ehrenfried Walther, Graf von Tschirnhaus. This outstanding chemist, the friend of Leibniz, is on the way to discovering the secret of 'true' porcelain, but cannot devise a kiln sufficiently hot to fuse the glaze and the body. He recognises Böttger's talents, and asks for his co-operation. The alchemist, to save his skin, agrees.

Over the door of this workshop Böttger hangs a notice:

God, Our Creator
Has turned a Goldmaker into a Potter.

In 1708 he delivers to Augustus the first specimens of red porcelain and, in the following year, the white.

In 1710 the Royal Saxon Porcelain Manufactory is founded at Meissen and begins work on a commercial scale. 'Arcanum' – a word usually employed by alchemists – is the official term for the chemical composition of the paste. The formula is declared a State secret. Almost at once, the secret is betrayed by Böttger's assistant – and sold to Vienna.

In 1719 Böttger dies, of drink, depression, delusion and chemical poisoning.

During the German inflation of 1923 the Dresden banks issue emergency money, in red and white 'Böttger' porcelain.

Utz had some specimens of the 'funny money' to show me. He dropped them, like chocolates, into the palm of my hand.

'Very interesting,' I said.

'But now I tell you something more interesting.'

Most porcelain experts, he continued, interpreted Böttger's discovery as the utilitarian by-product of alchemy – like Paracelsus's mercurial cure for syphilis.

He did not agree. He felt it was foolish to attribute to former ages the materialist concerns of this one. Alchemy, except among its more banal practitioners, was never a technique for multiplying wealth ad infinitum. It was a mystical exercise. The search for gold and the search for porcelain had been facets of an identical quest: to find the substance of immortality.

As for himself, he had taken up alchemical studies on the advice of Zikmund Kraus: both as a field for his polymathic impulses, and as a means of elevating his 'porcelain mania' onto a metaphysical plane: so that if the Communists took the collection, he would none the less continue to possess it.

Utz had read his Jung, his Goethe, Michael Maier, the ramblings of Dr Dee and Pernéty's 'Dictionnaire Mytho-

Hermétique'. He knew all there was to be known about the 'mother of alchemy', Mary the Jewess, a third-century chemist who is said to have invented the retort.

Chinese alchemists, he went on, used to teach that gold was the 'body of the gods'. Christians, with their insistence on simplification, equated it with the Body of Christ: the perfect, untarnishable substance, an elixir which could snatch one from the Jaws of Death. But was this gold gold as we knew it? Or an 'aurum potabile', to be drunk?

Jewels and metals, he said, were thought to mature in the womb of the earth. As a pallid foetus matured into the creature of flesh and blood, so crystals reddened into rubies, silver into gold. An alchemist believed he could speed up the process with the help of the two 'tinctures': the White Stone, with which base metals were converted into silver; the Red Stone which was 'the last work of alchemy' – gold itself! Did I understand that?

'I hope so,' I said weakly.

He shifted to a different tack.

What did I know of the homunculus of Paracelsus? Nothing? Well, Paracelsus had claimed to create a homunculus from a fermentation of blood, sperm and urine.

'A kind of test-tube baby?'

'More probably a kind of golem.'

'I knew we'd get back to golems,' I said.

'We have,' he agreed.

Would I now please reflect on the fact that Nebuchadnezzar had the burning fiery furnace heated to seven times its normal temperature when he put in Shadrach, Meshach and Abednego?

'Seven times, I ask you!' Utz waved his hands in the air.

'Are you trying to tell me that Shadrach, Meshach and Abednego were ceramic figures?'

'They could have been,' he answered. 'They certainly survived the fire.'

'I see,' I said. 'So you *do* think the porcelains are alive?'

'I do and I do not,' he sniggered. 'Porcelains die in the fire, and then they come alive again. The kiln, you must understand, is Hell. The temperature for firing porcelain is 1,450 degrees centigrade.'

'Yes,' I said.

Utz's flights of fancy made me feel quite dizzy. He appeared to be saying that the earliest European porcelain – Böttger's red ware and white ware – corresponded to the red and white tinctures of the alchemists. To a superstitious old roué like Augustus, the manufacture of porcelain was an approach to the Philosopher's Stone.

If this were so: if, to the eighteenth-century imagination, porcelain was not just another exotic, but a magical and talismanic substance – the substance of longevity, of potency, of invulnerability – then it was easier to understand why the King would stuff a palace with forty thousand pieces. Or guard the 'arcanum' like a secret weapon. Or swap the six hundred giants.

Porcelain, Utz concluded, was the antidote to decay.

The illusion was, of course, shattered by Frederick the Great who simply loaded the contents of the Meissen factory onto ox-carts and sent it, as booty, to Berlin.

'But Frederick,' Utz fluttered his eyelids, ' . . . and with all that musical talent! . . was really an absolute philistine!'

The room was almost in darkness. It was a warm night, and a soft breeze ruffled the net curtains. On the carpet, the animals from the Japanese Palace shimmered like lumps of phosphorescence.

'Marta!' he called. 'A light please!'

The maid came in with a Meissen candlestick, and set it carefully in the centre of the table. She put a match to the candle. Innumerable points of flame were reflected in the walls.

Utz changed the record on the gramophone: to the recitative of Zerbinetta and Harlequin from Strauss's 'Ariadne auf Naxos'.

I have said that Utz's face was 'waxy in texture', but now in the candlelight its texture seemed like melted wax. Things, I reflected, are tougher than people. Things are the changeless mirror in which we watch ourselves disintegrate. Nothing is more ageing than a collection of works of art.

One by one, he lifted the characters of the Commedia from the shelves, and placed them in the pool of light where they appeared to skate over the glass of the table, pivoting on their bases of gilded foam, as if they would forever go on laughing, whirling, improvising.

Scaramouche would strum on his guitar.

Brighella would liberate people's purses.

The Captain would swagger childishly like all army officers.

The Doctor would kill his patient in order to rid him of his disease.

The coils of spaghetti would be eternally poised above Pulchinella's nostrils.

Pantaloon would gloat over his money-bags.

The Innamorata, like all transvestites everywhere, would be mobbed on his way to the theatre.

Columbine would be endlessly in love with Harlequin – 'absolutely mad to trust him.'

And Harlequin . . . *The* Harlequin . . . the arch-improviser, the zany, trickster, master of the volte-face . . . would forever strut in his variegated plumage, grin through his orange mask, tiptoe into bedrooms, sell nappies for the children of the Grand Eunuch, dance in the teeth of catastrophe . . . Mr Chameleon himself!

And I realised, as Utz pivoted the figure in the candlelight, that I had misjudged him; that he, too, was dancing; that, for him, this world of little figures was the real world. And that, compared to them, the Gestapo, the Secret Police and other hooligans were creatures of tinsel. And the events of this sombre century – the bombardments, blitzkriegs, putsches, purges – were, so far as he was concerned, so many 'noises off'.

'And now,' he said, 'we shall go. We shall go for a walk.'

On my way out, I thanked Marta for cooking supper. A wan smile passed across her face. Without getting off her stool, she inclined her torso stiffly from the waist.

It was a very warm and sultry night, and moths were whirling round the street lamps. In Old Town Square, crowds of young people had congregated at the foot of the Jan Hus Memorial. They seemed fresh and full of vigour: the boys in white open-necked shirts; the girls in old-fashioned cotton dresses.

The stars came out behind the spires of the Týn Church and, to peals of organ music, more people began to file through the arcades of the Divinity School, on their way from Mass. 'Prague Spring' was almost a year away: yet I remember an atmosphere of optimism. I remember being taken aback when Utz turned on me, and bared his teeth.

'I hate this city,' he said.

'Hate it? How can you hate it? You said it was a beautiful city.'

'I hate it. I hate it.'

'Things will get better,' I said. 'Things can only get better.'

'You are wrong. Things will never get better.'

He shook my hand and gave a curt bow.

'Goodnight, my young friend,' he said. 'Remember what I said. I will leave you now. I will go to the brothel.'

That winter I sent Utz a Christmas card and got a postcard in return – of the tomb-slab of Tycho Brahé – hoping that when I next returned to Prague I would call him.

During the months that followed, as the world watched the activities of Comrade Dubček, I tried to imagine Utz's reaction to the events, wondering if he still stuck to his guns: that things would never, ever get better.

As the summer wore on, despite noises in the Soviet press, it seemed less and less likely that Brezhnev would send in the tanks. But one night, as I drove into Paris, the Boulevard Saint-Germain was closed to traffic, and police with riotshields were pushing back a surge of demonstrators.

The occupation of Czechoslovakia had been completed in a day.

I humped my bag up the stairs of the Hôtel Louisiane and told myself, sadly, that Utz had been right. In December I sent another Christmas card. I never had an answer.

Dr Orlík, on the other hand, was a positive nuisance. Always in a semi-legible scrawl, always on the notepaper of the National Museum, he pestered me for photostats of scientific articles. He commanded me to trace the whereabouts of some mammoth bones in the Natural History Museum. He demanded books: nothing cheap of course, usually monographs published at great expense by American university presses.

One letter informed me of his current project: a study of the house-fly (Musca domestica), as painted in Dutch and Flemish still-lifes of the seventeenth century. My role in this enterprise was to examine every photograph of paintings by Bosschaert, Van Huysum or Van Kessel, and check whether or not there was a fly in them.

I did not reply.

About six years later, towards the end of March 1974, I received from Orlík a black-bordered card on which he had scrawled: 'Our beloved friend Utz is dead . . .'

The word 'beloved' seemed a bit strong: considering I had known Utz for a total of nine and a quarter hours, some six and half years earlier. All the same, remembering how devoted the two friends were, I sent a short note thanking Orlík for the news, and hoping to share his sorrow.

This produced a flood of even more unreasonable demands. Would I send $1,000 U.S. to help the researches of a poor scholar? Would I agree to sponsor a six-month tour of Western scientific institutions? Would I send forty pairs of socks?

I sent four pairs.

The correspondence dried up.

At the end of last summer I happened to pass through Prague on my way back from the Soviet Union. The mood, especially in smaller cities along the Volga and Don, struck me as exceptionally buoyant. The Soviet education system, I felt, had worked all too well: having created, on a colossal scale, a generation of highly intelligent, highly literate young people who were more or less immune to the totalitarian message.

Prague was infinitely more mournful and gloomy. There were plenty of things in the shops: but the shoppers mooched up and down Wenceslas Square with the faces of a people disgusted with itself for having, if temporarily, lost hope. The works of the 'Prag-Deutsch Schriftseller', Franz Kafka, were unavailable in the bookstores. Monuments likely to be the focus of national sentiment – the Týn Church or St Vitus's Cathedral – were closed for reconstruction. Their façades had vanished under a blight of rust scaffolding – although very few workmen could be seen.

It was impossible to drive anywhere without being blocked by a 'road up' sign. The entire city – labyrinthine at the best of times – had been turned into a labyrinth of culs-de-sac. I had the impression of a mercantile city in mourning, not so much for its lost prosperity as the loss of its European role. It was a city at the end of its tether.

I am being unfair. Everywhere in Prague there were signs that the Czechs were uncrushable.

I think it was Utz who first convinced me that history is always our guide for the future, and always full of capricious surprises. The future itself is a dead land because it does not yet exist.

When a Czech writer wishes to comment on the plight of his country, one way open to him is to use the fifteenth-century Hussite Rebellion as a metaphor. I found in Prague Museum this text describing the Hussites' defeat of the German Knights:

> At midnight, all of a sudden, frightened shouting was heard in the very centre of the large forces of Edom who had put up their tents along three miles near the town of Žatec in Bohemia; in the distance of ten miles from Cheb. And all of them fled from the sword, driven out by the voice of falling leaves only, and not pursued by any man . . .

As I scribbled this in my notebook, I seemed to hear again Utz's nasal whisper: 'They listen, listen, listen to everything but . . . they *hear* nothing!'

He had, as usual, been right. Tyranny sets up its own echo-chamber; a void where confused signals buzz about at random; where a murmur or innuendo causes panic: so, in the end, the machinery of repression is more likely to vanish, not with the war or revolution, but with a puff, or the voice of falling leaves . . .

I was staying at the Hotel Yalta. Among the guests there was a French reporter on the trail of a Peruvian terrorist. 'Many terrorists come to Prague,' he said, 'for facial surgery.'

There was also a party of English 'dissident-watchers': a Professor of Modern History and three literary ladies – who, instead of watching animals in an East African game-park, had come to spy on that other endangered species, the East European intellectual. Was the creature still at large? What should one feed it? Would it compose some suitable words to help the anti-Communist crusade?

They drank whisky on their credit cards, ate a lot of peanuts, and plainly hoped they were being followed. I hoped that, when they did meet a dissident, they'd get their fingers bitten off.

On the following day, I checked for an Utz in the Prague phone book. There was no one of that name.

I ventured past the sickly stucco medusa-masks above the door of No. 5 Široká Street, past the ranks of overflowing dustbins in the entrance, and rang the bell of the top-floor apartment. Beside the bell-push, I saw the screw-holes where Utz's brass plaque had been.

On the landing below, I tried the bell of the soprano who, twenty years earlier, had appeared in a peony-printed peignoir. She was now a shrivelled old lady in a black, fringed shawl. I said the name 'Utz'. The door flew in my face.

I had got as far as the next floor when the door re-opened and, with a 'Psst!', she called me back.

Her name was Ada Krasová. The apartment was crammed with the mementos of an operatic career.

She had sung Mimi, Manon, Carmen, Aida, Ortrud and Lisa in 'The Queen of Spades'. One photograph showed her as an adorable Jenůfa in a lace peasant blouse. She kept fingering the tortoiseshell combs in her hair. In the kitchen a cat was being sick. There were arrangements of peacock feathers in Chinese vases. The profusion of faded pink satin reminded me of Utz's bedroom.

I came quickly to the point. Did she, by any chance, know what had happened to Utz's porcelains? She gave a little operatic trill, 'Oooh! La! La!' – and shuddered. Obviously she did know, but was not letting on. She gave me the name of a curator at the Rudolfine Museum.

The museum, a grandiose edifice from the 'good old days' of Franz Josef, had been named after the Emperor Rudolf to commemorate his passion for the decorative arts. Along the front façade, there were sculptured bas-reliefs representing various crafts: gem-cutting, weaving, glass-blowing. A pair of grimy sphinxes sat guard over the entrance; burdocks were sprouting through cracks in the steps.

The Museum was shut for 'various reasons' – as it had been shut in 1967. Only one room, on the ground floor, was open for temporary exhibitions. The current show was called 'The Modern Chair' – with student copies after Rietveld and Mondrian, and a display of stacking chairs in fibreglass.

At the reception desk I asked to speak to the curator.

Prague is hardly a stone's throw, culturally, from Dresden. I know that if I posed as an expert on Meissen porcelain, they would soon call my bluff. So I cooked up a likely tale: I was a historian of the Neapolitan Rococo and was writing a paper on the Commedia dell' Arte figurines of the CapodiMonte factory. I had once seen Mr Utz's lovely group 'The Spaghetti Eater'. Was there any way of knowing where it was?

A subdued female voice on the end of the line murmured, 'I will come down.'

I had to wait ten minutes before a homely, middle-aged woman stepped from the lift. Her head was wrapped in a deep lilac scarf, and there was a wen on her chin. She drew back her lips in a covert smile.

'It would be better,' she said in English, 'if we went outside.'

We strolled along the embankment of the Vltava. The day was cold and drizzly, and the clouds seemed to touch the spire of St Vitus's Cathedral. It was one of the worst summers on record. Mallard drakes were chasing ducks in the shallows. A man was fishing from an inflatable rubber dinghy moored in midstream, with the kittiwakes wheeling round him.

'Tell me,' I broke the silence, 'why is your museum always shut?'

'Why do you think?' She let out a quick, throaty laugh. 'To keep the People out!'

She gave a furtive glance over her shoulder, and asked: 'You have known Mr Utz?'

'I knew him,' I replied. 'Not well. I once spent an evening with him. He showed me the collection.'

'When was that?'

'1967.'

'Oh, I see,' she shook her head forlornly. 'Before our tragedy.'

'Yes,' I said. 'I always wondered what became of the porcelain.'

She winced. She took half a step forward, a full step sideways, and then leaned against the balustrade, apparently uncertain how to phrase her next question:

'Do I think correctly that you know the market of Meissen porcelains? In Western Europe and America?'

'I don't,' I said.

'Then you are not a collector?'

'No.'

'Or a dealer?'

'Certainly not.'

'Then you have not come to Prague to buy pieces?'

'God forbid!'

My answer seemed to disappoint her. I had a presentiment she was going to offer to sell me Utz's porcelains. She exhaled a deep breath before continuing.

'Can you tell me,' she asked, 'have pieces from the Utz Collection been sold in the West?'

'I don't believe so.'

A month or so earlier, I had called on Dr Marius Frankfurter in New York, in his overstuffed apartment atwitter with Meissen birds. 'Find me the Utz collection,' he had said, 'and we will make ourselves really rich.'

'No,' I said to the curator. 'If anyone knew, it would be Utz's old dealer friend, Dr Frankfurter. He said it was a total mystery.'

'Oh, I see!' She looked down at the water. 'So you know Dr Frankfurter?'

'I've met him.'

'Yes,' she sighed, 'it is also a mystery to us.'

'How is that?'

She shuddered, and fumbled with the knot of her scarf: 'All those beautiful pieces . . . ! They have gone . . . How would you say it? . . . Vanished!'

'Vanished!'

'After his death? Or before?'

'We do not know.'

Until 1973, the year of Utz's stroke, the museum officials were in the habit of paying routine calls on him: to check the collection was intact.

The visits seemed to amuse him: especially when one or other of the curators brought a puzzling piece of porcelain, on which to test his expertise. But in July of that year, his right arm paralysed, he agreed to sign a paper confirming that, on his death, the collection would go to the State.

He also agreed to import his 'second' collection from Switzerland: with the proviso that, since the visits now distressed him terribly, they would leave him thereafter in peace. The Director of the Museum, a humane man, consented. Two hundred and sixty-seven objects of porcelain were given special clearance through customs, and were delivered to Utz's apartment.

The funeral, as we know, began at 8 a.m. on March 10th 1974 – although there was some confusion over the timing of the arrangements. As a result, the Director and three of his staff missed the church service and the burial altogether, and were thirty minutes late for breakfast at the Hotel Bristol.

Two days later, when they kept their appointment at No. 5 Široká Street, no one answered the bell. In exasperation, they called for a man to pick the lock. The shelves were bare.

The furniture was in place, even the bric-à-brac in the bedroom. But not a single piece of porcelain could be found: only dust-marks where the porcelains had been, and marks on the carpet where the animals from the Japanese Palace had stood.

'And the servant?' I asked. 'Surely she must know?'

'But we do not believe her story.'

After breakfast next morning, I asked the concierge to call the National Museum to find out if a Dr Václav Orlík still worked there. The answer came back that Dr Orlík, although officially retired, continued to work in the mornings, in the Department of Palaeontology.

On my way to the Museum I took the precaution of reserving a table for two at the Restaurant Pstruh.

A museum guard conducted me through a maze of passages into a storeroom heaped with dusty bones and stones. Orlík, now white-haired and resembling a Brahmanic sage, was cleaning the encrustation from a mammoth tibia. Behind him, like a Gothic arch, was the jawbone of a whale.

I asked if he remembered me.

'Is it?' he scowled. 'No. It is not.'

'It is,' I said.

He left off scouring the mammoth bone and examined me with myopic and suspicious glare.

'Yes,' he said. 'I see it now. It is you.'

'Of course it's me.'

'Why you not reply to my letters?'

I explained that, since I was last in Prague, I had married and changed addresses five times.

'I do not believe,' he said flatly.

'I wondered if you'd like to lunch with me?' I said. 'We could go to the Pstruh.'

'We could go,' he nodded doubtfully. 'You could pay?'

'I could.'

'So I will come.'

He made the motion of running a comb through his hair and beard, set his beret at a rakish angle, and pronounced himself ready to leave.

On the way out he left a note saying that he had gone to lunch with a 'distinguished foreign scholar'. We went outside. He walked with a limp.

'I do not think you are distinguished,' he said as he limped along the pedestrian underpass. 'I think you are not a scholar even. But I must say it to them.'

Nothing much had changed at the restaurant. The trout were still swimming up and down their oxygenated tank. The head-waiter – could it really be the same head-waiter? – had grown a balloon-like paunch, and the disagreeable face of Comrade Novotný had been replaced by the equally disagreeable face of Comrade Husák.

I ordered a bottle of light white Moravian wine, and raised my glass to Utz's memory. Tears trickled down the creases of Orlík's cheek, and vanished in the wilderness of his beard. I resigned myself to lunching with a tearful palaentologist.

'How are the flies?' I asked

'I have returned to the mammoth.'

'I mean your collection of flies.'

'I have thrown.'

The trout, this time, were available.

'Au bleu, n'est-ce pas?' I tried to imitate Utz's weird French accent.

'Blau!' snapped Orlík, with a loud hoot of laughter.

I leaned across, and asked in a lowered voice:

'Tell me, what happened to the porcelains?'

He closed his eyes, and tilted his head from side to side.

'He has thrown,' he said.

'Thrown?'

'Broken and thrown.'

'He broke them?' I gasped.

'He broke and she broke. Sometimes he broke and she threw.'

'She?'

'The Baroness.'

'What Baroness?'

'His Baroness.'

'I never knew he was married.'

'He was married.'

'Who to?'

'He! He!' Orlík cackled. 'Guess it!'

'How can I guess it?'

'You have met the Baroness.'

'I met no one.'

'You have met.'

'I have not met.'

'You have met.'

'Who was she?'

'His domestic.'

'Oh no! No. I don't believe it . . . Not . . Not Marta!'

'As you say it.'

'And you're saying she destroyed the collection?'

'I am saying and I am not saying.'

'Where is she now?'

'Gone.'

'Dead?'

'Dead, maybe. Maybe not. She has gone.'

'Out of the country?'

'Not.'

'Where then?'

'Into the country.'

'Where in the country?'

'Kostelec.'

'Where's that?'

'Süd-Böhmen.'

'You say she went back to Southern Bohemia?'

'Maybe. Maybe not.'

'Tell me . . .'

'I cannot tell you,' he whispered, 'in here . . .'

Until the end of lunch, Orlík entertained me with an evocation of the mammoth-hunters who had roamed the tundras of Moravia in the Ice Age.

I paid the bill. We took a taxi to the Vrtba Garden where we sat on one of the terraces, beside a stone urn half-covered with a trailing vine.

Utz married Marta at a civil ceremony one Saturday morning in the summer of 1952, six weeks after returning from Vichy.

It was a dangerous moment. The Gottwald regime had let loose the self-perpetuating witch-hunt that culminated in the Slánksy trial. It was almost impossible for ordinary citizens not to fall into one or other of the categories – bourgeois nationalist, traitor to the Party, cosmopolitan, Zionist, blackmarketeer – that would land them in prison, or worse.

If you happened to be Jewish and a survivor of the death-camps, this branded you as a Nazi collaborator.

It was obvious to Utz that he would have to tread with great circumspection.

One morning, an order came for him to quit the apartment within two weeks: as a single man, he was no longer entitled to two rooms, only to one.

So it had come to this! He would be out on the street, or in some rotting garret with nowhere to store the porcelains. Marriage was the answer.

At the ceremony Marta was very shy, and very upset by the red flags in the Old Town Hall. 'The colour of blood,' she shuddered, as they came out into the sunlight.

On the following Monday, the newlyweds, arm in arm, joined the shuffling queue of house-seekers, and presented their marriage certificate to the bureaucrat in charge. They put on a drooling show of affection. The eviction order was cancelled.

Marta gave up her own room, and brought her bag to No. 5 Široká Street.

I cannot vouch for the authenticity of Utz's title 'baron'. Andreas von Raabe, a friend of mine who lives in Munich, assures me that the Utzes of Krondorf did marry, from time to time, into the minor German nobility. He cannot be certain if they were ever ennobled themselves.

Nor, after my call on Dr Frankfurter in New York, do I believe that Utz's annual pilgrimage to the West was quite so 'pure'. I must have been very naive to think the authorities would let him travel back and forth without a favour in return.

Dr Frankfurter's apartment, as I said, was jammed with Meissen and other German porcelain. It was clear that much of it had belonged to aristocratic families in Czechoslovakia and had been sold off, recently, by the State. The Czechs were always in need of hard currency to finance their various activities: espionage or subversion. I now suspect that the safe-deposit in the Union de Banques Suisses in Geneva was an unofficial shop – with a Mr Utz in charge – through which confiscated works of art were sold.

But I *can* state, categorically, that Utz did have a moustache.

Without the moustache, he might have remained in my imagination another art-collector, of fussy habits and feminine inclinations, whose encounters with women were ambiguous.

With the moustache, he was a relentless lady-killer.

'Of course he had a moustache!' Dr Frankfurter shook with smutty laughter. 'The moustache was the clue to his personality!'

Utz had grown the moustache after his adolescent disappointments in Vienna, and had never looked back. He was not the ineffectual lover I had pictured in Vichy. His entire life had been a successful pursuit of voluminous operatic divas: though, since singers of high opera were too temperamental and too obsessed with their art, he tended to settle for the stars of operetta.

A succession of Merry Widows and Countess Mitzis passed through his bed. And if the usual sources of erotic arousal left him cold, he would be driven to frenzy by the sight of a lower larynx, as the singer threw back her head to hit a high note.

He was an ordinary little man. The secret of his attraction to the divas was his technique – you could call it a trick of applying the stiff bristles of the moustache to the lady's throat so that, for her, the crescendo of love-making was as ecstatic as the final notes of an aria.

The part played by Marta in all this was a sad one.

She had adored Utz with a hopeless and blinkered passion from the moment he beckoned her into his automobile. Yet realising, with a certain peasant canniness, that to hope would drive her mad, she accepted her position. If she did not enjoy his body in this world, she would, with faith, enjoy his soul in the next.

She prayed and prayed. She went tirelessly to Mass. In the

Church of Our Lady Victorious she would weep in front of the Prague Baby Jesus: a greedy infant who appropriated pious ladies' necklaces and had his costume changed, weekly, by nuns.

Once, in an outburst of frustrated maternal passion, she offered to help the nuns undress Him, and was rudely rebuffed.

She dared not confess to Him the extent of her ambitions. She begged forgiveness for her husband's infidelities, and for her role in turning the bedroom of No. 5 Široká Street into 'something like a Polish bordel'.

She had never made love to a man – except for one brutal encounter behind a haystack. Yet she acquired a professional's skill in preparing the bedroom for ladies too proud, or too ashamed, to bring an overnight bag.

She applied her entrepreneurial talents on the black market to acquire scented soap, toilet water, talcum-powder, face-powder, towels, flannels and the assortment of pink crêpe-dechine négligés that unaccountably went missing from the laundry of diplomatic wives.

Sometimes, Utz's visitors found one of these luxuries too tempting to resist, and would stuff it into her reticule. Marta found it expedient to leave an immediate bait on the bed-table – a lipstick or a pair of nylons – and so preserved her more valuable stocks.

She would cook the dinner and wash the dishes. Then, as Utz began his routine with the Commedia figures and the music of 'Ariadne auf Naxos', she would slip out into the night.

Some nights she spent on the floor of her friend Suzana: a woman who kept a vegetable stall on Havelská Street.

There were worse nights at the Central Railway Station, her heart in shreds, crossing herself at the thought of thrashing limbs and pink satin.

Since the queue of ladies became more, not less, pressing over the years, the number of nights she had to sleep out increased. There was never a hint of reproach on her part. Nor, on his, the least acknowledgement that she had ever been inconvenienced.

She believed that, by marrying her, he had done her all the honour in the world. My impression is that, in her mind, and perhaps even in his, she played the part of the consort who is obliged to witness, with amused condescension, a succession of hysterical mistresses.

After moving into the apartment, she had slept under a quilt on the narrow Mies van der Rohe daybed. But one night, while reliving in a nightmare the horrors of Utz's arrest by the Gestapo, she landed on the floor with a reverberative wallop that set the porcelains clattering on the shelves.

Thereafter, she preferred a kapok-filled camping-mattress that could be rolled out in the hallway: any night intruder would have to tread on her.

I uncovered evidence of Marta's unwavering feud with the tenant of the flat below.

Ada Krasová, in the course of a tumultuous affair with Utz, had used her opera singer's privileges to import a bale of pink satin from Italy, and had decorated his bedroom in the taste of a demi-mondaine.

She then committed the solecism of installing herself on the floor below and, seriously believing she could outwit Marta, had pinched a bottle of Chanel No. 5. Marta countered this act of kleptomania with a bald statement, 'I shall not be cooking for her.' The lady was never invited again: and when I found her, thirty years later, she was still stewing in rancorous recrimination, among her souvenirs.

I don't know the exact date: but sometime in the mid-Sixties, at a performance of 'Don Carlos', Utz trained his opera glasses on the throat of a singer far younger than his usual prey: a substantial girl with an outstanding tonal range who, as Queen of Spain, had to conceal her golden, hawser-like plait within the folds of a black mantilla.

Next day, on his habitual visit to the opera café, Utz

summoned up the courage to address her – and recoiled from her stinging reply: 'Get away, you silly old fool!'

It was a lowering winter day. He had an attack of sinusitis and pink-eye. He glanced into the mirror of a shop-front and, in a moment of extreme disillusion, was forced to revise his image of himself as the eternal lover.

What passed between him and Marta, one can only guess. But, from that day on, she quit the camping-mattress and moved into the bed.

The pink art-silk dressing-gown was the emblem of her victory.

His embittered tone, as we parted in the Old Town Square, was perhaps conditioned by the fact that he and his wife had swapped roles. She was too tactful to make a public show, but was certainly the mistress of the household. Henceforth, if he wanted to go philandering, he would have to philander elsewhere.

She then made the victory complete.

She had been married at an atheistic – not to say pagan – ceremony, and had always felt cheated of her rights. In her mumbled conversations with the Infant of Prague, she confessed to having committed a cardinal sin: sleeping with a man to whom she was unmarried in the sight of God.

One day in April, as she and Utz were spring-cleaning some boxes stored on top of the wardrobe, she opened one containing the white lace veil that had been worn by brides of the Utzes since the eighteenth century.

She laid it out on the pink satin coverlet. She looked at him pointedly. He returned her glance.

Utz and Marta were married in the Church of Saint Nikolaus on an incandescent afternoon of plum blossom and hazy blue skies in the 'Prague Spring' of 1968.

She wore a white suit, with minor sweatstains under the armpits, and carried a bouquet of white lilacs and lilies-of-the-valley. The veil, pinned over her head, did not look incongruous. A lock of grey hair fell aslant across her brow.

To the Wedding March from 'A Midsummer Night's Dream', the priest, in ruffles and a wig, led the procession up the aisle.

They passed the inevitable cleaning woman who removed herself and her bucket into a pew, and waved them on gaily with her mop handle. They passed the pulpit, which was the colour of raspberry ice-cream, and arrived in front of the altar where a mitred statue of St Cyril was lancing a pagan with the butt of his crozier.

The onlookers, their curiosity piqued by the disparate sizes of the bride and groom, were taken aback by the elderly couple who turned defiantly to face them: as well as by the smudge of vermilion lipstick that Marta – using lipstick for the first time – had planted on her husband's temple, being too tall to reach his lips at the moment of the bridal kiss.

The organ poured forth Sigmund Romberg's 'When I'm calling you . . .' and as the pair came out into the sunlight, the crowd assembled on the steps broke into a round of hand-clapping.

Another wedding-party was waiting to go in. The young men wore sprigs of myrtle in their lapels. Marta's sharp eye registered that the girl was pregnant. She cringed at the applause, fearing, perhaps, that they were making fun of her. But the bridegroom, a friendly fine-boned boy, bade the Utzes to join them inside for the service, and afterwards at the Hotel Bristol.

A reception for one couple of newlyweds doubled into a reception for two. The revellers, drunk on Tokay, made a number of mocking toasts to the bear at the head of the table.

I am now in a position to add to my account of Utz's funeral.

Between the moment of death and the appearance of the undertaker, Marta had obliterated the porcelain shelves with draperies of black material. She called Orlík from the Museum, and the two sat vigil until the coffin was taken away.

Ada Krasová, meanwhile, conducted her own dirge on the floor below. Women from all over Prague, from Brno, from Bratislava; women who had detested each other, on the operatic stage, and as rivals for Utz's affection, were now united in their hatred of Marta for thwarting them of their final glimpse of the moustache.

They screamed. They hissed. They banged on the door. She was deaf to their entreaties.

On the eve of the entombment, she posted Orlík to guard her exit and entrance, and held a conference on the stairwell in which she informed the grieving women of the arrangements for the next day.

With inspired malice, she told them the service would be held in the Church of Saint Jakob instead of Saint Sigismund; the burial at the Vyšehrad Cemetery instead of the Vinohrady; and that breakfast at the Hotel Bristol – 'to which my beloved husband bade you all attend' – would begin at 9.45 a.m. instead of 9.15.

As a result there were two more hired Tatra limousines shuttling back and forth across Prague in the early hours of that bitter morning: one containing a group of retired operatic divas, the other crammed with officials from the Rudolfine Museum.

These two parties coincided at the entrance to the hotel dining-room at the moment when the widow Utz – having raised her Tokay glass 'To the Bear! To the Bear!' – was making her remorseless exit.

Taking her leatherette bag into the ladies' lavatory, she changed out of black into a suit of brown wool jersey. She took a taxi to the Central Station, a train to Ceské Budějovice, and went to stay with her sister who still lived in their native village.

When reconstructing any story, the wilder the chase the more likely it is to yield results.

Acting on a tip from Ada Krasová, who made a number of veiled allusions to the hammering that used to sound from Utz's apartment, I stationed myself on the corner of Široká and Maislova Streets, between one and two of a drizzly Saturday morning, to await the emptying of the dustbins.

In Prague, at least in the older quarters, many citizens have an obsessional relationship with garbage. An apartment building such as Nos 5 and 6 Široká Street – built for prosperous bourgeois before the Great War – retains, in the foyer, the original red and yellow marble facings. But where, in the old days, there might have stood a console with a vase of artificial flowers, now, in these less fastidious times, the visitor is greeted by a platoon of grey, galvanised dustbins, of standard size, and with identical articulated lids.

The garbage trucks of Prague are painted a vivid orange. They have been in service for about fifteen years. As a warning to motorists, they are mounted with revolving orange lights that flash their beams against the surrounding architecture. These lights, and the noise of the vehicles' crushing machinery, are the curse of light sleepers but a source of wonder to insomniacs, who will rise from their beds to watch the scene in the street below.

The dustmen wear orange overalls, with leather aprons to protect them as they roll the bins into the street.

I watched a young man remove the refuse of the kosher restaurant in the Jewish Town Hall before moving on to the Golem Restaurant where, earlier in the day, I had sent back a 'Kalbsfilet jüdischer Art' which was garnished with a slice of ham.

He was an energetic young man with laughing eyes and a mop of curly hair. He performed his task with an air of cheerful bravado. The light lit his face into an orange mask.

His companion was a big black Dobermann pinscher, his snout in a basketwork muzzle, who either sat on the passenger seat, or hurtled round the block chasing cats, or lovingly rested his forepaws on his master's shoulders.

Turning into Široká Street, the young man manoeuvred the truck arse-first against the kerb, on the opposite side to the Pinkas Synagogue. Then, having rolled out the dustbins from Nos 4, 5 and 6, he stationed them in groups on the sidewalk.

An orange arm shot forth from the truck; clamped its claws around the lip of the bin; lifted it upside down into the air; and, with a double *chu-unk!* . . . *chu-unk!* . . . jettisoned the contents into the vehicle's belly.

The bin returned to earth with a bang, while from inside the truck came the noise of gnashing, crushing, churning, compressing and the shriek of metal teeth.

The Doberman tried to lick my face but was unable to slide its tongue through the muzzle. The dustman was friendly to the man who had befriended his dog and, to my surprise, spoke English.

What was I doing here?

'I'm a writer,' I said.

'So am I,' he said.

Many of his colleagues were writers, or poets or out-of-work actors. They met on Saturdays to drink in a village near the dump. He gave directions how to get there.

'Ask for Ludvík,' he said.

The village was an oasis of orchards and cottage gardens in a waste of industrial pollution. In a garden of roses and hollyhocks, Ludvík was hosing down his truck.

He took me to the bar where his friends, in overalls of orange and blue, were knocking back tankards of Pilsen beer. Some read newspapers, some played chess. In a quiet corner two men were playing backgammon. They finished, and turned to greet us.

One of the men was a Catholic philosopher, Miroslav Žítek, who, as I knew from émigré publications, was the author of an essay on the self-destructive nature of Force. He was a broadshouldered man with greying sideburns and an open, pink face. He was smoking a meerschaum pipe. He told me how, in Socialist Czechoslovakia, everyone over the age of sixty had the right to a State pension, providing he had put in the required years of work. He and his friends preferred not to embroil themselves in white-collar squabbles: manual labour was better for the mind.

Žítek had worked as a gardener, street-sweeper and garbage-collector but, with two years to sixty, he found that kind of work exhausting, and had got a new job. He was a bike-boy.

The job was to take computer-software across Prague, from one computer-centre to another. The software fitted into one of his saddlebags, his philosophical treatise into the other. Whenever he made a delivery, the manager of the centre would set aside a room for him to work in. He would work for three hours. Sometimes, at the end of the day, he read a chapter to an audience of workers.

He had some strong things to say about certain Czech writers in exile who, assuming for themselves the mantle of Bohemian culture, neglected what was happening in Bohemia.

Žítek's backgammon-partner was a man with tremendous biceps and a grinning face latticed with scars. His name was Košík. He had gone to America after '68, to Elizabeth, New Jersey, but had returned because the beer was undrinkable.

It was he who, in 1973 – the year of Utz's first stroke – had done the garbage round in the Old Jewish Quarter. He would thus have emptied Utz's dustbins.

I now come to the most difficult part of my story. Once I took it into my head that the Utz Collection could have vanished down the maw of a garbage truck, my temptation was to twist every scrap of evidence in that direction.

Košík answered my questions with amused good humour. But I am doubtful, in retrospect, whether his answers were genuine, or the answers I wanted to hear. I cannot place much reliance on the image he spun for me: that, when clearing the bins of No. 5 Široká Street, he sometimes saw a shadowy figure flattening himself or herself against the back wall of the entrance lobby. One night, he said, a pair of figures appeared at the window of the top floor apartment – and waved.

I felt I was on firmer ground with Košík's second story:

here, at least, there was a measure of agreement among his drinking companions.

They agreed that ten or twelve years ago – more maybe – a taxi used to bring an elderly couple to the village for a Sunday afternoon stroll. The man was shorter than the woman, shuffled his feet, and had to be supported on her arm. They would walk along the lane, as far as the wire fence surrounding the dump, and then walk back to the taxi.

I walked along the lane.

The fields were overgrown with ragwort and willow-herb. Factory chimneys were churning clouds of brown smoke in the direction of the city. The sky was tied in a tangle of electric cables.

I came to the fence. A rank of bulldozers stood outside a shed. Beyond lay the dump: an area of raw earth and refuse, with seagulls screaming over it.

I walked back to the village, thinking over the various possibilities.

Had Utz or Marta smuggled the collection abroad? No. Had the museum officials smuggled it abroad? No. Dr Frankfurter would have known. Did Utz destroy his porcelains out of pique? I was doubtful. He loathed museums, but he was not a vindictive man.

But he *was* a joker! I felt it might have appealed to his sense of the ridiculous that these brittle Rococo objects should end up on a twentieth-century trash-heap.

Or was it a case of iconoclasm? Is there, alongside the tendency to worship images – which Baudelaire called 'my unique, my primitive passion' – a counter-tendency to smash them to bits? Do images, in fact, demand their own destruction?

Or was it Marta? Did *she* have the vindictive streak? Did she connect Utz's love of porcelain with his love for opera singers? If so, having got rid of one lot, she might as well rid herself of the other.

No. My impression is that none of these theories will work. I believe that, in reviewing his life during those final months, he regretted having always played the trickster. He regretted having wheedled himself and the collection out of every tight corner. He had tried to preserve in microcosm the elegance of European court life. But the price was too high. He hated the grovelling and the compromise – and in the end the porcelains disgusted him.

Marta had never given in. She had never once lowered her standards, never lost her craving for legitimacy. She had stayed the course. She was his eternal Columbine.

My revised version of the story is that, on the night of their wedding in church, she emerged from the bathroom in her pink art-silk dressing-gown and, unloosing the girdle, let it slide to the floor and embraced him as a true wife. And from that hour, they passed their days in passionate adoration of each other, resenting anything that might come between them. And the porcelains were bits of old crockery that simply had to go.

The village of Kostelec lies close to the Austrian border, near the watershed between the Danube and the Elbe. The wheatfields have been invaded by biblical 'tares': but the cornflowers, the poppies, knapweed, scabious, and larkspur make one rejoice in the beauty of European countryside as yet unpoisoned by selective weedkillers. On the edge of the village there are water-meadows and, beyond, there is a lake where carp are raised, half-encircled with a stand of pines.

The houses of the village have red-tiled roofs, and their walls are freshly washed with ochre and white. The women plant geraniums in their window-boxes. On the village green, there is a well-tended chapel with a tiny dome.

Beside the chapel there is the base of a monument which once would have borne the double K's – Kaiserlich und Königlich – of the Dual Hapsburg Monarchy. It now supports a rusty, lopsided contraption commemorating a Soviet foray into space.

A storm was passing. The thunderheads rolled away, and a rainbow arched over the water-meadows. The sun illuminated gardens of yellow rudbeckia, purple phlox and banks of white shasta daisies.

I unlatched a wicket-gate. A snow-white gander flapped towards me, craning his neck and hissing. An old peasant woman came to the door. She wore a flowered housecoat, and a white scarf low over her forehead. She frowned. I murmured a word or two and her face lit up in an astounded smile.

And she raised her eyes to the rainbow and said, 'Ja! Ich bin die Baronin von Utz.'

The Viceroy of Ouidah

Beware and take care
Of the Bight of Benin.
Of the one that comes out
There are forty go in.

Slayer's Proverb

One

The family of Francisco Manoel da Silva had assembled at Ouidah to honour his memory with a Requiem Mass and dinner. It was the usual suffocating afternoon in March. He had been dead a hundred and seventeen years.

The Mass was said in the Cathedral of the Immaculate Conception, a stuccoed monument to the more severe side of French Catholicism that glared across an expanse of red dirt at the walls, the mud huts and trees of the Python Fetish.

Turkey buzzards drifted in a milky sky. The metallic din of crickets made the heat seem worse. Banana leaves hung in limp ribbons. There was no wind.

Father Olimpío da Silva had come into town from the Séminaire de Saint-Gall. A white-haired presence in a crimson cassock, he stood on the south steps, surveying his relatives through steel-rimmed spectacles and swivelling his luminous bronze head with the authority of a gun-turret.

Not only a priest but an ethnographer by calling, he had attended the lectures of Bergson and Marcel Mauss at the Sorbonne; had published an intricate volume, *Les Sacrifices humains chez les Fons*, and was unable to begin a sentence without a qualifying adverb: '*statistiquement . . . morphologiquement . . .*'

Gravelly organ music floated by; the organist had a limited range of chords.

The Da Silvas had come from Nigeria, from Togo, from Ghana and even from the Ivory Coast. The poor had come by bus and taxi. The rich were in private cars, and the richest of all, Madame Hélène da Silva, better known as Mama Benz, now sat sprawled over the back seat of her cream-coloured Mercedes, cooling herself with a fan of 10,000-franc notes and waiting for the service to end.

Everyone in the family knew their ancestor by his Brazilian name, Dom Francisco.

He came from San Salvador da Bahia in 1812 and, for over thirty years, was the 'best friend' of the King of Dahomey, keeping him supplied with rum, tobacco, finery and the Long Dane guns which were made not in Denmark but in Birmingham.

In return for these favours, he enjoyed the title of Viceroy of Ouidah, a monopoly over the sale of slaves, a cellar of Château Margaux and an inexhaustible seraglio of women. At his death in 1857, he left sixty-three mulatto sons and an unknown quantity of daughters whose ever-darkening progeny, now numberless as grasshoppers, were spread from Luanda to the Latin Quarter. Yet, among those who gathered in the square, only five had travelled to Europe and none to the Americas.

Turbaned ladies hobbled towards the cathedral, scuffing the dust with feet too splayed and calloused to admit the wearing of shoes. Their cottons were printed with leaves and lions and portraits of military dictators. They hauled themselves into the teak pews.

Little girls tripped about in frilly dresses: their hair was balkanized into zones, each zone twirled up in a tinselled plait.

Their brothers wore tight pants and shifted from foot to foot, holding, but not wearing, the red-starred caps of the Jeunes Militants.

The younger men were in national costume, the old men in suits of white duck or faded khaki.

The lives of the older Da Silvas were empty and sad. They mourned the Slave Trade as a lost Golden Age when their family was rich, famous and white. They were worn down by rheumatism and the burdens of polygamy. Their skin cracked in the harmattan; then the rains came and tambourined on their caladiums and splashed dados of red mud up the walls of their houses.

Yet they clung to their képis and pith-helmets as they clung to the forms of vanished grandeur. They called themselves 'Brazilians' though they had lost their Portuguese. People slightly blacker than themselves they called 'Blacks'. They called Dahomey 'Dahomey' long after the Head of State had changed its name to Benin. Each hung Dom Francisco's picture among their chromolithographs of saints and the Virgin: through him they felt linked to Eternity.

Father Olimpío rose before the altar and intoned his annual message in a consoling baritone: the Father-of-Them-All had not died but come to Life Everlasting. He looked down on his Children from his Heavenly Resting Place. He counselled them from the infinite store of his wisdom, 'especially,' he added in an undertone, 'in this, your hour of need'.

At the *Credo*, the ladies sighed, heaved their thighs and got to their feet. Letters, lions, leaves and military dictators rustled and recomposed themselves.

Mrs Rosemary da Silva, the wife of a Lagos accountant, shut her ear to the blasphemies: she was a Methodist. She sat when they kneeled for the *Sanctus* and she sat through the *Agnus Dei*. Her husband, Ernest, was beside her, sweating into an English blazer, wishing she hadn't come. He felt a rush of love and pity for his own kind. She merely did her best to embarrass him.

She made a show of adjusting her straw boater. She smoothed the folds of her white piqué dress and clacked three ropes of glass beads against her bosom. When the Da Silvas went up to receive the Host, heads bowed in reverence, she looked airily up at the ceiling, wondering how long it would take to fall down.

The building reeked of decay. Seams of rust were splintering the iron pillars of the aisle. The blue planks of the roof were rotten. Someone had stolen the ivory Dove of Peace inlaid into the altar table. Though the Virgin still beckoned from her niche, her hands were tied in a tangle of cobwebs.

And there were one or two more conspicuous changes: a Red Star hovered over the Crèche; the faces of the Holy Family had been repainted the colour of Balthazar, and the confessional was full of scarlet drums.

After the Benediction, the family sang the canticle *Mido gbe we* (*Salve Regina*) in Fon. Father Olimpío slapped his missal shut and small boys scampered for the sunlight.

On the steps of the cathedral the Da Silvas posed for their annual photograph.

Agostinho-Ezekiel da Silva was in charge of the ritual. A bird-like gentleman of eighty-nine, he was one of the four surviving grandchildren of the Founder, and Head of the Family.

His skin stretched tight over a bald and shining skull and his toothless mouth was drawn to a perfect O. Silently, he waved instructions with a silver-headed cane: the old people would sit on chairs, the young would stand on the steps and their parents would fill the space between.

Two spindly boys helped him compose the group. Their names were Modeste and Pierre and they were having a terrible time with the ladies.

'*Mettez-vous là, madame!*'

'*Bougez, madame!*'

'*Ne bougez pas, madame!*'

But the ladies went on fidgeting, arguing, elbowing and shoving their sisters aside.

Nor were the men behaving any better.

Uncle Procopio, a retired flautist of the Dakar Conservatoire, was reciting his 'Ode to the Death of the Dahomean Republic'. Gustave the intellectual told him to shut up. Africo da Silva was describing his gas station. Karl-Heinrich said that Togolese State Railways ran on time, while old Zéférino, a Kardecist medium, spoke of the planchette conversation he had had with his brother, Colonel Tigré da Silva, in exile on the Champs-Élysées: as usual the colonel had been sipping champagne and eyeing the girls.

Meanwhile the photographer was getting desperate.

He was a young man called Cyriaque Cabochichi, with a shaved gourd-like head, skin so black it glinted blue and the most serious approach to his profession. On the back of his sleeveless orange jumpsuit were a purple lamb and letters reading 'Foto Studio Agnew Pascal'.

He stood behind his tripod, half-hidden under the black cloth, signalling with both arms to Modeste and Pierre to push the ladies from either end and squeeze them within the frame of his plate camera.

The boys got wildly excited. They shoved at the ladies' backsides. They slapped them. They pinched them. But the ladies took no notice: their attention was drawn to the Python Temple where a European tourist was photographing the *féticheur.* The old man stood on one leg, a blue cloth round his midriff, pulling a face of absolute contempt, with the python's head nuzzling his left nipple and its tail coiled round his umbilical hernia.

The sun throbbed and slid downwards, casting blood-red shadows and gilding the jagged edges of the papaya leaves.

'The light's going,' moaned Cyriaque Cabochichi, and brought the ladies to their senses.

Nothing was going to deprive them of their photograph. With a show of unity unimaginable a minute before, they turned sideways into a conga and the length of the line shrank.

Papa Agostinho set a picture of Dom Francisco on his knees. His chief wife, Yaya Felicidade, tried to control a wayward breast. Gustave tilted his bowler, Procopio twiddled his moustache. Modeste held up the green satin banner of the Société Brésilienne du Carnaval, and the ladies spread their mouths to the camera: flashes of white and gold burst through their lips.

Overhead the first fruit bats were flying towards the southeast. There was a vague smell of guavas and stale urine. Cyriaque Cabochichi lifted his lens cap and replaced it.

★

From the Place de l'Immaculée Conception the family set off for the Portuguese Fort.

Two boys beat a tam-tam. Smaller boys waved maracas, banged gongs, whirled bicycle tyres, and cartwheeled in the dust. Pierre carried a wreath of pink vinyl roses to place on the shrine of the Virgin.

At the end of the Rue du Monsignor Steinmetz, the procession made a detour round the carcass of a bombax. The Minister of the Interior had declared the tree 'a sorcerers' restaurant' and ordered it to be chopped down after a subaltern of the Gendarmerie caught an old man in the act of nailing a charm to its trunk: the charm had contained a bat claw, some crushed spiders and a newspaper clipping of the President.

The Da Silvas came into the Place du Marché Zobé. Mountainous mammas were sailing home in the opposite direction. Long-fingered Mandingo traders were folding lengths of indigo into tin trunks. The medicine man wrapped the excrement of a rainbow into a rag, and the state lottery salesman was making his final call to the 'fidèles amis de la chance'.

It was the hour when the fetish priests slaughtered a fowl over Aizan, the Market God, an omphalos of cut stone standing alone in an empty space.

It was also the hour for the intellectuals of Ouidah to gather at the Librairie Moderne and discuss the latest books, even though its stock had been reduced to back numbers of the La Femme soviétique; the Thoughts of Kim Il-Sung; a Socialist novel called Le Baobab; Racine's Bajazet; a complete Engels and some pots of macaw-coloured brilliantine.

And it was supper-time. A hundred smoky lamps had lit up the booths where optimistic matrons were ladling millet beer from calabashes, frying fritters in palm-oil, wrapping maize blancmange in banana leaves or grilling joints of agouti, a big rat with yellow teeth.

Their hands reached out for their customers' money – pink, moist and affectionate as dog tongues. Babies were tucked into their cottons. All were asleep: not a single baby cried.

One of the women plucked a wing-feather from a live fowl and twizzled it in her ear.

'It's to take away the human grease,' a small boy informed the European tourist: and the tourist, who was collecting this kind of information, patted the boy's head and gave him a franc.

'I like the Whites,' the boy purred, 'because the Whites repair me.'

Mama Benz went in the Mercedes: she was far too heavy to walk. As the chauffeur drew abreast of the mammas, she stopped for a snack of agouti in sauce, handing out a white enamel bowl to the woman, who handed it back.

The boy said, 'Mama Benz is a carnivore, heh?'

More little boys, teeth glittering in the half-light, kept up a deafening chorus: *'Ago! Yovo! Ago! Yovo!'* – which means, 'Go away, Whitey!'

Meanwhile the Da Silvas turned right up the Rue Lenine, past the Hotel Windsor, past the Hotel Anti-Windsor and came up to the Bar Ennemi du Soir, where Uncle Procopio slipped in for a drink.

Nailed to the wall was a rattan mat with three giraffes moving through a Chinese landscape, beside which someone had scrawled in blue chalk:

The dog howls
　The caravan goes by

Two Lagos taxis were parked outside, the Confidence Car and Baby Confidence. Earlier in the afternoon the groans of love were heard from behind the splintering shutters of the bedrooms. But now the drivers were drinking beer with the bar girls and, over the radio, the Head of State was barking the first of his evening monologues.

The smallest bar girl gasped and bared her armpit in astonishment as Uncle Procopio bowed, clicked his heels and said, 'Mamzelle, I need a green chartreuse.' She fixed her eyes on his incredible moustache, poured from the bottle as if by instinct, and held her gaze till he had downed the glass and gone.

All the young Marxists came out and ogled the Mercedes as it passed.

The Da Silvas finally reached the Fort and laid the wreath.

They inspected the Independence Memorial – the last Portuguese Resident's burned-out Citroën set up on a concrete plinth.

They looked out over the south bastion at the grey lagoon, at the mangroves and the line of surf beyond.

The flourish of Arab calligraphy was a canoeman punting home.

Soft lights were seen moving along the track to the beach, up which Dom Francisco had come, down which the word 'Voodoo' made its way to the Americas.

Then they went back to Simbodji.

The ancestral home of the Da Silvas was a mud-walled compound to the west of the taxi park, where, for a week before the Mass, the noises of rasping, thumping, grinding and sizzling had drowned the infernal chatter of weaver birds as Dom Francisco's descendants cooked the dishes he loved to eat.

Girls came back from market with pitchers of pigs' blood. Boys rode bicycles with strings of offal slung from their shoulders. Fishermen brought baskets of oysters and blue-clawed crabs. Old men brought leaves from the forest. Old women crystallized eggs in honey.

The six-year-old Grégoire da Silva pointed to a column of ants marching into an unplugged refrigerator and said, 'The refrigerator exists.'

Modeste and Pierre spent the week sloshing apricot lime-wash over the walls of Dom Francisco's private quarters – two long low buildings set at right-angles around the main courtyard.

Both boys stripped to the waist but wore dunces' caps of newspaper to stop the paint from caking in their hair.

They picked out the crosses over the lintels and took infinite care to mix the colour of the doors and shutters, a colour that was neither black nor purple nor brown but was the colour of themselves.

Then they set to work on the old gaming saloon.

They emptied the dead flies from a Japanese porcelain bowl. They mended a broken spittoon and nailed a hardboard sheet over the collapsed wicker seat of a sofa. They scrutinized the ruins of a billiard table, without being able to imagine how one played, and flicked an ostrich feather over the frames of the pictures – for the room was also a portrait gallery.

Around the blue-washed walls hung the heads of the Da Silvas, from the Founder to the present Chief.

Dom Francisco's knotted brow and scarlet skull-cap glowered from a canvas of treacly impasto, done twenty years after his death by a wandering Sicilian artist who got stuck in Ouidah in the 1870s and had obviously earned his living from ikons of Garibaldi.

A far more competent likeness was that of his son, Isidoro da Silva, the Second Chief, painted in Bahia to celebrate his twenty-first birthday in 1837. The young mulatto dandy was shown standing in a book-lined library, wearing a blue frock-coat, a velvet cravat, and with a flowered white satin waistcoat shining over his paunch. One hand clutched at his lapel, the other fingered the diamond knop of his cane.

The portraits of his brothers, Lino and Antonio, were also the work of the Sicilian dauber. There was a sepia photograph of Cândido, the Fifth Chief, in the uniform of an Honorary Colonel of the Portuguese Infantry. And lastly there was a framed page of the souvenir catalogue of the Paris Exhibition of 1900, where Estevão da Silva and his son Agostinho-Ezekiel were exhibited as 'Fils et Petit-Fils du Négrier'.

Dom Francisco himself lay sleeping under his bed, in a chamber that overlooked a garden of red earth and plastic flowers where lizards sunned themselves on the flat white marble tombs. The room was the preserve of Yaya Adelina, a laundrywoman, who would allow no one to enter without permission.

The bed was a Goanese four-poster with ebony uprights and a headboard set with ivory medallions. But the most arresting feature was a painted plaster statue of St Francis of Assisi, his brown cassock girdled with a rope of real knots, gazing at the mildewed sheets of his namesake and lifting his hands in prayer.

A white marble plaque, set into the floor, read:

FRANCISCO MANOEL DA SILVA
Nascido em 1785 Brazil
Fãlecido a 8 de março 1857 em Ajuda (Ouidah)

A wreath of arums bore the legend 'Pour Notre Illustre Aïeul!' and on a shelf stood a gilt crucifix, a yellowing Ecce Homo and a silver elephant, which was the family emblem.

Yaya Adelina carried her veneration of the ancestor to such lengths that she kept a bottle of Gordon's Gin open on the bed-table in case he should wake up.

Every morning, in case he wanted to wash, she refilled the silver water-jug cast from Maria Theresa thalers that melted when a British shell fired a warehouse in the 1840s.

From time to time she would remove the white cloth covering a rusty iron object resembling an umbrella, clotted with blood and feathers, and stuck into the floor.

This was an *Asin*, the Dahomean Altar of the Dead.

Two days before the celebration there was a moment of alarm when Lieutenant-Colonel Zossoungbo Patrice of the Sûreté Nationale burst in on Papa Agostinho's siesta and banned the celebration.

The colonel was twenty-four, and had long curly eye-lashes and knife-edge creases to his green paratrooper fatigues. Two grenades, the shape of scent-bottles, were slung from his belt.

Papa Agostinho wrapped a towel round his tummy and rocked his rocking chair, while the young revolutionary paced up and down, waving a North Korean sub-machine gun to emphasize important points:

Family festivals, he shouted, were the barbarous and fetishistic survivals of the colonial period . . .

But the afternoon was hot and the colonel was tired.

His voice rose to a childish treble. He was terrified of not making the right impression and, when Papa Agostinho made a very modest cash offer, was so relieved and grateful that he allowed the Da Silvas to go ahead – on one condition (he had to make a condition): they must listen to the Presidential broadcast at eight o'clock.

Then, with a smile of radiant innocence, he doffed his cap as if it were a schoolboy cap, and edged out backwards.

His boot crushed a begonia as he went.

The colonel's visit explained the brown plastic radio blaring martial music as the guests came in to dinner.

There was a table covered with red-chequered oilcloth. Kerosene lamps spread streams of yellow light over the aerial roots of the banyan. Two mango trees, glimmering with fireflies, cut arcs of blacker velvet in the sky.

Never, not even in the time of Dom Francisco, had Ouidah witnessed so unctuous a feast.

Pigs' heads were anointed with gumbos and ginger. Black beans were frosted with cassava flour. Silver fish glittered in a sauce of malaguetta pepper. There was a ragout of guinea-fowl and seri-flowers, which were reputed to have aphrodisiac properties. There were mounds of fried cockscombs, salads of carrot and papaya, and pastes of shrimp, cashew nuts and coco-flesh.

The names of Brazilian dishes were on everyone's lips: *xinxin de galinha, vatapà, sarapatel, muqueca, molocoto.* There were phallic sweetmeats of tamarind and tapioca, ambrosias, bolos, babas and piles of golden patisseries.

Yaya Adelina, her head shaved and her cottons whirling with the rings of Saturn, lumbered round the table, scooping up a sample of each dish into a calabash carved with totemic animals.

Uncle Procopio moved towards the *petits-pains au chocolat* murmuring, '*Byzance!*' He had all but thrust one through his moustachios when Adelina slapped his back:

'Shame on you, sir! Eating before the Father eats!'

She set the calabash on a table outside Dom Francisco's bedroom window and covered it with a cloth of broderie anglaise.

Everyone waited for something to happen.

A gong clanged. A drum rolled. Grégoire da Silva hurtled from the shadows shouting, 'Dom Francisco! Dom Francisco!' and a differently dressed procession filed into the yard.

Men in white loincloths came in with images wrapped in red stuff. Others carried chickens and a pot-bellied goat. Everyone was chanting the Founder's song: 'The Elephant spreads his net on land and sea . . .' Their bodies were smeared with white powder and their cicatrices stood up like lumps of candlegrease.

Three young drummers were calling the Ancestor back to Earth. The sweat stuck their shirts to their skin and dark patches spread from their armpits like ink on blotting-paper.

Papa Agostinho wore coral chokers and an opera hat sequinned with butterflies and a bleeding heart. His son, Africo da Silva, had on a yellow petalled crinoline, while Yaya Felicidade, in a headscarf of purple pansies, waved about a nineteenth-century English naval cutlass.

The drumbeats took the women and propelled them into the juddering movements of the dance. An effeminate in pink satin pants groaned, swayed and fell rigid as a plank.

Other women knelt before the window kneading the hamstrung goat and bellowing, 'Za! Za! Zanku! It is Night! Night!' Chickens squawked and fell silent. The knife fell on the goat's neck and its life gurgled away.

The shutters burst open to reveal Papa Agostinho standing inside his grandfather's bedroom. The women handed him the foaming red calabash. He sprinkled food and blood and feathers and Gordon's Gin over the bed, the grave and Altar of the Dead.

Africo called out, 'The Dead has eaten now!' Someone predicted that rain would water the maize, and from the far end of the courtyard could be heard the booming voice of Father Olimpío: 'Syncrétisme!'

Mrs Rosemary da Silva shook her fist and shouted, 'Ah no go fo com heah fo no juju!' and stamped off, followed by her husband.

Everyone agreed the Nigerians had no manners.

While the votaries dressed and changed, the band relaxed into a Brazilian samba. Father Olimpío took his place at the head of the table:

'Bénissez-nous, Mon Dieu, pour la nourriture que nous mangeons ce soir . . .'

Throughout dinner, the President's voice came in cracked bursts: there was something the matter with the radio. He called on the People to break the 'umbilical cord of International Imperialism' and, when lost for words, would howl, 'Down with Intellectuals!' or 'Death to Mercenaries and the Lackeys of Capitalism!'

Nobody took much notice.

Stuffing his face with compaste, Hermengildo da Silva

made no secret of the fact that he had sacrificed a goat to Gu, the God of War. Mama Benz hiccoughed. Adelina sneezed and sprayed pineapple juice over the table. Uncle Procopio offered to play Dvořák's *Humoresque*; and the twin brothers, Euclides and Policarpo, squabbled about whether the family motto should read, 'Flies are not visible in society!' or 'Flies are not acceptable in society!'

But as usual, the favourite topic was the loss of Dom Francisco's fortune; and as usual, the family's 'German', Karl-Heinrich (Gazozo) da Silva, set his fists on the table and began his annual dissertation:

'I have it on the authority of my late father, Anton Wilhelm, that Our Illustrious Ancestor deposited thirty-six million US dollars in a Swiss bank . . .'

'It wasn't a Swiss bank,' Agostinho interrupted. 'It was the Banco Coutinho in Bahia.'

'Petrification,' shrieked the President, ' . . . Paralysation! . . . Mystification! . . . Mummification!'

'And that your Uncle Antonio . . .'

'They weren't dollars. They were cruzeiros . . .'

' . . . lost the paper . . .'

'He didn't lose it. He drank it.'

' . . . to sensibilize . . . to organize . . . to mobilize . . .'

'I tell you, he burned the paper from the bank. He put it in a glass. Then he poured in a bottle of champagne and drank the lot.'

'I don't believe you.'

'It was a big glass.'

'And the fleet?' asked Yaya Adelina. 'What happened to the fleet?'

'Sunk by the British.'

' . . . to defeat this macabre plot to massacre our people . . .'

'Stolen by the Brazilian Government.'

'They should give it back.'

'They won't give it back.'

'We should start a process.'

' . . . to steal the incredible riches of our country . . .'

'Peanuts,' said Uncle Procopio.

'Peanuts?'

'We'd starve without peanuts.'

' . . . and the thunderous riposte of our Armed Forces . . .'

'And palm-oil . . .'

' . . . and our scientific and operational regime . . .'

'But peanuts give you cancer.'

'But they're all we've got.'

Africo da Silva said the President was giving him a headache. Gustave said you got headaches from the harmattan. Someone else said you got them from fruit bats, and Papa Agostinho wound up wearily by saying that Dom Francisco was ruined the year the United States stopped using cowrie-shells for money.

Mama Benz asked what a cowrie really was.

'Cowrie is a snail,' he said. 'It lives in a river called Mississippi. In the old days, the Americans would throw a slave in the river, the cowries would feed on the body, and then they'd haul it up and that's how they got money to buy more slaves.'

'Revolution or Death!'

'So when they passed the law, there were no more cowries . . .'

'Marxist-Leninism is our only philosophical guide!'

' . . . and that's how Dom Francisco was ruined!'

'Ah! *Cette chinoiserie de la Révolution!*' Gustave da Silva shook his lovely head.

'And the fleet?' wailed Yaya Adelina. 'Whatever became of the fleet?'

Two

At twenty-five minutes past eight, a woman's wail rose up from the belly of the compound.

'Ey . . . yeo . . . yo . . . yo . . . o . . . o . . . o . . . wo . . . wo . . . wo . . . !'

The diners widened their arms and went silent. A girl, all arms and legs, rushed in.

'It's Mama Wéwé,' she shouted. 'She won't eat.'

Shooing Muscovy ducks before them, the Da Silvas followed the girl down an alley to the house with purple shutters.

They peered in. Moths whirled around a glutinous patch of lamplight.

Dom Francisco's own daughter, Wéwé the White One, the proof that he was white, lay dying at the far end of the room.

Mademoiselle Eugenia da Silva, a skeleton who happened to breathe, lay dying on an etruscan couch of jacaranda wood carved with anacardiums and passion flowers. Beside her was a plate of shredded papaya, uneaten.

Her tongue had locked to the roof of her mouth. Her lips had sunk without trace into the crevasses of her chin. Only her nose was visible, rearing from the tatters of a black lace bonnet, and the great white hands lying between the bones of her pelvis in a hollow of black bombazine.

The Da Silvas gazed at the miracle. That she should continue to live was not incredible. She was not that much older than Sagbadjou the King, who lived with his wives and retainers in a bungalow behind the palace at Abomey.

That she should die was unthinkable.

Sometimes, on cooler evenings, her shutter would creak open. The boys playing naked in the yard would cluster round and a withered white arm would reach through the closed black curtains and feel for their heads.

Sometimes they saw her face, the skin transparent as a gecko's and the green eyes milky with cataracts.

She still had power in her fingers. They would skim over the tight curls, but if they touched a head of straight hair, they would stroke and caress it, and the second hand would pass through the curtains and reward its owner with a coin of Louis Napoleon or Queen Victoria.

She lived *en princesse*, they said, on a diet of bean paste and papaya, drinking a little mango juice or an infusion of citronella grass. Her only companion was a withered crone called Mãe Roxa, who prepared and tasted her food: Mama Wéwé was still terribly afraid of being poisoned.

In 1953, at the celebrations of her hundredth birthday, she had pointed a finger at her relatives and said, 'Remember you are Brazilians!' She had never spoken since. The years went by without her ever opening her mouth except for food.

Before she withdrew into silence, Papa Agostinho was the one man whose presence she would tolerate. He would listen as she rambled over the disordered events of the century: of Amazons drumming in the courtyard; of the arms of General Dodds, 'quite hairy for a mulatto', or 'that animal' by which she meant Mère Agathe of the Petites Soeurs des Pauvres.

But when Agostinho asked her about the existence of some lost papers and tried to steer the conversation to the events of March 1857, she curled her lip.

Exactly ninety-eight years ago she fell in love.

She was tall and beautiful. Her skin was golden and her black hair streaked with auburn. She had eyes of greenish amber, the colour of a troubled sea. The corners of her mouth lifted in a perpetual smile from pronouncing the slushed, suggestive consonants of Brazilian Portuguese. At the sight of her swaying walk men had to hold themselves – yet, at the time, she was a virgin.

One evening, when the harmattan was blowing, she met the English agent coming up from the beach. He told her of a merchantman at anchor in the roads. On board was a professor who had come to collect the plants and animals of Dahomey.

That night she lay awake and tried to picture the professor. At sunrise she put on a dress of white muslin embroidered with blue flowers. She tied a ribbon to her straw hat and went with Mr Townsend to the shore.

Crabs scuttled sideways as they trod down the scarp of white sand. Through the mist they saw the hull and rolling yardarms: as it cleared they saw the red of her ensign and black dots which were the passengers and crew.

But the surf was running high. No passengers could land and the krumen went back to their huts.

Five days later the sea was down. Mr Townsend signalled

the 'All Clear!' She watched the canoe prows rear through the foam, and the backs of the krumen in a fitful sun.

Sharks swam between the inner and outer line of breakers, waiting for a capsize: they were said to have a taste for white flesh. The fetish-man stood in the shallows rattling a chaplet as the first canoe came in. She prayed as well. She could hardly bear to watch the men paddling as they tried to keep it straight.

The canoe roared over a crest and thudded on the shingle: black arms whisked the passengers ashore before the next wave broke.

The professor shook hands with Mr Townsend, rubbed the salt from his spectacles and began checking his pile of equipment. He was a heavy man, purple in the face, wearing a jacket with a lot of pockets and a pith-helmet and a veil.

In the first rush of her disappointment, she did not take in the tall, freckle-faced lieutenant with his red moustache and blue eyes the colour of the market-women's beads – and then she understood the pounding of her heart.

That evening he came to Simbodji with a request for hammockeers: he was going to Abomey with a message to deliver to the King.

At dinner he wore the blue and gold mess uniform of the Queen's 2nd West India Regiment, which was stationed at Cape Coast Castle. She spoke a little English and he said, 'We'll soon put a stop to that pidgin.'

Slowly, so she should understand every word, he told her of the Queen of England and the City of London. She tried to imagine snow – soft and white like the down of the silk-cotton tree, but cold, how cold she could not guess.

She played the Swiss musical boxes that had once

belonged to her father. They watched the steel combs and the bristling brass cylinders that turned erratically because the combs were corroded with rust. He tried to sing Schubert's 'Trout', but the tempo was far too erratic and they ended up laughing.

Then she found the key to the box that played waltzes. Not knowing the steps, she let her feet drift and the weight of her body fall on his hand in the small of her back.

He played billiards with her half-brother Antonio and allowed him to win. She heard them murmuring in English and, when she looked in their direction, saw the avid blue eyes through clouds of Havana smoke.

Next morning he came with presents: two scarves of Madras silk, a marcasite necklace and a gilt toilet mirror – all intended for the ladies of the King.

At sunset they walked to the garden at Zomai where Dom Francisco had built a Chinese pavilion. The trunks of the mango trees had been whitewashed and the breeze stirred a glissando of coco fronds.

The pavilion had upturned eaves and round windows that were no longer round. The old gardener had swept it clean as if for a picnic. He slipped away as they came in and she thought, 'So my brother arranged all this.'

Her forelip tingled from the bristles of his moustache. His hands were gentle at first but she could feel them hardening. Her dress ripped as she tore herself away.

He dropped her in surprise. She did not scream. She ran from the garden into the red street, where some Fon drummer boys were practising. They jeered and thumbed her and struck up a thumping rhythm as she passed.

She shut herself in her room and lay face downward on

the brass bed covered with country cloths. Only when her pillow was wet through did she realize the extent of her loneliness.

Not that she had been ignorant of what to expect. Virgins were broken at Simbodji with the ease of bursting seed pods. From childhood she had known the coarse laughter of women as they sniffed the bloodstained rag. Her half-brothers had tried to force her. Her half-sisters pursed their lips if approached by anyone darker than themselves – yet they were always willing to whore to white sailors.

An unlearned code of honour had stopped her sinking to their level.

But when he came back in the morning, mumbling apologies, she fell, a lovely automaton, into his arms.

She said, 'Take me with you!'

'I will,' he said, and instantly regretted it.

The porters were ready to carry the expedition up-country.

The lieutenant and the professor lay on the blue-and-white striped hammocks. The porters lifted their weight as if it were nothing, and they set off with a clatter of gongs and retching of ivory trumpets. The last she saw of them was a khaki sleeve waving as they went out of sight.

For three weeks her mood varied from euphoria to despair. Then, late one night, a boy ran over from Mr Townsend's house: the younger white had come back sick, very sick; and the professor had been kept by the King.

The colour of his face had gone beyond the white of the bed-curtains. His eyes were yellow and his mouth was grey, foaming at the edges, babbling names that meant nothing to her. Mr Townsend diagnosed an attack of malaria that would, perhaps, be fatal. He had run out of quinine, but had the sense not to despise the remedy she fetched from the herbalist. He rammed it down the throat of the patient, who recovered.

As the fever left him, he would shout hysterically, 'Get me out of here! Do something!' and when Mr Townsend told him of a Dutch brig at anchor, he said, 'Get me aboard!'

None of the King's subjects was allowed to leave Dahomey without permission, so she had to go down to the beach under guard. His manner was correct but his voice was cold: from England he would send the passage money, and the bride-price.

It was a grey and windless day but the crashing breakers wafted a current of air that set her muslin dress flapping between her legs. She waved a scarf as the canoe shoved off. He did not wave back but stared out to sea, fixedly, at the waiting ship.

She waited six months, a year, two years. She learned the art of lace-making from a slavewoman freed from Bahia. Together they made headcloths, petticoats and napkins: she was anxious to possess every accomplishment.

She taught herself to read. She pretended to read, but though she could distinguish one page from another, though she could even memorize the letters on a page, she was never able to unravel the sense from the lines.

Hoping to master more English, she went each Thursday to the service of hymn-singing in the Methodist Chapel. The Reverend Bernabo was a Sierra Leone mulatto, who had Dundreary whiskers and had been educated in England. He taught her the scales on a tinny upright piano and soon, to the toc-toc of the metronome, she was playing 'Abide with

Me!' or 'Mine Eyes have seen the Glory of the Coming of the Lord!'

The missionary's daughters adored her. They would all wear white together and, when they sang, a wide-eyed crowd was sure to gather at the gate. She was bitterly upset to learn they hired themselves to pay for their father's drink.

She went on long walks alone.

On thundery afternoons, when perpendicular clouds towered high in the sky, she would wander through the palm-groves to the lagoon and watch the black-and-white kingfishers flutter over the dark water.

Sometimes she walked inland to the campsites of the Peuls. These were a light-skinned people who slept under the stars and kept their beauty into old age. The harmattan brought them down from the savannah to the coast. Their lyre-horned cattle moved through the grass with a crackling sound. She welcomed their coming: the dry season also brought Europeans to the shore.

Her eyes would question Mr Townsend but pride prevented her from asking for news. He tried to avoid her: the callousness of his countryman embarrassed him. Only when his company recalled him did he find the courage to tell her of the professor's letter: the lieutenant had resigned his commission, married and settled in Somerset.

'Oh!' she said.

He had expected an outburst of grief and held out a hand to comfort her. But she stared at him as if he were mad and ran off, singing and dancing barefoot in the sand, to where some krumen were landing empty palm-oil puncheons from a ship.

★

The years hardened the contours of her face into angular planes. A pinched look came into the corners of her eyes. Her skin stretched tight over her nose and cheekbones, and fell in loose folds down her throat. At thirty she was an old maid, but after that her appearance hardly changed: the Slave Coast takes its victims young or pickles them to great antiquity.

One by one, her acquaintance narrowed to her maid, her Mahi slave-boy, her father and the red-haired stranger. Unable to make the distinction between the real and the supernatural, she made none between the living, the absent and the dead.

For all she cared, her relatives were the masks of a nightmare. And in their turn, the Da Silvas looked on the white childless woman with superstitious awe.

They suspected her of the Evil Eye. They took care to burn their loose hair and nail clippings. The women said she prowled round Simbodji at night, scooping up earth impregnated with their spittle.

Since no one would sleep under the same roof, they left her in possession of Joaquim da Silva's old villa at the far end of the compound. She bought a bolt of black cloth and draped it round her room. She took to wearing black herself, a stiff dress reaching to her calves and a lace bonnet tied under her chin.

For years she had lavished affection on her father's macaw, a bad-tempered bird called Zé Piranha, which pecked at strangers and its own feathers till it died of inanition. She then transferred her love to a scabby bitch with mastitis that lay all day in the shade of a banana, but at sunset would sit by the steps and howl.

Simbodji decayed. The roofs collapsed and the walls crumbled. Livid weeds smothered the piles of rubble, which were left to lizards, scorpions and snakes. Deprived of their revenues from the Slave Trade, the Da Silvas sank into tropical torpor.

In 1882 a tornado hit Dom Francisco's house, whirled its pantiles in the air and scattered them over the town.

In 1884 a girl was grilling cashew nuts when one burst from her brazier and set a roof on fire. Thirteen houses burned to the ground.

In 1887 Cândido da Silva, one of Dom Francisco's youngest sons, was elected Head of the Family on the strength of his talent for repairing the fortune. He even got the King of Dahomey to put his cross to a document that turned Ouidah over to the Portuguese as a protectorate.

The colonizers came with a military band from the island of São Tomé, and staked out the site for a barracks. The King sent Cândido a flattering message inviting him up to Abomey. And he left, in his Portuguese Colonel's uniform, with his wives, children, umbrella-bearers, musicians and an Amazon guard of honour.

He did not come back.

The Portuguese major, who went to ask for his comrade-in-arms, was shown into a mud house with a pair of executioners' knives flanking the doorway. The honorary colonel sat trussed to a European chair, still in his epaulettes, with an iron chain round his neck and a wooden gag shoved down his throat. At his feet was a silver bowl, buzzing with flies.

'Into that bowl,' the officer was told, 'go the heads of all who trouble the Kingdom.'

Nine days later, a detachment of Amazons burst into Simbodji in uniforms sewn with the crocodile insignia of their brigade.

They fired their muskets in the air and danced the decapitation dance, warning the Da Silvas that if they dared sell one grain of Dohomean soil, the house would be broken, razed, obliterated; and they would be sent to work the Royal Plantations, or to tell the King's ancestors how things stood in this perfidious world.

For months Simbodji was wrapped in the silence of the tomb.

Senhorinha Eugenia took advantage of the catastrophe to carry off some of Dom Francisco's relics, as if, by collecting his possessions, she could restore him to life.

She took his silver-mounted cigar case; his pink opaline chamber pot; his ivory-handled slave-brand with the initials F.S.; his rosary of carnauba nuts; some scraps of paper covered with his handwriting; a lithograph of the Emperor Dom Pedro II; a picture of a Brazilian house, and a particularly bloodthirsty canvas of Judith hacking off the head of Holophernes.

Her fellow-raider on these expeditions was Cândido da Silva's ten-year-old son, Cesário. He had got left behind when his parents went up to Abomey, and was now an orphan.

With his green eyes and wad of blond hair, Cesário was a throwback to an earlier strain in the family. And as young buds will expel an albino from their nest, the other boys made his life a misery and pelted him with filth and rotten fruit.

The climate disagreed with him. The sun peeled his skin leaving pink patches. There was a permanent scab on the bridge of his nose, and his mosquito bites would come up in welts and go septic.

He came to her one morning with chiggers in his left foot.

She laid him down, sharpened a knife blade, cut through the leathery sole, and scoured out the sack of eggs. He didn't even whimper. She kissed him on the forehead and took him to live with her.

She had never looked after a child and each day brought something new. She recovered her lilting walk and dazzling smile. The colour returned to her face. She threw off her black, put hoops of gold in her ears, and strode through the market in a dress of bright flowers.

She dressed Cesário in long whites, made him wear a panama of palm fibre and, in this uniform, sent him to the French Fathers to learn how to read. He would come home with stories of railways and knights-in-armour and all kinds of useful information: the Ancestors were, in fact, Gauls; the cows of Haute-Savoie gave six times more milk than cows in Africa.

He particularly liked the story of Moses and Pharaoh and kept asking whether Pharaoh was the same as the King of Dahomey: he was unimpressed when told he was not.

On rainy days she would take out a colour print distributed by the Church Missionary Society in Abeokuta, and she would point to the greybeard beckoning the traveller up the 'Straight and Narrow Path' and say, 'Look! It's a picture of your grandfather!'

Or they would spread out a panorama of Bahia and he would read off the names: 'Casa Santa da Misericórdia . . . Monastery of São Bento . . . Convent of Santa Teresa . . .' while her eyes ranged over the domes, towers and pediments which reminded her of the New Jerusalem floating down from Heaven.

She tried to picture the house they would live in when they went back to the City. She spoke of dancing in Bahia, in a tall blue room lined with mirrors and pillars of gold – which was quite untrue, for she had never strayed further than Ouidah.

At other times they would call on the Germans. In 1890 a Hamburg trading company called Goedelt bought the concession of the old British Fort. The newcomers drank beer from stoneware tankards and, in the evening, their mess-room clouded over with pipe-smoke. A cuckoo clock, painted with red roses, hung on the wall and there were pictures of the Rhinemaidens and one of the young Kaiser Wilhelm II.

Cesário was the favourite of Herr Raabe the director, who thought of training him as a book-keeper. Whenever Eugenia went over to fetch him, she brought a chicken or some fruit and would stand on one foot, shyly, in the doorway, rubbing her calf with the other foot and staring at the wall.

The Germans thought she was waiting for the cuckoo. When the bird popped out of its hutch, they would say in English, 'That's enough now, old lady. Thank you. Time to go home!' and when the door shut, in German, 'My God, how that woman stares!'

But she had only been staring at the Kaiser.

One evening she and Cesário were crossing the Sogbadji Quarter in the stillness that precedes a storm. White flags hung motionless over a fetish. Some old men were crouching in the shadows, whitewashed all over, with their heads hung low. Unusual numbers of turkey-buzzards were converging on the town.

From one house they heard a low moan; from another mourners carried a corpse wrapped in a reed mat with the feet poking out. They saw a man dragging himself into the bushes. There were patches of vomit and yellow excrement all down the street.

The cholera had come ashore with the crew of a ship.

They hurried home. She bolted the door and would admit no one: she knew that much about contagion.

At dusk on the third day, Cesário felt dizzy and had to lie down. Within an hour he had fouled his bed. Sweat streamed from his skin leaving it cold, inelastic and clammy. His eyes sank in their sockets and gaped, expressionless, at the rafters. He did not lose consciousness and locked his shrivelled fingers tightly round hers.

The crisis came at that moment in an African dawn when everything is golden. Doves were cooing in the garden. A shaft of sunlight fell through the window and framed the woman in blue who kneeled by the boy's bed. Cramps racked his body and his ribcage writhed like a concertina.

She bent over and kissed him, slowly sliding her tongue into his dry mouth, praying for the disease to leave him and come to her.

He gasped, 'Do leave me alone,' and soon he left her.

She went on living.

She went to a Brazilian trader and bought a length of azure cloth, the colour the Angels wore in Heaven. She washed the body, which had already taken on a greenish tinge. She wrapped it and laid it in a coffin of iroko wood. She fluffed his hair round like a halo. She put a gold coin in his hand and her gardener nailed down the lid.

They buried him in the family cemetery, under Dom

Francisco's window, with a cross of palm-fronds set over his head. None of her relations took any notice, being too distracted by their own deaths.

Three days later, Raabe's assistant saw her walking on the beach, her chin pressed against her throat, muttering and watching the sand squeeze between her toes.

Then she laughed and held her hands wide and waved a black scarf at the birdless sea.

He asked what she was doing and she said, 'He's gone to Bahia.'

The next few years washed over her without disturbing her solitude.

She failed to notice the outburst of human sacrifice that marked the accession of the new King, Behanzin the 'Shark'. She ignored the French bombardment of Ouidah which killed a hundred and thirty people and dismembered a sacred baobab. Nor did she celebrate when Estevão da Silva hauled an improvised tricolour up the flagpole and started the family on their career as brown Frenchmen.

The events of her life were the palm-nut harvest and the festivals of the Brazilian Church. For three weeks before Saints Cosmas and Damian in September, she and her maid, Roxa, would sew frilly dresses for the twin sisters of the town, who were almost worshipped as divinities. In January, they would help paint the mummers' costumes for the Bumba-Meu-Boi. And every 3rd of June, on John the Baptist's Day, they sat outside the chapel of the Portuguese Fort grilling ears of new corn for the congregants.

Because these occasions repeated themselves year after year, she lost all sense of growing old.

Mãe Roxa died in the smallpox epidemic of 1905 after refusing an inoculation. Her place was taken by an eighteen-year-old 'Brazilian' girl, whose real name was Cristella Chaves, but Eugenia would make no concession to the change, called her Roxa and expected her to know all about the last fifty years.

By 1914 the Chapel of the Fort had fallen into decay. She had long coveted the image of the Baptist's head and, to preserve it from looters, she took it away for safe-keeping. The head had glass eyes and snaky black curls and was the work of an African sculptor in Bahia who had carved the aorta, the oesophagus and third neck vertebra with meticulous attention to detail. He had screwed it to a Minton meat-dish stencilled with mauve carnations: painted blood trickled into the scoop intended to catch juices from the roast beef of Old England.

Her next idea was to convert Dom Francisco's bedroom into a shrine.

She and Roxa made rosaries. They made reliquaries. They made wreaths of artificial flowers from sea-shells and they improvised a Holy Ghost from a Pirevitte teapot in the form of a chicken. They hung up the panorama of Bahia, the picture of Judith and some religious colour prints: Santa Marta with a pair of bleeding hearts; Santa Luzia smiling at her own two eyes lying in the palm of her hand.

The head of the Baptist they set on the altar table.

Then, with the work all but finished, she hit on the idea of buying a statue of St Francis to stand at the foot of her father's bed.

The palm-nut buyer, Monsieur Poidevineau, advanced some money on her share of the crop and sent off to Marseille to a company that specialized in sacred sculpture.

The Poverello arrived at the railway station in a stout box. The Brazil-town band beat out a samba and Mama Wéwé – as she was now called – stood smiling on the platform as the train drew in. For the first time in twenty-five years she was not wearing black.

The Fathers of Our Lady of Africa heard of this touching example of faith and offered their help. But she would allow no one in the shrine until she was ready for the consecration.

One morning Fathers Truitard, Boët and Zérringer walked down to Simbodji in spotless white soutanes and sandals. She unbolted the door and ushered them in with a gesture of triumph.

They saw the head of Holophernes, the head of the Baptist, the slave chains, a toilet mirror and the nails and bloodstained feathers. Father Zérringer, who was an amateur zoologist, looked over the reliquaries and identified a vulture's claw, a python vertebra, a fragment of baboon skull and the eardrum of a lion.

'*Ce sont les gri-gris du marché*,' he whispered.

Knowing him to be less liable to sectarian anger, Father Truitard's colleagues deputed him to tell her the truth. He was an embarrassed man, with a pitted face and kind brown eyes, who had spent years communing with waves and petrels on the island of Ushant. He knew some Portuguese.

Mother Church, he explained, could not allow the worship of idolatrous objects on Holy Ground. The Faith was there. The heart was willing and the Flesh was willing. But she did need some lessons in scripture. Nor was the choice of St Francis a wise one to stand over the grave of a slaver.

'But he sent them to PARADISE!' she screamed, and pointed to the panorama of Bahia.

'But St Francis, my sister, was a poor wanderer, who loved all men and the birds and the animals . . .'

She was not listening. A hoarse cry tore from her lips. Her arms lashed out and flapped helplessly. She hurled herself out into the blazing sun and fell down in a heap.

Two days later, Mère Agathe of the Petites Soeurs des Pauvres barged past Roxa and forced her way into Eugenia's room. She withdrew after five minutes, her face scratched to ribbons and her habit a massacre of carmine.

Mama Wéwé sat another sixty years in the curdled odour of rotting brocade, her eyes glued to her father's portable oratory of the Last Supper.

This was a glass-fronted vitrine, the size of a small doll's house and made by the nuns of the Soledade in Bahia:

The miniature room had sky-blue walls, mirrors and gilded pilasters. On the floor there was a marquetry sunburst and, under a glass dome on the mantelpiece, a clock. Wooden figures of Christ and the Apostles were sitting down to a meal of plaster-of-Paris chicken. The eyes of Our Lord were the colour of turquoise and his head bristled with real red hair. In her imagination she would contract her body and stand watching in the doorway – though she would step aside for the shifty mulatto who left in the middle of the dinner.

The years slipped by and nobody repaired the house. The thatch rotted, the shutters splintered and, when ants undermined the floor, her rocking chair would no longer rock. Weeds sprang up in the rainy season, bleached for lack of light. Patches of mould spread over the walls: a delta of red streams fanned out from the wasps' nests in the rafters and cut across the termite trails.

Only once, in 1942, was there a break in the rhythm of her days.

After a noisy *vin d'honneur*, the Resident's wife, Madame Burlaton, mistook the accelerator for the brake of her Peugeot and distributed Aizan, the Market Fetish, in pieces all over the square. The *féticheurs* demanded a human sacrifice for the reconsecration. Her husband refused. There was a riot.

A platoon of Senegalese spahis fired, killing a goat and wounding a woman in the leg. Roxa heard the shots and, four hours later, ran to the barracks with a message for their commanding officer: Mademoiselle da Silva would be delighted to receive him.

Lieutenant André Parisot had heard of the mysterious white woman whom nobody had seen. He took some time to macassar his hair and put on his best whites.

'Lieutenant,' she said. 'I shall play to celebrate your victory. Roxa, fetch me my piano!'

Roxa carried in a white plank painted with thirty-five black keys, and the lieutenant chewed his lip as her uncut fingernails scratched the arpeggios and dust fell out of the wormholes.

Dom Francisco's wardrobe, held together by its paint surface alone, lasted until 1957, when it collapsed, revealing a wreckage of whalebone stays and shreds of black taffeta that fluttered upwards like flakes of carbonized paper.

Spiders had turned the parrot cage into a grey tent. The pictures were peeling, and all Twelve Apostles eaten away to leprous stumps.

Yet, from the head of Christ, like the periscopic eyes of certain fish, two blue glass beads stood out on stalks.

*

Her own eyes were too tired to see the faces peering in at the window. But she had seen the same faces long ago, and they were all there, as she imagined.

Unscrewing a silver phial, Father Olimpío da Silva gave extreme unction and the room resounded with his prayer. Modeste swung a censer and the clouds of blue smoke disturbed the wasps and set them buzzing.

She was not sweating. Her face was still. No one would have thought that, under that papery skin, there were veins and arteries and a pumping heart.

Then her lips opened with an audible pop. The Da Silvas heard a rustling sound. At first, they were uncertain if it were the rustle of her skin, the rustle of black bombazine, or the start of the death rattle.

A word detached itself and floated around the room. A second word came clear. A string of words, faint as the wind in distant palms.

'The papers,' they whispered. 'Ask her about the papers.' Papa Agostinho put his ear to her mouth. He got up and tiptoed to the window.

'She's speaking Portuguese. Who speaks Portuguese? Doesn't anyone speak Portuguese?'

Three

The man who landed at Ouidah in 1812 was born, twenty-seven years earlier, near Jaicos in the Sertão, the dry scrubby cattle country of the Brazilian North-East.

The Sertanistas are wild and poor. They have tight faces, sleek hair and sometimes the green eyes of a Dutch or Celtic ancestor. They hate Negroes. They believe in miraculous cures, and their legends tell of a phantom king called Dom Sebastião, who will rid the earth of Antichrist.

Like all people born in thorny places, they dream of green fields and a life of ease. Sometimes, with light hearts, they set out south for San Salvador da Bahia, but when they see the sea and the city, they panic and turn back to the badlands.

Francisco Manoel's father, a hired hand on a ranch, was killed while driving steers at a round-up. His leather hat caught in the fork of two branches: the chinstrap slipped round his neck and throttled him. Friends following the tracks of his riderless horse found the body dangling with the feet just clear of the ground.

His son was one year old.

The mother was a very bad-tempered woman. Her hands were worked raw. Blue veins stood out on her temples and her thinning hair failed to hide the wens that had sprouted in several places on her scalp. Years of drought had set her mouth in an expression of rage – rage for her shrivelled breasts; for the bast sandals instead of shoes; for the feather bed she would never own, or the white metal crucifix that should have been made of gold.

She spent most days crouching in the speckled shade of an acacia, smoking a stone pipe.

The house had a grass roof and walls of packed mud and scantlings and stood in open country in a clump of umbu trees. The shutters were painted a cool blue, but the coolness was an illusion.

A barricade of bromelias fenced in the yard. Nearby, there was a cattle-tank with duckweed and, beyond that, the thornscrub, rising and falling in grey-green sweeps, punctuated here and there by black candelabra cacti.

The three rooms were bare, whitewashed, flyblown. Folded hammocks hung like hams from the rafters: the saddles, hats and halters hung in the porch. There was a statuette of Onuphrius to guard the door and one of St Blaise to keep off ants. The woman kept a white cloth on the altar table long after she had stopped praying for anything in particular.

Within weeks of her husband's death, she took up with an Indian half-breed called Manuelzinho, who came to the house one day and asked for water. He had a hare-lip and teeth like bits of rusty metal. The tie-strings of his jerkin stretched taut across his chest, and people thought they were going to snap. He killed snakes for a living and sold the flaky white flesh at market.

His horse had one ear clean off, and when they asked,

'What happened to that horse's ear?' he'd say gloomily, 'It got eaten by bugs.'

The boy's first memories were of watching the pair, creaking night and day in a sisal hammock: he never knew a time he was not a stranger.

Yet whenever the man satisfied her, the woman's voice became less rasping and her mouth would ease into a smile. She took trouble with meals, combed her son's hair for lice, and told the old stories of Dom Sebastião and the Princess Magalona.

Remembering happier times, she told him the riddles she had learned as a child: the avocado which had the 'heart of a bull'; or the 'girls in a castle clothed in yellow', who were a bunch of bananas. And then there was his particular favourite:

> Igrejinha bem rondinha
> Bem branquinha
> Não tem porta
> Não tem janela
> Dentro dela tem tesouros
> Um de prata, outro d'oro.

– a little round white church, without a window and without a door: yet inside it had two treasures, one of silver, one of gold – to which the answer was 'Egg'.

But Manuelzinho was a born wanderer. After a week of captivity he was ready to move on. He would pace round the yard glaring at the sun as though it were setting late. Or he would flay the dust with a whip, or sit throwing knives at a log.

Then as the woman watched him dwindle to an ash-coloured speck, her fingers would claw the table top and the splinters got in under her nails.

Many years later, chained hand and foot in the King of Dahomey's prison, Francisco Manoel would remember the year of the drought.

That summer – he was seven at the time – the clouds banked up as usual and burst. For five days rain drenched the earth, seedlings sprouted and there were clouds of yellow butterflies everywhere. Then the clouds went away. The sun quivered in a blue metal sky. The mud cracked.

One sunset, mother and son watched the formations of duck flying south. She hugged him and said, 'The ducks are flying to the river.'

Hot winds blew, hiding the horizon in dust and blowing pellets of goat dung across the yard. When the tank dried up, the cattle stood around the patch of green slime, groaning, with their muzzles full of spines.

In a cabin behind the house lived an old Cariri Indian called Felix, who looked after the widow's few animals in return for food and a roof. One evening, he collapsed in the kitchen and, in a hoarse and hopeless voice, said, 'All of them are dying.' He had cut lengths of cactus, stripped them of spines, and set them out for fodder; but the cattle had gone on dying.

Blood flowed from their flanks from the little pink lumps that were ticks. They slashed themselves trying to reach a single unwithered leaf and, when they did die, the hides were so tough that carrion birds could not break through to the guts.

Fires tore through the country with a resinous crackling,

leaving velvety stumps where once there had been trees. The flames caught Felix as he was hacking out a firebreak, and they found him, charred and sheeny, with a grimace of white teeth and green mucus running out of his nose. The woman dug a grave, but a dog unearthed the body and chewed it apart.

Rats ran down the boy's hammock strings and bit him as he slept. Rattlesnakes came into the yard, attracted by anything that still had life. When a column of driver-ants swept through the house, the woman had only the energy to save a saucepan of manioc flour and some strips of wind-dried beef.

Finally, when she had lost hope, Manuelzinho rode out of the thornscrub, where he had lived on the half-roasted bodies of rodents. He dug deeper down the well-shaft and came back with a dribble of foul ferruginous liquid. But within a week all three water jars were empty.

The boy's mouth cracked and ulcerated. His eyelids blazed. His legs went stiff. They gave him mashed palmroots to eat but they swelled in his stomach and the cramps forced him to lie down. All the moisture seemed to have drained from his body. There was no question of being able to cry – even as his mother entered her death agony.

They woke that morning to find her left leg hanging limply over the lip of her hammock. Manuelzinho lifted the cloth that covered her face from the flies. Unspeaking, and with the terrible tenderness of people pushed to the limit, she pleaded for the son whom she had starved herself to save.

Her oases were not of this world: she died in the night without a groan.

The boy watched Manuelzinho bury her. They started

south for the river. They passed knots of migrants too tired to go on. Black birds sat waiting on the branches.

The horse died on the second day, but men are tougher than horses.

They reached the river at the ferry station of Santa Maria da Boavista, where Manuelzinho left the orphan with the priest and rode away.

The boy remembered nothing of the journey, yet for years he would keep back a lump of meat and sleep with it under his pillow.

Santa Maria da Boavista lay on the north bank of the São Francisco River as it sweeps in a great arc through the provinces of Bahia and Pernambuco.

It had a single street of pantiled houses strung out along a rocky ridge. Below, the muddy waters sluiced by, carrying rafts of vegetation from a greener country upstream. A white church crowned the highest point: above the scrolls of its pediment, a plain blue cross melted the sufferings of the Crucifixion into a cloudless sky.

The boy's guardian, Father Menezes Brito, was a fat conceited Portuguese, who had been exiled here for some misdemeanour: his one amusement was to baptize Indian babies with his spittle. He fed Francisco Manoel and let him sleep in a shed. Hoping to claim him for the Church, he taught him to ring a carillon of bells, the rudiments of Latin, some simple mathematics and the art of writing letters in italic script.

He told him of Bahia and its three hundred churches, of the city of Lisbon and the Holy House of Rome. He made him play the role of St Sebastian at Corpus Christi processions.

He called him 'my green-eyed angel' yet made him grovel and confess the blackness of his soul. Sometimes he led him into a bedroom reeking of incense and dead flowers, where he kissed him.

The village boys called the newcomer 'Chico Diabo' and were always plotting to hurt him: he had only to glare in their faces and they shrank back.

His one friend was the black boy, Pepeu, whom he held in thrall. Together they plucked finches alive, made certain experiments with the flesh of a watermelon, and shouted obscenities at the girls washing tripes in the river.

Once, they tried crucifying a cat, but it got away.

On market days, they went down to the slaughterhouse where old hags would be fighting with pariah dogs over offal. The butchers wore red caps and breeches of blue nankeen that were always purple, and they would splash about in the blood, puffing at cigars and poleaxing any animal still left standing.

The cows stared unamazed at their murderers.

'Like the Saints,' said Francisco Manoel.

He knew, far better than the priest, the meaning of Christ's martyrdom, and the liturgy of thorns and blood and nails. He knew God made men to rack them in the wilderness, yet his own sufferings had hardened him to the sufferings of others. By the age of thirteen, he wore an agate-handled knife in his belt, took pains to clip his moustache, and showed not a trace of squeamishness when he went to watch a flogging at the pillory.

Every October, as the cashews ripened in the last of the rains, the cowhands from the outlying ranches would round up their herds and begin the long trek south to the markets of Bahia. Files of cattle converged on the town. They were cumbersome animals, with swinging dewlaps and hides the colour of cornmeal; and the men would ride around in clouds of dust yelling, 'É . . . Hou . . . Hé . . . Hé . . . O . . . O . . . O . . . O . . . !'

Sometimes, in the lane leading to the river, a tired cow would lie down and the other cows would spill sideways, break fences and trample the villagers' bean patches. Women rushed from their houses and shook their fists, but the riders took no notice: the cattle-men never seemed to notice gardens.

Francisco Manoel liked helping them winch the animals aboard the wherries. Then, after dark, he would listen to their stories of bandits and pumas. But if he asked to go along, someone was sure to say, 'The boy's too young,' and he went back to the hard bed and disapproving crucifix.

He had made up his mind to run away when a rider came into town with news that his mother's old companion was dying at a ranch some leagues into the bush.

Outside the shack a sorrel stallion chomped at the hitching post. He pushed back the cowhide that served as a door and saw a shrunken figure laid out on a pallet. A crust of pustules covered his face and his eyes were closed.

Feebly, Manuelzinho gestured to his saddle, his quirt, an ocelot waistcoat, a waterproof made of boa skin and a leather hat sewn with metal medallions.

'Take them,' he said.

The boy rode off with some passing horsemen. He did not say goodbye to the priest. Nor did he ever go back.

★

For the next seven years, he drifted through the backlands of the North-East, taking odd jobs as butcher's apprentice, muleteer, drover and gold panner. Sometimes he knew a flash of happiness, but only if it was time to be departing.

Duststorms burnished his skin. His clothes reeked of sour milk and horses. When drought tore at his throat, he soothed it with an infusion brewed from the tail of a rattlesnake.

Faces he forgot, but he remembered the sensations: the taste of the armadillo meat roasted in clay; the shock of aguardiente on the tongue; the pleasures of hot blood spurting over his hands, or of pissing down the leg of his horse.

He lived in Indian villages. He rode with gipsies who sold dud slaves and scapulars of St Anthony. For a season he washed gravel, working shoulder to shoulder with Negroes, at a diamond-camp. It astounded him to find their fetor so exciting: he would compare their uncreased foreheads with the battle raging inside his own.

He knew he was brave. One night, a face loomed red in the firelight: he was amazed by the ease with which his knife slid into the man's belly. Another time, bivouacked on the Raso da Catarina, he shared his meat with a bush-wanderer whose clothes were a patchwork of green silk and whose fingers were stiff with gold rings. The man walked eighteen leagues a day, barefoot through the cacti:

'I trust no one,' he said. 'Why should I trust a horse?'

Not for months did Francisco Manoel realize that this was the bandit Cobra Verde who robbed only rich women and only for their finery.

And he too believed he would go on wandering for ever: yet, on Santa Luzia's Day of 1807 – a grey, stifling day that held out the promise of rain – the aimless journeys ended.

He had been riding through the village of Uauá when the potter's daughter rushed from her house with an apronful of green oranges. A week later he brought her trinkets: within a month they had married.

He found work on a ranch nearby. His employers were a family of absentee landlords called Coutinho, who had ranched in the Sertão for two centuries, but now lived on their sugar plantation by the sea.

He learned the equations of grass and water; the flight of birds around a stricken cow, or the presence of an underground spring. For leagues around he could distinguish all the neighbours' brands: it was a point of honour to return a lost animal no matter how far it had strayed.

Not far away, along the river-bed, there were cotton fields worked by poor sharecroppers. Knowing him to be cool and resourceful, they came to him when they were cheated and he would force the landowners to admit their miscalculations and pay up. But when the sharecroppers came again, with gratitude and humble presents, a bitter taste rose up his throat, and he brushed them aside.

The Coutinhos paid no wages, but each round-up entitled the cowhands to one calf in four.

For two years he sold his animals, preferring coins in his pocket to wealth on the hoof. But for the third season he ordered a branding iron from the blacksmith and set about 'humanizing' his property.

He coralled young bulls, tied their legs and lashed them to a wooden post. He sliced off their testicles and sawed the tips of their horns. They slavered and moaned as the iron sizzled into their flanks: it gave him pleasure to rub the hot tallow into his own initials.

And he enjoyed his simple house with its gourds and melons straggling over the porch and its ochre walls that sucked up the sunlight. After a hard day he would unhook his guitar and strum the old songs of the Bandeirantes.

His wife dressed always in pink. She could sew, plant vegetables, cook, and squeeze the poisonous juice from manioc. Yet her movements were stiff and mechanical. Making love meant no more to her than sweeping the floor. A dazzling set of teeth froze the words in her throat. She would make her eyes glitter if she wanted something, or cloud them over if ever she was afraid. More often, she sat, staring into the distance, stroking an orange cat.

She would wake in the night and scream, 'Father! Father!' Twice a week she went to see the potter and came back red to the elbows in clay.

The strain of living with her told on his nerves. The sight of her vacant smile made him pale with anger and tempted him to sink his fingers in her throat. He took to sleeping rough, hoping to recover his equilibrium under the stars.

He woke one sunrise on a patch of stony ground and, squinting sideways, was surprised to see, so far from water, a green frog crouching under the arm of a cactus. Its back was the colour of new grass, its belly mauve, and when it crawled, patches of orange and turquoise flashed from under its legs.

He poked the frog with a stick. It stiffened with fright. He watched its eyes suffuse from silver to purple. He took a stone and pounded it to a blood-streaked slime and, for a whole week, regretted what he had done.

His wife was expecting a child.

The women of the village came with advice, with bunches of rue to keep off witches, and a crucifix to place under the mattress. But the prospect of witnessing the birth disgusted him. He made an excuse to go on a journey and, afterwards, could never believe that the child, who curled her fingers round his, was his own daughter.

He was alone in the house one afternoon sewing a patch on a leather horse-frontal. Rain smacked on the roof tiles and cut winding channels in the earth. From time to time he looked up, and watched the black clouds streaming past the window frame. Suddenly, the cat was sitting on the sill.

He went on sewing but the cat stared in his direction. When it miaowed, he felt as if a scalpel were scouring the inside of his skull. It bounded over and started sharpening its claws against his breeches. He shivered as its head nuzzled his calf. One hand reached under its forelegs, the other for a knife.

The blood was warm and sticky on his hands. He wiped the dark drops coagulating on the floor. He put the cat over his saddle and rode off to get rid of it. Then he stood for hours, hopelessly alone, in the cloudbursts.

The woman looked for the cat but soon forgot about it.

One evening she tucked the baby into her cradle and, balancing a waterjar on her head, went off to refill it at the tank. He watched them go, two undulating forms, receding down an alley of agaves into an orange sunset. He sat savouring the silence, and then began to twang at his guitar. The baby cried. He stopped playing and the baby stopped. But when he touched the strings again, the cries redoubled.

He held the guitar above the cradle, waited for the crash

of splintering wood, then checked himself and broke it across his knee.

He had gone before the woman came back.

He went back to his solitary wanderings. Believing any set of four walls to be a tomb or a trap, he preferred to float over the most barren of open spaces.

He passed through valleys of white dust where merlin white went digging for tubers. Jerked beef was his food, dried fruits and wild honey: water he pressed from the roots of the umbu.

Sometimes there was water and no grass, but sharp sedges only and the horses falling from hunger. The journeys were endless, over empty horizons: the sound of hoofs on chips of silica, the crack of dead branches, the crack of rainless thunder, the shriek of a vulture – whatever broke the silence was sadder than silence.

And when he did go to the towns, the noises oppressed him: the dances, the music, the lively talk and laughter – he would crouch on his haunches and swig at a bottle.

And in the evenings he would stroll past houses and peer into the lamplit rooms, where fathers played with children, men played cards and women smiled as they braided their hair. He craved their simple pleasures of touch and trust; but if a woman saw the green eyes glinting in the darkness, she closed her shutters and bars of light slid through the jalousies and striped his face.

One Lent he passed the sacred mountain, Monte Santo, where the Capuchin Father, Apollonio of Todi, found mysterious letters carved in rock.

Pilgrims in sky-blue rags came here from all parts of the Sertão to climb the white quartz *via sacra* to the chapel on the summit where, every Good Friday, the Virgin shed tears of blood.

He heard their litanies. He heard their cries as they flailed themselves with nettle-spurge. He watched them crawl the four miles on their kneecaps and the path becoming redder as they neared their goal.

He longed to perform some similar act of mortification, or simply to unburden his load. He would gaze for hours at wayside crosses. He never passed a village without dismounting to watch a congregation at prayer – yet he could never join them.

Once, at Jeremoabo, he stopped to speak to some women laying lilies on the altar. The guardian of the church was a young mulatto with skin-covered bones for legs, who propelled himself in a wood-wheeled cart, always looking over his shoulder as if someone, perhaps Death, were coming to collect him. He introduced the visitor to his companions: Santa Rosario in green lace; Sts Theatriel, Uriel and Barakiel; St Moses the Black with his foot on Pharaoh's windpipe; or St Anthony of Padua, whose tortured image would appear to runaway slaves and tell them to go home.

The cripple pushed himself up the aisle, unlocked the chest under the altar, and rolled back the shroud of mildewed velvet to uncover the cadaver of Christ.

The body was smooth and white, the belly taut, and the palms held inarticulately outwards. Black hair, graceful as a girl's, swirled about the shoulders. Red paint gushed from the lance wound and the knees were crimson scabs.

'Dead!' the cripple whimpered, and the tears welled up,

out and around his cheeks, and pattered among the wreckage of his legs on to the boards of the cart.

Francisco Manoel laid a hand on the hunched shoulder. His mouth crinkled and he too, suddenly, burst out crying.

A cassock swished past.

He bolted for the door.

He had not cried since before his mother's death: the tears relieved his sorrow. The fear that he would turn into a killer left him. He began to drink in bars, to laugh and play cards, though still he would not trust himself with a woman.

He was drawn towards the cities of the coast.

He went as far south as Tucano, where the cacti grew stunted and the big trees began, and where his old employer, Colonel Octávio Coutinho, owned a factory for making jerked beef. There, as if to purge himself in blood, he worked with the butchers and the salters, and would hang the slabs of meat to dry on copper wires. The grease boilers covered the town in a pall of smoke. Healthy men died of fever and the survivors drank.

From time to time caravans came up from the coast to buy beef for the slaves on the sugar estates. One January evening the Colonel's heir came to fetch a load for the family plantation at Tapuitapera: he had been sent along with the muleteers to toughen him up.

Joaquim Coutinho had dark wounded eyes that watered in the wind. His clothes were coated with a bloom of dust. His buttocks were in agony – he was unused to long journeys in the saddle – and the slave boys snickered as they watched him dismount.

That night he and the backlander struck up a friendship

that could only be explained by the attraction of opposites. Next day, when the panniers were loaded and the men were ready to leave, Joaquim said he would like to stay on.

Francisco Manoel taught him to lasso steers, to braid rawhide whips, to break colts and ride down rheas and snare them with slingstones. Yet he, in turn, sat tongue-tied to hear Joaquim prattle of his lineage and latifundias, and of the Tower at Tapuitapera that had stood two hundred years.

One day, Joaquim said, 'You should ride with me down to the coast.'

He held back: secretly, he dreaded setting eyes on the sea.

Then he said, 'Yes.'

Tapuitapera, so named after a rock on which the Tapuya Indians once sharpened their axe-blades, was a hump of red sandstone about seventy miles north of Bahia and three miles inland from a beach of white sand. On the summit was the shadow of something dark and solid half-seen through the shining trees.

The sea was always blue and dotted with the sails of outriggers, and offshore breezes soughed through woods of mango and cashew trees.

The Coutinhos' plantation house had cross-lattice windows and walls of pink stucco. Green silk curtains rustled in its flower-stencilled apartments. On the verandah there were aviaries of song-finches; and in the dining room vases of blue-glazed porcelain, gilded pilasters and panels the colour of lapis lazuli.

The scents of rose and lily drifted through the garden. Humming-birds sucked from scarlet honeysuckle. Morpho butterflies fluttered over the morning-glories and, after dark, in a Chinese loggia, black choirboys in snuff-velvet breeches and lace jabots would sing Pergolesi's *Stabat Mater*.

And Francisco Manoel imagined he had stumbled on Paradise.

The Colonel welcomed him as a good influence on his son, treated him as one of the family and put him in charge of his stables.

The Colonel was a magnificent wreck.

As a young man, frenzied at the thought of horizons unpopulated by his own cattle, he had extended his ranches into the green void of Maranhão, where horses sank to their withers and his ranch-hands died of anal gangrene. A parchment map of his empire still hung in his office. But his desk was stacked with copies of unpaid rent demands and, every month or so, word would come from some ranch up-country that the tenant had annexed it.

Fifty years of peppery food and pitching in the saddle had so inflamed his haemorrhoids that he could move from his hammock neither to dine, to sleep, to shit, to pray nor play cards with his chaplain. His one pleasure was to have his hair washed by a lovely mulatta, who would run her fingers through the stiff waves as if peeling the outer leaves off a cabbage.

Francisco Manoel did his best to humour him. He put on freshly laundered whites for dinner. He took care to lose every other game of backgammon, and listened with attention to his stories of killing Indians.

The two young friends fought gamecock: and trained a pack of hounds to hunt for capybaras in the forest. Returning, hot from the chase, they would wave up to Joaquim's sisters, who lounged on feather hammocks or fed slips of custard-apple to their pet marmosets.

On rainy days they explored the Tower, a gloomy granite colossus built in 1602 by Francisco Coutinho the First, whose leathery face stared out from the walls of the portrait gallery.

Or they would leaf through volumes with vistas of European cities, or visit rooms where precious objects were strewn in disarray: Venetian glassware, silver from Potosí, crystal and cinnabar and black lacquer cabinet sloughing pearlshell.

Francisco Manoel could not account for what he saw. He had never thought of owning more than his knives and a few silver horse-trimmings. Now, there was no limit to his thirst for possessions.

In March the time came round for the harvest. The hills and valleys flashed silver with the beards of sugar cane and, from the House, they could see lines of black backs and the glint of machetes. The blacks hacked at the wall of yellow stalks twice the height of themselves. The leaves slashed their skin and, by afternoon, the blood had mixed with the sweat and cane-juice and attracted swarms of flies.

A thick smell of molasses hung over the mill. Vats bubbled. Pairs of yoked oxen turned the rollers of the cane press, and the slaves staggered towards it, bowed under the weight of the sheaves, with their neck-veins bulging.

One afternoon, a man got his hand caught in the rollers and the overseer had to hack it off at the wrist. His screams silenced the valley as his friends took him back to his cabin. The overseer shrugged and said, 'Not another!'

When the chapel bell clanked at six, the slaves downed

tools and trudged uphill to say an evening prayer to the Virgin. They filed past the Colonel and raised their hats. Opaque, husky voices repeated his 'Boa Noite!' in unison.

The chapel was dedicated to Nossa Senhora da Conceiçao, and on the altar was the portable oratory of the Last Supper that would end its days at Ouidah. The nuns, who made it, had used as their model the dining room of the Big House. For some reason Francisco Manoel wanted to own it more than any other object he had seen.

Lying awake one night, he heard a sound of drumbeats in the hills.

He dressed and followed the sound to a forest clearing where some slaves were calling their gods across the Atlantic. The dancers wore white metal masks and white dresses that glowed orange in the firelight. They whirled round and round until Exu the Messenger tapped them between their shoulder-blades. Then, one by one, they shuddered, growled, crumpled at the knees and fell to the ground in trance.

Their priest, a Yoruba freeman called Jerónimo, was a votary of Yemanja the Sea Goddess and he slept beside her mermaid image in a chamber bursting with corals and basins of salt water.

Nothing gave Francisco Manoel greater pleasure than to sit with this androgynous bachelor and hear him sing the songs of the Kingdom of Ketou in a voice that suggested, not the gulf between continents, but planets.

Jerónimo showed him the loko tree, sacred to Saint Francis of Assisi, whose writhing roots were said to stretch under the ocean to Itu-Aiyé, to Africa, the home of the Gods. Sometimes, a slave on the plantation would hear his ancestors calling through the rubbery leaves. At night he would creep among the branches and, in the morning, they would find his body, hanging.

Jerónimo told him stories of mudbrick palaces lined with skulls; of tribes who exchanged gold dust for tobacco; a Holy Snake that was also a rainbow, and kings with testicles the size of avocados.

The name 'Dahomey' took root in his imagination.

And it was time for him to move from Tapuitapera.

The Colonel was sick and bad-tempered, and Joaquim bored by his company. He would deliberately pitch the conversation above his head, only to stop himself and say, 'Now why am I telling you that?'

His mother, Dona Epiphania, hated to see her son mix with inferiors and took her meals alone. She was a big woman with blotchy skin, black wings on her upper lip, and teeth corroded to thin brown wafers. She kept a silver-handled whip in her embroidery basket and, while a slave girl circulated the air with a leafy branch, would sit on a reed mat and plan vengeance on her husband's mistresses.

She called Francisco Manoel 'The Catamite'.

When he first came to the house, Joaquim's sisters blew him kisses and signalled love-messages in the language of the fan. But soon, their mother encouraged them to pick on his weak points. They mimicked his accent. They mocked his efforts at conversation and would screech with laughter when he used a knife and fork. They said, 'We do have chairs, you know,' if he squatted on his hams. Often, as he entered the room, they would cry, 'Hurry! Hurry! It's the Brute!' and dash for the door in a rustle of taffeta.

One evening, Joaquim told him his father had had a stroke and that Dona Epiphania insisted he leave the house.

Their eyes met.

Francisco Manoel flushed with anger, but saw it was useless to argue and bowed his head.

He went to Bahia.

He drifted round the City of All the Saints in a suicide's jacket of black velveteen bought off a tailor's dummy. Flapping laundry brushed across his face. Urchins kissed him on the lips as their fingers felt for his pockets. His feet slipped on rinds of rotting fruit, and puffy white clouds went sailing past the bell-towers.

He would stroll down the cobbles of the Pelourinho to watch the street-boys practise shadow-wrestling. The 'Beautiful Dog of the North' was a dyed blue poodle that played cards; and after dark there was always an excuse to let off fireworks.

His principal amusement was to follow funeral processions. One day it would be a black catafalque encrusted with golden skulls. The next, a sky-blue casket for a stillborn child, or a grey corpse wrapped in a shroud of banana leaves.

He lodged in a tenement in the Lower City and got a job with a man who sold the equipment of slavery – whips, flails, yokes, neck-chains, branding-irons and metal masks: the shop reminded him of tack-shops in the backlands.

His green eyes made him famous in the quarter. Whenever he flashed them along a crowded alley, someone was sure to stop. With partners of either sex, he performed the mechanics of love in planked rooms. They left him with the sensation of having brushed with death: none came back a second time.

The lineaments of his face fell into their final form.

His right eyebrow, hitched higher than the left, gave him the air of a man amazed to find himself in a madhouse. A moustache curled round the sides of his mouth, which was moist and sensuous. For years he had pinched back his lips, partly to look manly, partly to stop them cracking in the heat: now he let them hang loose, as if to show that everything was permitted. The fits of anger had left him, not so the remorse. He wanted to go to Africa, but would not take a conscious decision.

Whenever a ship from Guinea anchored off the Fort of São Marcello, he would stroll round the slave quays and watch the blacks being rowed ashore. Dealers from every province elbowed forward shouting themselves hoarse as they identified the consignors' brands. They calculated the numbers of the dead; then made the survivors run, stamp, lift weights and bellow to show the soundness of their lungs.

The defectives were sold off cheap to gipsies.

Francisco Manoel made friends with one of these gipsy slave-copers, who taught him some tricks of the trade: how to hide bloody dysentery with an oakum plug, or a skin disease by smearing it with castor oil.

But when he talked to old Africa hands, every one of them shuddered at the mention of Dahomey.

One December afternoon, for lack of anything better to do, he helped some hired ruffians hang a straw-filled effigy of the British Consul: it was four years since Parliament passed the Abolition Act, but only in recent months had the Royal Navy started seizing Brazilian slave ships.

The crowds worked themselves into a fury and, when a

platoon of militia dispersed them, they set on a Scottish sailor and dumped him in the harbour. Perhaps Francisco Manoel's strongest memory of Bahia was of leaning over a balustrade and watching the red head bobbing amid a lattice of masts and spars.

A fortnight later, he was drinking a glass of sweet lime outside the slave auction on the Rua dos Matozinhos when one of the lot numbers, a Benguela houseboy, ran off in the middle of the bidding. Joaquim Coutinho was among the buyers and, as the sales clerks chased the fugitive, he spotted his old friend and tapped him on the shoulder.

They renewed their friendship: in fact, whenever Joaquim came to town, the two would spend an evening together and a night with the whores.

On one of these visits, he said that the Colonel had died, leaving the family affairs in a terrible state, and forcing Dona Epiphania to sell her diamonds. Hoping to repair the fortune, he had joined a syndicate of army officers, whose aim was to corner the market in dried beef and invest the profit in faster slave ships.

The most valuable slaves came from Ouidah – and Ouidah, by terms of the Prince Regent's treaty with England, was the one port north of the Equator where it was legal to trade: the only problem was the King of Dahomey, who was mad.

Francisco Manoel made it clear he had only the haziest idea where Dahomey was.

'You should go there,' said Joaquim. 'You'd soon find out.'

Three weeks later, Francisco Manoel found himself in a room at the Capitania, where the city's founding fathers peered from the dark panelling and Joaquim's partners were seated round a table.

A man in gold epaulettes and a red sash got to his feet, twirled a terrestrial globe, pointed to the Fort of St John the Baptist at Ouidah, and raised the candidate to the rank of lieutenant. The commission carried no salary, but came with two free uniforms, a passage to Africa and permission to trade in slaves. None of the officers knew what had happened to the Governor of the Fort, or to its garrison. At the end of the interview, everyone rose to their feet to congratulate the man they knew would be a corpse.

On his last night ashore, with the slaving brig *Pistola* stowed and ready for sea, he went to a farewell Mass at the Hospice of Boa Viagem.

The church was lit by a double row of crystal chandeliers and the walls were covered with panels of blue-and-white tiles. The tiles were painted with galleons – galleons dashed on rocks, toppled by waves, lashed by leviathans or battered in gunfights – yet always saved by the Blessed Virgin who hovered in an aureole above the masthead.

The captain and sailors sat in the front pews.

All were men with blood on their hands; yet all gazed longingly at the milk-white body of Our Dying Lord, identifying His Agony with their agony and calling on Him to pacify the sea.

The priest said a short prayer to the Patron of Slavers, St José the Redeemed, and a longer one for the souls of the Black Brethren who would be ransomed for the Christian fold. Nasal responses rose to the roof, where the Prophet Elijah, in spirals of smoke and flame, continued his chariot journey towards the Almighty.

Candles blazed on the altar, and the light flickered on the golden wings of angels.

From his seat at the back, Francisco Manoel saw the priest exhibit the ciborium and the crew file meekly towards him: 'Corpus Domini Nostrum Jesum Christum . . . Corpus Domini Nostrum . . .'

Without a second for reflection, he joined them – making a treaty with the hand in lace cuffs and letting the wafer wetten on the tip of his tongue.

Outside, the storm had blown over. Stars shrank and expanded in the blue void. Lightning flashed over the island of Itaparica, silhouetting the ship's yardarms out in the fairway.

The Mass ended, and the sailors stood outside the church holding up the ship's mizzen topgallant by its tack and clews. The choir sang an anthem and the priest's golden chasuble detached itself from the angels and was seen moving slowly down the aisle.

The procession passed through the green doors.

Boys in purple cassocks carried a silver cross, a stoup and a palm-frond aspergillum.

Drops of Holy Water pattered on to the canvas.

'Bless, O Lord, this ship Pistola and all who sail in her. Bear her as you bore the Ark of Noah over the floodwaters. Give them your hand as you gave it to the Apostle Peter when he walked upon the waters of the sea . . .'

Four

He landed at Ouidah between two and three of a murky May afternoon smelling of mangrove and dead fish. A band of foam stretched as far as the eye could reach. Inland, there were tall grey trees which, at a distance of three miles, anyone might mistake for waterspouts. He was the only passenger in the canoe: the crew knew better than to set foot in the Kingdom of Dahomey.

At the start of the voyage he had gazed at the new element with the innocent awe of the landsman. He saw boobies. He saw fleets of medusas, ribbons of sea-wrack, the prismatic colours on the backs of bonitos and albacores and the pale fire of phosphorescence streaming into the night.

Then, as the ship sailed into the horse-latitudes, the sails hung slack, shark fins swirled on an oily sea, everyone lost their tempers, and the mate smashed a sailor's teeth in with a marlin-spike.

A shower of red rain spattered the deck the day they sighted the African coast, and a locust got caught in the rigging. On his last night aboard, Francisco Manoel woke up covered in his own vomit: the ship had narrowly missed the tornado that covered the shore with dead fish.

He brushed aside the krumen who helped him from the canoe. He refused to 'dash' the outstretched hand of the fetish-man. He refused to let the porters carry him across the lagoon, and with black ooze coating his thighs he strode up the track to the Captains' Tree.

Waiting in the shade of this decrepit ficus were some underlings of the Yovogan, the Dahomean Minister for the Slave Trade. Decanters of claret, madeira, rum and distilled palm-wine were laid out on a card table missing most of its baize.

He drank their toasts and soldiers fired their muskets in the air. A royal eunuch with silver horns on his temples tilted his head, asked what presents he had brought from Brazil, and gasped when the answer was 'None!'

A palaver followed, and everyone seemed quite friendly, but when he reached the Fort he found the place in ruins.

The flagstaff was broken, the Royal Arms defaced. Walls were roofless and smoke-blackened. The shutters were wrenched off their hinges and the cannon had come adrift of their emplacements and were sinking through the swish walls.

Turkey buzzards flapped off as he stepped into the yard. A pig was teasing the rind off a jackfruit. A dog pissed against a tree and started howling.

Through the door of the chapel came a gangling pox-pitted figure in a drum major's shako and the remains of a Turkish rug. He blinked at the newcomer; then, curling his lips back over a set of loose yellow teeth, whooped, 'Mother of Jesus Christ and All the Saints be praised!' and bounded over to paw the apparition and make sure it was real.

Taparica the Tambour was the only survivor of the garrison.

A Yoruba freeman who had joined the 1st Regiment of Black Militia, he told his sad story in the lilting cadences of plantation Portuguese: of how the Governor died of fever, the lieutenant in a skirmish by the shore; and how the King had let his soldiers loot the Fort.

They stole the bells, cut the eyes from the Prince Regent's portrait, unstoppered the rum barrels, buggered a cadet, and marched the men off to Abomey where, for all he knew, their heads were on the palace wall.

Thinking he knew the secret of buried treasure, the Dahomeans put ants on the Tambour's chest, pepper under his eyelids and burned his tongue with the tip of a red-hot machete. They were about to do their worst when someone explored the powder magazine with a lighted firebrand. Seven bodies were taken from the wreckage, and they left him thereafter in peace.

In the last of the light he walked his rescuer round the garden where there were mounds of red earth, each set with a rough wood cross. Then they barricaded the gate with palm-trunks.

Francisco Manoel slung his hammock and lay under a muslin net listening to a symphony of frogs and mosquitoes. And he congratulated himself: for the first time in forty-seven days, he rocked to his own rhythm, not that of the ship.

At seven in the morning the Yovogan's messenger came with an order for the Brazilian to present himself at once.

Taparica shook his head.

'King him need gun,' he said. 'Yovogan him come you.'

The Kingdom, it so happened, was passing through one of its periodic bouts of turmoil. The people had had enough of the King's blasphemous ways. He had failed to 'water', with blood, the graves of his ancestors. He was a coward and a drunk. Food was scarce, the army was out of ammunition while, from the east, the Alafin of Oyo was threatening to invade.

The messenger shouted abuse and went away, only to return with word of an official visit.

Puffs of musket smoke preceded the Yovogan, a frail octogenarian who rode to the Fort in a costume of pink satin, propped up by the grooms, sitting sidesaddle on a starved grey nag. A man led the beast by a grass halter. Another twirled a blue umbrella. A noisy entourage followed.

It was raining. Boys splashed alongside carrying the old man's cigar case, his stool, and the card table and decanters. Once inside the gate he signalled his wish to dismount, and the groom lifted him from the saddle, sat him down and removed his black tam-o'-shanter.

The Yovogan clicked his fingers in salutation, then proposed his own King's health in palm-wine and the Queen of Portugal's in Holland's Gin. He did not drink himself but poured the contents of both glasses down the gaping mouth of an acolyte.

The interview began in broken Portuguese. The Yovogan's face turned grey as he registered his disapproval at the lack of presents.

What about the barquentine full of silk? What about the coach and horses? Or the trumpets? Or the silver hunting-gun?

'There are no presents,' said Francisco Manoel.

'Not even the greyhounds?'

'Not even greyhounds.'

Nor would there be any presents, until the King released the prisoners, repaired the Fort and resumed the sale of slaves.

Everyone was confused, then angry. A man shouted,

'Death to Whites!' and an Amazon whirled her cutlass round her forefinger and brought it close to the Brazilian's face.

But when the Yovogan raised his hand, the crowd melted away muttering.

That same afternoon, a hubbub of shouts and whiplashes awoke Francisco Manoel from his siesta. Peering over the north bastion, he saw a crowd of naked men piling up bundles of reeds, planks, baskets of oyster shells and buckets of swish: the Yovogan had sent a corvée of captives to make good the damage.

In the weeks that followed Lieutenant da Silva worked in heat that would have driven most whites to their hammocks or their graves. Even on quivering afternoons, when the sun sucked out the colour of earth and leaves, he would strip to the waist, bark orders and shoulder the heaviest loads himself.

The blacks were amazed to see a white man work.

They thatched the roofs, whitewashed the walls and mucked out the cistern. Again the cannon gleamed with blacking and palm-oil. Again ships offshore saw the 'five shields' of the Braganzas floating from the flagpole, signalling that the Fort of St John the Baptist had slaves for sale.

The first batch were criminals convicted of stealing the King's palm-nuts and condemned to be fed on them till they burst: none seemed the least unhappy to be leaving Dahomey.

More slavers came – the *Mithridate*, the *Rinoceronte*, the *Fraternidade* and the *Bom Jesus* – each carrying crates of muskets, rum, tobacco, silks and calico. The Alafin of Oyo did not invade. The King went to war against some defenceless millet planters in the Mahi Mountains and, within two years, Francisco Manoel had sent no less than forty-five slave cargoes to Bahia.

Joaquim Coutinho had the sense to offer him a place in the syndicate.

Da Silva took to the Trade as if he had known no other occupation. Having always thought of himself as a footloose wanderer, he now became a patriot and man of property. No word of congratulation came from his superiors in Bahia. Yet he believed it was his heaven-sent vocation to fuel with black muscle the mines and plantations of his country, and he believed they would reward him.

He persisted in this illusion with the obstinacy of the convert. Often on sleepless nights he would lie and listen to the groan and clank of the barracoon, only to remember the sweet singing in the chapel at Tapuitapera and roll over with his conscience clean.

He lived in the Governor's suite of rooms; he restored the chapel and imported a Portuguese padre to say Mass before the start of each voyage.

As major-domo of the Fort, Taparica dressed in a green frock-coat, sailor pants of white canvas and a black felt bicorn with a cockade of parrot plumes. Whenever they passed through the town, he would stride ahead of the hammockeers, clanging an iron bell and shouting, '*Ago! Ago!*' to clear the path.

He slept on a mat outside his master's room. He cooked and tasted his food, controlled his drinking habits and emptied his slop-pail. He found girls for his bed, aphrodisiacs if the weather was exceptionally sticky, and warned him not to make lasting attachments.

Francisco Manoel would use the same girl for a night or two, then send her home with a present for her family.

His profits – and reputation for straight dealing – exasperated the veterans of the Trade. One year, a Captain Pedro Vicente begged him for a shipload of slaves without money or goods to pay. He swore to return but squandered the proceeds in Bahia and did not come back. Some time later, on hearing that the same man was in Lagos with an unseaworthy ship and a mutinous crew, Da Silva sent his cutter with a message: 'Come over to Ouidah and I will refit you. Nobody cheats me twice.'

Nor was he less straightforward in his dealings with the King.

The two men never met: a taboo forbade Dahomean monarchs setting eyes on the sea. But if the King wanted twelve gilt chairs, they were sent. If he wanted twenty plumed hats, they were found. And he even got his greyhounds, which came specially from England – though, on their way up to Abomey, the dog was bitten by a rabid bitch.

Every month or so an invitation came for Francisco Manoel to visit the capital. He would read each letter through and politely decline: on the first one, the King's Portuguese scribe had written a warning in the margin:

'I, Antonio Maciel, have been sixteen years a prisoner of this cruel king without seeing another of my countrymen . . .'

The King went to war in January and the chain-gangs started reaching Ouidah towards the end of March.

The captives were numb with fright and exhaustion. They had seen their homes burned and their chiefs slaughtered. Iron collars chafed their necks. Their backs were striped purple with welts; and when they saw the white man's ships, they knew they were going to be eaten.

The Dahomeans' mindless cruelty offended Da Silva's sense of economy. Time and again, he complained to the Yovogan that the guards were ruining valuable property, but the old man sighed and said, 'It is their custom.'

On arriving at the Fort, the slaves were housed in a long shed, roofed with dried grasses and fenced in with a palisade of sharpened stakes. Each was manacled to an iron chain that ran in bights down the length of the structure. The thatch came lower than a man's waist and, when the buyers peered in out of the sunlight, all they could see were eyes in the darkness.

Every morning, after the Angelus, they were fed from a cauldron of millet gruel and driven to the lagoon where they washed and danced for exercise.

Taparica cured the sick and calmed their fears: in a dozen dialects he would burble of their country-to-be where everyone danced and cigars grew on trees. He taught his master to distinguish the various tribes by their cicatrices. He could tell any man's age by the state of his gums; and if in doubt, would lick his cheeks to test the resilience of his stubble.

The loading was done in the cool of the evening, when the sea was down – the same scene repeated year after year: the ship, the waves, the black canoes, the black men shorn of their breechclouts, and the slave-brands heating in driftwood fires.

Francisco Manoel preferred to do the branding himself, taking care to dip the red-hot iron in palm-oil to stop it sticking to the flesh.

The chains were struck off at the water's edge, so that, in the event of capsize, one man would not drag the others down. Only occasionally, in a final bid for freedom, would one fling himself to the breakers; if, later, his shark-torn carcass was washed ashore, Taparica would bury it in the dunes, sighing, 'Ignorantes!'

Five years went by, of heat and mist and rain. The British stopped recognizing Ouidah as a slave port; and when a frigate of the West Africa Squadron boarded the brig Borboleta, becalmed off Ouidah with five hundred slaves aboard, Da Silva watched the fight through his telescope and said, 'At least something has happened.'

Often the Brazilian captains had to wait weeks before the coast was clear but their host spared no expense to entertain them. His dining room was lit with a set of silver candelabra; behind each chair stood a serving-girl, naked to the waist, with a white napkin folded over her arm. Sometimes a drunk would shout out, 'What are those women?' and Da Silva would glare down on the table and say, 'Our future murderers.'

The sight of white men disintegrating in the tropics disgusted him. How he hated their hollow laughter! And as their warted contours dissolved behind clouds of cigar smoke, he would make an excuse to slip away and be alone.

On Thursdays he put on his regimentals and went to dine with the Yovogan in an open courtyard frescoed with ochre chameleons.

The old man was so old he could remember the piles of skulls put up to celebrate the Dahomean conquest of Ouidah in 1741 – and, to amuse his guest, would croak a refrain about using the dead king's head as a mortar:

Doli dohò mè sè
Boli sà boli sè

He liked his white friend so much that he took him to his bed-chamber to show off his blunderbuss and the nine rosaries of human molars, the souvenirs of his bloodthirsty youth. But he was equally fond of his European presents – the porcelain teapot of the Brandenburgers or the cruet-stand presented by the Royal Africa Company – since they reminded him of the days when ships of every nation crowded the roadstead.

The Yovogan trembled at the mention of the King's name. But one day, he unwrapped a framed engraving of the guillotine in the Place de la Concorde, the parting gift of Citizen-Governor Deniau before he left for France.

The idea of chopping off a king's head in public struck the old man with the force of a revelation. Deniau had explained that a tyrant forfeits the right to live, and, though he never understood the logic of that argument, it was an awesome precedent.

And Da Silva was always dreaming of Bahia. Whenever a ship sailed, he would watch the yardarms vanish into the night, then light a pipe on the verandah and sink into a reverie of the future: he would have a Big House, a view of the sea, grandchildren and the sound of water tinkling through a garden. But then the mirage would fade. The sound of drumbeats pressed against his temples and he had a presentiment that he would never get out of Africa.

He confided his fears to no one. To convince himself they were unreal, he would sit, red-eyed into the night, writing letters to Joaquim Coutinho, tearing up sheet after sheet in an effort to express himself:

These people must be the biggest thieves in the world. I would live on any other continent but this one. I would live in the lands of ice and snow, anywhere to be away from their gibberish . . .

Or:

I cannot begin to describe this cretinous existence of mine. Nor how lonely it is to be without family or friends. Perhaps next year I shall come back and marry . . .

He pleaded for news, any scrap of news, to keep his memories of Brazil from fading: but Joaquim's replies were invariably cold and commercial:

By our brig *Legitimo Africano* I have this day received your consignment of 230 items (144 m 86 f), also 41,500 cola nuts (female). I regret to report losses of one third owing to an outbreak of the bloody flux. I would like your opinion as to why the females do so much better than the males. In the meantime the above items will be sold for the highest possible price and your share returned in flintlocks, tobacco and iron . . .

But why, his partner wrote back, had they not made him Governor of the Fort? How he longed for one word that they were aware of his existence! 'My conduct, I can assure you, is irreproachable.'

The officers had not forgotten him. But since they were profiting, privately, from his activities, public recognition was out of the question.

At an official level, the Fort at Ouidah had ceased to exist.

Gradually Africa swamped him and drew him under. Perhaps out of loneliness, perhaps in despair of fighting the climate, he slipped into the habits of the natives.

He wore long pantaloons instead of the breeches that gave him prickly heat in the groin. He wore amulets against the Evil Eye. Taparica taught him to shuffle his feet at the phallus of Papa Legba and, together, they went to the diviners.

The fear of illness obsessed him. But since his servant was an adept in the mysterious medicine of excrements, and since he trusted him in everything, he had no choice but to swallow his own piss for a liver attack; piss and yams for malaria; and when he had a sore throat, he would say a prayer to St Sebastian and flavour his coffee with fowl droppings.

Some evenings they went to the Python Temple to watch the novices sink their teeth into the necks of living goats. The spectators screamed with laughter as boys somersaulted on one another's backs and mimicked the motions of sodomy. When the lightning danced, the votaries of the Thundergod would axe their shoulder blades, then writhe and rear their buttocks to the sky.

He never knew what drew him to the mysteries. The blood? The god? The smell of sweat or the wet glinting bodies? But he was powerless to break his addiction and, realizing that Africa was his destiny, he took an African bride.

Her name was Jijibou.

She was sixteen.

Dehoué, her father, was a chief of the krumen, whose one ambition was to possess a white son-in-law. He had come four times to the Fort to propose yet another of his daughters. When turned down a fourth time, he had threatened to go on strike: the Yovogan said it was most insulting to refuse an offer of wives.

One December evening, Dehoué came again, this time with musicians and a figure muffled in white cloth. The town was silent but for the howl of breakers on the bar. Swifts were slicing the green air. The girl brushed past the spectators and tore off her veil.

She had owl eyes, a pouting mouth and shell-pink fingernails that fluttered at her finger-tips. Gold hoops shone in her ears. Her neck was a perfect cylinder. Her legs gleamed like metal rods and her torso, clad only in an indigo loincloth, was hard yet flexible as a hinge.

Her shoulders shuddered at the first roll of drums. Then she spun round. She pirouetted. She strutted. Her arms pumped the air, her feet kicked the dust. Sweat poured from her breasts and a musky perfume gusted into the Brazilian's face: not once did she let her gaze fall away from him.

The drummers stopped.

She stood before him, on tiptoe, swaying her hips and languidly laying out her tongue. Her arms beckoned. She bent at the knees. Then she arched her spine and bent over backwards till the back of her head brushed the ground.

Francisco Manoel caught her father's eye and nodded.

Taparica rattled his teeth with horror, said, 'You not know this people,' and moped about in a sulk. But Da Silva put his reaction down to jealousy and went ahead with plans for the wedding.

That midnight he left her panting behind the bed-curtains and chucked the red rag to the crowd of her relatives who had drunk far more rum than he had bargained for.

In the morning, Taparica prayed the blood came from his master's scratched and bleeding face, but his hopes fell on hearing the guffaws of the bride's mother as she inspected the night's work.

As for Francisco Manoel, he welcomed the change. The south-west angle of the Fort now echoed with the thumping of mortars and the ivory merriment of ripe women. He liked Jijibou's peppery messes. He liked twisting his tongue round the dissonant syllables of Fon. And when he loved her, she would rub her calloused heels, one after the other, down the depression of his spine.

She tightened her lips if ever he tried to kiss them. Yet her nostrils would quiver with pleasure at the sight of a new present. She would swan about begging approval for a new bandanna of Cantonese silk: what the eye saw, the fingers grabbed and played with, childishly.

One Thursday he gave her a Dutch looking-glass and she stared at herself, tossing her head this way and that way till Saturday, till she let it slide to the floor and shiver to bits.

Her stomach swelled and she gave birth to a boy the colour of pink coral. They called him Isidoro and the midwives buried his umbilical cord under the roots of a baobab.

But the delivery of a male heir was the signal for her relatives to move in. Not a day passed without some new cousin requiring to be fed. Jijibou stole the key to the liquor store and gave it to her brothers. He asked her to restrain them, but she said, 'Stealing from a white man isn't stealing.' And when he complained to the Yovogan, the old man looked dreamily over the chameleons and said, 'It is their custom.'

Late one night, they heard howls coming from the Yovogan's compound. He had died of delirium and the body had swelled up and gone green. Taparica knew which particular cactus had provided the poison, said it had 'not taste' and begged his master board the Brazilian brig at anchor in the roads.

But Francisco Manoel was unwilling to abandon his property.

There were bad days ahead: the King had fresh troubles and was blaming them on the foreigners.

He replaced the Yovogan with a Commander of the Atchi Brigade, a man all mouth and no neck to speak of, who, at their first meeting, kept the Brazilian waiting five hours hatless in the sun. When asked to settle the King's debt, the man folded his arms and said, 'Dahomeans never sell slaves to white men.'

Within a month only a few cripples could be seen hobbling round the barracoon. People shut the doors in Da Silva's face. Boys darted across his path shouting, 'Road closed to whites!' The officials made him pay a toll to go down to the beach and a far bigger toll to come back. One morning, a headless black cock appeared on the altar of the chapel.

'Life here', he wrote to his partner, 'is not what it was a year ago, when a delicious life cost us nothing and we made good money. We are subject to the most humiliating searches and the Blacks are full of envy and hatred for the Whites. In addition, our friend the King of Dahomey has turned robber. He buys but does not pay. He owes me for the rifles of the *Atalante*, for the whole cargo of the *Flor da Bahia*, and hasn't sent one captive to the coast in nine months. I cannot say what I should do. Perhaps I should move to Badagry and trade with the King of Oyo? My man Fernandinho will tell you all, for he has been one of the victims . . .'

But Fernandinho did not get aboard with the letter. The customs men stripped him of all he possessed before they allowed him to board. And ten days later – the time it took to have the handwriting deciphered – a detachment of soldiers arrested Francisco Manoel and hauled him before the new Yovogan.

The rain had fallen all day and, all over town, naked men were lathering each other in the purplish puddles. In the outer yard some boys were sorting cowries into grass-cloth bags. He heard a raucous cry. A weight pressed on his shoulders. The last thing he remembered was a foot rammed hard against his windpipe.

He recovered consciousness lying in the mud with a red film covering his eyes: his head had hit the rim of a mortar as he fell. His right hand had swollen solid, where they had wrenched off the ring of his Brazilian marriage. Then they hobbled him with chains and put him in a stinking hut.

The guards pinched him, pulled his hair and kicked him in the kidneys. Pus oozed from the head wound. He dribbled dysentery. The small boys laughed.

He lost all sense of time and waited for death as one waits for a friend. Instead a messenger came with orders to take him to the capital.

His memories of the journey melted into a colourful blur.

For seven days he tossed in his hammock, feverishly eyeing the runnels of sweat that poured from his bearer's back. At one village there were heads on poles: at another, women pointed up a tree to where a crucified man croaked for water in a library of sleeping fruit bats. Crossing the Great Marsh, there were weedy meres where red birds perched on dead branches and blue dragon-flies darted over the nenuphars. A porter missed his footing on the causeway and the mud peeled from his thighs in thick grey flakes.

It was night when they came into Abomey.

The palace of Abomey had tall walls made of mud and blood but very few doors. It lay at a distance of twenty-three thousand, five hundred and two bamboo poles from the beach. In its innermost compound lived the King, his eunuchs and three thousand armed women.

The guards put their prisoner to lodge in a low thatched house. When his strength returned, they took him for walks about the city, but the drumbeats, the headless victims, and stench of putrefaction made him dizzier and dizzier and he had to go back to his bed.

Sometimes the King passed by on the far side of the wall, but all Da Silva saw was a white parasol frilled with jawbones.

He asked, 'When will I see the King?' and the guard lowered his eyelids and drew his forefinger across his Adam's apple.

Then, one morning at cockcrow, three eunuchs came and told him to dress. Hardly daring to look right or left, he followed their swishing orange robes through courtyards crammed with hollering tribesmen: everywhere an architecture of white skulls outnumbered the heads of the living.

They came into the presence of the King.

The King lay lounging on a bolster of carmine velvet, thronged by naked women, who fanned him with ostrich feathers and wiped the perspiration from his forehead.

He was a tall sinewy man with dry red eyes, automatic gestures and the bonhomie of the seasoned slaughterer. The rising sun shone on his chest. His fingernails curled like cocks' feathers. His loincloth was purple and his sandals were of twisted gold wire. At his feet were the heads of a boy and girl, sent half an hour earlier to tell the Dead Kings that their descendant had woken up. He glared at the Brazilian and spat.

All the commoners lay on the ground and, when he lifted his baton, they rubbed their noses in the dirt and bellowed, 'Dada! Breathe for me! Dada! Steal from me! Dada! Dada! Break me! Take me! My head is yours!'

A troubadour crawled forward, pointed at Da Silva, and said in a hollow voice, 'The bird who leaves her nest cannot carry away the eggs.'

An albino dwarf jumped up, saluted crazily, screeched white man's talk and gurgled as if he were being garrotted.

The executioner ran his fingers up and down his knife-blade.

But the prisoner knew better than to show fear and, as if

by suction, drew the monarch's mouth into a cracked tobacco-stained smile.

By the end of the audience he was the King's friend.

Not that he was set free, merely that swarms of people clustered round his house – to see him, to feel him, to beg for medical treatment and give him food. Ministers came to call, princes came. A man came with a tumour the size of a loaf, and a woman kept coming with fruit and said, 'I am your mother.'

He found the Portuguese prisoners and noted down their names: 'Luis Lisboa . . . Antonio Pires . . . Roque Dias de Jordão . . .' but when he tried to get them released, the King said, 'You are my friend. Don't speak about my enemies.'

The King said he loved him 'too much' and made him stand at his side to watch every ceremony of importance. So, Francisco Manoel saw the Horse Sacrifice and the Platform Sacrifice, at which the victims were trussed in baskets and toppled to the executioners. He saw the spirits of Dead Kings moving with the slow disjointed gait of skeletons. He saw the Dead Queen Mothers, who were much more colourful and lively; the King's 'Birds' who twittered and wore white, and the Lady Pipe Smokers who looked rather ill.

Often, the King would dance himself, rolling his scapulars and weaving his steps around the skulls of his favourite victims. Or he would amuse himself by teaching little boys to chop heads, and when they made a mess of it shout, 'Not that way, you fool! Think of chopping wood!'

Then he would nudge his friend in the ribs and bellow, 'Ha! Whiteman! I drink from your head also.'

The courtiers cackled at his buffooneries, and Francisco Manoel wondered where the farce would end.

Yet he was not alone; for there was a young man who kept trailing him wherever he went.

His forehead was high and wide, his eyebrows were glistening arches and his teeth shone. He wore an iron ring on his upper arm. A pink tunic, slit at the sides, revealed the slabs of his back and chest, and a hunter's knife hung loosely from his belt.

His one defect was a cast in the right eye, which was veiled and bloodshot.

He seemed to be signalling a message, but when Francisco Manoel returned the smile, the face collapsed in idiotic blankness.

A guard said he was Kankpé, the King's mad half-brother.

A friendlier guard whispered that Kankpé was only shamming madness; that he was the rightful king, and only waiting for an omen to raise the rebellion.

In April, the month when purple arums reared their hoods in the yamfields, there were fresh rumours spreading through the city.

The diviners who foresaw the future in egg-yolks and the surface of water were predicting catastrophe or change. At Sado, a woman gave birth to a boy who was half a leopard. The war against the Egbas had produced a total of five captives – and the King's behaviour had surpassed even Dahomean limits of tolerance.

He had tied up his two chief ministers, the Mingan and Meu, and spat rum in their faces. He had castrated a soldier whose hips were too wide. His sons had defiled a royal tomb, and he had opened the belly of one of his wives to prove her foetus was a boy.

One morning levée, an old man pushed through the crowd and raised a finger at the throne. His cheeks were hollow. His chest was smeared with white paste and white rags hung limply from his hips.

'Who are you?' asked the King.

'Can you not recognize Adjaholanhoun?' the man answered. 'It was I who obeyed your orders to poison your father. Now the Dead Kings have put me in prison for helping your crimes.'

The King shuddered and called for food for the stranger. But the old man threw the cornpastes over his left shoulder and said, 'The Dead eat so.' Then he poured the palm-wine over his right shoulder: 'The Dead drink so.'

The crowd parted, he walked into the mist and no one could find a trace of his footfalls.

All through that month the hyenas came into the streets at night and the city was silent by day. The King had played with his prisoner for a season and now had grown tired of his plaything. And the prisoner looked on death as a face unfolding from a mirror: he let himself hang limp when they dragged him out and threw him on the ground before the throne.

The King stood over him, his shadow falling in a dark diagonal stripe:

'Why has Portugal sent three hundred and thirty-five ships to attack Ouidah?'

'It hasn't.'

'Why did you kill my greyhound?'

He opened his mouth to speak, but the guards stoppered it with a wooden gag.

'So you think you're a white man?' the King sneered, and ordered him off to prison.

The guards shaved his head and dipped him in a vat of indigo.

To make sure the dye reached every pore, they made him submerge his head and breathe through a straw. They dipped him five times in a single moon, but each time, when they scrubbed him, the skin showed up grey underneath and they put him back to soak.

Then, since there was no precedent for beheading a white man – and since white was the colour of death and all whites were half-dead anyway – they left him to die without water or shade or food.

His legs withered. His stomach stretched taut as a drum. His skin erupted in watery pustules: whichever way he turned was agony. Phosphorescent centipedes crawled over him at night; and the vultures spattered him with ammoniac droppings, shuffling for position along the wall, and flexing their pinions with the noise of tearing silk.

He dreamed of walking through a line of airless rooms and, in each room, seeing his own head, crawling with meatflies, laid out on a silver dish. His fingers would push back the eyelids and a green light would flash and set the flies buzzing till they dropped, ping . . . ping . . . and exploded in wisps of smoke.

Sometimes he saw Prince Kankpé, standing full-face as if frescoed on the wall, smiling and showing the gap between his two front teeth.

Memories of Brazil kept passing before his eyes: the miserable mud house, the pendulum of his dead mother's leg, the cries of his child, the penitents at Monte Santo, the treasures of the Coutinhos – and as he counted the wrong turnings that had brought him to this end, he choked with self-pity and promised to take the cowl if ever he got out of Africa.

Or he would shriek with laughter at the absurdity of dying in this charnel-house, where the dead were more alive than the living.

And when death came, it came quietly, at night. It loosed his chains and lifted him gently up a ladder, up and over the prison wall and laid him on cushions below.

Kankpé had stolen the wickerwork litter used for carrying cowrie-shells to count the annual census. No one, not even a customs officer, was allowed to look inside. The bearers headed north-west and had crossed the frontier before the alarm went up.

Francisco Manoel woke from his drugged sleep and let his eyes wander over the chaff-flecked walls of a mud hut. A cock crowed. He heard the burble of women's laughter and, from over the valley, the trills of a flute.

A shadow passed across the door, and a grey-haired man came in with a calabash of foaming milk. The foam stuck to his beard; he wiped it with his arm and went back to sleep.

Later, the same man revealed the identity of his rescuer: he was to wait in the village till Kankpé could join him.

He went for walks in the sere rolling hills where longhorned cattle were grazing. Far to the west an escarpment crinkled the horizon into facets of purple and blue. The land reminded him of the Sertão, but here the thorn-trees had orange bark and the thorns were long and white and seemed to be shining.

He woke one morning to hear news that Kankpé was hunting in the bush not far away. He walked with the boy till sunset, till they came to a water-gourd poised by the roots of a tree.

They heard him before they saw him, striding through the grass-blades. A freshly killed antelope widened the trapeze of his torso: a breechclout of brown leather merely emphasized his nakedness.

Kankpé flayed the animal in the half-light, throwing the fat to the dog and burying the entrails so the soul should rest in peace. Then they ate the meat, grilled over a grid of green saplings.

A leopard barked in the bushes. He crawled to the edge of the clearing and barked back, and for a second they saw the spotted face flickering in the firelight.

'My father,' he said, and stretched out to sleep.

For the next five days they went out hunting together, feeling for affinities to break the lines of colour and custom.

Kankpé showed him the spoor of various antelopes – gazelles, kobs, waterbuck, guibs and bubals. He would steal up on a herd, now running, now crawling, now freezing motionless as an anthill if an animal reared its snout to sniff the wind. He would plunge into a marsh to drive out a warthog, or clamber up a tree to keep clear of a buffalo. He never threw his spear unless certain of his target. He despised the hunting gun as the weapon of a coward.

On the fifth night they swore a blood pact.

The moon in its final quarter smeared its light over the

lumpy trunk of a baobab. Somewhere a hornbill rattled its beak and, not far off, there was a jackal howling.

The two men knelt facing each other, naked as babies, pressing their thighs together: the pact would be invalid if their genitals touched the ground.

The moon glinted on the black thighs and biceps, but white skin absorbs the moonlight evenly.

Kankpé fumbled in a leather bag and took out a skull-cup. He set it in the space between their knee-caps and added the ingredients of the sacrament: ashes, beans, baobab pith, a thunderstone, a bullet taken from a corpse, and the powdered head of a horned viper.

He half-filled the skull with water. Then they split each other's fingers and watched the black blood fall.

They drank in turn, running their tongues over the bullet and thunderstone.

Kankpé rolled his eyes and muttered curses: 'A dâ la . . . A dâ la . . .': blood-brothers live together and together they must die.

Francisco Manoel drank with the light-heartedness of the man who has skipped from certain death. It took another thirty years for him to realize the extent of his obligations.

Five

He made his way to the coast of Anecho, a slave port to the west of Ouidah in the territory of the Popos. The factory beside the lagoon belonged to a Mr George Lawson, a hunchback mulatto and son of an English captain called George Law. The house was still full of English knick-knacks, but the English ships no longer came and guinea-fowl had nested in the saloon.

He wanted to get out, to forget, to begin again. He would scan the horizon with Mr Lawson's telescope, watching for a blur to break into the two half circles of grey, but a ship was a long time coming. In the evenings he played chess, and the stories he told about Abomey distracted his partner from his moves.

At last, an old felucca flying Portuguese colours dropped anchor and sent a boat ashore. She was bound from Lagos to Bahia but a storm had washed her waterkegs overboard and she needed replacements. The Captain agreed to take him: the crew took him for yet another madman in an African port.

On his last night ashore, he could not sleep for thinking of Bahia. Already he saw the harbour, and the churches and the grog-shops of the waterfront. But towards daybreak he remembered he would be going back a pauper. He remembered his promise to help Prince Kankpé and, by morning, he was in the mood for revenge.

His letter to Joaquim Coutinho made light of his sufferings and told the syndicate of their chance to rid Dahomey of a monster and replace him with a candidate of their own.

The syndicate replied with a shipment of muskets, rum and tobacco. Teams of porters met Prince Kankpé's partisans on the frontier. A length of scarlet silk, torn into pennons, became the symbol of the revolt.

Francisco Manoel waited and went on playing chess: he had just begun a game with Mr Lawson when the new King's messenger burst into the saloon and blurted out the news.

Not five days before, the two Chief Ministers had attended the levée, but instead of grovelling and throwing dust on their heads, shouted, 'The Dead Kings have deposed you!' and each removed one of the golden sandals that only a King could wear.

The King winced at his ancestor's verdict, abdicated and allowed himself to be shut up in prison – where he would linger on another forty years, ordering imaginary executions and slumped in a torpor of compulsive eating.

Mr Lawson spat out the tamarind pod he had been chewing and said:

'All Dahomeans are liars and new King will be bad king same as old one.'

Francisco Manoel shuddered at the thought of Abomey and refused to leave with the messenger. More messengers came, offering honours and a monopoly of the Slave Trade. Again he refused.

Nor would he relent until the evening a black canoe came gliding through the fishweirs and grounded at Lawson's Landing. A leggy figure stepped ashore. It was Taparica.

Master and servant flew along the path and smothered each other in an embrace that astonished both of them. They talked all night and, though their talk was unexhausted by the morning, Taparica convinced him he had nothing to fear.

The bearers brought up his hammock; yet, as he lay down, Francisco Manoel turned to his host and said:

'You'll see. One day I shall end up his slave.'

They passed through the West Gate of Abomey, riding in an open landau hauled not by horses, but men. A twenty-one-gun salvo was fired off. Umbrellas were broken in the crush.

The new King stood smiling to greet them in a toga of grey silk slashed with silver crescents: around his neck there was a single blue glass bead. He seemed to have grown taller and now trod the earth as if honouring it with his footfalls. He guided them to some chairs, thanked Taparica for 'landing the Big Fish', and, without warning, invested Francisco Manoel with the regalia of a Dahomean chief.

The clamours of the crowd increased in volume: '*Viva o amigo do Rey.*'

At sunset the King took them to a fortress where, peering from a platform, they saw the deposed monarch, reeling drunkenly round the yard, spitting balls of phlegm into the dust.

The King said:

> The hyena howls
> The elephant goes by

– and from that hour the Dahomeans called Francisco Manoel Adjinakou the Elephant.

Within a year he was the King's Viceroy at Ouidah and had turned Dahomey into the most efficient military machine in West Africa.

As long as he stayed on the coast, he assumed the manners and style of a Brazilian seigneur. From Cape Verde to the Bonny River, drifters of every colour came to feed at his table and test the resources of his cellar. Though the title 'Dom' was usually reserved for members of the Portuguese Royal Family, everyone called him 'Dom Francisco'.

He gave Ouidah the air of a civilized town by ordering drains to be dug and streets cut through its maze of pestilential alleys. He planted oil palms and coconuts, and introduced the pineapple. The flatlands were a sea of maize and manioc, and there were rice-paddies along the lagoon.

Because he forbade the lash on his plantations, his own workers adored him. On their way to the fields, they would file past his window and chant his litany:

> The Elephant spreads his net
> On land and sea
> He buys mothers, fathers, sons
> And the hyena howls in vain
> Friends gather round the smells of his kitchen
> Monkeys dance when they drink palm wine
> He is the Good Sponge who sponges us clean
> He hardens his walls with fire
> He gives us pearls when we give him a mosquito

In one day he sold all the slaves in Ouidah
His well will never run dry.

No captain could evade the vigilance of his coastguards. None could load a slave without paying an export tax, or land a bale of cotton without paying him a due. His promissory notes were honoured by bankers in New York or Marseille. Alone or in partnership, he commissioned a fleet of Baltimore clippers.

These new ships were designed to out-tack any cruiser of the Royal Navy. They had tall raking masts, sleek black hulls, and he named them after seabirds: *Fregata*, *Albatroz*, *Gaivota*, *Alcatraz*, or *Andorinha-do-Mar*.

But they sailed at a sharp angle of keel: even in a moderate sea, the crew had to batten the hatches and close the gratings. The temperature in the hold shot up, and the cargoes died, from heat, from dysentery and lack of air.

Like every self-respecting slaver, he blamed his losses on the British.

Each year, with the dry season, he would slough off the habits of civilization and go to war.

His first task had been to reform the Dahomean army. He and the King got rid of the paunchy, the panicky and the proven drunks. And since Dahomean women were far fiercer fighters than the men – and could recharge a muzzle-loader in half the time – they sent recruiting officers round the villages to enlist the most muscular virgins.

The recruits were known as the 'King's Leopard Wives'.

They ate raw meat, shaved their heads and filed their teeth to sharp points. They learned to fire from the shoulder not the hip, and never to fire at rustling leaves. On exercises they were made to scale palisades of prickly pear, and they would come back clamouring, 'Hou! Hou! We are men!' – and since they were obliged to be celibate, were allowed to slake their lusts on a troop of female prostitutes.

Dom Francisco insisted on sharing all the hardships of the march.

He crossed burning savannahs and swam rivers infested with crocodiles. Before an attack on a village, he would lash leaves to his hat and lie motionless till cockcrow. Then, as the dawn silhouetted the roofs like teeth on a sawblade, a whistle would blow, the air fill with raucous cries and, by the end of the morning, the Amazons would be parading before the King, swinging severed heads like dumb-bells.

Dom Francisco greeted each fresh atrocity with a glassy smile. He felt no trace of pity for the mother who pleaded for her child, or for the old man staring in disbelief at the purple veil spread out over the smouldering ruins.

For years he continued in this self-directed nightmare. But one day, before the sack of Sokologbo, he was hiding behind a rock when some small boys came skipping down the path, waving bird-scarers to shoo the doves off the millet fields. He would never forget their gasps as the Amazons pounced from the bushes and garrotted them one by one.

All that morning, as the Dahomeans did their work, he buried his face in his hands, muttering, 'No. Not the children!' and never went to war again.

But the King became a warrior more frightful than any of his ancestors.

He broke Grito in 1818, Lozogohé in 1820 and Lemón in 1825. He killed Atobé of Mahi, Adafé of Napou and Achadé of Léfou-Léfou. He made the Atakpameans eat their fathers in a stew. He swore to defeat the Egbas in their stronghold at Abeokuta, and he told the Alafin of Oyo to 'eat parrots' eggs'.

He was not cruel. He too sickened at the sight of blood and would avert his eyes from the executions. He longed to end the cycles of war and revenge – yet he could never resist the temptation to acquire more skulls.

The skulls of his enemies assured him that he was alive in the world of real things. He drank from skulls, he spat into skulls. Skulls formed the feet of his throne, the sides of his bed and the path that led to the bed-chamber. He knew the name of every skull in his Skull-House and held imaginary conversations with each in turn: the lesser enemies were piled on copper trays, but the great ones were wrapped in silk and kept in whitewashed baskets.

Not that he could have spared many victims had he wanted to. The war-commanders eyed him for the first sign of weakness, and a body of priests was always on hand to advise which captives should go to the Deadland, and which to the Americas.

Dom Francisco would think up ways to save them from the knife: he found the best plan was to divert the nobles' attention with some novelty imported from Europe.

One year, when the palace architects were planning a skull-mosaic, he suggested using porcelain plates instead. At first, the King was overjoyed at the idea of 'breaking' such valuable property and dashed a whole pile to the ground. Then, as if he heard his ancestors growling, he frowned, his dead eye drained the light from the live one, and he barked out:

'War is for taking heads, not selling them attached to bodies.'

Gradually the two friends lost the art of communicating except through presents. But though Dom Francisco's presents usually pleased the King, the King had nothing to offer but women – and such were his ideas of friendship that he posted spies inside the Fort at Ouidah to make sure each one was used. The mistress of the seraglio was still Jijibou.

She had weathered the upheavals and grown into a big-jowled woman, shapely as a horse, with a satiny gloss to her skin. She spent her days in the shade of her hut, muffled in orange cloth, and was never seen to smile.

Her father, the kruman, had died. He drowned the day his canoe capsized and, even if Jijibou suspected her husband of selling him to a slaver, she did not allow her suspicions to interfere with her household duties.

She would inspect the girls to make sure they were virgins, calm their fears and lead them to the bedroom. She brought each new baby to its father, but their squalling only reminded him of his Brazilian child, and, as their tiny fingers clawed at his beard, he would grit his teeth and stop his ears and hurry off.

To uphold the decencies of the Church, he insisted on Christian baptism and made Jijibou go through a fiction of being the real mother. He tried to read her thoughts as she stood by the font. But if she caught him glancing in her direction, her eyes would narrow and the facets of her mouth turn down.

By 1835 the size of his family had outgrown the Fort. So, work began on the mansion he had been cheated of building in Brazil.

Simbodji – which means 'Big House' in Fon – lay open to Atlantic breezes on a sloping site between the King's Baobab and the Captains' Tree.

The house that emerged from its chrysalis of palm scaffolds was a replica of Tapuitapera except that, for want of stone foundations, it was unsafe to build a second storey. The pink walls were the same, the upturned eaves, the blue dining room, and the cross-lattice windows that were painted green.

The houseboys had never seen glass windows before, and when they saw the reflection of the setting sun, they thought they were ablaze and doused them with water.

Dom Francisco imported jacaranda couches, an opaline toilet set, the Swiss musical boxes and the Goanese bed. A piano came from Germany. The billiard-table came through the surf on a raft of three canoes lashed together.

His own rooms were tall and cool, and stripes of sunlight filtered through the shutters. The verandah gave on to a garden of night-scented flowers, and there was a path that led through the wall to the seraglio.

Facing his bed, he hung up a panorama of Bahia, but the sight of it made him homesick and he replaced it with an engraving of the boy Emperor Dom Pedro II. His desk was stacked with old Brazilian newspapers. He tried to puzzle out the politics of the new Empire. The names meant nothing. He gave up and only read the advertisements.

One night, in a flash of inspiration, he wrote to Joaquim Coutinho, asking if the nuns of the Soledade could make a replica of the oratory of the Last Supper.

Joaquim, it so happened, was delighted at being spared the embarrassment of his partner's return. He lost no time in sending a crate with a letter:

My consort and I take pleasure in sending the original, with our blessings for the Christian community established at Ouidah . . .

A portrait of Dom Francisco at the age of fifty would have shown a man strangely unaffected by the climate. A scar fanned out from his right temple. A deep furrow split his forehead into two. But his skin, though yellowish, was unwrinkled. His hair and beard were black and glossy, and he moved with the easy strides of youth.

He took not the slightest trouble with his clothes. By day he wore a planter's suit of grey calico, an old pair of boots and a bandless straw hat with holes in it. He would make his dinner guests wear freshly laundered whites, only to insult them by turning up in a dirty chintz housecoat and pantaloons that trailed over his Moorish slippers.

Not that he had no other clothes. In his bedroom was a wardrobe painted with Chinese landscapes, stuffed full of the clothes he ordered from the tailors of London and Paris for the receptions he would never attend. Some nights, behind a bolted door, he put on evening dress and would extend a white-gloved hand to the cheval-glass that flaked and pitted far faster than his own face. Then, when the moths and silverfish began their work, he would tell Taparica to burn the lot and write out fresh orders to his agent.

He wore no watch. He knew the time from the sun or the constellations; and even when the sky was overcast, he could peer into the darkness and say, 'Three hours left till dawn.'

Yet he kept a collection of watches in a leather box beneath the bed – gold fobs and half-hunters; watches with rock crystal dials, or painted with scenes of the Turkish harem.

His favourites were the Swiss musical clocks; and when his women heard the tiny birds twittering under the mattress they thought they were the spirits singing.

He would wind them up before retiring, taking care to set each one to a different hour: he was so much obsessed with the passage of time.

There were other nights when he would take out his rings, putting on one after the other till his fingers were stiff with the wild light of emeralds.

Afterwards he would stare moodily at his bare hands and call out, 'Taparica! Soap and water!' Then he would lie in his nightshirt, waiting for the creak of boards on the verandah: on the bad nights, the game of breaking virgins was his only hope of consolation.

The Da Silva boys were allowed to play naked till the age of seven. After that, their father dressed them in whites, put them to sleep in a dormitory and sent them to the padre's schoolroom to learn how to read.

They were lively boys and they learned easily. They learned their catechism and the verses of Camoens, but most days they came back from their lessons with blank, bewildered faces.

Twenty years of mission work in Angola had given Father de Lessa the appearance of a bird of prey and biblical convictions on the subject of Blacks. He had the habit of conducting scripture lessons in the form of rhetorical questions:

'Can the Ethiopian change his skin?' he would shout. 'Or the leopard his spots?'

Was not black the colour of night? Of the Devil? Was not black skin the very mark of Cain?

Dom Francisco guessed what was wrong and, one morning, sat outside the schoolroom and listened to the padre's peroration. Then he poked his head through the window and said, 'But blacks believe the Devil is white.'

His eldest son, Isidoro, was sent to Bahia to finish his studies with the Coutinho boys. The family now lived in a big white mansion on the cliffs overlooking the bay. But Isidoro's wildness – and African toilet habits – so terrorized the ladies of the household that his guardian packed him off to a gloomy seminary in the hills.

There, in classrooms reeking of incense, he learned to parse a Latin sentence wearing a white cassock emblazoned with a red cross. He would come back for the holidays sunk-eyed and flabby. His coughing fits reminded the Fathers of consumption and, finally, they sent him away for good.

Back in Bahia, he soon recovered his spirits in the bars and brothels of the Pelourinho.

'I have decided,' Joaquim Coutinho wrote to his partner, 'to shut my eyes to your son's indecencies, since the only means I have of controlling them would be to hand him over to the civil authorities, which, as a guardian, I am loath to do.'

But when the young mulatto staggered into the house, drenched with blood and his clothes ripped to ribbons, he was thrown out and sent to lodge with a slave-broker in the Lower City.

Joaquim Coutinho used Isidoro's behaviour as an excuse to break up the partnership: by 1838 slave-trading was no longer an occupation for a Brazilian gentleman.

It had been a criminal offence for ten years. But though it

flourished without prosecution, though the Southern coffee-planters were crying out for slaves, the business had got into the hands of Portuguese nouveaux riches, whose business methods made them highly unpopular.

Brazilian liberals hated slavery on moral grounds and the conservatives mistrusted it for practical ones: there were far too many Blacks in Brazil.

In 1835 a slave revolt had all but overwhelmed the city of Bahia. The leaders, it turned out, were a cabal of Muslim fanatics who had infiltrated the Black Christian Brotherhoods and declared a Holy War. But in fashionable society the name of Toussaint-Louverture was on everyone's lips, while at Court the Emperor's ministers were known to favour German immigrants over Africans.

Apart from his ships, Joaquim Coutinho was the owner of ranches, a diamond mine, a bank, streets of town property, and he was thinking of building a railway. He had also set his heart on a title, lived in dread of compromising himself and was particularly sensitive to his nickname, 'Old Meat'.

On a visit to Rio he bribed the imperial chamberlains. Then he cut his old associates and sold his fleet. He built two churches in the Gothic style; he endowed a convent, put his name at the top of every subscription list – and, finally, he had his reward.

One evening at Simbodji, as Dom Francisco leafed through the latest copy of the *Jornal do Rio de Janeiro*, he read that the well-known Bahia financier and philanthropist had been created Baron of Paraíba. A line engraving showed a spade-bearded man, coffined in a frock-coat, with gold chains round his paunch and the Order of St Boniface round his neck.

'Not the boy I knew,' he said.

He decided to risk a letter of congratulation, though five months passed before the reply came – a curt note regretting that public and private pressures no longer allowed him to attend to the African trade.

The new Baron of Paraíba did at least have the grace – or the self-interest – to find an agent in Bahia for his ex-colleague.

José de Paraízo was a Portuguese who had learned from the experience of exile the art of making himself indispensable. His first action was to rescue Isidoro da Silva from the gutter. He bought him a new set of clothes, and made him pose in them for his portrait. Then he sent him to Marseille as an apprentice to a shipping company.

He also excelled in finding things to keep the King of Dahomey amused. In the same consignment as the portrait, he sent some lustre-ware kettle-drums, a Noah's Ark and a barrel-organ that played the Psalms. Next, he bought up the costumes that were sold off by the Rio Opera to defray its costs; and for a season, the court functionaries of Abomey swanned about dressed as characters from Rossini's *Semiramide*.

Another time, perhaps as a joke, he sent the canvas of Judith and Holophernes, but Dom Francisco kept it back:

'These people,' he wrote, 'have so little humour. His Majesty might not be amused.'

Nor was there any way of telling if the King was pleased with a present; for he would frown at each one and lift an eyebrow, as if to say, 'What have you kept back this time?'

All the serving girls at Simbodji were royal spies: whatever went on in the household the King was the first to know. So, when Dom Francisco bought for himself a silver swan that gobbled up fishes to the airs of Bellini, it vanished overnight, only to be sent back from Abomey with the neck off, the mechanism overwound and a warning never again to send anything broken.

The King had no use for gold. Gold was the currency of his enemy, the King of Ashanti, whereas Dahomey used cowrie-shells that could neither be faked nor adulterated.

But the Cubans and Yankees who came to buy slaves in Ouidah always preferred to pay in gold: ingots, doubloons, louis d'or, napoleons, sovereigns and sometimes the coins of the Great Moghul. Dom Francisco kept his hoard in money barrels buried under the bedroom floor: it alarmed him terribly when the King commanded one of them to be taken up to Abomey.

The King peered at the coins, one after the other, and let them slide through his fingers. He learned the names of Louis Philippe, the Elector of Brandenburg, Tsar Paul and the young Queen Victoria. Then he rolled his eyes and threw the lot to the ground, snorting, 'I wouldn't let anyone walk off with my head,' and never spoke of gold again.

In the rainy season of 1842 Father de Lessa went mad.

He would come into the schoolroom naked and mortify himself with a leather flail. Or he could be seen stalking round the Python Temple, in a mud-spattered soutane, shrieking, 'I will make this city desolate. I will smite the abominations.'

One Sunday, as he was preparing the sacrament for Mass, he found a python curled up in his vestments and staved its head in with the butt of his processional cross. The fetish priests hauled him out of the chapel and, by the time Dom Francisco had rescued him, he was out of his mind.

He kept seeing an animal called the Zoo.

The Zoo had the head of a monkey, a dog's body, leopard claws, and it would sprawl lecherously across his path and twitter like a bird.

Dom Francisco decided to ship him back to Bahia. But the Zoo was also in the sea; for when they strapped him aboard the canoe, he was still screaming, 'The Zoo! The Zoo!'

About this time Isidoro came back from France with the airs of a dandy and a head full of schemes for starting a palm-oil factory: by the 1840s the middle classes of Europe had discovered the blessings of *savon blanc de Provence*.

A Marseille trading company, Mm. Binet and Poncetton, sent a scout to report on the palm plantations of the Slave Coast: it was through Isidoro's help that a thin-lipped young man called Blaise Brue reoccupied the old French Fort of Saint-Louis-de-Grégoy.

Blaise Brue played an excellent game of boston and was a welcome dinner guest at Simbodji. It was he who suggested turning Ouidah into a French protectorate.

As for Dom Francisco, he jumped at the chance of making clean money in the oil trade. He put his entire workforce at the Frenchman's disposal, and they went into partnership. They unchoked old palmeries and they planted new ones. From distant villages women converged on the Fort with oil calabashes balanced on their heads. In the first season, four thousand barrels were rolled to the beach, and Dom Francisco was seen again to smile.

He smiled as the palm nuts ripened the colour of

embers and he smiled to watch the glutinous yellow liquid rise to the surface of the vats. Often, he would turn to his sons and say:

'One day palm-oil will make us rich beyond the dreams of avarice.'

But the young mulattos were stranded in a limbo. They hated their father. They hated any kind of work and, having no outlet for their energies, turned sour and moody, stole from the storerooms, or took to drink and discovered the pleasures of the knife.

Dom Francisco's love-affair with France reached a climax when Louis Philippe's second son, the Prince de Joinville, landed off the frigate *Belle-Poule* to inspect the French factory.

That night at dinner, he served a Château Margaux of 1811 and provided a silver tooth-pick holder in the form of a porcupine for each officer to take as a souvenir.

The Prince made everyone laugh by telling scandalous stories about the English when he went to fetch the body of Napoleon off St Helena. He discussed the problem of cooling champagne in the tropics and the origin of the expression '*Perfide Albion*'. Then he drew a pencil sketch of his host – the basis of all future portraits – and retired to bed in the Goanese four-poster.

Next morning, when he came to leave, the Da Silva boys shouted 'Vivas!' The girls garlanded him with frangipani; and, presenting him with a box of his best Havanas, Dom Francisco asked him to put in a good word with his brother-in-law, Dom Pedro of Brazil.

'I shall tell him everything,' the Prince said.

It came as a terrible shock when Blaise Brue got a message

from his company in Marseille to drop his association with the infamous slaver.

'I am sorry, mon vieux,' – and that was all he had to say.

In despair Dom Francisco turned to the British, hoping that if he helped them, they would help him in return.

When a Bristol barque went ashore four miles down the coast at Jacquin, he cleared the beach of looters and helped the crew salvage the cargo. He rescued a Methodist mission stranded at Lagos, and looked after Mrs McCalvert when her husband blew his brains out. He even entertained the Englishmen who came with Lord Palmerston's draft treaty for abolishing the Slave Trade.

The first 'Englishman' to visit the King was a Freetown 'trouser black', the Reverend Tommy Crowder, who was forced to witness the annual sacrifices and came back scared out of his wits. He did, however, just manage to stammer out the greetings of the Great White Queen.

The King's reply, which the clergyman transcribed into a kind of English, asked after the Queen's health and that of 'His Daughters and His Sons and His Mother and His Grandmother'. It agreed that selling slaves was 'BAD'; that Brazilians were 'BAD PIPPLE ONLY WANT SLAVE FOR MONEY'; and that 'Him Queen' should send a man with a 'Big Head to hear King Palaver and write Book Palaver and same way King of Dahomey send messenger to Queen bye and bye'.

The man with a 'Big Head', Captain William Munro, arrived six months later in the uniform of the 1st Life Guards. He had ginger hair, candid blue eyes, a tuft of ginger whiskers on the bridge of his nose, and his conversation was full of the stock phrases of Abolitionist literature. He had brought the King a present of a pair of peacocks, and a spinning-wheel from his mother in the Highlands.

Over dinner he tried to convince Dom Francisco that the soil of Dahomey was ideal for growing cotton.

'Yes. Yes,' his host replied. 'It will come. It will all come. You will bring them railways and make them very happy. You may even stop them killing each other. But that will take a long time, and I am much too old and tired to try. All I can do, my dear young friend, is offer you the hospitality of my simple house.'

He was laid up with rheumatism the day the mission left for Abomey; but calling the Captain to his bedside, he gripped his hand and whispered, 'Do, please, commend me to the King.'

Afterwards, no one knew if the interpreter was to blame, or Munro's naivety, or the King's desire to please. But the Foreign Office got the impression that the King was a 'just and humane man', who longed to be rid of the 'detestable Da Silva' and take up the peaceful arts of agriculture.

In his turn, the King had the pleasing vision of an annual subsidy of three thousand pounds from his White Sister, which would allow him to make war and take as many heads as he liked without the troublesome business of selling captives.

His letter to Queen Victoria promised to expel all the slavers from Ouidah; and since the Queen's heart was a 'BIG CALABASH overflowing with palm-wine for the thirsty man', he needed a big tent and a golden carriage – now.

Three more English missions came, each worse-tempered than the last, and a Vice-Consulate was set up at Ouidah in the old British Fort.

The King promised one thing, then another, but never put

his cross to the treaty. No tent came from England, nor did the golden carriage. Instead Consul Crosby took the King a suit of chain mail, some gutta-percha masks of Punch and Judy, a contraption called Dr Merryweather's Tempest Prognosticator, and a copy of the *Illustrated London News* covering the Great Exhibition.

The meanness of these presents shocked the King into asking Dom Francisco what three thousand pounds would pay for:

'Your household expenses for one week.'

The Vice-Consul was a sour-faced man, who held himself excessively erect and had cheeks that looked as if they were pumped full of grease. He earned Dom Francisco's undying hatred when he pointed at Taparica and said, 'I see, sir, that you keep a performing monkey.'

His orders from Lord Palmerston were to insist that Dahomey refrain from attacking the city of Abeokuta, where there were Anglican missionaries. The King, however, had promised his ancestors to leave Abeokuta a pile of ashes – and he promised the English nothing.

At his last audience, Crosby made the mistake of lecturing on the evils of war, at which the King produced a framed engraving of the Battle of Waterloo and said, 'Whose war, Mr Consul? Whose war?'

The Consul's reply was to present the King with a native hoe together with some comment about 'doing a useful job of work'. The King then flew into a rage, threw a necklet of bat wings in the envoy's face and bellowed, 'Take that for the old woman!'

Consul Crosby broke off negotiations and closed the Consulate.

The King went to war.

Two missionaries stationed at Abeokuta, Messrs Bickersteth and Smith, gave the Egbas lessons in arms drill and provided ammunition. On March 3rd 1851, five thousand Dahomeans were killed below the Sacred Rock. It was the worst defeat in their history.

The West Africa Squadron then blockaded the port of Ouidah and the King's ministers blamed Dom Francisco for letting the Englishmen into the country.

But worse troubles were to come from the 'Brazilians'.

The first 'Brazilians' in Ouidah were a shipload of ex-slaves, who had bought their freedom and chartered an English merchantman to take them back to Africa. They landed near Lagos, hoping to go upcountry to their old homes in Oyo. But the fetid swamps were far from the paradise of their grandmothers' tales. Villagers stoned them and let loose their dogs. They panicked at the thought of being sold again. They were homesick for Brazil but, with one-way passports, had nowhere else to go.

Dom Francisco heard of their plight and sent his cutter to offer them asylum.

He met them on the beach, the men in stove-pipe hats, the women in white-lace crinolines with their hair ironed flat. He gave them parcels of land and soon their cheerful farms dotted the countryside all the way to Savi.

The 'Brazilians' turned Ouidah into a Little Brazil. They went on picnics. They gave dinners. They planted pots of love-lies-bleeding and the marvel of Peru. They decorated their rooms with pictures of St George and the Dragon and, at Carnaval, would pelt each other with waxed oranges full of scented water.

The whole town changed colour. Instead of dull pinks and ochres, the houses took on the hues of a Brazilian garden; and as the women leaned over their half-doors, they seemed to be wearing them as an extension of their dress.

On the hot days they would lounge on their balconies, fanning themselves or scratching their backs with ivory backscratchers. Sometimes, a chain of captives came clanking by with dogs at their heels – and the 'Brazilians' would fling flowers into the street, shout '*Boa Viagem!*' and sigh for the great houses of Bahia and Pernambuco.

Every Saturday, Dom Francisco gave a dinner for the leaders of the colony. All of them agreed that Simbodji was gloomy, old-fashioned and vulgar.

The newcomers were very fussy about their health and, for the first time, Ouidah had a doctor.

He was Dr Marcos Brandão Ferraez, a harassed young mulatto, gone grey at thirty, who could be seen hurrying on his rounds with a green carpet-bag. Back in Brazil he had eloped with a Sertanista from a small town in Ceará: they decided to go to Africa when her brothers threatened to kill him.

The couple were childless and lived in two neat rooms above their pharmacy, where they put a plaster bust of Hippocrates and rows of blue pottery drug jars inscribed with Latin names; and they had a macaw called Zé Piranha.

Dona Luciana kept a spotless kitchen. No one knew better how to make guava marmalade or stuff a crab. She sang as she pounded her spices and, when she sang, her upper lip lifted in an enchanting way. But they were all sad songs. She had sung them as a girl, when she ached to get out of the backlands – to which she was aching to return.

After a while, she seemed to shrivel away in the heat. Her hair hung in rat-tails and her face came up in a rash. She was terrified of going out, mistook scorpions for snakes and would sit, miserably fingering her crucifix, till her husband came back.

One midday, as Dom Francisco was walking home with Taparica, he stopped dead in his tracks. Clearly and slowly, through the pharmacy window, came the words of a song that untied knots in his memory. It was a song his mother sang, about the gipsy woman who walked from fair to fair; and when Dona Luciana came to the final stanza, he joined in the last two lines.

She froze.

He peered in.

She took one look under the brim of his hat, saw the eyes and afterwards swore she had seen the Devil.

On the other hand he was always welcome for a glass of sweet lime at the house of Jacinto das Chagas, a half-Yoruba mulatto who had been a clerk on a sugar estate and had a lovely daughter called Venossa.

Jacinto's calm smile, his gentlemanly bearing, his temperance and clean cotton suits made a lasting impression on the Dahomeans. Years of deference had taught him how best to worm his way into another's confidence, or play on another's guilt. Whenever he spoke of the Slave Trade, he would splay his long bony fingers over his heart and sigh, 'My brothers! My poor black brothers!'

Because of his reliability, and his head for figures, Dom Francisco took him on as his assistant. He trusted him with commercial secrets he would never have shared with his sons. And he even trusted him on confidential errands to the King.

At first the King was infuriated by the idea of black men in shoes, but when Jacinto told him of the 'Brazilians'' marriages in the chapel, he too said he needed a Christian bride: the whole colony was disgusted by Jacinto's decision to sacrifice his own daughter.

One drizzly morning, veiled so no one should see her crying, and driving her fingernails through a purse of blue satin, Venossa das Chagas said, 'I will,' between sobs; and she walked down the aisle on the arm of Dom Francisco, who stood proxy for his blood-brother in a black morning coat.

An Amazon guard of honour escorted her to Abomey where, forty-nine years later, a French army officer found her, bent double before a crucifix in an attitude of prayer.

It was she who ruined the Da Silvas.

A month after the marriage, her father picked a quarrel with his employer, made friends with the French, and set up as a palm-oil exporter on his own. The King gave him land and slaves. He built a house with white columns and filled it with furniture from Paris. Soon, under the cover of the oil business, he started selling slaves to dealers from the United States.

Dom Francisco heard his monopoly was broken, and thought he was going mad. He burst in on the Das Chagas family at luncheon and sneered:

'Where are your black brothers now?'

'Those were Mahis,' Jacinto replied, 'not my people.'

In message after message, Dom Francisco tried to get his rival expelled but Jacinto had taught the King the true value of gold. And he had hinted that half the Da Silvas' fortune was already in Brazil – a capital crime in a country where every scrap of property was royal.

Without warning the King's tax-collectors swarmed into Simbodji and removed all the silver and gold. A month later, a steam-frigate of the West Africa Squadron boarded the last Baltimore dipper: it was obvious that Jacinto had tipped the British off.

The women of Simbodji said, 'The Big Tree is falling,' for quite suddenly the master was old.

And Taparica was dying.

His head drooped. His skin shrivelled and red crescents showed up under his eyeballs. Some days he peered like a lost child, not knowing where he was. When the end came, Dom Francisco would not let him die on a mat, laid him down on the Goanese bed and held his scaly hand through three suffocating nights.

The voice croaked through the curtains:

'You not know this people. You not learn them never.'

Taparica tried to explain the various kinds of poison and their antidotes. But the seabird part of him had flown, back to his island in the Bay of Bahia, where he had once licked the armpit of the woman who had taught him the mysterious medicine of excrements.

Dom Francisco buried him at dawn in a grave among the flowerbeds. A clammy mist enveloped his private sorrow, and he stared at the mud-stained shroud.

From over the wall of the seraglio, he could hear the women wailing, but the wails sounded more like a song of triumph.

*

A worried Dr Brandão Ferraez appeared one morning before breakfast to report a case of yellow fever in a 'Brazilian' house where a girl had entertained a Cuban sailor.

Within a week groans and muffled prayers sounded in every street. The disease struck down hundreds of blacks and mulattos but left the whites alone. The 'Brazilians' hung purple cloths from their balconies and, if they strayed out of doors, tied sponges soaked in vinegar under their noses. Isidoro and his half-brother Antonio lit bonfires to stop the contagion, but the sparks set fire to a roof and burned down several houses.

Ten Da Silvas died of the disease; and the doctor was the last of its victims.

He came home from calling on a case, his cheeks concave and his eyes congested and yellow. He said, 'Don't touch me! Don't come near me!' and lay down on his bed.

By noon he was writhing on the floor with streams of black vomit, black as coffee grounds, spilling from his lips. Towards evening there was a storm. The clouds were the colour of mud. The palms bent and hissed. For another hour he lay quietly. Then he screamed as if an arrow had pierced his throat, and he died.

In the crowd watching the body as it came feet first through the pharmacy door was a hysterical woman who had lost all her children. The second she saw Dona Luciana, she shrieked out, 'Witch!'

The mob smashed the drug jars and the bust of Hippocrates lay headless in the street.

Dom Francisco heard the pandemonium and guessed the cause. Half an hour later, he and the houseboy carried in a bundle of rags and clotted blood, which they set on the Goanese bed.

For ten days Dona Luciana wavered between life and death, though she ate greedily what food was put before her. When she was well enough to recognize her rescuer, she shut her mouth so tightly they had to feed her by force.

Whenever he came into the room, she would cringe like a nocturnal mammal brought into the sunlight. It took weeks for her to get used to his presence. Then, suddenly, overnight, the man who had been the Devil was transfigured into her Guardian Angel.

He took care not to touch her, not even to touch her sleeve or her hand. Yet, joining two miseries in one, they took comfort from each other's company and could not bear to be apart.

He let her live on at Simbodji. She slept in the bed, while he slept next door on one of the jacaranda couches. He had the door of the seraglio walled up, and they stayed indoors and saw no one.

They lived as a man and a wife who have sworn themselves to chastity. She made an altar table and put vases of white flowers on either side of the oratory of the Last Supper. She kept a candle burning, and she promised to save his soul.

She would read from the New Testament the stories of Christ's forgiveness for sinners, with the sunbeams falling over her widow's weeds and her chignon of flaxen hair. Her neck was very white: around it, on a velvet ribbon, hung a locket of her husband's curls.

Dom Francisco listened, while Zé Piranha perched on his shoulder and poked his mandible into his ear: when the macaw's feathers came out, he would stroke his poll and say softly, 'Poor bird! He wants to go back home.'

In the rainy season, his attacks of rheumatism got worse

and for weeks he would be too stiff to move. She applied hot compresses to his spine: she knew any number of remedies, but had lost her medicines in the pharmacy fire.

The women of Simbodji hated their rival. Even in a rainstorm, Jijibou would bang and bang on the door, clamouring to be let in. She made such a row that Dom Francisco had to send for Isidoro who calmed his mother down and, for the first time, earned his father's gratitude.

Of all his children he cared only for two twin sisters by a mulatto woman who had died. Their names were Umbelina and Leocadia and they were growing up to be beauties. Dona Luciana said, 'Let them come and live with us. Twins will bring us luck,' and she gave them a mother's love.

She sewed them frilly white dresses and tied satin ribbons in their hair. She taught them to embroider their initials on handkerchiefs. Together they made a picture of the Virgin Mary, using Zé Piranha's moulting wing-feathers for the robe, and his breast for the halo. Often, they took a picnic to the Chinese pavilion at Zomai. All four of them would sing the songs of the Bandeirantes. And how the girls screamed when their father told the story of the Goblin-with-hair-for-hands!

On one of these picnics, Dona Luciana asked if he ever thought of going back to Brazil.

'If God wills it,' he said. 'I would give anything to die in my country.'

From that day onward she could think of nothing else. She was full of schemes for slipping past the King's guards, who now watched over them night and day. But he, the man of action, seemed incapable of action. He would press his fists against his temples and say, 'But how? How? How?'

But she knew there had to be a way.

He still owned property in Brazil – a cigar factory at Magarogipe, a ranch, a sawmill and a few town houses – which his agent had bought as an investment when the price of slaves was up. Not without misgivings, he wrote to José de Paraízo asking him to buy a house in Bahia for his retirement, begging him keep it a secret.

Six months later, together with a copy of the title deeds to No. 1 Beco do Corto, Barra, came a crudely painted canvas, still reeking of turpentine, with a pink villa in a garden going down to the sea.

Dona Luciana clapped her hands as they unwrapped it, and asked what were the squiggles in the sky.

'Birds,' he said.

The first half of Paraízo's letter listed the furniture and the names of the household slaves: he had kept back the bad news for the end.

Because of an oversight by the Baron of Paraíba, Dom Francisco's citizenship had been allowed to lapse. The Governor of Bahia had turned down his petition for a passport. Slaving was now a criminal offence: they would arrest him the minute he landed.

And yet, Paraízo continued, perhaps there was no cause for alarm: a contribution to charity would surely solve the problem. Another year passed. But when the *Jornal da Bahia* reported the opening of the sailors' hospital, Dom Francisco read the text of the Baron's address – and not a mention of his name among the donors.

In letter after letter, Dona Luciana appealed to the Governor, to the Baron and even to the Emperor himself: if all failed they would travel to Rome and lay their case before the Apostle Nunciate.

In her imagination she saw the great golden church, the choirs, the angels and the sunlight slanting sideways on the altar. The smell of incense already tingled in her nostrils. Then a figure in shining white would get up from his throne, and raise his hand in benediction, and say, 'Rise, Francisco! Reborn in the body of our Saviour!'

They went on waiting for news and there was none.

Umbelina and Leocadia were too frightened to go out. Their half-brothers would jeer them, push them against the wall, and pretend that they were wanted by the King. Their father feared for their safety. Firmly, he ordered Dona Luciana to take them to the house in Bahia, where she would lobby for his pardon and he would, one day, join them.

The Da Silvas were overjoyed to see the back of her: her departure was a scene of jubilation. But when she saw the ship slewing in the swells, and the tears in his eyes, she threw her arms around his neck and said, 'No. I cannot go.'

The setting sun had coloured the waves a milky golden green. The canoes looked like giant black centipedes as the crews heaved them down the scarp of the beach. Gently, Dom Francisco disentangled the moaning girls and led them to the water's edge. He gave the Captain a note for the Baron of Paraíba, commending them to his care. Flecks of foam blew on to Dona Luciana's black taffeta dress. And they stood, arm in arm, on the sand, watching the brown arms waving from a wavecrest and falling into the trough beyond.

That night she accepted an old man's love.

Two months later, she felt faint and had a twinge of pain in her stomach. Not till she started to swell would she believe what her instincts told her: she had always believed herself to be barren.

The pregnancy was difficult – and dangerous for a woman in her forties. Yet after a painful struggle, on January 21st 1854, she gave birth to a daughter. The baby was sickly: they had her baptized in the bedroom in case she failed to live.

But Eugenia da Silva clung to life and greedily took the teat of her wetnurse, though, at the same time, her mother had daydreams of falling into a slimy pit.

Eventually, the pardon came – a sheet of paper signed by the Emperor himself, acknowledging Lieutenant da Silva's 'many years of zeal and useful service at the Fort of São Jõao Baptista da Ajuda'. In the first rush of excitement, they did not take in the content of Paraízo's letter, with its catalogue of debts to the Banco Coutinho, the failure of the cigar factory, the disease that had killed his cattle, the landslide, and the decision of the Bahia Society of Commerce to declare him bankrupt.

He said, 'They have robbed me,' and let fall the sheet of paper.

He wrote, for the last time, to the Baron of Paraíba:

> Please, my dear friend, be patient with me. I would give you all I possess in Bahia. But what would people say? Everyone would turn against me if they knew I had nothing. They would say I could no longer count on you, my most trusted friend and protector over all these years. I ask you, I implore you, not to sell my furniture or my slaves, but put the house out to rent, so that my life may not be criticized. And I beg of you take care of my daughters . . .

The Baron did not reply to this letter. His bank foreclosed the mortgage. The bailiffs carted off the furniture, and the house and slaves were sold, unadvertised, at public auction. There was one bidder, Senhor Ricardo Paraízo, the agent's brother, who opened the place as an academy for young ladies.

But Umbelina and Leocadia did not attend classes at that school, or at any other school. They did not live in the Coutinho household, even as servants. Instead, they were sent to a famous personality called Mãe Andresinha, who taught them a trade on the cobbles of the Pelourinho.

'Whores?' their father howled at the captain, who told him that news. 'Whores? My darling daughters? Whores?' And he set his fists on the table and watched his whitening knuckles, and he choked with sobs.

On the night of February 15th 1855, disguised as masked carnival dancers, he and Dona Luciana tried to smuggle themselves and their baby aboard a Brazilian ship. The night was cloudy, but the moon came out as they crossed the lagoon, and the sentries brought them back, as prisoners, to Simbodji.

Dom Francisco was stripped of his wealth and privileges though he was allowed to live on in rooms bare of all but the bed. He was the King's blood-brother: it was a crime to touch a hair on his head, yet even his own sons spoke of him in the past tense.

On the hot days, he would lie in the shade of a mango and let little Eugenia clamber over his belly and tug at his beard. His eyes were weak. His hands weighed heavily under a network of grey veins.

He would shred the petals of a rose or bury his face in a hibiscus flower. If his old gardener passed by, he would open his mouth to bark an order, but no words came. Or he would listen to the howling of the surf, and bang his head against the wall. At night, he saw rows of bloodshot eyes glaring at him out of the darkness.

Some nights he lay under the tree till dawn and, by morning, the snails had left silvery threads over his legs. On tatters of paper, he scribbled incoherent prophecies, which Isidoro had his houseboys collect in case they contained information about the Brazilian fortune:

In 1860 the thorns will bear fruit but there will be few heads on bodies. – In 1870 there will be no heads to fill the hats. – In 1880 the slaves will sell their masters and buy wings. – In 1890 the Emperor will send a ship for his friend, but the sea will run red and the sky will turn to mud. And there will be a rain of stars and the ship will sink. – In 1900 the Holy House of Rome will crumble and bodies will choke the streets of Bahia and Jerusalem.

And Dona Luciana was sick and could do nothing to help him.

She had a bitter taste in her mouth and headaches so terrible that the sutures of her skull seemed to crack. She said, 'It's nothing. It must be the clouds. If only the clouds would go away.' She tried to smile, but the strain of forcing a smile made the pain much worse.

Then the skin flaked off her arms and legs, and left humid patches covered with a mouldering blush. Then her toes went numb, and her fingers, and the patches of skin turned black.

She could hardly breathe. Giddily, and with her pupils distended, she would gasp to Eugenia's wetnurse, 'Wash my arms! Look! Look! The spots are eating my arms!' Or in bursts of euphoria, she would cling to the bedposts, and bare her gums and chant Alleluias! at the top of her voice.

One morning, he saw threads of dark green mucus trailing from her mouth. Dimly, he remembered Taparica's dying words and murmured, 'Poison!'

She said, 'I'm so tired,' as she passed into a coma.

He clung to the body, but the grave-diggers tore him away and he flapped his arms and cawed like a wounded bird.

He never saw the smile of triumph spread over Jijibou's shining face. He had run off into the canebrakes and went missing for days. Search-parties failed to find him. Then a man coming home from his yam-patch saw something blue in the undergrowth. Brushing the branches aside, he made out a matt-haired figure on all fours, with a big bird perching on his shoulder.

Zé Piranha bit Isidoro's hand when they came for his master. But they overpowered the old man and chained him to a tree beside the Chinese pavilion at Zomai. Only later, when the rage went out of him, did they let him wander freely round the town.

He would hobble round Simbodji crying, 'My daughters! What have they done with my darling daughters?' But the women hid little Eugenia so she should not see her father.

One woman gave her a wooden doll and, at sunset, she would lay it down, wrap it in a scarf, stroke the tippet of white fur stuck to its chin, and whisper, 'Sleep, Papa! Sleep!'

With rags falling off his body, he would skulk round the

Legba Fetish. Only when no one was looking would he filch the offerings of cowrie-shells and buy himself a mouthful of food. He never ate Jijibou's scraps for fear that they were poisoned.

He talked to the waves on the beach. He even threw himself to the waves, but the waves threw him back; and they found him, bitten raw by sandflies and the crabs crawling over his body.

Gasping for water one day, he saw the King come towards him, smiling and showing the gap between his two front teeth. The King was young again, and was wearing his pink hunting costume. He laid a cool hand on his old friend's forehead and unstoppered his water-gourd.

Dom Francisco reached out both hands to receive it, only to wake and see the black pig snuffling round his toes.

March 8th 1857 was a white-hot day with the wind kicking up dust-devils in the street. Dressed in their best black frock-coats, Isidoro da Silva and his brothers were giving a luncheon to thank Jacinto das Chagas for smoothing out their problems with the King.

Dragging his left leg, Dom Francisco came through the Brazil Quarter, mobbed by a gang of boys chanting, 'Bom Dia, Yovo! Yovo, Bom Dia!' and making the sign of the knife.

There were scabs on his kneecaps.

He passed the plaster elephant over the front gate. He limped over to the gaming saloon, where some of his Swiss musical boxes lay undisturbed on a table. And he wound them up, one after the other, till the room was bursting with random sound.

The door of the dining room opened and his sons stood before him. He peered at the faces filling the doorway. Some of them had napkins tucked into their collars. Jacinto excused himself and slipped away.

The old man was crying. Tears sped down the creases of his cheeks, only to be sopped up in the mud that had caked in his beard. He opened his mouth to speak, but his lower lip hung slack, and the music whirled, round and round his skull, as he reeled from the room, out into the light and dust and hawks and dark and nothing.

Six

This is what Mama Wéwé remembered as she lay dying:

She remembered the rags, the scabbed legs and the swift, spiralling shadows on the ground. The women were wailing and there was an odour of burning. They burned the crops and the canebrakes. They set the chairs on the table, so there would be no place for the old man's soul to sit – for once he sat down, he would sit there for ever.

She never knew if she remembered – or if they told her later – of the King's great grief: blood-brothers go together when they go to the Big House. Perhaps he knew that he would die within the year.

Or the Amazons howling. 'No. No. No. It was not the leopard that killed him. Not the buffalo that killed him. It was Night. Night that killed him!'

But she could see clearly again the mourners carrying goats and chickens; the grave-digger shovelling spadefuls of soil through the bedroom window; and the rum barrel – it was Antonio's idea to bury him in a rum barrel; and the shaved white head with wads of kapok stuffed up the nostrils.

Once again, they were all around her, the cringing men

and the set, fanatic faces of the women: it was not to be a Christian funeral.

Again hands lifted her for one last look – at the head bobbing in the barrel and the boy and girl standing beside it, whimpering. They put her down when the sacrificer came with a knife.

Then she was running, faster and faster down a wet red tunnel with no light at the end. A door opened. A cool draught blew in her face. A mulatto in a white suit brushed past her, turning his face to the wall.

And she stepped into a tall blue room lined with mirrors and pillars of gold. A dinner-party was ending. A man rose from the head of the table. He had red hair and his eyes were the colour of the market-women's beads. And he held out both his hands and said, 'I have waited a long time.'

Lieutenant-Colonel Zossoungbo Patrice heard the screams from his office in the Sûreté Nationale. His fatigues were drenched with sweat. He stopped composing his list of possible traitors. The President was coming to the end of his broadcast:

> Victory to the People!
> Glory to the People!
> Power to the People!
> Ready for the Revolution!
> Ready for Production!
> And the fight continues!

Fixed to the wall were a pair of handcuffs and a broken guitar. There was also a stuffed civet cat, nailed, in mockery of the Crucifixion, with its hind legs and tail together and its forelegs stretched apart.

Above the desk hung the scarified face of the President.

The colonel got up and made a gesture which, if anyone had seen it, would have landed him in jail.

Then he paced up and down, waving to an imaginary crowd, creaking the floorboards and crushing a cockroach under the heel of his combat boot.

penguin.co.uk/vintage